IT'S DEFINITELY NOT ALIENS

A<small>T LEAST,</small> R<small>AVEN</small> B<small>ARRISTER'S</small> *PRETTY* <small>SURE IT ISN'T.</small>

Between double shifts, looming exams, and an embarrassingly intense crush on her way-too-attractive bartender coworker, Sky, she doesn't have time for alien nonsense, anyway.

But everything changes the night she crashes into a UFO. Suddenly there's a glowing artifact, a robot that isn't from around here, unexplained lights in the sky…and Raven's starting to think maybe it *is* time to put the extra in extraterrestrial.

Marked with strange symbols and haunted by memories no one else has, she doesn't know what to believe. The only person with answers may be the one guy she's no longer sure she can trust: Sky.

He's hiding something. Something big.

Too bad nobody gave her the study guide for cosmic chemistry, galaxy-sized problems, or…you know, what to do when your crush might not be from this planet.

It's definitely not aliens…*but what if it is?*

STARDUSTED
It's Definitely NOT Aliens
Book 1

ELLE DEYESSO

Published by Waking Dream LLC

PO Box 15065

Fort Wayne, IN, 46885, United States

Cover design by Danielle Shafer

Interior design and formatting by Danielle Shafer/Vellum

Editing by Danielle Fine – Design by Definition

For more information, visit: www.elledeyesso.com

 Formatted with Vellum

To all the ones who grew up wanting to be Rebel scum, a Brown Coat, or join Starfleet Academy—the ones who stayed up for meteor showers and memorized constellations and secretly daydreamed about alien boyfriends…it's our time.

And my husband. You're my own personal slow burn love story. I love you more than I can put into words.

CODE YELLOW (suspected contact)

Grid D442: high-speed aerial anomaly, heading W-SW.
Likely Type-2. Spotters activate. Hats on, eyes up.

 Got visuals? Tag #FETRfinds
Form 3-C optional. Just text Dave (Rhonda's on vacation).

Visit FETRHQ.com for updates
⚠ Don't use skywatch.com. It's been hacked again.
To unsubscribe, reply STOP
We are the Friends of the Extraterrestrial Races.
👽 The truth is up there. Probably.

DELIVERED: 6:35PM

Chapter 1

THE NIGHT EVERYTHING WENT WAY WRONG

"**Kelly**, it's definitely *not* aliens," I said, rolling my eyes.

It was definitely aliens.

Not that I knew that yet.

At the time, the idea seemed ludicrous. Improbable. Arguably the most insane explanation for what was going on in One Willow. Let alone the world.

But you know what they say: ignorance is bliss.

And speaking of ignorance…

"You don't *know* it's not aliens," Kelly said. "Like, not for sure, Rae-bae."

Ugh. Not that stupid nickname again.

I fought the urge to swear and shoved open the swinging kitchen doors a little harder than necessary, bracing for the wave of sizzling beef smoke and heated grease. The cacophony of classic rock, shouting, and clattering utensils swallowed the muttered curse that slipped out despite my best efforts.

My name was Rae. Not Rae-bae. Raven, technically. But only professors and the DMV called me that. And my mother when I was in trouble.

Everyone else just called me Rae.

Everyone except, of course, Kelly. She'd insisted on that cringe nickname since the day I'd landed the waitressing job at Oasis Bar and Grill six months ago.

And, like a fly to a glue strip, it stuck.

I'd given up fighting it. Just like I was ready to give up on this stupid debate.

I reached the ready line stacked with waiting orders, Kelly hot on my heels. After a glance at the digital screen, she handed me the plate of Hula fries for table three. I mumbled a thank-you, and she turned to face me, one hand on her curvy hip, her serving tray clutched at her side.

Like me, she wore the tropical-themed uniform: an aggressively green minidress printed with pineapples and surfboards and her waitressing apron.

Unlike me, she pulled it off.

Then again, Kelly could wear a paper bag and still look like she'd stepped off a modeling gig. She kept the top two buttons of the dress strategically undone to showcase cleavage. The best push-up bra at Victoria's Secret wouldn't help me emulate that. Trust me. I'd tried.

I gave her a flat look, and in response, she pursed her lips. They were painted a bright Barbie-pink today.

Our staredown lasted a full ten seconds, during which angry rock music raged.

Kelly broke first with a disgusted click of her tongue, like my refusal to give in was a personal affront.

"Okay, fine," she said, flipping a long lock of golden blond hair over her shoulder. "So everyone *says* it's some kind of solar storm. That's what the news is reporting, sure. But how do we actually know that's what's happening? How do we know for real? How do we know it's not just what the media wants us to believe? Haven't you seen the reels?"

God. Not the *reels*. Next, it'd be Reddit threads and blurry YouTube videos of alleged alien sightings.

"Because," I cut in before she could start citing message-board experts, "it doesn't make *sense*, Kelly. Aliens aren't invading."

2

I was still holding the Hula fries. Sighing, I angled my tray and slid them on top. The rest of my order still wasn't ready yet. The kitchen was backed up.

Could this night get any worse?

I dug deep for patience and came up short. Like she sensed it, Kelly's pale blue eyes narrowed. She was waiting for me to crack.

I was closer than I wanted to admit.

Ignoring her, I shifted my attention to the digital screen. Still no coconut shrimp or Hawaiian burger. I could practically feel my tips shrinking with every passing second.

Kelly hadn't moved. Her stare hadn't wavered. Pretending she wasn't there didn't work, either. I dragged my gaze away from the frazzled cooks and turned to my blonde nemesis.

"Fine," I said, massaging my aching temple. "If you really want to talk about this, here's how I know it's not some giant conspiracy: Because *science*, Kelly. Science knows what a solar flare is. You've seen the footage. The actual satellite images of the sun, you know, flaring?"

She waved off my very reasonable explanation with a flick of her pink-tipped fingers. "That's what they want you to think. That could all be computer-generated. A cover-up. AI can do crazy things."

I was going to lose it. Right here in the kitchen.

I pinched the bridge of my nose and forced back a string of colorful curses that would've made the line cooks proud. "Who's they, Kelly? You think every single news source and government agency is colluding in one giant lie?" When she opened her mouth, I held up a hand. "Don't answer that."

She gave a dramatic shrug.

"Let me get this straight," I said, fixing her with an incredulous look. "The entire world is under alien attack, and their master plan is…disrupting our cell signals? Making us resend a few texts?" I snorted. "Yeah, you're right. You can't check your views on socials. It's the apocalypse."

"That's the media talking," Kelly replied primly. "You have to do your own research these days, Rae-bae."

Lord help me. She was serious.

Before I could respond, Tony, one of the kitchen staff, piped up from her other side. "Don't forget the power outages." He'd finished slicing an onion and was now leaning on the prep table, wiping his watering eyes on his shoulder. And also apparently injecting himself into this conversation. "There were grid issues over in Logansport and a whole thing in New York. And that's just in the States. I read on Spiral that it's been happening in other countries, too."

"What countries?" I demanded, glaring.

But, *damn it,* I had heard about that. The outages. Brief mentions on the news. I'd brushed them off because power outages happened all the time. Because electromagnetic interference *could* disrupt the grid…

Oh, no. They were sucking me in. Like a sensationalized whirlpool.

Well, I wasn't jumping into that water. I was too smart for this.

"That's just a coincidence, Tony," I said, shaking my head. A dull ache pulsed at my temple. Work stress. School stress. This whole, stupid debate. "Logansport's an hour from here, and New York is literally across the country. They're not related."

"The military base is *here,* though, Rae-bae." He sniffed, eyes still glistening with onion tears. "Maybe aliens are poking around for a long-lost spaceship the government's hiding."

"Do not call me that." I sharpened my glare. "And nobody's hiding a UFO at the base! It's mostly shut down now anyway. My dad worked there."

The pang was quick, stabbing. I shoved it aside. I was too deep in this ridiculous argument to pause for grief.

Was I the only sane one left in this restaurant?

"Yeah, and Roswell was a weather balloon," Tony said, pointing the knife at me. "Don't be such a sheep."

My mouth dropped open. He did *not* just call me a sheep.

Before I could unleash a scathing retort about herd mentality, Jackie appeared on the other side of the ready line, their hands full of Kelly's order. The tall, stocky lead cook slid the plates onto the warming shelf and sent me a solemn look. "They only tell us what they want us to know, Rae-bae. Remember that."

No. Not Jackie, too. They were *always* on my side!

I stared, frozen mid-sentence. I was outnumbered. No way I was winning this one.

While Tony and Kelly exchanged triumphant grins, I closed my eyes. Maybe if I didn't look directly at them, they'd forget about this stupid argument. A girl could wish.

Sighing, I rubbed my forehead.

My headache had been lingering since my bio-anthro lecture this morning, and the Tuesday night dinner rush wasn't helping— nor was this absurd conspiracy-club conversation I'd stumbled into. If I hadn't needed the cash to pay Bob rent, I'd have begged one of the other waitresses to take the rest of this closing shift.

But I didn't have that luxury. Not with midterms coming and the study days I'd already planned to take off.

One more year. One more year before I earned that bachelor's in basic anthropology. Then came the real fun: applications, scholarships, and *hopefully* a master's in archaeology. And then—

"Order up! Hawaiian burger and a coconut shrimp!"

Jackie's voice jolted me out of my daydreams about the future, and I startled, nearly dropping the Hula fries. Nobody said anything else, but I swept a warning scowl around the room anyway and gathered up my order, hoisting the tray to my shoulder. Without a word, I turned my back on the peanut gallery.

Kelly snickered. I resisted the urge to stick my tongue out like the dignified adult I was, lifting my chin and pushing through the kitchen doors instead.

Aliens. *Please.* How ridiculous.

There would always be people who obsessed over conspiracy theories.

The solar storm had shown up on my feed earlier that week, and everything they'd described—the flickering power, the signal issues —lined up perfectly with what NASA had explained. I'd even watched the educational video. *Twice.*

Recalling it chased away the last of that creeping doubt. It was embarrassing I'd had any at all. Kelly could be persuasive when she wanted to be. One of her dubious superpowers.

Some people just weren't content with the simplest explanation. Me? I liked things that could be weighed and measured, tested and proven. I liked science.

Kelly could go chase ET into traffic for all I cared.

I dismissed the whole ridiculous conversation and left the employee area, glancing toward the bar before catching myself.

Because *he* was working tonight.

The sweeping counter stretched to my left and curved around the corner, packed with stools and patrons leaning in toward the flickering fake tiki lights and bottles stacked along the mirrored wall. Tonight's bartender moved with smooth, practiced ease behind the glassy black surface.

Tall. Dark. Handsome—

I wrenched my attention away, but the urge to sneak a second glance almost overpowered me. My face went hot.

Speaking of embarrassing. I couldn't even look his way without blushing. I needed to pull it together.

Clearing my throat, I directed my eyes forward and marched into the dining area.

Like the bar, the floor was busy tonight. The crowded four- and six-top tables and the booths lining the far wall were mostly full. Conversation and laughter mingled with the tinny island music floating from speakers hidden among the plastic palm trees, twinkle lights, and fake vines. Every so often, a prerecorded bird squawk or monkey call echoed across the dining room.

The track repeated every fifteen minutes. I would know. I heard it in my sleep. My nightmares, even. Especially the ones where I showed up at work without pants on.

I pasted on my server smile and wound my way through the sea of patrons to my section. A middle-aged couple sat waiting. Impatiently. The woman's pinched face confirmed my fear about their tip.

Inwardly wincing, I slid the tray off my shoulder and adopted my most apologetic tone. It came out a bit more stilted than I'd intended. "I'm so sorry for the delay." I set their food down and glanced at their drinks. Still good. "Is there anything else I can get you?"

"No," the woman huffed, patting her bright red curls as she reached for her fork. "I'm *starving*."

The man dove into his burger without comment.

Somehow, despite my souring mood, I managed a real smile. "Well, I'll be back by to check on you—"

The lights chose that exact moment to flicker and go out.

Darkness fell, sudden and deep. My heart skipped a beat. The music cut off mid-strum. Gasps rippled through the dining room, followed by the murmur of startled voices.

I turned in place, blinking rapidly to get my eyes to adjust.

What the hell?

It took a second to register. But then...

Great. A power outage. Just *great*. I could practically *hear* Kelly's I-told-you-so.

Before I could decide on an action, the emergency lights kicked on at the exits, splashing white into the shadows as a jumble of complaints and questions echoed across the dining room and bar. In the dimness, I scanned for the familiar lime-green of my fellow waitresses and spotted Kelly's svelte shape darting through the chaos alongside a few others, doing their best to placate guests. The frustrated clatter from the kitchen swelled, along with crashes and shouted curses. I winced.

"What's going on?" snapped the angry woman at my own table.

I'd almost forgotten she was there. I blinked then scrambled to cling to professionalism when all I really wanted to do was throw my tray and scream. Somehow, I summoned a soothing tone. "I-I'm not sure. I'll find my manager. Just...please stay here and, um, keep calm. I'll be right back."

Before she could fire off more demands, I turned on my heel and hurried toward the kitchen. This night just kept getting better.

As I moved, I searched for tonight's manager, Sandy, but of course she was nowhere in sight. Typical. She had a sixth sense for disappearing when things got hectic. She had to have noticed the blackout, though. Hard to miss the entire restaurant going dark.

Grumbling, I veered toward the office behind the bar. She was probably holed up in there, scrolling her dating profile. Again.

If the outage dragged on, we'd have to comp food, hand out free drinks—meaning we'd need Sandy to emerge and pretend to do her job for at least five whole minutes. That, or finally appoint an assistant manager like every single one of us had asked her to do. Control freak, party of one.

The lights blazed back to life, sudden and blinding. I flinched as they stabbed my already tender skull. The jarring screech of monkey calls and music returning mid-chorus followed, painfully loud after the shocked silence. Guests groaned, hands went up to shield eyes, and I paused mid-step, trying not to stagger.

Sandy chose that moment to materialize, brushing past me with a customer-service smile plastered on her face, eyes wild. From the far side of the room came the unmistakable crash of breaking glass. I twisted just in time to see Emily's expression crumple in horror as the rest of her tray hit the floor. Serving ware, fried fish, and lemonade flew everywhere.

As if on cue, Jackie bellowed, "Good-for-nothing freeloader!" from somewhere in the kitchen. A pair of old ladies gasped like they'd just witnessed murder. My headache intensified.

I needed a minute.

Spinning, I stalked toward the back of the house, passing tables murmuring about "solar flares" like they were the harbingers of doom. I caught a glimpse of Kelly heading in my direction, her smile frighteningly triumphant.

Nope. *Not today, Satan.*

I took a hard right into the prep closet, slammed the door behind me, and sucked in a breath.

Sanctuary.

The closet was tiny but blessedly quiet, packed with cases of sealed bar bottles, stacks of silverware, and boxes of condiments. More importantly, it was out of view. No guests. No Kelly. Just peace.

Or what passed for it in restaurant life.

Short of chain-smoking in the alley or crying in the bathroom, hiding in here was the best it got. I'd wrap a few silverware bundles, give myself two minutes to pull it together, and hope the pain ricocheting around my skull would dull into something tolerable.

At least the door muffled Sandy's screeching and the din of annoyed customers. The lamp in the corner cast a pale yellow glow over the space. I sagged back against the wall and let myself breathe. Taking this double had seemed like a good idea at the time. One morning class and a full night of tips—a done deal. If I hadn't needed the money so badly…

Muttering an oath, I dropped my tray onto the folding chair and glanced at the stack of neatly rolled napkins. Someone else had clearly shared my plan. I had, if I was lucky, a few minutes to myself before I had to resurface and pretend I hadn't been contemplating that aforementioned cry in the women's bathroom.

It was just a power flicker. Not the end of the world.

Definitely not aliens.

Sighing, I pulled my phone from my apron pocket. No missed calls. No texts. Not that I was expecting any. Amelia was still visiting her dad, but she'd be heading back soon. I debated texting her a vent-rant about the night but decided against it. Instead, I glanced at my signal.

Full bars. Still no sign of an intergalactic takeover. Take that, Kelly.

I snorted and tucked my phone away again before grabbing a fresh napkin and set of silverware.

But before I could start folding, the door behind me creaked open.

My shoulders tightened. She'd found me *already?* So much for hiding.

"Well," I said with a sniff, "your alien friends sure didn't hang around long." Sneering, I started to turn. "If they were going to shut off our lights, they at least could've stuck around long enough to close the—"

Only it wasn't Kelly.

My eyes landed first on a broad, well-shaped chest. Wide shoulders attached to a tall, lean frame.

It wasn't Kelly at all.

It was *him*.

Sky Acosta—broody bartender, unspeakably hot coworker, and subject of my private, embarrassing obsession—stood framed in the prep room doorway, backlit by the dim restaurant lighting like he was the actual embodiment of every overactive fantasy I'd ever denied having.

He was looking right at me. Frowning, actually.

All the blood in my body rushed upward, setting my face on fire. My mouth hung open. My fingers stopped working mid-bundle. I forgot how to breathe.

Of course it was him. Of course it was now.

Chapter 2

THE BABY CHICKEN DISASTER

WHEN I SAID NOTHING, just gaped at him like a moron, Sky rocked back onto his heels and tipped his head to the side, one hand still holding the door. His tousled, mink-brown hair fell over his eyes.

Eyes that looked a little...bewildered.

Okay, and a touch concerned.

Which was fair. He'd just found me hiding in the prep closet mid-dinner rush, launching conspiracy theories like badly aimed bottle rockets at whoever opened the door.

Conspiracy theories about *aliens*.

Oh my God.

I'd just ranted about aliens to Sky Acosta.

Kill me now. Just bury me in the silverware basket and call it a night.

With a quick look over his shoulder at the dining area, Sky released the door, leaving it propped open. It let in enough light to illuminate the way he swept an assessing glance around the closet. Like he was searching for a hidden-camera prank-show host.

I stared at him, caught in a confusing quagmire of horror and fascination.

"Sorry. I didn't realize anyone was in here," he said. His quiet, deep voice filled the small space in a way that made it feel smaller. More...*intimate*.

When I continued to stare, Sky blinked a couple times and rubbed the back of his neck, which caused his bicep to bunch up beneath his short-sleeved shirt. I noticed because the universe hated me and I, tragically, had eyes. I yanked my attention away from the ripple of muscle...only for it to get caught on the lock of dark hair that'd fallen across his forehead. It looked soft. My fingers itched to brush it back.

He was giving me a strange look now.

Maybe because I still hadn't answered him.

"Um," I said brilliantly, finally managing to close my mouth but failing entirely to stop myself from checking him out.

Bartenders didn't have to wear the ridiculous neon Hawaiian uniforms like the rest of us. I suspected management let it slide as an offering to keep our very skilled, very efficient drink-slingers happy. After all, nobody looked great in lime green.

If anybody was going to, though, it'd be Sky.

His dark shirt clung to the sculpted muscles of his upper body, tapering into a narrow waist and faded jeans. He was built like a swimmer: long-limbed, broad where it mattered. Practically meant for tiny scraps of Spandex.

My mouth went dry. Not only had I launched into a crazy-person rant, I was now gazing directly at his abs and imagining him in a Speedo. A *Speedo*. Seriously? What was *wrong* with me?

I closed my eyes.

Could a person die of embarrassment? Possibly, if my growing numbness was any indication. At least sweet death would spare me the rest of this interaction.

Alas, I remained alive for the time being. Needing something—*anything*—to do with my hands, I turned around and dropped the silverware bundle in the general direction of the basket. It bounced off the side and hit the floor with a dramatic *clang*, unspooling.

Before I could scramble to grab it, Sky spoke again.

"That's an interesting theory."

Amusement. That was amusement coloring the casual statement. My flush returned with a vengeance, the blotchy kind. Sweat beaded on my forehead.

What was he talking about?

Oh. Right.

The alien thing. *My* alien thing.

Out of *every* possible thing I could've said to Sky Acosta, I'd gone with the tinfoil-hat manifesto.

My back to him, I opened my mouth to do some damage control, but all that came out was a tiny, squeaky noise that sounded suspiciously like a baby chicken. A *meep*.

Okay, maybe skip the silverware-basket burial and just chuck me right into the dumpster. Because this whole night was trash.

Dread pooling in my stomach, I gave up on the fallen silverware and slowly turned his way.

Sky scanned my face, as if taking stock of my slow descent into mortification. He wasn't laughing, per se, but there was a softness to his mouth as he studied me. I could see the thoughts churning inside his sapphire eyes.

His eyes had always been my favorite. That deep, clear indigo, like ocean water right before nightfall. You could write songs about those eyes. Those chiseled cheekbones, too.

I mean, I couldn't. I wasn't Ed Sheeran. And also, I was currently mute. Except for poultry sounds.

We looked at each other in silence, me screaming internally, him entirely too composed and seeming more amused by the second.

The faintest smile finally broke free and tugged up the corner of his full mouth.

"Aliens, huh?" he said, flashing white teeth in a slight grin.

Say something, Rae. Say anything. *Stop being a malfunctioning Roomba.*

"Um," I said again. *Stellar.* My gaze slid sideways to his shoulder, a safer place to focus than those *eyes*. "No. I mean, yes. Well, Kelly said...I don't actually think..."

What had Kelly even said? What was *I* saying?

I trailed off, certain I was about to spontaneously combust from sheer shame. Not that I wanted to die. I couldn't die. I was finally talking to Sky, *actually* talking to him, and not just the standard "here's your shift drink," "table four wants a whiskey on the rocks," and "have a great night."

Six months of stolen glances and overthinking everything. Six months of mentally scripting this very moment, and this was what I delivered. My rehearsals in the shower had gone so much better. In those, I was witty and clever and absolutely *zero* percent baby chicken.

God.

It wasn't like I didn't know how to talk to guys. I wasn't a nun. I'd had my share of boyfriends. A few casual flings. Amelia and I had hit the party scene hard when we turned twenty-one. There had been experiences.

None of them had looked like Sky Acosta…but still. I wasn't a virgin. I wasn't some teenager wallowing in new hormones.

And yet…this was *Sky*. And Sky was different.

It wasn't just me. I wasn't the only one who'd noticed him. If you swung that way, it was impossible not to. Even Kelly, whose standards were somewhere in the clouds with Everest, had pointed him out my first night.

"That's Sky Acosta," she'd whispered, yanking me around the corner and motioning to where the guy in question was making a dirty martini. His profile was to us, his attention on the pour, but I still felt myself flush—despite the fact we were hiding behind a fake palm tree, lurking in the faux foliage.

"He lives above the place," Kelly continued, stage-whispering like we weren't clearly stalking him. "Rents the apartment from the owners. He always does his own thing, keeps to himself, never stays after to hang out. Never comes when we go out to Crescent or anything."

The last part came with a pout.

That's when I discovered she'd tried her luck with him and struck out. Hard. Kelly didn't get turned down often (read: ever) and Sky's polite but distant rebuff hadn't gone over well.

She wasn't wrong, either. I'd never seen him at work events. He had no social media, no online presence at all. No one ever came in to visit him like with the rest of the bartenders. He was, for all intents and purposes, a loner. A quiet, sexy-as-sin enigma.

The crush had been instant. And since then, it'd only grown. I'd caught myself watching him during our shifts more times than I could count. Occasionally, he'd caught me, too. I'd panicked each time, slapped on a weird grimace-smile, and fled like a scared rabbit, but hey—eye contact! That had to count for something.

At this point, he probably thought I had a staring problem. Or a personal vendetta.

And now he probably thought I didn't know how to talk, period.

Crap. I was still gazing stupidly at him.

Focus, Rae.

I forced out a shaky breath and scooped the silverware from the floor, crumpling the napkin in my palm. The cutlery clinked as I shoved it into my apron pocket for a later sink dunk. The napkin went straight into the hamper and landed clean.

"Nothing but net," I muttered.

Small wins. I'd take any size tonight, on the shittiest of all nights.

I faced Sky again.

I'd imagined this moment more times than I could count. Since that first night I'd watched him behind the bar, I'd fantasized about mustering the guts to flirt…or, in some wild reality, telling him how I felt, even though I knew better. Sky Acosta was miles out of my league. He was GQ-level intimidating. Deeply uninterested in any of us mere mortals.

But once—*once*—he'd said my name.

Well…almost my name.

Okay, he'd called me Riley. But he'd gotten the "R" right, and I was hanging onto that.

Like I said, small wins.

But this? This tiny room with three feet of air between us and no one else in sight? This was a first.

Even as I stared at the wall beside the door, I could feel his attention on me. Like a spotlight. It made my skin buzz. I inhaled slowly and caught a whiff of his cologne. Spicy and earthy, mixed with something uniquely him. Like night air.

My stomach fluttered. With effort, I turned, tried a smile, and picked up my tray, using the moment to gather my thoughts enough to form words.

"Sorry. I'm...well. Whew, you know? One of those shifts, and I was just taking a quick break." I hunched a little, preparing to slip past him. "I'll get out of your way."

"You're not in my way," he said without missing a beat. His easy tone surprised me enough that I looked up and met his eyes without instantly melting. That felt like progress.

He'd leaned a shoulder against the doorframe and crossed his arms, his biceps doing that flex thing again that should honestly be illegal. For once, he didn't seem distant. He seemed...curious. About me?

Then he said, "Tell me more about this alien theory of yours."

I plummeted straight from cloud nine back to Earth. In flames.

Oh. That checked out. That was why he was still here. He wanted to hear the crazy girl's alien rant. Fascinating stuff.

Of course he wasn't interested in *me*. He probably thought it was funny. He was mildly entertained, at best.

I unbent my spine and stood tall. I wasn't going to melt. I wasn't going to spiral. I was going to be calm and rational and—

I rolled my eyes. At myself. At him. At *this*. Everything.

"It's not my theory," I said, trying for confident and landing somewhere near defensive. "I don't believe in aliens."

Sky's brows slowly angled upward. "Oh, really? That's... interesting."

Something flickered in his expression too quickly for me to recognize. That gaze was direct but unreadable. Trained on me.

My fluster was coming back, tangling my tongue into knots.

"Well, not *these* aliens." I took a deep breath. "This is something some online nutjob posted. Kelly buys into it. I don't. It's ridiculous." I shook my head and gestured weakly. "I mean, yeah, *okay*, sure. My texts haven't always been sending the last few days. But I don't immediately assume we're being invaded by the Borg." No little green men or massive *Independence Day* ships had been spotted. Kelly and the rest of these people were just...delusional. I twisted my lips. "If aliens were going to make a dramatic entrance, I doubt they'd start by screwing with the power grid…"

I blinked. Sky was the one staring now. Too late, I realized I'd made a Star Trek reference. Great. All I needed was a phaser to go with my tinfoil hat and I'd complete the look.

Everything about this night was officially Too Much. Capital T and M.

Shoulders slumping again, I dropped my gaze to my white canvas shoes. "Excuse me, Sky. I need to check on my tables."

"In a minute. They're fine. Sandy's bribing everyone with hand-delivered Seaside Samplers. Jackie's losing their mind."

None of that was surprising. I huffed a weak laugh. What *was* surprising, though, was Sky stopping me. Surely he had better things to do than talk about conspiracy theories in the prep closet.

I dragged my eyes from the floor, back up to his face. His mouth was still curved in that close-lipped half-smile as he studied me. Intently. A whisper of uncertainty stirred in my gut.

"Whose theory did you say it was?" he asked.

Why was *everyone* so hung up on this ridiculous alien crap?

"Kelly's," I muttered, shifting my grip so both arms wrapped around the tray like it was a shield. Maybe it could block the tide of ridiculousness sweeping through this place.

When Sky gazed at me blankly, I tilted the tray aside, lifting one hand to mime curves in the air. "Blond. Hot. Pink…well, every-thing. That Kelly."

"Oh." Recognition lit his face—predictable, albeit annoying—and he nodded. "Right. Kelly. She came up with that?"

I snorted. "Hardly. She probably saw it on a reel. She loves reels." Focusing on my shoes again, I pinched the inside of my cheek between my teeth and nodded at the door. "Look, I really need to get back to work."

I stepped forward, waiting for him to move. There was a chip in the doorframe, like someone had slammed it hard once. Relatable.

I wanted to slam something.

"Yeah, sure," Sky said, after a beat had passed. "Sorry."

Finally, he stepped aside, arm extended like some kind of gallant knight, gesturing me through. I was going to have to pass close. Like, inches close. A fresh thrill of nerves zinged up my spine.

Swallowing hard, I darted a glance up.

He gave me that same infuriatingly dimpled smile, a slight tug at the corner of his mouth so smooth I'd believe he'd practiced it in a mirror. His dark eyes sparkled. "After you. Good talking to you, Rachel."

Rachel. Not my name, but another random one that started with an R. Talk about adding insult to injury.

I ripped my gaze away, gripping my tray hard enough I was surprised the plastic didn't creak. I felt the weight of his attention on my downturned face. Like he was willing me to look up. Which, of course, I didn't.

Damn it. *Rachel*. Really? I was wearing a *name tag*, for God's sake.

I didn't even correct him. Didn't bother. Just tucked my chin and brushed past, heat burning up the back of my neck. Somehow, I felt worse than before. Like I'd lost a contest I hadn't known I'd entered. Like someone had taken the air right out of my shiny balloon.

Dejected, I shuffled to my section. Everywhere I turned, Seaside Samplers sizzled.

I made it two steps before I couldn't stop myself from looking back over my shoulder.

Sky was gone. Along with what remained of my dignity.

This night was officially the worst.

If Kelly was somehow right about the aliens, maybe a spaceship *should* come get me. At this point, getting abducted sounded better than surviving the rest of this shift.

I snorted a bitter laugh.

Of course, that was about to become cosmic-level ironic.

Chapter 3

SWERVING RIGHT INTO THE TWILIGHT ZONE

"**AND** THEN HE CALLED ME RACHEL," I mumbled into the phone wedged between my shoulder and ear. As I walked, I wrestled with the knot in my apron. That sucker was tied *tight*. "And before you ask, no, I didn't correct him. I was too busy trying to get the hell out of there."

On the other end, Amelia made a sympathetic *hmm* noise. "At least he remembered it started with an R?"

I'd thought the same thing earlier. It sounded even more pathetic out loud.

Still, I conceded, "I guess there's that."

I puffed my cheeks in an exaggerated sigh, the sound lost in the rush of green-lit traffic turning off Main onto Broadway. Despite the hour, a steady stream of headlights flowed past Oasis. The bar and grill sat on the corner between a car lot and the water treatment plant.

The temperature had dipped with the sunset, and late-fall air nipped at my arms and lifted goosebumps. I quickened my pace, canvas shoes crunching across the chip 'n' seal parking lot.

The far streetlamp cast a yellow halo over my beat-up blue four-door, spotlighting the rust around the rear wheel well and the fresh bird poop decorating the back window.

Just one more reason I couldn't afford to miss these shifts. Faith, short for Old Faithful, was showing her age. As much as I hated it, I needed to start thinking about a new vehicle.

"Well, don't sound so depressed, Rae," Amelia said, her voice crackling through her car speakers. She was finally on her way home from visiting her dad at one of his fancy vacation homes. "Sky *talked* to you. That's something, right?"

"Yeah, about a ridiculous alien invasion theory spawned in the darkest pits of the internet." I wheezed a humorless laugh as I conquered the apron string's knot and yanked the whole thing off. "And I entertained it. How hard up does that make me for a guy's attention?"

We both knew the answer to that. I hadn't had a date in over two months, and it'd been even longer since I'd had a good one. I'd given up on the Matcher app everyone else swore by. The few matches who didn't bolt after our first chat had either been way too much too fast, or they'd just wanted to get into my pants.

Which was fine and all. Just not what I was looking for.

Maybe I was destined to be single. Maybe if I could just *accept* that, I could stop turning into a Neanderthal every time Sky got within ten feet of me. No—worse. At least Neanderthals could communicate. I could only gape like a dying fish.

A desperate, dying fish.

I didn't realize I'd said any of it out loud until Amelia let out a groan. "You're not desperate, and you're not destined to be single. Stop it right now. You're just picky. And there's nothing wrong with that. You've got way more important things to focus on than boys, anyway. Like a real academic career."

Easy for you *to say*, I thought, but I swallowed the pettiness before it reached my tongue. I felt guilty anyway.

Amelia had no issues in the dating department. She was the full package. Fun, smart, funny, and effortlessly stunning. Long, shining black hair, mile-high legs, olive skin with a megawatt smile and a sassy attitude to match.

I, on the other hand, was average height, average build, with below-average curves. My hair was that not-quite-blond, not-quite-brown color that always looked better on Pinterest than in real life, and my eyes were the exact shade of mud. While Amelia was full of confidence, I was…not timid, exactly. I knew my mind. But I was quiet. Reserved. Maybe a little too sarcastic for my own good sometimes.

Amelia had always made me feel like I was enough, though. She had that aura, the kind that drew people to her and made them feel…wanted. Interesting.

We'd hit it off back in sophomore chemistry at the private school I'd gotten a scholarship to, and in the seven years since, she'd become the sister I never had. Despite the fact she owned designer clothing and I shopped secondhand, she'd always picked me first. She may have grown up well off, but that kind of thing didn't matter to Amelia. Quite the opposite, in fact.

She was my sister in all the ways but blood. I couldn't imagine my life without her.

"So how close are you to home?" I asked, changing the subject as I slung the apron over my arm and dug into my purse. My keys had buried themselves somewhere deep. "How are Vorn and Estelle?"

Amelia sighed, long and gusty, full of annoyance. "Oh, you know. Living the aristocrat's dream. Estelle's disappointed I changed majors. She was really banking on me becoming some sort of breakout fashion star." She snorted. "At least my father seems blasé about media communications. Which, you know, is a glowing review from him. I'm sure he's already calculating how he can absorb me into his PR branch. I'm just waiting for him to give the ultimatum."

Amelia's forever struggle with her dad's expectations was only getting worse the longer she resisted his wishes. Vorn Delarosa wasn't used to not getting his way. It's how he'd ended up on Forbes lists, after all. He expected the same of his only offspring, too. Even if Amelia didn't want it.

I thought of my own mom, who'd never batted an eye at my dream of becoming an archaeologist, even knowing how underpaid, underfunded, and overworked I'd probably be. I was lucky. I knew it.

I tightened my grip on the phone. "It's your career, not hers, A."

"Her career consists of sitting poolside and spending Dad's money," Amelia said with a trace of venom.

I bit my lip. Estelle was her dad's fourth wife, barely older than Amelia herself, and had a holier-than-thou streak that made her even harder to like. Amelia had tried. If she couldn't find it in her to pretend, it was safe to say it was pretty hopeless.

"You think you'll make it to class tomorrow?" I asked, reaching Faith and fumbling with the key. The automatic locks were out again; my mechanic brother said something about a relay. I didn't know what that meant, but I heard dollar signs and mentally sobbed.

"Yeah, I'll be there. We still meeting for coffee after your comp class?"

"Yep." I finally got the door open, the hinges shrieking in protest. "Sounds good. Gotta run to the bank and dump this cash. I'll catch you tomorrow. Drive safe."

"You, too. And hey—don't get abducted by any aliens on your way home."

She laughed at my disgusted growl and hung up.

Shaking my head, I tossed my apron and purse into the passenger seat before sliding behind the wheel. And, because I was weak and apparently a glutton for punishment, I paused with the door open and glanced back toward Oasis.

No lights glowed in the second-story windows on the left side where Sky's apartment was located. I didn't think he was home. He'd vanished after the dinner rush and left the other bartender, Derek, to close. Not that I'd been watching.

Who was I kidding? Of course I had. I hadn't *stopped* watching him.

Ever since the incident in the prep room, I'd been painfully aware of his presence across the restaurant. More so than normal. Not even the steady crush of customers had dulled the lingering embarrassment still simmering under my skin. Or the faint twinge of relief that'd followed when he'd left for the night, off to do whatever it was criminally attractive, alien-obsessed bartenders did after work.

"Well, it's over now," I whispered to myself as I started the car. Faith coughed in protest before the engine caught and rumbled to life.

Best to put the whole night behind me. Including the world's weirdest backroom chat with the guy I'd spent months fantasizing about. I was sure he'd already forgotten the girl whose name he couldn't remember, anyway.

I adjusted the crooked rearview mirror and backed out of the space.

THE TRIP to the bank took no time. But as I rounded the stretch leading to Cherry Street and the small apartment I rented above Bob's garage, I groaned. Of course there would be a train tonight. And a parked one, no less. I knew from experience it could sit there for close to an hour before creeping forward. The cross-guard lights blinked like taunting little eyes in red and yellow.

"Screw this."

I glanced behind me—no cars—and threw Faith into reverse, executing a clunky three-point turn. Even the long way home through the back roads would be faster than waiting forever for the freight train. It wasn't even eleven, but after tonight, I felt like I'd been awake for three days. I was ready for my bed and oblivion.

Houses gave way to open land while the radio played a throwback hit from last summer. I hummed along, tapping my fingers on the wheel. The familiar tune chipped away at my scowl. With the city lights fading behind me and the stars brightening overhead, I spotted the boxy shape of the Big Dipper easily. It hovered just above the tree line. I couldn't help but smile.

My dad had always pointed out that constellation when I was little. It reminded me of him every single time I noticed it up there.

I'd grown up thirty minutes away in Maryville, a two-stoplight town whose biggest claim to fame was its grain mill. One Willow, with its mall, medical centers, and not one but two Walmarts, had been the nearest thing to civilization. My dad had worked on the military base there for years.

A large part of my childhood had been spent making the drive into One Willow, first for my fancy school, then my dad's appointments...and after that, for his longer treatments.

Eventually, for the weeks he never came home.

After all this time, the ache that lived in my chest had softened into something gentler. Familiar. I adjusted my grip on the wheel, keeping one eye on the Big Dipper like I had as a kid riding shotgun.

When Amelia and I applied to The Willow University, I knew moving here was the right choice. Close enough to visit my family. Far enough to start over. Amelia had wanted me to move into her father-funded luxury apartment downtown, the one she'd fought him on and lost. I'd passed. I loved her, but I knew better than to test the roommate gods. Too many horror stories.

Besides, I needed my solitude. My space.

That's when I'd found Bob's ad in the local paper. A retired widower, he needed help with yard work and grocery runs. In return, he offered a discounted rate on the fully furnished garage apartment. It was too good to pass up.

Except when dumb trains got in the way.

The landscape outside my windows turned rural—clusters of trees, quiet fields, the occasional farmhouse. Faint glimmers of porch lights shone in the distance. My headlights skimmed golden corn stalks as I turned down 100E, a stretch of road so empty it felt like it existed outside time. Harvest season was in full swing, and soon these fields would be flat and barren.

I liked the city and its conveniences, but there was something peaceful about the country's heavy quiet. It was its own kind of beautiful. At least it made the long way home enjoyable—

My car speakers exploded in a burst of static so loud I yelped and instinctively lifted my foot off the gas. Light danced off my passenger window, there and then gone. Recovering, I checked my mirrors. No one behind me. Nothing at all besides fields and stars.

Just me on this lonely lane. *Weird.* I could've sworn I saw lights.

The static swelled again, and a garbled voice cut through the white noise. Impossible to make out, gone just as fast. Interference.

"See? Just the solar flare," I muttered, pressing a button to change the station. Static.

The next station. More static.

I frowned, turned the volume down, and tightened my hands on the wheel. It was nothing. Electromagnetic interference.

Chalk it up to science.

Could also be my shitty car's even shittier antenna. Either way, nothing beyond the realms of normalcy here. Nothing to put the *extra* in extraterrestrial.

The road narrowed and sloped into a dense cluster of trees, branches crowding the edges of the pavement like reaching fingers. The crescent moon vanished behind them, leaving my headlights to carve through the black.

The path curved sharply ahead, and I slowed, glancing once at my rearview. Still empty. Still alone. A tingle of unease prickled between my shoulder blades.

But then I clicked my tongue in annoyance. Screw Kelly and her stupid conspiracy theories. Screw Tony and his smug little grin.

Screw that dumb conversation with Sky, of all people, for…well, being the rotten cherry on top.

Aliens weren't scary. They weren't even real. What were they going to do, mess with my Spotify queue?

I snorted at my own joke. Loudly.

And that was when the sky lit up.

A blinding sphere of multicolored fire exploded through a gap in the trees, as if the sun had suddenly risen again and then decided to drop from the sky. It careened to a stop in the middle of the road ahead, hovering.

Glowing pink, green, yellow, blue.

In front of my windshield. *Right on top of me.*

Time slowed.

My heart stopped beating as I slammed on the brakes.

Faith's tires shrieked in protest, the wheel shuddering violently in my grip. I let out a short scream and braced myself as the back end fishtailed, the car veering sideways across the road. Air punched from my lungs. My shoulder mashed into the door, and the seatbelt cinched tight across my chest, biting deep. I caught a blur of those lights, rainbows of flickering color, then Faith lurched with a bone-rattling crunch and ground to a halt in a spray of gravel. The jolt flung me forward into the steering wheel.

For a moment, I couldn't move. I hung there, lungs heaving, ears ringing with static and my own frantic heartbeat.

I didn't know how much time passed before I lifted my head. Still wheezing, I blinked hard and squinted out the windshield.

Faith sat crooked, her front end in the ditch, back tires on the shoulder, headlights spearing through a patch of red-leaved oaks. Beyond them, broken stalks of corn jutted up like jagged teeth in the dark.

I'd just wrecked my car. Something had flown out in front of me. But *what*?

Adrenaline surged, snapping me into motion. My chest ached as I drew a deeper breath and threw the car into park. Where was my phone? Had I tossed it into my purse?

I twisted to look over my shoulder. Then froze.

The ball of light was still there.

Blazing, suspended in midair over the road, it pulsed in steady rhythm—pink, blue, yellow, green—glowing too brightly for me to stare at it directly. Still, I couldn't look away. Couldn't blink.

Couldn't breathe.

It was silent. Motionless. Radiating like a fallen star.

"No freaking way," I whispered.

My fingers shook as I fumbled with the jammed seatbelt. On the third try, it gave way with a loud click. I shoved the door open with a trembling hand. The ding of the keys still in the ignition echoed loudly in the otherwise eerie quiet.

I half-fell out of the car, legs wobbling. My knee cracked against the doorframe, but I didn't feel it. My limbs tingled with pins and needles as I dropped into a crouch and sucked in another shaky breath.

I should call someone. Make sure the car was okay. But I couldn't. Not yet.

I had to *know*.

My shoes sank into the damp leaves and wet ground as I crawled up the embankment, driven by that stupid, innate curiosity.

Surely I hadn't seen what I thought I had.

I hesitated at the top, crouching just before the ridge. A spooky, flickering glow spilled from the other side, bathing the trees, the car, the crumpled, wet grass. I couldn't see the source from here.

I'd seen it in the road, though.

Scrambled possibilities flitted through my brain, too fast to process. What if I'd imagined it? I could've mistaken a different light…a bright star, a meteor. Hell, even Starlink. Those satellites always looked creepy.

Or…or maybe I was concussed.

Maybe that shitty dinner shift had caused a mental break. Maybe I'd lost my mind. Nobody could blame me after the night I'd had.

Or maybe…just maybe, it'd been…*real*.

Panic swelled, and I braced my back against the back wheel well's rusted metal, forcing myself to breathe. The static of Faith's radio buzzed faintly, and the taillights bathed the pavement in red. The crimson glow illuminated the harsh, black skid marks that showed exactly where I'd swerved right off the asphalt.

That had been *before* I hit my head. Which ruled out a concussion.

A mental break was still in the running.

Also, I was delaying the inevitable. I had to look.

I stayed crouched there, though. Tall trees loomed over me like dark sentinels, and each pulse of light made their trunks ripple. A faint charge hung in the air, humming on my skin. The scent of ozone filled my lungs and mingled with the burned-rubber stench and Faith's exhaust.

I had to see.

But my knees wouldn't cooperate. My stomach twisted with nausea, fear, and something else. Something electric.

I wanted to run.

I wanted to *look*.

"Come on, Rae," I whispered, closing my eyes. "There is no try."

With a grimace, I shoved up just enough to peek over the trunk, peeling open my lids.

And I gasped.

Because the road was *empty*.

The ball of light was gone.

Chapter 4

WE'RE NOT SAYING THAT ACRONYM OUT LOUD

I BLINKED. Once. Twice.

Nothing. No blazing orb of questionable origin. Not even a meteor impact crater. Nothing that explained why I'd swerved hard enough to leave those snaking black marks on the asphalt.

No *anything*. Just flat, empty road.

"What the f—"

I shot to my feet, steadying myself on the car's trunk before stepping onto the lane. The air curled around me, cool and biting, drying the clammy sweat on my forehead. The wind carried the scent of distant bonfires and damp earth, and fall-painted trees rustled overhead, their dead leaves whispering. The stars were vivid chips of ice.

The night was still. Completely still and unnervingly quiet as I turned in a full circle.

There was nothing out there.

"You've got to be joking." My voice felt extra loud in the loaded silence.

I'd seen it. I *knew* I'd seen something.

I left the roadside and made my way on trembling legs to where the orb had hovered, and I crouched to get a better look. In the red glow of the taillights, the pavement glittered with something like wet sand or ground glass.

Chilled, I extended a hand, then hesitated. Afraid to touch the ground. Afraid of what I'd *feel*.

But I couldn't let it go. Not yet.

Bracing myself, I pressed my palm to the asphalt.

And immediately hissed through my teeth, yanking my hand back and curling it against my chest.

The ground was hot.

Not warm. *Hot.* Like sunbaked blacktop at the peak of a July afternoon. Like something had burned there a second ago. Something glowing and pulsating and…impossible.

Could it really have been a…?

Climbing to my feet, I scrubbed my hand against my uniform skirt like I could remove the sensation. I couldn't tear my eyes from the spot. All I could see was that ball of light, that blazing glow, and shock buzzed in my ears.

Which was why I didn't hear the engine until it was too late.

The low growl of a vehicle registered a split second before headlights burst into view, swerving around the bend.

Coming right for me.

I stumbled back with a scream, but it was too late to run. Too late to get out of the way. I'd been squatting like an idiot in the middle of the road, and now I stood rooted in place by the searing white light hurtling around the curve.

This was it. This was how I died, on the shittiest of shitty days, pancaked on a lonely country road. Splattered while chasing after strange lights—

Tires *shrieked.*

I shrieked, too, short and hoarse. The chemical scent of burning rubber stung my nose again, and I shrank in on myself, throwing my arms over my face like they could somehow save me. Like I could hide from my inevitable doom adorned with halogen bulbs.

This was it. I waited for the pain. Readied myself for the impact. Hoped my family, my friends, wouldn't be too sad because this was the end.

Only the end didn't come. Neither did the impact.

One second passed. Then another.

Somehow...somehow, I was still upright. Still breathing. My heart pounded so hard it hurt, but I was alive. Very much not a pancake.

I pried open one eyelid, gasping.

Headlights burned into my retinas. Behind them, I could barely make out the hulking shape of a larger vehicle, an SUV maybe, idling inches from where I stood.

It'd stopped.

It'd actually *stopped*.

I didn't know how, but it hadn't splattered me across its grill.

Shuddering, my knees finally unstuck enough for me to stagger backward, arm raised to shield my eyes. My hand trembled. Somewhere behind that blur of vicious brightness, a door slammed, the sound echoing against the watching trees.

"What the hell were you doing?" a familiar male voice snapped. "I almost hit you!"

I knew that voice. A shockwave sizzled through me. *No.* No way.

A tall figure stepped into the glare, blocking part of it. My eyes adjusted just enough to make him out: messy dark hair, broad shoulders, black T-shirt, faded jeans, boots. A body I'd imagined in Spandex not two hours prior to this unfortunate incident.

Sky Acosta.

Because why not? If I could've moved, I'd have thrown both hands into the air and given up on this entire day.

But I didn't move. I stood there gaping while he stalked toward me, his head turning as he took stock of our surroundings. Then he stopped short as his eyes locked on mine and flared wide.

"It's...you," he murmured, barely audible over the rumble of his car's engine. He took half a step toward me, then tilted his head and asked, louder this time, "What are you doing here? And why were you standing in the middle of the road?"

"I was..." Words failed me. Those were both two great questions I didn't have answers to. I wrapped my arms around my middle and scrambled for dignity. "What are *you* doing here?"

He didn't reply right away. He took a step toward me, out of the light. Shadows fell over most of his face, masking his expression. "Apparently, nearly turning you into roadkill."

Right. He'd just nearly killed me.

Also: he'd nearly *killed me.*

The delayed adrenaline roared through me like an angry tidal wave. My stomach knotted itself up, and my throat clamped tight. Head swimming, I stumbled the last few steps to Faith and collapsed over the top of her rusted trunk.

I was going to be sick. I was going to puke up the shift-comped fish sandwich I'd wolfed down. Right here. Right now. In front of Sky.

I fought it with willpower born of desperation. Instead, I pressed my flushed cheek to the cooler metal and focused on breathing.

Because somehow, I *was* still breathing.

What had I just seen? Could I even trust my memory? Everything had happened so fast. The light, the wreck. The mysteriously appearing bartender.

A scuff of shoes behind me roused me from my descent into madness. A soft curse reached my ears, then—

"Hey, are you okay? Do I need to call someone?"

The world had stopped swimming, so I cautiously straightened, leaning heavily on the car's bumper. The fish sandwich stayed where it belonged, at least.

My eyes tried to drift back to that empty spot in the road, where I'd nearly been hit while chasing after something that couldn't be real. It couldn't be. When my sandwich pitched dangerously, I made myself focus on where Sky stood near the ditch, his outline bathed in white-blue from his headlights. His hands rested on his hips as he scanned my vehicle.

When he saw I was upright, he pivoted in my direction, and his voice had softened when he asked, "Are you hurt?"

Was I? I didn't think so. My limbs trembled with lingering fright, and that stupid headache still throbbed, but considering the alternative—i.e. *pancake*—I'd take it.

I shook my head and wiped a shaky hand across my damp forehead. My braid had mostly come undone, and frizzy strands stuck to my sweaty face. I was sure I looked like a hot mess.

Why *him*?

I licked my lips and croaked, "No, I'm fine. I just…thought I saw something in the road. I overcorrected."

"Something?" His tone was careful. Careful enough that I glanced his way.

His dark eyes were almost black in the shadows, and he wasn't looking at me. He was scanning our surroundings again, searching the fields and road. The empty sky.

Almost like he was looking for something.

A chill swept over me.

"Yeah. Something." I rubbed my arms and lifted a shoulder. "I'm not sure what it was."

Because what I *thought* I'd seen…couldn't have been real. A fresh wave of shivers wracked my body, and my teeth chattered.

Sky faced me again, but he didn't press. Gravel crunched when he stepped off the road's shoulder and made his way around Faith, as if checking the angle of the ditch. Clutching my middle, I watched him. When he cocked his head, that chunk of his dark bangs flopped over his brow.

Twice in one day, he'd ended up in the place I'd least expected him. We'd spoken more in the last twelve hours than we had in the six months we'd worked together. In other circumstances, I'd be excited. Happy, even.

It was hard to feel happy while questioning my sanity, though.

My pulse had begun to slow enough for me to breathe normally by the time he circled back to me. Embarrassment, my old friend, was beginning to creep in. He probably thought I was even *more* of an idiot now than he had when I'd ranted about aliens in the prep room.

My stomach flipped at the A-word. I swallowed hard.

Oblivious, Sky gestured at my car, his jacket rustling. "It doesn't look too bad. I'll pull my SUV over, turn on the hazards. We can probably get it out, if you're up for it. You steer, and I'll push. Just put it in reverse and give it easy gas when I say."

When I didn't move, just gazed up at him, feeling dazed, he shifted closer. Leaned down and angled his chin to meet my eyes. Concern furrowed his brow. "Are you sure you're okay to drive? I can call someone. A family member. Or the cops. Whatever you need."

That unexpected gentleness made something soft and traitorous flutter inside me, but I pushed it aside. Along with the suggestion. My mom didn't need a panic attack. My brother didn't need to wake his very pregnant wife. And as much as I loved Amelia, I wasn't ready to explain this. Not yet. She'd take one look at me and know I was hiding something.

Calling the cops wasn't an option, either. I really didn't want my insurance to find out about this. I needed that good driver discount like I needed air.

"No, it's okay." I caught his dubious expression. "I'm good. I swear." I swallowed and squared my shoulders. "I can do it. And… thank you."

"Okay." Sky gave a faint smile, the barest tilt to his lips that seemed more worried than anything. "And don't mention it."

But as he turned back toward his SUV, I caught him studying me sidelong. Like he wasn't entirely convinced I hadn't lost it.

That made two of us.

Chapter 5

ONSTAR? MORE LIKE HOTSTAR

A FEW MOMENTS LATER, I sat behind the wheel again, white-knuckling it.

Through the windshield, I had a clear view of Sky giving the world's hottest emergency roadside service. If I hadn't been questioning the reality of my entire existence, it would've been a lot more enjoyable.

The blink of his SUV's hazard lights cast rhythmic flickers, and my own headlights illuminated his tall silhouette in front of Faith's hood. Despite the heat blasting from the vents, I couldn't stop shivering, and I didn't think it was just the cold air spilling through my open driver's side window.

I couldn't wait for a hot shower. Possibly a glass of wine—or six—if that bottle Amelia had brought over was still in the fridge.

"All set?" Sky called, and I nodded. He pushed up his jacket's sleeves, and added, "Remember, keep the tires straight and don't hit the gas until I say go."

"Roger that!" I said brightly, then winced at myself. *Roger that?* If he thought it was a weird thing to say, he didn't react. He splayed his palms on Faith's hood, leaning in.

Blowing my bangs out of my eyes, I adjusted my grip on the wheel.

The whole situation felt surreal. Sky Acosta, pushing my car. After nearly hitting me. After that…that thing in the road.

Out of all the people who could've come across me…why did it have to be him? What was he even doing out here in the boonies? Maybe he had a girlfriend who lived in the country. Jealousy curled in my chest before I caught myself and rolled my eyes.

Seriously, Rae? Now was *not* the time.

"Get it together," I muttered, disgusted with myself.

"What was that?" Sky glanced up from in front of the car.

"Nothing. I was just…nothing."

He frowned, squinting as if trying to see me through the windshield. "Right. Are you ready?"

"Yes. Ready. Whenever you are."

He bent back into position. "Now!"

I tapped the gas, and the car lurched but didn't go far. My gaze flew to Sky. He dipped his head in acknowledgment, braced again, and strained with another push. His jacket pulled taut across his shoulders. Good God, they were a thing of beauty.

Okay, maybe I could enjoy it a *little*.

"More gas!" he shouted over the engine's rumble.

Averting my gaze, I pressed harder. With a grinding whirl, the wheels caught, and Faith yanked herself out of the ditch. My tires bumped over the uneven ground, jolting me hard enough I winced as I jammed the brakes. But we were out. Shaky with relief, I eased into park, headlights now facing the still-running SUV.

Looking at it, I had the wildest urge to laugh. Seeing it parked there felt almost as crazy as seeing the unidentified—

Nope. Not going there. Not yet.

I put it aside to analyze later, when I had time and privacy for a mental breakdown. Gathering myself, I climbed out on watery legs. Sky made his way to me, brushing his hands off. When he reached my driver's side, he flashed a tentative, close-lipped smile.

"It worked."

"Yeah. Thank you," I said, hugging my midsection. I should've grabbed a coat before work. I hadn't exactly anticipated loitering on a country lane after dark, though.

He gave me a once-over, the curve to his lips fading. "You sure you're okay to drive?"

I opened my mouth to say yes—

But then Faith's engine sputtered and died.

My stomach plunged. Spinning back to the door, I yanked it open. "No, no, no…"

This couldn't be happening. I dropped into the seat and turned the key. Something in the car's innards clicked twice and then nothing. Not even a flicker. I pumped the gas. Tried again.

Click-click-click. Then silence.

I let my head fall forward, resting my forehead on the wheel.

The universe officially hated me.

"Did you run out of gas?"

I jumped. I'd been too caught up to realize Sky now stood right outside my driver's door. I didn't look at him, though. I glanced at the very full gauge instead and shook my head. "No. I have plenty of gas. I just filled up."

Sky didn't say anything. Just waited. I felt him scrutinizing me through the open window.

"I'm fine," I said, answering the unspoken question. "You've done enough. I'll just—"

Leaning into the passenger seat, I rummaged in my purse until I found my phone. I lifted it.

Somehow, I wasn't surprised to find the screen blank. Despite the fact I could've sworn I had at least half a charge left, it was very dead. My shoulders collapsed in.

Dead, like I'd almost been. Like I would've been if Sky hadn't stopped in time. Like I wanted to be after this stupid, *stupid* day.

I stared at the blank screen I held. My throat tightened. My lower lip gave a telltale tremble. I was going to lose it, finally—

"Come on. I'll take you home."

Hinges squeaked, jerking me from my spiral. I yanked my head up as Sky opened my door the rest of the way. He stooped a little to peer in, raising his brows when I didn't move.

I kept my butt firmly planted, though, and my protest came out hoarse. "No, really—"

"I'm not leaving you out here alone in the middle of the night with a dead car," he cut in firmly. "If you're not going to let me call someone, I'm taking you home. Do you have someone who can get you back here in the morning? Maybe give you a jump?"

The brusque tone startled me enough that I blinked. My grip on my dead phone tightened in reflex.

But then I caved a little, considering it. Because what other option did I have?

"My brother," I said, licking my lips. "He's a mechanic. I'll call him in the morning. I don't have class until later, so—" I realized I was rambling and took a deep breath. "Yeah, I can figure it out."

"Okay." Sky tapped the car's roof before stepping back. "Come on, then. Grab your stuff and make sure to lock it up."

An order. A gentle one, sure, but an order. When he turned back toward his SUV, I frowned after him.

This version of Sky was...unexpected.

Bossy. Take-charge. A little commanding. Not what I was used to seeing behind the bar. He'd always seemed so...laid-back. Reserved.

I narrowed my eyes, watching his lanky form waver against the SUV's lights. He opened the driver's side door and leaned in. It was too dark to see what he was doing.

Kelly had once theorized he was snobby, but I found that hard to believe. He'd always been polite and pleasant enough. I'd always been more inclined to say shy. *Aloof*, maybe, but he'd certainly seemed nice enough.

This serious, authoritative version of him was...different. It had my nerves ratcheting up even higher. It was a reminder I didn't really *know him* know him.

Despite all the hypothetical conversations we'd had in my head.

I jumped when he slammed his car door and headed back toward me. He drew near enough for me to make out the faint line between his dark brows, maybe because I was still sitting behind the wheel.

I chewed my lip. Going with Sky made the most sense. Even if I imagined it'd be the most awkward ten-minute drive of my life.

Suppressing a sigh, I grabbed my dead cell, purse, and apron. After one last scan of the car to make sure I hadn't left anything important behind, I pressed down the manual lock and climbed out. Ahead of me, Sky bent over the hood, scribbling something on a piece of paper. I watched, puzzled, as he walked around me and slid it onto the dashboard.

"A note, in case a cop or a Good Samaritan stops by," he said, catching my confused look. The thud when he shut the driver's door echoed. "You lock it?"

I nodded, and he turned away. With one last glance at Faith, I trailed after him. Wind swirled through the rustling cornstalks and tugged at my hair. Gravel crunched softly beneath my shoes. My pulse still hadn't quite evened out.

The night was so still. So quiet. Deceptively quiet, considering how hazardous it'd been so far.

I tore my attention from the deserted stretch of road when we reached the SUV. Sky surprised me by opening the passenger door. For me. I blushed for absolutely no good reason and climbed in. When he closed it again, I was alone in the car.

The interior smelled like him. Spice and leather and something cool and fresh. A low, sultry beat whispered from the speakers, and I took in the gleaming chrome, buttery leather seats, and touchscreen dash.

It was all...nice. Pretty nice for your average bartender's paycheck.

Did Sky come from money? Or was he just that good at mixing Old Fashioneds?

Maybe he moonlighted as a male stripper.

A second later, I started guiltily when he opened his door and slid behind the wheel. I cleared my throat and looked out the window, trying to pretend like I wasn't just imagining him shirtless and gyrating to a Ginuwine song.

He was quiet as he settled into the driver's seat. With him in it, the SUV's interior suddenly felt much tinier. I shivered and not entirely from the cool fall night.

He noticed. "Cold?" His smooth voice wrapped around me like velvet.

"I think it's just the adrenaline." My teeth promptly clicked together, proving me a liar.

Out of the corner of my eye, I watched him tap a button on the console, and the seat warmed beneath me. Heated air surged from the vents, and I began thawing out almost immediately. Some of the tension in my back released.

"Better?" he asked, buckling his belt.

"Yeah. Um, thanks." I tucked an escaped hair behind my ear, feeling suddenly shy, which was completely ridiculous in the circumstances. He'd just seen me nearly puke up a fish sandwich. And yet here we were. Or I was. Blushing furiously just because I was sitting next to him.

Sky's eyes met mine. The dashboard's glow traced the sharp edge of his high cheekbones, the graceful lines of his strong jaw.

Be normal, Rae. Be normal.

"Seriously—thanks," I said in a rush. "For everything. You didn't have to do all this. And I'm sorry about earlier, about being in the road. There was…" *Oh boy.* Where to begin. "I'm not sure…"

That was all I could manage. In another life, this would be a dream come true. On another night, when I hadn't just had a near collision with a…a…

I may as well admit it, at least to myself.

I'd seen a UFO.

An unidentified flying—no, *floating*—object. I'd seen an Unidentified Floating Object, which, in my book, still counted. Same acronym.

Even inside my head, though, it sounded ridiculous. Saying it aloud? Forget it. Kelly would die of smug satisfaction. Amelia would question my caffeine intake. My mom would schedule a therapy session. Bob would probably blame it on the government.

But I'd seen something. It'd been real.

And then it'd vanished.

Shaken, I glanced up again—only to find Sky still staring at me. He hadn't said a word. His eyes appeared nearly black again in the dim light, and his expression was just as impenetrable.

He was watching me so intently, I jumped when he leaned his elbow on the steering wheel and twisted my way. "So what did you *actually* see?" he asked evenly.

Chapter 6

MORTIFICATION AND OTHER
POSSIBLE EXPOSURE SIDE-EFFECTS

THE QUESTION LANDED LIKE AN ASTEROID IMPACT BETWEEN US, even with his level tone. He'd trained a stare on me that was so direct and stripping, it momentarily froze me in place.

God, I considered answering him, too.

My lips parted, and the words welled up. Something about the way he was looking at me expectantly—as if he already knew what I was going to say—made me *want* to tell him. To spill my guts and all my too-insane conspiracy theories come to life.

I leaned toward the center console.

And then I stiffened.

No. No, I'd already made the mistake of yapping to Sky about UFOs once tonight. I wasn't about to go two for two. Besides, I wasn't sure. I wasn't absolutely, irrevocably *positive* that was what I'd seen.

And if I was going to spout that kind of thing to the man I'd been pining after for the better part of a year, I'd better be pretty damn positive.

Swallowing, I straightened, clutching my apron tighter in my lap. "I'm not really sure. It all happened so fast. Probably just...an animal. Or a trick of the light. I'm tired. Dinner rush was crazy today. And I've got midterms. Lots of studying."

I trailed off, remembering too late how much I sucked at lying.

Amelia always said I advertised my emotions like a walking, talking billboard. I fought hard to meet Sky's eyes, hoping my poker face was better than usual tonight.

His skeptical expression told me it wasn't. For a second, I thought he might call me on the meandering lie. His gaze stayed on mine, sharpening slightly. A far-too-astute study that threatened to peel back the layers of my barely-there composure.

There was something beneath it. Something calculating. Something that breathed a ghost of wariness over my nape.

But he only sat back without a word. Didn't push.

I turned away, too, pretending to study the snaking tire tracks illuminated by the flickering emergency lights.

I couldn't lie to myself, though. I'd seen something.

The seat squeaked as Sky shifted again. I turned my head just in time to see him nod at my knee.

"By the way, you're bleeding."

I was? Pressing my thighs together instinctively under the offensively neon-green dress, I followed his gaze, surprised to find he was right. I must've scraped my kneecap open when I'd banged it on the doorframe after the crash. The small cut trickled a thin rivulet of red down my shin. My whole leg was filthy, a mess of drying blood and dirt from the ditch. I'd probably left a Rae-sized smudge on his shiny leather seat.

Embarrassed, I tugged at the hem of my skirt, grimacing. "Sorry. I didn't notice…"

The apology faded when he leaned over me to open the glove box. The movement brought him close. So close I felt his body heat and nearly let it out as another baby chicken squeak. Luckily, Sky didn't seem to notice.

He pulled out a handful of napkins and a small red box, then shut the compartment again. The back of his forearm brushed the top of my thigh as he withdrew, just a quick, accidental touch, but still enough to send a wave of tingles through me.

He didn't react.

God, I was really that hard up for attention. An incidental graze, and my stomach felt like a down pillow had exploded in there.

Looking as cool and collected as ever, Sky eased back into his seat and extended the bundle across the center console. The dim light made it hard to read his face, but his voice was calm, perfectly polite. "You can clean it up with that if you want. There should be some antiseptic wipes in there."

"Oh. Thanks," I murmured, looking down at what he'd given me.

The little red box turned out to be a mini first-aid kit. Sky Acosta carried a tiny first-aid kit in his glove box. How...responsible of him. Did Oasis's mysterious bartender often find himself patching up crazy girls on the road? Or was I just special?

I barely managed to stifle my snort and instead focused on setting my things aside. While I busied myself wiping off my knee with the tiny moist towelette, Sky reversed onto the road again, flipping off the emergency lights.

The next song that came on was darker, a heavier beat thrumming through the speakers.

"Where to?" he asked over it.

"Cherry Street." I balled up the wipe. The gash had stopped bleeding, at least, though I couldn't do much about the grime. "415 Cherry. The blue house across from Franklin Park."

He nodded, eyes on the road.

I leaned back into the seat, the leather warm now beneath me thanks to the heater. I hadn't realized how cold I was before. I could get used to this. Faith was a few decades too old to have butt warmers.

As Sky drove us down the winding country road, back toward the glow of town, I scanned the sky.

Nothing. No multicolored fireballs. No pulsing orbs. No signs of *anything* out of the ordinary. Only stars and moonlight.

Could I really have imagined the whole thing? Maybe Kelly had gotten under my skin more than I'd thought. Maybe the stress of midterms, work, and life had finally broken me.

But I hadn't imagined the heat of the pavement. My fingertips tingled at the memory of touching it.

"So...class?" Sky asked suddenly.

I jumped, whipping my head his way. "Sorry—what?"

He glanced over with a raised brow. "You said you had class in the morning. And you'd mentioned studying, too. Are you at TWU?"

"Oh." I fiddled with the edge of my apron. "Yeah, I go to Willow. I'm majoring in anthropology...well, archaeology, eventually."

"Archaeology, huh?"

I braced for the usual judgment, waving the hand holding the crumpled-up wipe. "I know, I know. It's hard to find a job. Doesn't pay well. I'll have to get a master's—"

"I was going to say it's cool."

"Oh." I eyed him. He was still looking ahead, but a smile played over his lips. They were nice lips. I stared at them because he was distracted and why not?

"It's a fascinating field," he said, with another quick look my way.

I tore my gaze from his mouth when his small smile deepened, revealing that rogue dimple in his right cheek that shouldn't be wielded around small children.

He turned his head back toward the road. "Do you have an area of specialty?"

My brain seemed to catch on then, and I realized he was... asking me about myself.

Was this real life? Had I died back on that road and this was heaven?

My cheeks heated again, and not the ones cozied into his seat warmer. "Not yet. I've been leaning toward cultural anthropology. I don't know. I find studying different cultures interesting. It's like... looking into a different world."

We reached the edge of town. Stadium lights from the high school's football field bordered on blinding after the country dark. The SUV rolled to a halt at a stop sign.

Sky was quiet for a beat. I glanced over, half-expecting him to look horrified with boredom. But instead he tilted his head a little and said, "It *is* interesting."

Then we were moving again, and he was driving, which was a good thing because I was gawking at him.

It was just small talk. Polite chatter. You know, the kind a bartender like him did all the time to keep those tips flowing. This didn't mean anything. He was only doing me a favor and filling the awkward silence.

His...*interest* couldn't be real. Even if I desperately wanted it to be.

It sobered me. I watched the houses blur past, quiet and draped in the deep night's shadows. When they got even more familiar, I leaned forward.

"It's that blue house there on the corner," I murmured, pointing.

He took his foot off the gas, and we slowed. "Your parents?"

"My what?" I frowned at him.

"Is this your parents' house?"

"Oh. No." I smiled a little and gathered my things. "I rent the apartment over the garage."

"Cool."

He pulled up beside the small two-story with its overgrown yard. I needed to mow before Bob tried to do it.

Speaking of the cranky old man, the porch light glowed warmly. He must've left it on for me. Classic Bob. My little apartment over the garage was dark, waiting.

"Thanks again," I told Sky, tucking that loose strand of hair behind my ear again as I juggled my purse, apron, and dead phone.

I reached for the handle, pushed the door open, went to step out—

—and forgot the damn seat belt.

I yelped when it snapped taut and yanked me back into the seat.

To his credit, Sky didn't laugh. He didn't say anything, in fact, as he leaned over and pressed the release, freeing me. The belt hissed like a snake as it retracted.

I muttered another thank you, avoided eye contact, and shifted to climb free before I could do anything else to embarrass myself.

Apparently, the options were endless tonight.

"Are you sure you're okay?" he asked, the quiet question stopping me before I could escape.

Bracing myself, I turned to face him. In the streetlight's soft glow, his eyes sparkled the deepest, jeweled blue. He rested a wrist casually on the steering wheel and hit me with a direct, unblinking look.

And then he completely rocked my world.

"Do you want my number?" he asked. "In case you can't find anyone to get you to your car tomorrow. I've got jumper cables at home, and I don't clock in until seven for the late shift. I can help."

Did I want his *what*?

His number? Like…the one to his *phone*? *That* number?

Fiery blood rushed from my chest to the tips of my ears. My brain lagged behind my mouth, which was moving and betraying me—

"No. No, it's fine. I'm fine. I don't want your number."

The silence that followed was nothing short of catastrophic.

I went rigid, wide-eyed.

Too late. It was too late to take the words back. I'd just said *no*.

Maybe if I stayed perfectly still, the moment would glitch and reset. Maybe if I focused hard enough, the universe would rewind.

But today, on the shittiest of all days, I wasn't that lucky.

Sky blinked, clearly thrown. His mouth opened, then closed, as if he didn't quite believe what he'd heard. But after a beat, he shook his head and gave me a crooked half-smile. Bemused. Maybe even a little impressed. "Right. Sure. Okay," he said lightly. "Well…I'll see you around then, Rae."

Oh my God.

I'd just turned down his number.

I wanted to throw myself across the center console and scream, *"I meant yes! My alter ego Rachel said no!"* But it was too late to backpedal without making it worse.

My skin burned, and my heartbeat did a tap-dance of doom.

"Thanks again," I managed to choke out before scrambling from the car like it was on fire right along with the rest of my life. I nearly dropped my pile of things, but I managed to hang on as I shouldered the door shut. I practically sprinted across the street, tripping a little on the curb.

Sky's SUV idled behind me, purring like a patient cat. He hadn't pulled away yet, and I was hyper-aware of him watching me.

Staring, probably. Wondering what the *hell* was wrong with me. I wished I had that answer.

I fumbled with my keys as I reached the stairwell door, my hand shaking as I jammed the correct one into the deadbolt. I slipped inside without a backward glance.

Only when the door shut behind me did I hear the low rumble of his SUV rolling away. He'd waited until I got inside.

Like a gentleman.

I leaned back against the door and shut my eyes, groaning.

I'd seen a UFO.

I'd wrecked my car.

And for some reason, for some unknown and *completely* idiotic reason, I'd told Sky Acosta I didn't want his phone number.

What a freaking day.

But…he'd called me Rae. There was that. I snorted a breathless laugh.

At least he'd remembered my name.

Chapter 7

DENIAL, SHMENIAL

IN THE MORNING LIGHT, everything about my night before felt like a dream. A very bad, very embarrassing dream. The kind where you're walking around naked or all your teeth fall out.

Except worse. It was the kind where I'd acted like a crazy person in front of Sky. Twice. And it wasn't a dream.

If I hadn't been missing my car and sporting a gash on my knee, I might've been able to convince myself...but no such luck, Chuck.

It'd happened. The floating orb. The car accident. Me, you know...laughing in Sky's face when he offered me his phone number. I cringed.

At least the pale blue sky came with a surprisingly warm morning sun. Its rays beat down on my shoulders as I made short work of the mowing. I inhaled the sharp scent of cut grass and gasoline, held it, then exhaled, forcing away the mortifying memory. The heavy drone vibrated through my palms while I sheared another straight line through the front yard.

It helped that I'd managed to reason out the entire mysterious-light-in-the-road incident.

After failing to drown myself in the shower last night, I'd gone down a research rabbit hole on ball lightning, and now I felt moderately convinced my sanity was intact. There were actual documented cases of ball lightning occurring outside of storms, and a late-autumn storm *had* passed through One Willow yesterday afternoon, bringing the warm front I was enjoying now.

Ball lightning. A perfectly plausible explanation. Atmospheric phenomenon.

Science. Boom. Mic drop.

Any lingering details that didn't quite fit could easily have been tricks of the imagination. Exhaustion. I'd pulled a double after a two-hour class. In the middle of cramming for midterms.

No UFOs here. *Suck it, Kelly.* This was just science and maybe a touch of sleep deprivation.

As for Faith, my brother already had her in the shop. He'd even borrowed the tow truck from his boss, Harry.

I'd handled it. All of it. I felt...*better.*

Mostly. A few things still smarted.

Grimacing, I pushed the temperamental mower back up the hill, the drone of its blades drowning out the pop song blasting from my earbuds. Too bad they couldn't drown out the last piece of my sucky night.

I'd turned down his number.

I'd literally said, *I don't want your phone number.* To Sky Acosta.

My insides curled like a dying spider.

I could've done without that particular memory in the clarity of morning. But no, there it was again. His face. The way he'd stared in utter confusion. The sheer bewilderment.

He probably didn't get turned down often. Not with a face like that. Not with those arms.

And then I'd gone and *bolted* from his car like *he* was the crazy one.

I resisted the urge to facepalm, veering into the next neatly spaced row. Would he talk to me at work tonight? Or would he go back to vague smiles and polite nods? Wednesday nights were usually slow, more chatting than serving, and he *had* said he was working the late shift. I was closing, too. So that meant...

Yep. Interaction was inevitable. And so were the nerves that came with it.

Oh hey, Sky. It's me, Raven. You know, the girl who ranted about aliens in the prep closet, threw herself in front of your SUV, and then ran away in terror when you offered your phone number? Yeah, that girl. Can we hit undo on all that?

I squeezed my eyes shut and shoved the mower faster. Was he the type to tell people what had happened? Would I show up to Oasis and hear Tony reenacting my panicked death scream in the kitchen?

The thought didn't quite congeal. I didn't think Sky was that guy.

Honestly, he'd probably just act like nothing had happened. Keep to himself behind the bar, pouring drinks with quiet professionalism. And I'd avoid eye contact like a boss.

That was the plan. Forced smiles. Feigned chill.

I could do that. I had *practice*.

That was it. We would go back to normal. He'd forget my name again, and I'd pretend I wasn't one awkward outburst away from a restraining order.

With that plan in place, I felt noticeably lighter as I finished the front yard and moved to the small patch in back. I'd be done before Bob even got back from his diner breakfast.

Humming along to my peppy music, I let myself zone out to the mowing vibes.

IF ONLY FORGETTING it all were that easy.

"Did you hear about the UFO lights last night?" Amelia asked as she plopped down across from me at the picnic table I'd claimed outside Kepler Hall. Her Coach bag clanged on the metal surface, but I barely heard it.

The words sank in. I inhaled a mouthful of rapidly cooling coffee and immediately sputtered, hacking.

When I could breathe again, I gaped at her through watering eyes. "What? What *lights*?"

All around us, TWU students lounged in scattered clusters across the courtyard, hemmed in by the four main buildings. It was a beautiful fall day, warm enough that I'd tied my emergency cardigan around my waist.

Now, though, goosebumps prickled across my arms. I fought off a shiver.

"The spooky UFO lights." Amelia wiggled her fingers in mock-suspense, showing off her new red manicure. She snickered and tossed her hair. "Apparently, people saw them all over the country roads last night?"

The last bit came out question-marked, like she wanted to bait me. Her grin said as much.

"Ball lightning," I muttered, setting my cup down a little too hard.

Her smug grin faltered. "What?"

"I said, it was probably ball lightning."

"Ri-ight." She tapped her nails on her cup and studied me with narrowed eyes. "You look tired. Up late thinking about a certain enigmatic bartender, *Rachel?*"

"Ha. Funny." If only she knew. "Hardly. I've got midterms and work all week."

"You've got Saturday off, though. Our plans aren't until later that night. Just spend the day being a lazy bum."

"Yeah, but I'm going to see Mom…and Dustin and Lisa."

I checked my phone instinctively, scanning for a text back from my brother. Nothing yet. I'd sent a groveling thank-you along with a promise of cheesecake this weekend. He and Harry had dropped Faith off at Bob's just in time for me to make it to class.

Turned out the culprit was a faulty battery. Which didn't make sense; it was less than a year old. It wasn't like I'd left it running for long in that ditch. But Dustin had looked everything over and had only found the electrical relay issues, the slipping transmission, and the slow oil leak. Which meant there was nothing *new* wrong with my car.

The point was it'd been a fluke, and Faith was still kicking. We both were. It was over.

Ish.

I leaned back, twirling my pencil while pretending to read my notes.

"Earth to Rae!" Amelia snapped her fingers in front of my face.

"What? Sorry."

"You sure you're okay?"

"Yeah! Just tired. What were you saying?"

She sipped her latte and leaned her elbow on the table again. "Just that even the One Willow PD got called. They mentioned it at the nail salon this morning. The lights, I mean. A dozen people called them in. And a bunch more only admitted to seeing them after hearing *other* people did. They were worried they'd sound crazy or something." She waved a hand as if *that* was the ridiculous part of everything she'd just said. "But now it's like the whole town saw them. People are saying it has to do with the base."

"That doesn't make any sense. The base is mostly shut down. Has been since Dad worked there." I waited a beat and summoned my most casual tone. "But what were these lights supposed to look like?"

Amelia paused, eyeing me like she was deciding how far to push. "Most people said yellow and pink, some said blue and green. Big glowing ball. But get this..." She suddenly dropped her elbow and leaned in.

I abandoned all pretense and bent forward, too.

"There's a farmer out on 100E who said he saw *something*. Not just the lights. Said it was silver and shaped like a saucer."

I stared at her before a snicker escaped. Then another. I laughed until I snorted and had to stop to breathe. "You're telling me people are claiming they saw *flying saucers* now?"

Amelia arched a microbladed brow. "I'm just telling you what I heard."

"Come on, A." I sighed and clasped my hands together. "Weird light phenomenon? Sure. I'll buy that. But flying saucers? Seriously?"

"I'm just relaying what I heard while getting my nails done!" She shoved her phone across the table, pointing at it. I glanced at it long enough to register the grainy video of a blurry ball of light against a dark background before looking away. She jabbed a finger in the screen's direction. "You have to admit—it looks legitimate. And it's a little creepy how things have been glitching. TVs. Phones. Radios. And then these lights?"

"There's a solar storm happening—"

"Yeah, yeah. Magnetosphere, blah blah, electromagnetic interference. But what if it's not that?"

I groaned. "Please don't tell me you've gone full Kelly."

"Is it really so hard to believe there could be something else out there?"

"No." I shook my head vehemently. "Not at all. It makes total sense that something else is out there. Space is huge. The universe is infinite. It'd be dumb to think we're the only ones floating around out here."

"Okay," Amelia said slowly, sipping her latte while she studied me over the rim. She swallowed then cradled the foam cup. "So your problem is just…what? That they're *here*?"

"Yes. Exactly. Why would they waste their time on Earth? We can't even get to Mars. We're still debating if aliens *could* exist. What's so interesting about humanity that someone would travel lightyears—like, thousands and thousands of *lightyears*—just to… mess with our internet and light up some cornfields?"

The more I spelled it out, the better I felt.

It made no sense. Aliens *being here* made no logical sense.

Sure, I'd freaked out last night, but that had been in the moment. After a double shift. In the dark. In a ditch. Now, in the daylight, with coffee in my veins and Google in my pocket, it was obvious. So obvious.

I'd fallen under Kelly's conspiracy spell. Temporarily. Embarrassingly. I made a silent pact to never, ever admit it to her.

Amelia considered it for a moment before shrugging. "Who knows? I mean, if we're being real, any alien race advanced enough to get here would be, like, majorly ahead of us in a lot of ways, right? Trying to guess *why* they'd come is like asking an ant why a human stepped on their hill."

I blinked. Morbid. But also…disturbingly fair.

I thought back to all the anthropological studies I'd read. Ones where scientists embedded themselves into different societies to observe them. It always came with a power imbalance. A more "advanced" culture studying one deemed "lesser."

Maybe, if someone had crossed the stars to get here, they were an explorer. A scientist.

Or maybe the paranoid ones were right, and *Independence Day* had it nailed. Maybe they were just here to wreck the anthill.

Hypothetically.

I sighed and ran my fingers through my hair, the strands still wavy from air-drying after my shower. No matter what I wanted to believe, the facts remained: I'd witnessed something. A whole bunch of people had.

What that *meant*, though, was still up for debate.

Right along with my sanity.

Chapter 8

WAR OF THE WORLDS

I WAS *STILL* THINKING ABOUT IT HOURS LATER.

Mostly because I didn't have a choice, thanks to my company.

I sat at the specimen table in the anthropology lab, sorting through pottery sherds from a nearby Paleolithic site. The overhead lights buzzed slightly, just enough to be annoying.

Not nearly as annoying as the subject at hand, though.

Across from me, Landon Martz filed his nails.

"And Louisa May—you know, the clerk at the gas station? She said there are, like, twenty different YouTube videos of it up now. They're calling it the *One Willow Visitation*." He made air quotes. "Pretty badass name, if you ask me."

I hadn't. But that didn't stop him.

"How cool would it be to see a real-life UFO? Ugh. I wish I hadn't been elbows-deep in the new season of *Put a Ring on It*."

No. It was not cool. I could confirm firsthand: it was very uncool. Terrifying. Unsettling.

Not "badass."

I bit my lip and bent over the next pottery piece. "Yeah, I don't know, Landon. It all just sounds so…"

"Awesome?"

I closed my eyes and counted to ten. I was *so* done hearing about this. Worse, I was starting to wonder why I was the only one *not* convinced.

Maybe I was in denial.

But I'd done the research. I'd read the studies. I'd found an explanation. Ball lightning and atmospheric interference. Stress-induced hallucination, if I wanted to get psychological about it.

I wasn't going to let Kelly and the rest of the internet loonies drag me down into the void with them. Whatever mass delusion was sweeping through One Willow—the world—I refused to be part of it.

I adjusted my grip on the tweezers and focused on the sherds. "You know what this sounds like, Landon? A hoax. An internet-fueled case of mass hysteria. Ever heard the story about the original broadcast of *War of the Worlds*?"

Landon's brows rose. "The what? No. I have no idea what that is."

"In the 1930s, they aired a fake alien invasion as a radio drama. But people didn't realize it was fiction. They tuned in partway through and thought it was *real*. People thought we were being invaded by monsters from outer space."

The scraping sounds of his nail file stopped. "No shit?"

"Real shit. It caused panic. Tons of chaos. Pissed people off, too. But my point is a lot of these alien stories work the same way. One person's nightmare gets blown out of proportion. They talk, it gets passed on, and someone else's brain latches on and builds it bigger. Alien abduction dreams? That's textbook phobia manifestation. Shared hallucinations. And now, with all the crap online, it spreads even faster."

When Landon didn't reply, I looked up.

He crossed his skinny arms over his black My Chemical Romance tee. "Anybody ever tell you you're a nerd, Raven?"

"Yes, actually." I sniffed. "But that's rich coming from you. Don't you have a *World of Warcraft* raid to get to?"

"Not on Wednesdays," he shot back, resuming his manicure with a scoff.

Technically, he was supposed to be helping. We both got credit for this extra lab study. But we also both knew I was better at it, and I worked best when I ran the show. So instead, Landon hung out and provided commentary while I cataloged the collection, and everyone stayed happy.

Except for today, that is.

He finished shaping his nails and pulled out a bottle of black polish. "Hey, speaking of nerdy, did you hear about the prof's new project?"

That piqued my interest. I looked up from my sorting. "No. What is it?"

"That's the thing." He swiped a stripe of paint on his middle finger and squinted at it, then met my eyes with a dramatic head tilt. "Nobody knows. It's some hush-hush thing. Rumor is it's connected to the base."

"The base? The military base?" I rolled my eyes. "Why is everyone suddenly obsessed with that place? It's been on life support since before I was born."

"Apparently not enough for them to stop running secret experiments."

I snorted. "And those would be…?"

"Nobody knows. It's top secret."

"Of course." I raised a brow and leaned back on my stool. "But if that's true, how do *you* know?"

"I have my sources." At my look, he smirked. "I don't kiss and tell, beautiful."

I rolled my eyes. "Uh-huh. And your *source* says there's some mysterious project happening right here in One Willow?"

"With *Professor Stern* of all people."

"Wait. Stern?" I straightened, my sneer fading. "The paleoastronomer? Why?"

That was such a specific niche. Basically the study of how ancient civilizations viewed and tracked space. How they incorporated it into daily life. Of course, it required way more math than I cared for, but it was still fascinating. And totally out of place here.

TWU was a good school, but not exactly a research titan. This wasn't Harvard.

And the claim that the base was involved? No way.

Somebody had to be lying. Exaggerating, at the very least.

Landon just waggled his brows, giving me nothing. I leaned forward and tapped the tweezers pointedly on the table. "You're such a tease."

"Guilty." He beamed. "You know you love me. But if I hear anything else, you'll be the first to know. Especially if it's got anything to do with our recent ET guests. I know how much of a fan you are."

Muttering a curse under my breath, I bent back over the tray.

His delighted laughter echoed off the lab walls.

I WAS NOT HIDING in the work bathroom. For the record.

I was just...lingering.

I tucked a strand of honey-colored hair behind my ear and leaned closer to the mirror, wiping under my eye where my eyeliner had smudged in the kitchen's greasy heat. Satisfied that it was as good as it was going to get, I raked my fingers through my frizzed-out waves and fluffed them into place around my shoulders.

It would have to do.

I stepped back and gave myself a critical once-over. My chin was a little too round, my eyes a bit too big for me to ever be called classically beautiful like Amelia or Kelly. With a swipe of gold shadow and a heavy hand on the eyeliner, I could maybe manage the girl-next-door look. If the girl next door wore training bras and didn't know how to apply lipstick.

Sighing, I spun away from the mirror.

Not that it mattered how I looked tonight. I wasn't trying to impress anyone.

Sure, Sky was coming in at seven. And it just happened to be six fifty-eight. Complete coincidence that my stomach felt like a butterfly exhibit mid-tornado.

I slipped out of the bathroom and detoured past my single table.

My two margarita-loving ladies were still chatting away, so I left them to it and continued toward the kitchen entrance.

I nearly turned and walked the other way when I caught wind of the conversation happening by the prep room.

"I heard there were three ships."

"That YouTube video looked like at least two."

"Jackie's dad chased it! He made it all the way to Lake James before it vanished into the clouds."

I tried to ghost away, but Kelly spotted me at the edge of the group and lit up like a Christmas tree with perfect hair and too many teeth. "Rae-bae! There you are. Tell me you believe me now!"

"The truth is out there, Kelly," I intoned, managing to keep a straight face.

If she caught the *X-Files* reference, she didn't show it. I resisted the urge to snort.

If I was going to be trapped in this circus of conspiracy theorists, I could at least entertain myself.

"What, you don't think it's aliens, Raven?" Emily asked softly, peering at me through her thick-framed glasses. Her straight-cut bangs bounced when she tilted her head. "How come?"

"Rae-bae here is too scientific for aliens," Kelly answered for me, rolling her eyes like having a logical mind and a healthy amount of skepticism was a tragic personality flaw.

"Right," I muttered through gritted teeth, then turned back to Emily with more patience. "I just think there are better explanations than little green men zipping around One Willow."

Kelly waved a hand like I was a lost cause. "Whatever. You closed last night, didn't you? You see anything on your way home? This all happened right around that time."

I hesitated. Just for a second.

But in that second, the image of that glowing fireball bearing down on me blazed to life behind my eyes. My mouth went dry.

I started to deny all of it—

And then my gaze snagged on a pair of dark blue eyes watching me intently from across the room.

The knot in my stomach unspooled into something light and

floaty. Faintly effervescent, like I'd chugged a glass of champagne. Which, if true, would also have explained my thoughts blurring. But alas...no champagne.

Just Sky. And the effect he always had on me.

He leaned against the edge of the bar, a good ten feet from the group. Far enough not to be involved, but close enough to be clearly listening. His arms were folded over his chest, his gaze on mine. There was no smile, just that quiet, unreadable intensity—the kind that made my pulse skip and brain short-circuit.

And, naturally, I stared back with my classic deer-in-headlights look.

Somehow, in the past twenty-four hours, I'd managed to forget just how absurdly attractive he was. His gray button-down hugged his sculpted chest like it had been tailored for the occasion, sleeves rolled to his strong forearms, collar undone enough to show the hollow of his tanned throat. Dark jeans. He was also very much looking in my direction.

And I was checking him out again. Subtlety was *not* my middle name.

I slammed my mouth shut and forced my eyes away. Tried to focus on whatever the hell Kelly was saying. I could feel him watching me.

I couldn't help it. I risked another glance Sky's way. This time, a slow sliver of a smile tugged at the corner of his mouth. Not full-on smirk level, but close. He'd noticed my fluster.

Fantastic.

I turned stiffly back to Kelly. "Sorry. What?"

She rolled her eyes, huffing. "I asked if you saw any lights last night since you closed."

I was shaking my head before she'd even finished, because denial wasn't just a river in Egypt; it was also my middle name. "No. I didn't see anything last night."

For a split second I wondered why I couldn't just admit it, but then Kelly made a sound like a squeal, and I nearly gasped.

"Oh my God. Rae-bae, you're a *terrible* liar!" She pounced and snatched up my wrists. "You *so* saw something! What was it?"

"I didn't…" I tried to dislodge her. She clung like a pair of pink-painted handcuffs.

I slumped, biting back a slew of curses. I was useless at lying. Everyone knew it. The glint of triumph in her eyes said it all.

Something about it made me dig my heels in.

"You *have* to tell us!" she said, grip tightening. "What did you see?"

I ground my molars. "Nothing."

A bright light where there shouldn't be light. Ball lightning. A hot bartender. I glanced Sky's way again.

He hadn't moved. He was still watching, arms now uncrossed, hands tucked into his back pockets like he was settling in for the show. Unease twisted in my gut.

Was he hoping I'd spill about what happened last night? About the near-vehicular-manslaughter-meets-UFO-encounter? What part was he waiting on: my recap of his involvement…or what had caused the entire thing?

He obviously hadn't shared the deets on our late-night rendezvous. Gossip spread like wildfire in this place. If he'd said anything, Kelly would've been the first to blab it to the world.

So he'd kept quiet. So far.

Maybe he was just being a nice guy, and the purpose of keeping it on the down-low was to avoid embarrassing me.

Or maybe he was watching now and hoping I'd tell the story myself. Make him look like the hero. Maybe he had some kind of weird modesty complex.

Or *maybe* I was wildly overthinking everything, and he was just bored and mildly entertained by a prep area full of waitresses hyped up on alien YouTube.

Damn it. I'd stared at him a little too long. Long enough that the girls around me followed my gaze before I could fake disinterest. When Kelly saw who I was looking at, she dropped my forearm and sent me an *oh really?* look.

He hadn't looked away, as if he didn't notice the dreamy looks from the other waitresses.

Or maybe he didn't care.

He gave me a nod. "Hey, Rae," he said, quietly but loud enough to cut through the background hum of music and customer chatter.

My lips parted on a soundless inhale. For one golden second, all reason drained away, replaced by a buzz of happiness. He really *had* remembered my name.

Then I shook myself. It wasn't *that* big of a deal. Remembering a person's name was common courtesy, for God's sake.

Besides, I was sure I'd left an impression yesterday. Probably not a good one, but enough to stick, it seemed. He'd rescued me off the side of the road, and I'd responded by turning down his phone number.

I wailed inwardly.

Only one way to fix this: rip off the awkward bandage. Get it over with.

On autopilot, I stepped forward, giving Kelly's shoulder an absent pat on my way past. Sky watched me approach, and my heart played hopscotch in my chest. Out of the corner of my eye, I saw the other girls gawking. Turning my back on them, I stopped in front of Sky and tipped my head back to meet his gaze.

He angled his chin down, a shadow of scruff roughening the planes of his handsome face.

"Hi."

"Um. Hi. Hello," I said, immediately regretting everything. I bit my inner lip and hooked my thumbs into my apron pockets. Why not throw in a howdy while I was at it?

Sky gave me another faint smile.

"Hey," he said. The tiny grin hitched up higher. "Think we've covered most of the standard greetings now."

Damn it. He'd noticed.

"Yeah, look at that. We did. So...um, funny." I cleared my throat and shut my mouth before I could say anything else mortifying.

We just...looked at each other. Oasis's canned music track played a jaguar growl before transitioning into a steel-drum samba interspersed with monkey calls. Somewhere beyond the kitchen's swinging doors, an incensed Jackie shouted that whoever chopped tomatoes must've used a machete to butcher them.

Sky's mouth twitched like he was trying not to smile even wider —either at the cook's tirade or because I was still gazing up at him like a lovesick idiot. My cheeks went up in flames. I scrambled for something—anything—to say.

Thankfully, Sky took pity on me and broke eye contact. He shot a glance over my shoulder, where the others still loitered, before running a hand through his thick hair.

"So...you didn't answer them," he said, jerking his chin toward the group of waitresses. "You seemed pretty shaken up last night. Any idea what caused you to spin out like that?"

Some of my flustered embarrassment faded away, and I straightened, brow furrowing. He'd already asked me that. In the car. I'd told him I didn't know.

Unless he hadn't believed me.

Oh no. Not him, too.

He looked as serious as ever as he studied my face, like he was trying to read something in it.

I folded my arms across my chest, irritation flickering to life. "I already told you last night. It was nothing. I only caught a glimpse. It was an animal or something. Ball lightning."

"Ball lightning," he said, his dubious tone making it clear what he thought of my theory.

I pursed my lips, scoffing. "God, Sky. It wasn't a—" I stopped. I couldn't bring myself to say *spaceship*. Not with all the ears around us. But I refused to look away.

His dark eyes held mine. This close, I could see shards of silvery gray and inky black inside the sapphire.

And because I'd already made a mess of things, I went ahead and said what I was thinking.

"I can't believe you're falling for this ridiculous conspiracy. Aliens? Really?"

"You said it. Not me." His hands stayed in his pockets as he rocked back on his heels. "I just wondered..."

He trailed off as he glanced behind me again. I heard the subtle shuffle of shoes as the rest of the crew drifted closer.

His gaze flitted back to me, and when he spoke next, his voice was significantly more casual. "How are you feeling today? How's your car?"

The shift in topic caught me off guard.

"My car? Oh. Right." I rubbed the side of my neck. "I'm fine. It's fine. My brother said it was the battery." Toying with the end of my braid, I peeked up at him. "Thanks again. For the ride and everything. You didn't have to do all that."

"It was no problem."

"I mean it." I transferred my weight from foot to foot. "You really helped me out. I appreciate it."

"No problem," he repeated, offering a polite smile. His eyes flicked away from mine.

That spark I'd glimpsed earlier faded. He looked…distant now. Guarded. Back to the same cool demeanor he wore behind the bar.

I hated how much that bugged me.

But then I remembered that look from last night—the one he'd given me right after I told him I didn't want his number. Maybe he was being distant and guarded because I'd come just shy of flipping him off after he'd offered me his digits. It checked out.

Sky opened his mouth, hesitated, then closed it, studying the floor. When he looked up again, there were too many thoughts churning in the pensive stare he gave me. I couldn't decipher a single one.

An even heavier silence stretched between us until I gave up and jabbed a thumb over my shoulder.

"Well, I should go check on my people." I gestured vaguely behind me, at the mostly empty tables. "My, um, section."

He eyed me. "Sure. Yeah." He stepped back toward the bar. If I didn't know better, I'd think the slow movement was reluctant. "Catch you later, Raven."

With another ghost of a practiced smile, he turned away, slipped behind the counter, and rounded the corner. He didn't look back. I frowned after him until he was out of sight. The whole thing left me unsettled.

Why did it feel like he'd had more to say?

I had only a second to process before Emily and Kelly swarmed me.

"Since when are you and Sky *friends?*" Emily asked, her voice hushed and reverent.

Were we? I glanced back, but he was gone. I didn't think we qualified as friends. He'd only avoided running me over. That didn't make us friends...did it?

Kelly zeroed in, her mental wheels clearly turning. "What did you mean, *thanks for the ride?*"

I sighed. Loudly. "We're *not* friends, Em. And it's nothing. I had some car trouble after work, and he happened to be driving by. He gave me a ride home."

"Car trouble? Last night?" Kelly's grin turned predatory. "You mean, *during the time the UFOs were spotted?*"

"I know where you're going with this," I said, grabbing a tray. I turned and headed into the dining room, calling over my shoulder. "And I'm not going there with you."

"Sure. Just a coincidence, right?" she called after me, her voice dripping smug satisfaction.

But it wasn't.

I knew it wasn't.

I just didn't know what to make of it.

Chapter 9

CURIOSITY KILLED THE ANTHRO
STUDENT

THANKFULLY, I HAD A NEW MYSTERY TO CONTEMPLATE THE NEXT MORNING.

I unloaded bread from the reusable fabric grocery bag, glancing through the window. The sun peeked from behind puffy gray clouds that'd been gathering, and hazy light illuminated Bob's small kitchen. The smell of strong coffee and the faint, sweet scent of the carnations I'd grabbed hung in the air. Lord knew he could use the cheer.

Behind me, Bob set his mug down on the round kitchen table and cleared his throat in that pointed way of his. I braced myself for a lecture—

And was not disappointed.

"You should really see about a new car, Raven. Pretty girl like you shouldn't be worried about being stranded on the side of the road. There's some downright shit people in this world."

"I know, Bob. I'm working on it." I shoved his chicken noodle soup into the pantry and hung the bananas on the little brass hook I'd added under the cabinets.

Technically, none of this was in the rental agreement, but after a couple years of living above Bob's garage, we'd slipped into a routine. I'd gotten used to his grumbling, too. I almost enjoyed it. He was rough and gruff, an ex-soldier turned full-time curmudgeon. And yet, somehow, he'd gone from landlord to my grouchy, honorary grandfather.

Judging by his current tone, he felt the same.

"I told you, girl. I'll help you out."

"Absolutely not." I shoved up my sleeves, grabbed his dirty egg pan, and gave him an exasperated look over my shoulder. "I've already told *you* I'm not letting you help with a car loan. You already undercharge me for the fancy apartment above your garage."

"Bah." Bob huffed into his coffee.

I shook my head and turned back around, dunking the pan into the soapy water. At least he didn't swat me with the newspaper anymore when I did his dishes.

"You hear about these damn UFO lights?" he asked.

I could've done without *that* particular subject change, though. Apparently there was no avoiding it.

Resigned to it, I lifted a shoulder. "Yeah. I...heard about them. Everybody's talking about it."

Literally. Everyone.

Bob snorted. "Probably scouting before they drop a nuke."

"Nobody's going to nuke One Willow, Bob." I rinsed the pan and reached for the plate. "It's probably just the solar flare. That's what the news is saying, and that makes the most sense to me."

Liar, liar. Pants on fire.

I'd barely slept again last night. My brain wouldn't stop spinning. No matter how much I wanted to ignore it, I couldn't deny something was going on in One Willow. And it wasn't looking very...terrestrial.

Bob wasn't buying the solar flare theory either. "Then it's that there base," he muttered. "Always thought that place was trouble. No offense to your pops. Rest his soul."

"It's not the base. And thanks." I sighed, setting the plate on the rack.

I'd given in and done another internet search. The lights had been seen all over the county. Different locations, but eerily similar in description and timing.

And while the rational side of me screamed *coincidence*, my gut whispered otherwise.

After all, that was an awful lot of ball lightning.

I'd seen something. I'd *felt* the heat lingering on the road below where it had hovered. The brightness had stung my eyes. The hum, the electric buzz in the air—it'd all felt real.

All too real. Visceral, even now.

I tried to shake off the memories, but they clung like cobwebs.

Occam's Razor said the simplest explanation was usually the right one. But there was *nothing* simple about glowing balls of fire causing car accidents. Or floating all over the city.

I needed to understand what was happening.

Problem was, I had no idea where to start.

"I reckon you're right," Bob said when I stayed quiet. He snapped his newspaper straight. "You know more about this stuff than I do with all your fancy schooling. Speaking of those folks—sounds like that anthro-whatever professor of yours has some secret project going on. You know about that?"

The plate I was scrubbing slipped from my fingers and plopped into the water.

I twisted to stare at him, up to my elbows in suds. "What? How'd you hear about that?"

"Went to the diner yesterday for my Tuesday pancakes. Lettie said her son Dan—you know, young guy on the force—had to set up some escort for a delivery to the university. Something about the military working with the school's lab. Even got guards there. Crazy stuff."

The military? I jumped when Bob slapped his paper down.

He didn't seem to notice. "Whole thing sounds mighty suspicious, if you ask me. Lot of air traffic around that base lately, too, and that place's supposed to be practically shut down."

He was right. The base was supposed to be a ghost town. I swallowed hard, my pulse speeding.

After Landon's offhand comment yesterday, I hadn't thought

much of his claim that Professor Stern was involved in something fishy. But now...? Hearing it twice like this couldn't just be a fluke. There had to be some truth to it.

So what the hell would the professor be working on that would need *military* escorts and guarded deliveries?

I'd taken a few of his classes. He taught some of the two-hundred-level courses I'd needed for prereqs. Nice enough guy. Fair grader. Liked tweed jackets and overhead projectors. Nothing about him screamed *top-secret liaison to the government.*

I racked my brain for his last published study. Something about the placement of Native American burial mounds aligning with ancient constellations.

Ancient constellations.

Unidentified flying objects.

Solar flares.

A chill tiptoed down my spine. No. There was *no way.*

...Was there a connection?

"You okay, kid?" Bob's raspy voice cut into my thoughts, and I realized I'd been staring into space. I blinked and met his rheumy eyes. He squinted at me with clear concern. "You look like you've seen a ghost."

Not a ghost. Maybe aliens, though.

"Sorry." I turned back around and fished out the plate, rinsing it and moving on to the silverware. "That's just...surprising. Weird."

Weird. But...

A glance at the clock told me I had a few minutes before I needed to head to class. I mentally reviewed my schedule. There was a decent break between my last lecture and my shift at work.

Perfect.

I'd go to Professor Stern's office. I'd just *ask.*

What was the worst he could say? That it was classified? *I could tell you, but I'd have to kill you?*

I snorted.

There had to be a logical explanation.

I just had to find it.

·   ·   ·

THE ANTHROPOLOGY WING felt abandoned when I stepped from the stairwell hours later.

The elevator was still out—surprise, surprise—so I'd taken the stairs three flights down to the bottom of the Finke Building. My heart pounded from exertion, not nerves. Probably.

It was definitely nerves that had me eyeing the corridor lights when they buzzed and flickered. If they went out, it was going to be extra dark in this basement hallway. I patted the phone in my pocket, just in case.

The empty hall was at least a lot quieter than the upper wings had been. Devoid of alien gossip and people laughing over UFO memes. I ground my teeth in annoyance. My social media feed was full of them. Everyone was still obsessed.

Hopefully not for long. The electrical problems and blackouts had stretched across the Midwest, but according to the latest news clip, they were already tapering off. The solar flare, the newscaster claimed, was weakening.

If there was one at all.

I adjusted my bag and shoved away the thought. Who even was I? That wasn't me. I didn't fall prey to conspiracy theories. I certainly didn't let them make me jumpy like this.

My old Converse squeaked with each step, the sound echoing off the cream-colored linoleum. Closed doors lined both sides of the corridor. I didn't see *anyone*. The few staff members working down here must've been out to lunch or at some off-site department meeting.

Still. It was weirdly empty. Maybe that was on purpose. Maybe it had something to do with Professor Stern's project. I hadn't seen any of the guards Bob had claimed were here, though.

And yet the quiet went from feeling peaceful to…unnatural. Foreboding.

Shrugging off the chill, I focused on the familiar: flyers and event posters tacked to the corkboards, blurbs about local digs and conference dates, and the peeling edge of a laminated map. The unease lingered anyway.

A door slammed somewhere nearby.

I jumped and sucked in a sharp breath, halting mid-step.

Rolling my eyes, I straightened my spine and began walking again with renewed determination. It was someone closing a door, for Pete's sake. Perfectly normal. I was just on edge.

On the bright side, at least someone else was down here. It made the emptiness of the cramped basement wing feel a little less intimidating.

Then I rounded the corner—

And caught a glimpse of a dark figure vanishing through the double doors marked *Lab 3*.

They'd moved fast, a blur of motion, but I saw enough to register a tall, masculine form. The doors they'd passed through swung gently.

I paused at the bend in the hall, worrying my bottom lip.

That was weird. It almost looked like they'd been running. Maybe someone was late for a lab. Or a meeting with a professor.

"Professor Stern?" I called.

No response but the echo of my own voice. The fluorescent lights above buzzed and dimmed. I glanced up at them, breath catching. A half-second later, they flickered back to full power, as if nothing had happened.

Just a power blip. *Again.* I glared at the panels like they'd personally betrayed me.

Squaring my shoulders, I approached the double doors. No glow seeped from behind the opaque glass windows, but the panels still swung gently in the wake of whoever had passed through.

Instinct prickled at the back of my neck.

I reached out, then hesitated.

You're being ridiculous, Rae. I pushed the nearest panel open, braced myself, and stepped into...

Nothing. An empty lab.

No one waited on the other side.

I exhaled slowly and shoved the door wider. The front lab was dark. Light from the hallway spilled in, casting long shadows over the metal shelving and rows of white tables, each cluttered with carefully labeled boxes and stacks of notes. At the back of the room, a row of computer screens glowed softly in sleep mode, their pale light barely illuminating the space.

I licked my dry lips. "Hello?"

No response.

The door on the far side of the room stood slightly ajar. I knew where it led: a hallway connecting the staff offices, the storage room, and beyond that, the temperature-controlled, authorized-personnel-only lab.

All this alien talk was seriously getting to me. I shoved the sensation of creeping dread aside and moved around the nearest table, skirting the clutter as I headed for the far door.

Out of habit, I fumbled for my phone, pulling it from the back pocket of my jeans. For half a second, I considered calling Amelia for the illusion of company. Just in case.

I dismissed the urge, annoyed by my own jumpiness. I'd never been the paranoid type. It was only a dark hallway. One I'd been in before. And that figure had just been another student.

Simplest explanations.

I reached the far door and nudged it open with my shoulder, peering through.

Bright fluorescent light poured from the narrow corridor beyond. It stretched in a clean, sterile line to another set of double metal doors at the far end. Empty.

To my right: Professor Stern's office.

To my left: the drinking fountain and single-stall bathroom. The lock read VACANT.

"Professor?" I whispered. "Hello?"

Why was I whispering?

Somebody had to have come this way. I'd *seen* them. My throat tightened as I crept forward. One step, then another. I peered through the square window in Stern's office door.

It was empty. Dark, too. He hadn't just stepped out; he wasn't in. Only the cold glow of his sleep-mode monitor lit the stacks of books, artifacts, and mess of half-filed papers on his desk.

Another cautious stride brought me alongside the bathroom. Without thinking, I reached for the handle and pulled.

And screamed.

It echoed, slicing through the suffocating silence, but I barely heard it over the ringing in my ears. Flinging the door away, I stumbled backward until my heel caught my other foot. I crashed onto the linoleum, landing hard on my back. Books jabbed into my spine through the fabric of my bag, and the wind rushed from my lungs.

I lay there, stunned and breathless, struggling to comprehend what it was I'd just seen.

Because it turned out I wasn't alone down here after all.

Chapter 10

THIS DEFINITELY WASN'T ON THE SYLLABUS

THE BATHROOM DOOR SWUNG THE REST OF THE WAY SHUT WITH A QUIET *CLICK*, a sound far too gentle for how violently my heart was beating.

Sitting up, I pulled my knees to my chest.

The door might have closed, but what lay beyond was burned into my brain.

Three people dressed in military fatigues, armed, unconscious, and pale, had been crammed into the single-stall bathroom like discarded mannequins. The closest, a young man not much older than me, had a gash above his eyebrow. Blood smeared his temple.

From that single, horrified glimpse, I hadn't been able to tell if any of them were breathing.

What if they *weren't?*

Oh God. Had I just stumbled onto a murder scene?

My stomach pitched and rolled. For a long second, I thought I might throw up.

Breathe. In through the nose. Out through the mouth. I clung to the action, forcing the nausea down. Forcing my brain to work. To process.

They weren't campus security. The uniforms were all wrong.

Campus security wasn't in need of camo *anything*. I didn't even think they carried real guns.

My unconscious friends had to be the military guards Bob had mentioned. The ones Landon had hinted at. Here because of whatever project Professor Stern was working on.

So who the hell had *done* this to them?

And why stuff them in a *bathroom*?

I glanced around, gulping air. Sweat broke out on my forehead as I eyed the closed door. I needed to know if they were alive. Needed to know I hadn't just found dead guys in this college basement.

Using the wall for support, I hauled myself upright. My legs felt strangely weak, and a rock settled itself low in my gut. The idea of seeing those pale, bloody faces again made me lightheaded, but I forced myself to move.

I gripped the handle. Opened the door.

Another scream tried to rise, but I swallowed it, crouching beside the first guard. My arm shook as I reached for his neck.

Please, please…

Warm skin met the pads of my fingers, and my shoulders slumped, a sigh of relief escaping. He had a pulse. A strong one. He was alive.

I rocked back and balanced my elbows on my thighs, examining the others. They were all alive. Their chests rose and fell with shallow, steady breaths.

I hadn't found a pile of dead bodies. Thank God.

But I *had* found bodies. Someone had still attacked them and stuffed them in there. I'd seen a dark figure running, but I hadn't come across a single other soul. Hell, I hadn't gotten a clear look at whoever was booking it in the hall, either.

Which didn't matter. What mattered was the fact I needed to get help. Pronto.

Digging my phone from my back pocket with trembling hands, I raised it.

No signal.

A strangled sound lodged in my throat, half sob, half curse. Of course I didn't have signal. Reception in the anthro basement was crap on a *good* day. A day *without* mysterious electromagnetic interference.

Plan B. *Get out. Get help.*

I glanced at the bathroom. No way could I drag them upstairs by myself. Not quickly. Not safely. But leaving them didn't sit right, either. What if whoever did this came back?

Or...or what if they were *still here?*

I stiffened. That cold ripple of apprehension ran through me again, and common sense finally broke past the shock—along with the urge to *run*. If they were still there, then I was also in danger of being knocked out and stuffed into some basement crevice.

I had to get the hell out of here. I turned on jelly legs and staggered back toward the lab entrance.

Only to stop short as something crashed just beyond the double doors.

Thump.

My heart lurched. I slapped a hand to my chest.

Whirrrrrr-CLANK.

A metallic groan echoed through the door. Unnatural and high-pitched, like metal grinding against metal. Then another whoosh, like a hydraulic lift pressing down.

Then silence.

The hair on my arms stood straight up. I backpedaled, shoes squeaking, breath rasping as I stared at the doors.

Someone was in that lab.

No, not some*one*. Some*thing*.

I didn't wait to find out what. My survival instinct finally kicked into overdrive.

I turned the other way and ran.

My backpack bounced behind me with each step as I sprinted deeper into the basement, aiming for the double doors at the far end of the hall.

I'd only been down here a few times, but I remembered the layout. The storage room waited beyond those doors. And the clean lab past that.

Another way out.

Behind me, that mechanical shriek sounded again—closer now. They were moving faster.

Clank. Grind. Whir.

I didn't look back. I didn't want to see what was chasing me. *Gaining on me*, if the loudness was any indication.

I crashed into the storage room doors, and they squeaked once —short and loud—when I rammed them open. The ringing in my ears muffled the sound as I stumbled forward. A single white light shone down at the entrance, blinding me to everything except the concrete beneath my shoes. I veered to the side and broke into a sprint, bolting past the first set of shelves until I reached the end, near the wall.

Only then did I pause, chest heaving. I pressed against the cold edge of the metal rack and gripped my book bag strap in a death grip. Hiding.

From *what*?

I didn't know. All I knew was that my instincts were screaming and dread coated my throat. A waiting, ominous silence had fallen.

I squeezed my lips together to quiet my breathing and reached for my phone with shaking fingers. When I thumbed the screen on, wincing at the harsh blue glow, there was still no signal.

Damn it.

Panic rising, I shoved it back in my pocket and closed my eyes, the back of my head knocking against the cool shelf.

Okay. Think. Focus. Keep breathing.

I mentally mapped the room. Rows of shelves stretched across the massive space, all labeled and catalogued with meticulous care. I remembered from my first volunteer tour that the far side housed the more sensitive artifacts. The clean lab entrance waited just around the side of the shelves.

…and there was an emergency exit in there. Stairs. I distinctly remembered the glowing sign.

Which was great, since this definitely counted as an emergency.

Shit. Except I also remembered the lab room's door had an electronic lock. The professor had said something about getting authorization if you needed access. I hadn't.

My stomach sank, and I leaned my head back.

So I was trapped. If whatever I'd heard came in here...I was screwed.

That was it. I was about to join the unconscious guards crammed into the bathroom.

Or worse. I was about to become a permanent exhibit in the archive room.

But when I peeked around the edge of the shelf, I inhaled sharply. Wait. The far doors—the lab's doors—were propped *open*. I wouldn't need an access card after all.

Why? Who'd opened them? My brain snagged on the risk of unfiltered air damaging the specimens before lurching back to more immediate concerns. I couldn't care about the artifacts. Not right now.

I cared about surviving.

Another moment passed. I didn't hear anything. Either whatever had been following me had vanished...or I'd been imagining things.

Suddenly, I felt silly.

Maybe I'd just fled from a noisy HVAC system. The pipes down here *were* old.

Either way, I didn't need to know which possibility was the truth. It didn't matter. I pushed off the shelf. What mattered was getting the hell out of this basement. Because even if I wasn't being chased, somebody had knocked out some guards and stuffed them into a bathroom, and that could *not* be good—

BANG.

The double doors behind me slammed open. A choked squeak caught in my throat as I backpedaled, smashing myself against the shelf again. I barely felt the impact when my temple glanced off the frame.

I didn't dare breathe.

So much for a noisy HVAC. That wasn't an air handling unit that'd entered the room.

A harsh creak sounded, like rusty hinges being forced to move. My heart hammered.

CRASH.

I flinched as something shattered, a muted tinkle like glass or pottery hitting concrete. Seconds later came more: the heavy *thud* of boxes, the shriek of Styrofoam, the rending of cardboard. The shelf I pressed against trembled.

Whatever was in here was tearing the place apart. And they weren't just vandalizing. No, this sounded rhythmic.

Deliberate. Methodical.

They were searching.

Destroying, too, in the process.

I gritted my teeth and pressed harder into the shelf. My fists clenched at my sides.

Then, beneath the sounds of destruction, came that other sound. That mechanical *whir*, low and guttural. A *grinding groan.*

The same sound I'd heard before. My heart seized.

I wasn't running blind anymore. I *had* to see.

Slowly, so slowly, I inched around the corner. A crash rang out from the far side, and I dropped lower, instinctively ducking. The shadows between shelves swallowed me whole.

Clank. Whir. Rip. Thud.

And then—

A voice.

Not a shout. Not a murmur. Something…*else.*

Garbled. Digital. Warped like a bad radio signal, yet still undeniably a voice. That was speech.

Ice flooded my veins. Because that speech wasn't…

Human.

Mechanical and deep, it spoke again, each syllable guttural and foreign. Another crash followed, this one accompanied by the pinging of smashing glass. I caught my breath, dizzy with fear. My pulse thudded in my throat, my limbs, everywhere.

What the hell was that? And what was I supposed to do *now*?

I backed another step into the shadows and checked my phone again. Still no signal.

Then, as I watched, the battery drained in real time. The screen went black. Not even the charge symbol flashed.

The air vibrated, buzzing along my skin like a live wire, stinging enough I sucked in a sharp breath.

I knew that feeling. It was the same thing I'd felt on the side of the road.

Overhead, the bulbs flickered once, twice, then the one by the doorway sizzled and popped, going out. I barely bit back my yelp as —one by one—the rest followed, plunging everything into pitch-black.

Only the light from the propped-open lab doors glowed like a beacon in the dark, still within running distance.

But could I make it?

Someone—*something*—had taken out three armed guards. I'd seen the blood on that guy's forehead. Whatever was tearing through the shelves behind me...I didn't want to meet it in a dark alley. Or anywhere, really.

Even if I made it inside, the lab doors stood wide open. One of those things could already be in there.

I had to think. I was trapped. The destruction grew louder, each crash marching closer, like it was working its way down the rows.

Any hope I'd held that this was just Professor Stern, bumbling around was long dead. Professor Stern had a soothing, NPR-on-decaf voice. This thing sounded like a blender and a V8 engine had produced a baby, and that baby was *pissed*.

I shoved my useless phone into my pocket and crouched low, shuffling along the shelving. I couldn't make out much in the inky dark, but I kept moving, feeling my way along the metal frame.

Another crunch sounded, right on the other side of the shelf.

Way too close.

My legs shook with every step, but I slid along the racks, eyes on the end of the row. Almost there. Another few steps, and I was free.

Even better, I could see it now. There was a clear path.

The open lab doors waited. I wasn't a sprinter, but I could hustle. I waitressed doubles on Saturdays. I had stamina. I could do this.

As quietly as possible, I jogged to the next set of shelves and flattened against the end cap. Holding my breath, I listened. More rustling. Then—

Silence.

For just a split second before a motorized whine shattered the quiet, followed by metal striking stone. Once. Twice. Three times.

Shit. *Footsteps.* Those were *footsteps.*

The garbled voice returned, and something primal clenched in my gut. Closer now. The shelf at my back shook with each thudding step. My legs shook along with it.

Screw this.

I broke and ran.

Chapter 11

THE WORST LAB PARTNER EVER

I RAN LIKE MY LIFE DEPENDED ON IT. Odds were, it did.

My soles slapped concrete, and my pulse roared in my ears. Behind me came that awful, terrible mechanical whine.

The steps resumed. Faster this time.

Crunch, whir, creak. Crunch, whir, creak.

Oh my God. It was chasing me.

I didn't look back. I didn't have a second to spare—

I rounded the shelf's corner and stumbled over Styrofoam and paper filler. Somehow, I stayed upright.

A warped roar split the air behind me.

That sound was definitely not from human vocal cords.

"Oh *shit*," I gasped. My side cramped, chest seizing in terror. I reached the double doors at a sprint. My foot caught the box that had propped them open, knocking it flying. Without it, the doors banged shut behind me and sealed with a hiss.

My terror-hazed brain registered the cleanroom: two long black tables lit by sterile spotlights, one bearing a skeleton laid out like it was waiting for me to join it. The other held a plastic specimen box. The EXIT sign over the far door glowed like a beacon.

And someone else was in there.

Some*thing.*

A tall, dark blur stood over the nearest table and the open plastic specimen container atop it. In front of me. Not behind me. The figure I'd seen before all this chaos started?

Before I could focus—before I could even *process* whether what I'd glimpsed was real—I tripped over a stool, slamming into the table on my way down. The specimen box slid off the edge and crashed to the floor, and I caught a glimpse of the figure melting away like a trick of the light before I hit the ground, too. My knees and elbows took the brunt of it, cracking against the linoleum hard enough to tear a choked cry loose.

But terror swallowed everything when the floor trembled. *Impacts.* Those clanking, heavy footsteps were back, and they were coming, growing nearer by the second—

Driven by pure fight-or-flight, heavy on the flight, I scrambled on all fours underneath the table.

Just in time.

Something struck the sealed entrance hard enough to crumple the frame. Protesting metal shrieked, and cinderblock and drywall cracked. Another blow, and the flimsy card-access lock didn't stand a chance against whatever ripped through. The small viewing windows erupted, pelting shards everywhere, and chunks of door and wall exploded outward.

With a gasped curse, I huddled beneath the table, covering my head.

The room quaked. The air. Possibly the whole freaking world.

The spotlights popped in rapid succession. Pale orange sparks rained past the table's edge. Somewhere to my left, display cases shattered, and the pair of computer screens beside them flickered violently, sizzled, and died. Curls of acrid smoke rose like ghosts of processors past.

But worst of all, mechanical whirring thuds struck the ground in a rhythm I already knew too well. The thing was coming into the room. Dread unfurled greasy wings in my gut as I uncurled from the fetal position and finally made myself look.

Every muscle locked. The last, fading sparks drifted to the floor like falling stars.

What I was seeing couldn't be real.

Because those were supposed to be feet.

At least...something close. Feet designed by some nightmarish artist. Birdlike in shape but scaled like mini dinosaurs, they were made of interlocking metal segments flecked with blue, red, and black. Each of the four silver, talon-like toes tapered to scalpel-sharp points that gouged the tiles with every step. As I watched, whirring gears and levers twitched at the joint, and the ankle rotated in a fluid, too-smooth motion, lifting the foot and slamming it back down again.

Bipedal, I catalogued numbly, as the other foot landed with a crack that jolted through the floor and into my bones.

Crunch. Whir. Creak.

The cadence made my skin crawl.

What. The actual. Hell?

Cold sweat slicked my armpits and stuck my shirt to my spine. I inched backward as silently as I could, deeper beneath the table. It brought me closer to the far exit.

Past those legs and feet, the doors had been obliterated, pieces warped and jagged like a wrecking ball had been used to open them.

That thing *was* the wrecking ball.

A murderous wrecking ball with nightmare chicken feet—

Except...wait. I stilled.

Something new was happening.

The air thickened. My skin buzzed, and pressure gathered at the base of my skull. The hair rose on my arms.

An invisible tug lurched deep in my middle.

And then...a whisper.

Come here.

A distant part of me recoiled, but it was too late. That tether snapped taut, and I gasped.

The pulling sensation was strange, electric, and *familiar*. Familiar in a way I couldn't name, a mutter skating the edge of memory. Like a voice calling my name in a dream I couldn't quite recall.

The mechanical footsteps faded into the background.

That tug—that draw—it was coming from right behind me. I turned before I even registered the impulse.

The specimen box I'd knocked off the table lay tipped on its side. The same one the figure I thought I'd seen had been standing over when I barged in. Crumpled packing material spilled out.

Later, I would struggle to remember clearly what happened next.

My thoughts were foggy. Shrouded. Like something had slipped inside my mind and taken over. Fear unraveled into nothingness. My blood pulsated in my ears. My body moved on its own.

And like I was a spectator to my own actions, I watched my hands reach out. My fingers gripped the box's edge and shoved it aside.

I didn't remember sliding out from under the table. I didn't remember crawling forward, either, but the linoleum bit into my knees as I hunched over the container.

Behind me, metal groaned and whirred. Talons cracked against tile. Something *roared*. The table I'd hidden under was knocked clean across the room, crashing into the wall.

But I didn't flinch. I didn't move.

I leaned over the box and looked inside. Whatever lay in there was buried. It whispered furiously. I didn't recognize the words, but the urgency was clear.

Out of the corner of my eye, I spotted movement. An unyielding metal grip clamped down on my upper arm from behind. A hand. It was too big.

Fingers. Strange and multi-jointed. Squeezing too tight.

Muffled panic ignited, but I still couldn't tear my gaze from the box. Couldn't stop myself from shoving aside the sterile gel packs cradling its contents.

Those whispers grew louder.

Pain flared where the steel grasp dug into my bicep, but I'd already reached inside the tote with my other hand. It closed around a smooth stone tablet.

The moment I lifted it, a jolt shot up my arm.

The crushing grip vanished. The thing behind me snarled a string of harsh, mangled syllables in my ear. That massive metal hand swept past my shoulder—it had *six fingers*—reaching for the stone tablet. At the same time, something slammed into my back, hard enough to send me flying.

The impact spun me, and like it'd broken a spell, sound, sensation, *thought* rushed back.

What had just happened?

I hit the floor on my side, bouncing on my hip. Somehow, I held onto the object, curling my body protectively around it.

And then I looked up...

And up.

All the blood drained from my head. My vision grayed at the edges.

I couldn't move. I didn't dare breathe.

I could only *stare*, clutching the stone plate to my chest like it could somehow save me.

Which wasn't happening, because I was completely, thoroughly, and cosmically effed.

There was a monster in the lab with me.

A towering mechanical monster, at least seven feet of mismatched metal, gleaming in shades of shiny blue and black. A jigsaw of junkyard pieces cobbled together, Frankenstein-style. I caught a glimpse of what looked like a car alternator jammed next to something that resembled a melted iPhone case before my gaze climbed higher still.

A jagged crown of spikes scraped the lab ceiling. Dust rained down as it straightened with a grinding whine of gears. The crests on its head glittered beneath the lab lights.

It was...a robot.

That was the only word I could find, but even that didn't quite fit. It had a vaguely humanoid structure, two powerful mechanical legs ending in those deadly, talon-tipped feet, two arms made of segmented plating. Six-fingered hands. But its head...

Its head was wrong.

Triangular, mantis-like. Its mandible-like mouthparts clicked together and drew back, releasing another stream of inhuman language. Two eyes, glowing, bulbous orbs of electric green, locked on me.

That insectoid head tilted.

It studied me. *Weighed me.* As if assessing whether to crush the ant.

Oh, God.

I was the ant.

A high-pitched moan clawed its way from my throat as I clutched the tablet tighter. I kicked my heels against the floor, scuttling backward.

I didn't get far.

Despite its size, the thing crouched in one smooth, terrifying motion, metal folding with unnatural ease. It was *looking* at me. Sparks popped in the smoke-filled air.

It barked another unintelligible command and reached out. Reached for me.

Nope. *Nope nope nope.*

I rolled to the side and scrambled to my feet. I couldn't feel my legs. Couldn't feel anything besides horror and an overwhelming urge to escape before those talons ripped me apart.

The exit. The emergency exit at the room's back.

I ran.

Metallic footsteps thundered behind me. The robot let out a roar, louder than anything I'd ever heard. It shook the room, shook my *brain.* I couldn't breathe. The emergency exit waited ahead, visible through smoke.

My shoes slipped on dust. I was too slow, and it was right behind me—

I was still clinging to the tablet like it was life itself.

Then—

A voice.

A *shout.*

I thought it was my name. But it couldn't be.

I risked a glance over my shoulder just in time to see a silver-and-black blur explode from the far side of the lab, past the murderous robot bearing down on me. The blur moved so fast it barely seemed real, just a streak against the madness.

And then everything *lit up.*

Electricity spiderwebbed across the room, splitting into branching tendrils of lightning that danced along the floors, the walls, the ceiling. A beam of neon pink energy shot out from behind me, searing my vision. That scream I'd been holding in finally burst free as I dropped to my knees—

Not a moment too soon.

The beam of light tore overhead, slamming into the far wall with a devastating *crack.* Plaster and stone detonated. The pink lance traced a glowing arc of molten concrete, and the wall blackened in its wake, trembling. Ceiling chunks rained down. I threw my free arm over my head, the other still pressing the tablet to my chest.

That was…that was a laser beam.

The robot had just shot a freaking laser beam at me.

Somehow, the walls held, but blue lightning still writhed across them like snakes made of cold fire. Smoke thickened, bitter and burning. It scalded my lungs and coated my throat, stinging my eyes.

Tears streaming, I staggered sideways across the quaking floor. My shoulder smacked the wall, and a pulse of current bit into my skin. Arcs of lightning whipped around me in a chaotic, silent storm.

But I was getting out of this damn lab. I fought through it, fought forward. The door. The exit was right there. If I could just move—

But it was like pushing through a wall of static pressure. There was electricity *everywhere.* Had a wire gotten severed? Where the hell was it coming from?

I couldn't gather my senses. Light and sound crashed in around me, too loud, too much. Everything tilted, the room fading in spots.

God, I was going to black out. Right in front of that *thing*—

My knees buckled. I threw out my arms to catch myself, the artifact held tightly in my right hand. I landed by the exit and rolled to my side. The tablet clattered to the floor beside me.

For a moment, I simply lay there, gasping the smoke-laden air, my vision wavering.

The stone slab lay inches from my face. Close enough I could see hairline fractures had formed across its surface. Time seemed to slow.

That pull. It was back. That enigmatic, whispering *urge.*

The world around me roared and broke apart, but I couldn't look away.

A strange, nostalgic ache bloomed in my chest. I raised my head, frowning at the markings carved across the tablet's surface. I didn't recognize them. They looked like they could be Sumerian, the crude shapes, dots, glyphs. But it wasn't quite a match. Maybe a version I'd never seen before.

And then there was the fact they were *glowing.*

I couldn't look away from this weird stone artifact despite the murder-robot raging nearby. Roars, crashes. Bangs. The room shook with impacts. If I didn't know better, I'd think there was a fight raging behind me.

But I couldn't look. I was trapped. Stuck in some invisible web.

And the stone *was* strangely beautiful.

A pale, purple-pink light bled from the grooves and swirls like it was lit from within. In a daze, I reached out, fingers splayed over the surface without quite resting on it. Heat pulsed beneath my palm.

It reminded me of how the asphalt had felt beneath my hand two nights ago. The night everything changed. Otherworldly heat, impossible and eerie.

Now, the glowing lines moved. No, not the symbols...the surface itself. The stone's grainy texture shifted, rippling beneath my touch as the glow intensified.

Gently, ever so gently, I brushed my hand over it.

And then it crumbled. Or at least...the *shell* did. The façade of stone disintegrated, flaking away to reveal what lay underneath: a smooth, glassy slab the same shape as it'd been before, except smaller. And crystalline. Like a beautiful, pale amethyst run through with veins of pink.

That same purplish light radiated from within it, pulsing like a heartbeat. Like it was *alive*.

It had all happened in the span of a breath. An instant.

The reaching, the light, the collapse.

I knew without a doubt—this was what had called to me. This glowing crystal.

I could still faintly hear the chaos beyond. Metal screeching. A garbled roar. The boom of falling debris. The linoleum vibrated under me, and smoke and dust spun in spiral eddies. Electricity snapped and popped.

But none of it touched me.

The tablet sang to me. Called. I brushed my hand over it. It was warm, bordering on hot.

I gasped.

The glow surged—

And then it *erupted*.

Blinding, searing light, like a miniature star igniting beneath my hand. Time and space snapped. The world fell away into white fire. For one impossible second, I saw *something* in the light.

Writing I didn't recognize.

Shapes. Lines. Symbols.

Stars, constellations, a swirl of planets in orbit.

So much white light.

Those were voices, too, calling out.

And then just *heat*.

Raw, surging fire. Everywhere. My skull split with pressure, like somebody had squeezed my temples in a vise grip. Screams rang through the air, mechanical, inhuman. Maybe mine, too. The walls shook.

I couldn't care about anything other than the fact my hand was on fire. My *palm*. Molten heat so agonizing, it had to be melting skin off. Tissue beneath. Tears blurred my eyes. I couldn't see. I could only clutch it to my chest, the pain ricocheting through every nerve ending. I thought I may have shrieked again, but the sound was swallowed in a rush of static and thunder—

I had the briefest thought about how shitty this whole damn week had been so far.

And then...there was nothing.

Chapter 12

A MINOR EXPLOSION, BUT A MAJOR
EXISTENTIAL CRISIS

MY HEAD *POUNDED*.

Hard. Like my brain was trying to carve its way free from my skull with an ice pick. It made it hard to think. Hard to do anything but fight the urge to throw up.

Gradually, though, the agony subsided enough for me to register low murmurs nearby. I managed a strangled mutter, and a second later, a cool, gloved hand gently pressed against the inside of my wrist.

Somewhere in the distance, a shrill alarm bell rang, harsh and piercing but weirdly muffled, like someone had stuffed cotton into my ears. And my mouth.

This was worse than any hangover I'd had. Even my tongue hurt when I licked my lips. I frowned at the gritty taste. Dust.

What...what happened?

The last thing I remembered was walking down the hallway in the anthro wing, searching for—

"I think she's awake," said an unfamiliar feminine voice.

"Er, Raven?"

I recognized those dulcet tones. They could've been straight from a BBC literature special. And when I cracked open my eyes and found a concerned gaze behind thick-rimmed glasses, I recognized that, too. Not to mention the tweed.

"Professor Stern?" I croaked. "What...?"

Then it all rushed back.

Everything slammed into place. Terrifying and impossible. Images straight out of my favorite sci-fi movies.

But it hadn't been a movie. It'd been *real.*

I gasped and shoved myself upright.

Too fast. The world spun into a colorful blur. Acid swelled in my throat, and my heart rabbit-kicked my ribs.

I'd seen...

What *had* I seen?

I clawed at my sternum, fighting for air. That charred-ash taste —it was everywhere. That and panic. Because none of this could be *real—*

"Careful, Miss Barrister." A calm female voice broke through my spiral. "You're experiencing shock. Let's take it slow. Breathe in and out with me."

No shit. I was experiencing a hell of a lot more than just *shock.* But it was either that or start screaming and never stop, so I squeezed my eyes shut and obeyed.

In. Out. Again. Once more.

Gradually, the tightness eased. The trembling lessened enough for me to raise my head.

I blinked, dazed.

An older woman in a blue EMT uniform knelt at my side. Behind her, Professor Stern hovered, his dark skin several shades paler than usual. He was flanked by other professors I half-recognized and a wide-eyed student I'd had a class with once. Firefighters moved in the background, their breathers off, shouting instructions and checking walls. Two police officers stood farther back, one scribbling in a notepad.

But it was the three strangers standing just beyond them who caught my eye: two men and a woman, all in fitted blazers and slacks, not a logo or badge in sight. Beside them, a gray-haired man in military uniform watched me silently, eyes unreadable behind wire-rimmed glasses.

They looked…out of place.

Then again, *I* was out of place.

I blinked again and focused on the crooked bulletin board on the wall across from me.

"Why am I in the anthro hall?" I rasped, glancing between the EMT and Professor Stern. My voice sounded strange. Hoarse, like I had already been screaming. Which checked out. I had the urge to scream again, too.

Because I might be out of place, but I knew this hallway. I was slumped against the wall outside the stairwell I'd first walked down that morning. Dust smeared the walls. The scent of fried plastic and bitter smoke hung in the air. My book bag lay beside me, looking a little worse for the wear. I was sure I did, too.

None of this made sense.

The last thing I remembered—

I grimaced and pressed my fingers to my temple. *No.* I knew where I'd been. I'd been in the lab. The *cleanroom* past the storage room.

I remembered falling. The lights. The smoke. The sound of everything *breaking.*

I hadn't crawled out of the lab—especially not all the way here. Not without remembering it.

Goosebumps rose across my skin.

How the hell had I gotten here?

A glove touched my arm, and I jerked back, gasping.

The EMT gave me a wary look and held up her hand. "I'm sorry. But Miss Barrister, we've got an ambulance out front. Maybe you should come with us. It's possible you have a concussion, which would explain some of the confusion."

Confusion. That was the understatement of the year.

I let out a breathless laugh. It rubbed against my sore throat like sandpaper on its way out. "No hospitals."

"But—"

"How did I get here?" I interrupted, trying to fight back the rising tide of terror. Waking up in a strange place was bad enough. But the robot, the freaking lasers, the weird light and dissolving tablet? Those absolutely impossible memories felt real. Real enough that they were threatening to dissolve me into a pile of blubbering goo.

I wrapped my arms tightly around my middle to hold myself in a solid state. Both officers were watching me now, the one with the notepad stepping closer, his eyes sharp.

The EMT sighed and shifted back on her heels. "Well, what *do* you remember?" she asked, drawing out a penlight. "Any memories of the explosion?"

I winced as she aimed the tiny flashlight directly into my eyes. Why did they have to do that? And had she said *explosion?* I didn't remember any explosion. Memories played like a movie on fast-forward. The robot. The artifact. The white glow. The guards.

That...*thing* that had looked like it wanted to turn me into mulch. If there had been an explosion, it should have taken a back-seat to *that*.

My heart started racing all over again.

Those security guards. My stomach curled in on itself, and I reached for the EMT's arm.

"Was there...anything—anybody else in there? Is anyone hurt?"

Instead of answering, she exchanged a glance with the cop edging closer. When she turned back to me, she asked, "Did you see the security guards before the explosion? We've already taken them to the hospital."

My breath hitched. I had seen them, all right. Unconscious. At least one had been bleeding.

But for some reason, I didn't say that.

Instead, I heard myself murmur, "I think so. Are they okay?"

Professor Stern moved then, crouching beside me. His expression was tight, his brown skin ashen, deep lines creasing his forehead. "They're a little out of it, but they're all right," he said, examining me like he might a curious lab specimen. "They were knocked out by the explosion near the back hall's entry. We're very lucky it doesn't appear anyone was in the lab itself during the actual blast. You were very fortunate. We all were."

Fortunate?

But...but I *was* in that lab.

I blinked, trying to piece together the fragments of memory whirling around my aching skull. Something didn't add up.

Mainly: *Why the* hell *wasn't anybody talking about the terrifying freaking robot?*

Whatever crossed my face must've registered, because the professor's frown deepened. "Raven, did you see anything that might help us understand how this happened? Anything strange? We're trying to determine what sparked the explosion."

I had the urge to laugh hysterically. Possibly cry. Yeah, I'd seen something strange, all right.

And there it was again. That word.

Explosion.

I squeezed my eyes shut. The massive metal creature flashed through my mind, the blinding pink beam of light, the glowing tablet. My temples throbbed so hard I nearly whimpered.

"You're set on not going to the hospital?" the EMT asked when I rubbed at my forehead.

I nodded wordlessly, and she sighed.

"Well, if you're refusing medical care, do you want us to call someone for you?" Her radio crackled. She reached for the dial and turned it down before continuing. "You're not showing physical signs of a concussion, but it's still best we check you out thoroughly."

I shook my head, raising my eyes to hers. Even the dim lighting down here felt too bright. "No. I'm fine, really. What...so there *was* an explosion?"

The officer lingering nearby stepped closer, raising his voice over the distant drone of the fire alarm. "Far as we can tell, something in the clean lab went up. Sprinklers kicked in and suppressed the fire, but the whole floor took some damage. The lab and storage room got hit hardest."

I looked up at him from where I half-sprawled on the dusty

linoleum. He couldn't have been much older than me. His sandy hair was buzzed close to his scalp, and his name tag read *Brown*.

He adjusted his belt and flipped open a small notebook, licking his thumb to turn a page. "Professor here says your name's Raven Barrister," he said, glancing down at me for confirmation. I nodded. "Anthropology student, right?" Another nod. "Okay. So what's the last thing you remember, Raven? Did you see anyone else down there? What were you doing in the lab? Professor says it's usually off-limits."

"I was…looking for him," I mumbled.

And I hadn't seen anyone else. Except the guards. Except that *thing*.

None of this *made any sense*.

"I didn't see an explosion," I added, softer.

No, I'd seen something impossible.

A sentient robot. Its garbled voice. Wreckage and sparks and light.

But no one else was mentioning that.

"Aren't there cameras in the lab?" I asked, lifting my gaze to Officer Brown.

He hesitated, exchanged a look with Professor Stern, then shrugged. "There was an electrical malfunction. None of the cameras recorded anything."

Of course they didn't. The panic that had just barely receded clawed back up my throat.

The guards were okay. Their injuries had been blamed on the explosion. *They'd corroborated it.*

But I'd seen them stuffed in the bathroom. Alive. Unconscious. An explosion clearly hadn't deposited them all in there.

And why had they been hidden away?

If that robot-thing had been the culprit, why not just finish the job? They'd gone full demolition mode on the rest of the floor. Why spare the guards?

Why spare *me*?

None of it made sense.

My gaze drifted past the officer, down the ruined hallway. Debris littered the floor: collapsed bulletin boards, shredded papers, ceiling fragments. Chunks of scorched plaster were smeared with soot, and it hit me—

That was soot. Black and fine and coating the hallway walls. I was wearing it.

My stomach bottomed out.

That could be from an actual explosion. Maybe I *had* been knocked out. Maybe everything I remembered was some twisted trauma response.

Maybe I'd lost my mind.

My pulse fluttered sickeningly fast. The whole nightmare, sparkling stones, ancient glyphs, robotic monsters…maybe it was all something my brain had made up to make sense of whatever had *really* happened.

Far down the hall, emergency strobes still flashed, flooding the space with cold white bursts. I stared straight into them, and for a second, I saw *another* light. One that had pulsed *inside* me. That soul-deep resonance.

I shuddered and pressed my fingertips into my eyes, trying to shut it out.

A hand touched my back, and I jumped.

The EMT crouched beside me again, concern etched into her expression. "I think you hit your head, Raven." She paused. "Can I call you that?" When I didn't respond, she continued, "Maybe it's best you come with me to the hospital. We can check you out—"

"No!"

I flinched at my own voice. It came out too harsh, too loud. I pushed upright, fisting my hands in the front of my hoodie. The once-white fabric was dust-streaked and scorched around the sleeves.

"No hospitals," I repeated more calmly. Not if I could help it. Not since Dad. "I'm fine. Really. Just…shaken up."

I forced a slow breath, and when I looked away from her, I met Officer Brown's astute hazel eyes instead. He still stood above me, watching the interaction with a narrowed, keen gaze. Waiting, I realized, for me to finish my story.

"Sorry. Um, so I was coming down here to find Professor

Stern," I said, gesturing toward the professor. I blinked hard and tried to find the words. "I had just opened the door and…"

My voice abandoned me.

For one, stretched-out moment, I considered telling the truth. All of it. The car accident. The robot. The glowing, crumbling tablet. The whole damn alien conspiracy theory, served up with a caution-tape bow.

And then I imagined their faces. The disbelief, the concern, and the polite, pitying looks that would quickly morph into suspicion. My credibility would be shredded. Any chance at scholarships would be gone. I'd be lucky not to end up institutionalized and whispering about mechanical monsters to someone with a clipboard.

Shit.

I was going to lie. Flat-out. To a police officer. To the EMTs. To Professor Stern. To *everyone*.

Even to my mom, when I called her later.

It was an explosion in the lab. That was it. The only explanation I could give. The only one they'd accept.

There was no sign of the robot. No evidence. Even the guards thought it had been a blast.

Hell, maybe it *had* been. Maybe I needed to see a person with a clipboard, after all.

The officer tapped his pen on his notepad, the sound loud enough to drag me back into the present. "You opened the door and…?" he prompted, eyes steady on mine. He was reading me. I knew it.

Here went nothing. I tightened my hold on my hoodie like it could ground me.

"Sorry. I, um, I opened the door, and then I remember being thrown backward. I think I hit my head and then…"

I shrugged, doing my best to sound dazed and not full of absolute crap.

But my heart jolted as I forced my face to stay neutral. I was a terrible liar, and I *knew* it. But if I could hold it together for just this one moment—

An eternity passed.

Then Officer Brown looked away and nodded, pen scratching across the paper, though I didn't miss his brief hesitation. That was fine. I'd given my statement. I let out a slow, shaky breath.

I'd done it. I'd lied.

My gaze drifted past him. The trio of suits still stood near the stairwell. I hadn't seen them speak to anyone. Hadn't even seen them move. But the woman with the severe bun now had her eyes locked on *me*.

There was something about her stare. Not curious. *Knowing*.

A chill chased up my spine, and I looked away.

"Am I..." I started to rise then hesitated. Still seated, I turned to the EMT then to the professor. "Am I in trouble or something? Can I go?"

Professor Stern shook his head and extended a hand. "Of course you're not in trouble, Raven. Here, let me help you up, if you're ready."

I was. The adrenaline had nowhere left to go. It crawled under my skin, leaving me jittery and twitchy. I reached up and let him pull me to my feet. The EMT rose with me, reaching to steady me if needed.

The hallway tilted like a funhouse. I managed to stay upright, though. My body ached but nothing felt broken, just bruised. My head throbbed. My knees screamed. I was going to be a walking patchwork quilt tomorrow.

But I was alive.

For now, that was enough.

"I'm sure this has something to do with the solar flare," the professor said, patting my arm awkwardly before letting go. "There's just..." I didn't miss his glance toward the suits. "There's been extra security. I was working on a project that had some important people's attention."

But then he exhaled a long, quiet sigh. "Sadly, everything in the clean lab is destroyed. Invaluable artifacts. We'll have to start over. I'm glad no one was seriously hurt, but it's still a tragedy."

The tablet.

I swallowed hard, his words muffled. Was this shock? I didn't know, but the memories were playing on a loop.

That strange stone. That *thing* hidden inside. The bright white light.

Could that have been part of his project? It had to be.

Could it have been why that creature was here?

God, this was like putting together a thousand-piece puzzle without the box to look at.

The professor bent and retrieved my book bag, handing it to me. "Now, what did you need to see me for, Rae?"

It took me a second to process the question.

Oh, right. I'd said I was here to find him.

And I had been.

But the questions I'd had didn't matter anymore. Whatever he'd been working on, whatever had been going on here, I had a solid feeling it was gone now.

I'd watched that strange artifact crumble.

I'd seen something emerge that defied explanation.

Pushing the memory aside, I cleared my throat. "Oh. It was nothing. I had a question about a chapter for, uh, a different class I thought you could help with, but…" I forced a weak laugh and slid one bag strap over my shoulder.

My arm twinged. Right where those cold, inhuman fingers had gripped me. A reminder. A bruise that didn't just live on the surface.

"It's not important now," I said.

Nothing was.

This changed everything.

Chapter 13

I SURVIVED A KILLER ROBOT, AND ALL
I GOT WAS THIS BRUISE

IT WASN'T UNTIL MUCH, MUCH LATER—after I'd given Officer Brown my contact info and signed some liability waiver for the university, and *after* I'd recapped my lie twice and submitted to one last EMT checkup (while resisting her push for a hospital visit *again*)—that I managed to escape.

I sat in the parking lot a full twenty minutes without starting Faith's engine.

Mulling over, for one, how I was racking up near-death experiences like they were free drink stamps at the college coffee shop. And they were getting more and more...out of this world.

The afternoon sun had finally broken through the low-hanging clouds, warming the air and chasing away some of the chill. I was still shivering, though, when I tilted my head back against the seat and finally let myself *breathe.*

And I finally let myself remember every single fantastical, horrifying, sanity-challenging detail.

There'd been no explosion.

There'd been a *robot* in the lab.

A giant, seven-foot-tall mechanical creature had wrecked the storage room and come after me. Chased me. *Grabbed* me.

I knew I wasn't crazy. Because I had *proof.* It throbbed beneath the sleeve of my hoodie every time I moved.

I needed to see it.

Even lifting the arm hurt. Wincing, I tugged the hoodie over my head anyway, tossing it into the passenger seat beside my dust-covered book bag. Bracing myself, I looked down and...

"Shit," I hissed, extending my arm all the way.

A bruise had already formed, ugly and dark, in the unmistakable shape of a huge six-fingered hand. My pulse took off in a sprint, and sweat bloomed at my temples.

Real.

There was my undeniable proof that *it was real.* I hadn't imagined any of it.

Just like I hadn't imagined what had run me off the road the other night.

I couldn't deny anything anymore. Not with this purple mark on my skin completely wrecking any excuses I could come up with.

I lowered my arm and slumped back in the seat, every nerve buzzing. My body flooded with another round of adrenaline, like fight-or-flight hadn't gotten the memo it was too damn late for either.

There'd been a robotic *monster* in the school lab.

An angry, robotic monster made of weird metal parts.

So...what now?

Was the university covering it up? The cops? Those creeps in the black suits? The guy in military dress? Did *any* of them know how I'd ended up all the way back at the student stairwell, on the opposite side of the building from the lab?

Maybe I did need a tinfoil hat because a small part of me was starting to think maybe all of Kelly's ridiculous theories were spot on after all.

I gripped the steering wheel with both hands, flinching when the motion tugged at my bruised flesh. Outside the window, campus life carried on. Students streamed down sidewalks and filled the lots, laughter and voices mixing with the low rumble of traffic. People headed in and out of classes. Just another weekday.

Police had been stringing caution tape across the entrance to the Finke building when I left...but the rest of the university carried on. Business as usual. The staff and administration must've been clinging to that illusion with both hands.

But *how?*

Normalcy had officially taken a nosedive the moment I was chased by Optimus Prime's smaller, *much meaner* cousin.

Everyone else moved like gravity still worked. Meanwhile, I was floating in orbit, watching my life spin out below. Watching my skepticism, my thoroughly vetted alternative explanation for all this chaos, dissolve just like the tablet had.

Glowing green eyes, too-sharp claws...

My lungs squeezed tight again, that lightheadedness creeping back in. Sweat blurred my vision. I fumbled with the ignition and jammed the window button, lowering it. Cool, bracing autumn air swept in, carrying the scent of imminent rain.

I gulped in a breath and held it.

It helped. A little. Just enough.

Steadier, I stared out the windshield, jaw tight, and finally said the word, the one I'd been choking on since I woke up on that hallway floor. Maybe even longer. Since the moment on the country road when the ground had smoldered under my palm.

"Aliens."

There it was.

The strange light that had run me off the road.

The terrifying creature in the lab.

The white-hot light. The glowing tablet.

After all of it...

Kelly *was* right. There were freaking *aliens* here.

I sniff-laughed, a pitiful, half-hysterical sound teetering right on the verge of a sob, before leaning my head back again.

There was no *way* I was telling her. In fact, I wasn't telling *anyone.*

Not Mom. Not Dustin. Not Amelia. Not until I knew what the hell I was dealing with.

Squaring my shoulders, I tried to think, really *think*, like the version of myself who still believed in logic and evidence. I cataloged the things I did know.

Like, for one, the robot had clearly been after the weird tablet I'd pulled out of that box.

It had reached for it. Like it recognized and wanted it. Too many coincidences for the truth not to be right there. That *had* to be what Professor Stern had been working on, too. That was what the military escort had delivered. That was why security had been crawling all over the anthro wing.

Maybe even why the suits were there. Not for the robot, but for the tablet. Could it be they didn't even know the robot had been there? Maybe that's why no one was freaking out about it.

So if that was the case, what the hell *was* that artifact? It'd looked just like a rock slab at first, covered in glyphs. Like a weird Rosetta Stone, except with only that single language on it.

Until it'd cracked open to reveal…something else.

Was it some crazy alien object? A power source? …a weapon?

It couldn't be *that* dangerous. I'd found it in a foam box, packed like someone's leftovers. It wasn't exactly sealed in a vault.

Then again, I'd seen what it did. I'd felt it.

Had the robot taken it when I passed out, or had whatever caused that brilliant flash of light vaporized it? Maybe that light had been the explosion.

Maybe there *had* been one, something real. Something destructive. But if so, it'd come after the rest. After the lab had already become a battleground.

I blew out a long breath.

Okay, but that still didn't explain how I'd ended up back in the hallway without a scratch on me, short of the bruises where the thing had grabbed me.

No, where the *alien* had grabbed me.

I tried the word out in my head again and shivered.

Now that I was calmer, the memories were clearer. I frowned.

I *swore* something else had been in that room, too. Besides me, Mr. Robot-from-Hell, and whoever's skeleton had been artfully splayed across the table. I'd seen a dark figure when I'd first entered the lab. And again, right at the end, before the white light crashed in and wiped my brain clean like an ice scraper across a frosty windshield.

I stared out the window without really seeing anything, too absorbed in replaying the events.

A dark blur. Then a flash of silver. A streak that might've been a *body*. At the very least…a form.

It had all happened so fast. There'd been so much flashing light. Electricity.

Fear.

Frustrated, I leaned back and gripped the steering wheel. I'd think better at home. After a hot shower and ten pounds of pizza. Maybe even a glass—or three—of wine.

I started to reach for the ignition, then froze, a new kind of fear slinking its way down my spine.

No, surely I'd seen wrong.

I sat back. Slowly, I twisted my right hand until my palm faced up, and my insides pitched, stealing my breath.

Dull daylight glanced off faint, pearlescent white shapes on my skin, swirls in a vaguely geometric pattern. So faint, they were nearly invisible unless I tilted my hand just right.

There were markings on my palm.

Numb, morbidly fascinated, I traced them with the fingers of my left hand.

Nothing. No raised edges. No pain. No heat.

But they were there. Dots and slashes and elegant loops, just barely visible at the right angle. Embedded. Like scars. Or… symbols.

Glyphs like those I'd seen on the tablet? No. These were different.

I'd never seen anything like them.

Maybe I could just…I used the hem of my tank top to scrub at them, my heart in my throat. It didn't work. The marks didn't smear or fade. They didn't even smudge. There was *nothing* to scrub off.

They weren't *on* my skin. They were *in* it. My scalp prickled.

This was the hand I'd touched the artifact with.

It had to be a burn. That was the most logical explanation. Something to do with the heat, the light, the electricity. Maybe the weird charge that'd zapped the entire lab.

I'd just read about ball lightning burns, and some of those had looked like strange, intricate designs. *Lichtenberg figures*.

Yes. That made sense. Sort of.

The fact that it looked like alien artwork could be a coincidence. Pareidolia. My brain searching for patterns in chaos.

That was all it was. Had to be.

Except…it didn't hurt. It didn't *feel* like a burn. Or a scar. Or anything at all.

My fingers trembled. I dropped my hand into my lap and slumped against the seat.

Yeah, I was definitely going to need that wine.

My movements were as mechanical as the robot that'd nearly killed me when I started the engine and drove home on autopilot. Just me and one more gigantic piece of a weirdness puzzle to deal with.

I was going to need that whole bottle of wine.

Chapter 14

FINE. THE ALIENS ARE REAL.

I CALLED SANDY FIRST AND USED THE EXPLOSION AS AN EXCUSE TO SKIP MY SHIFT. She gave a token protest, but I didn't care. In my six months at Oasis, I'd only called in once. And I fully believed I was entitled to a day off after a traumatic, brain-melting alien encounter.

Next, I called my mom, mostly to get ahead of the local news. She was predictably panicked, and it took a solid fifteen minutes of reassurance and promises to see her at Dustin's this weekend before I could hang up.

Then I sat in silence.

Aliens.

I huddled in the corner of my hand-me-down couch, lifted the bottle of Moscato, and drank straight from it. I'd read somewhere you weren't supposed to drink with a head injury, but I wasn't convinced I had one.

And if I did...well, at least I'd go out calmer. The wine was helping.

But honestly? If aliens couldn't kill me, fermented grapes seemed like the least of my worries.

I snorted and took another swig.

The TV played on mute. The local news showed footage of yellow, blue, green, and pink lights hovering low over a harvested cornfield. Timestamp: two nights ago. Same night I'd had my own close encounter.

Aliens.

Fear bubbled in my gut, and I tucked my bare legs beneath me, curling into a tighter ball. I'd changed into plaid shorts and a T-shirt after showering. Despite the hot water and soft clothes, the paranoia that'd followed me home hadn't budged.

I'd closed every curtain, turned on every light in the apartment. Not a single shadow survived in my tiny space above Bob's garage.

The place was cozy. Faux-wood floors, neutral walls, granite countertops I never used. Bob had designed it himself, right down to the stainless-steel fridge I mostly ignored in favor of peanut butter sandwiches, ramen, and scavenged leftovers from work.

Tonight, though, I'd splurged. A pepperoni and olive pizza. Half of it had disappeared in record time. So sue me. Comfort carb therapy was a thing. Now, the greasy remains sat on my cluttered coffee table.

My appetite was gone. The second those lights had bobbed and weaved across the screen, my stomach had flipped. Now, the pizza twisted into a knot and threatened a second appearance.

Not that I blamed it. Nothing was settling right. After all, I'd had two days of close encounters of the really messed-up kind.

What were aliens doing here?

Also…why hadn't anyone else reported seeing a robot? You'd think *they*, more than strange lights, would've made for some sensational five o'clock news. Unless…

Unless my earlier suspicion was right, and nobody else *had* seen them. Just their lights in the sky.

I was assuming they were related, anyway. It made the most sense.

Maybe these robotic alien visitors were intentionally staying hidden. It made sense, in a terrifying kind of way. People didn't usually grab their rifles over floating orbs. But an army of evil mech-beings? The kind that could shoot laser beams, trash storage rooms, and leave six-fingered bruises on human flesh?

Yeah. People with guns would show up for that.

The pizza tried to make a reappearance, and I chugged more wine to force it back down. My phone dinged, and, gasping, I nearly launched the bottle across the room. I bobbled it, snatched it by the neck just in time, and set it next to the pizza box, sighing.

Pull it together, Rae. Text tones are not alien sounds.

No, they were more…mechanical. Garbled and warped and—

Blowing out a sharp exhale, I dug my phone out from under the pizza box. It was a text from Amelia.

> You sure you don't want company?

Then, true to form, another one came through. She never just sent one text.

> I'm all done with the broadcast class for the night so I'm free.

I chewed my lip.

Having my best friend here was tempting. Very tempting. But I needed time to figure out what the hell I was dealing with before I even considered telling her the truth. And even then, would she believe me?

I'd already told her I was there during the explosion in Finke, because it was all over the news. But I hadn't told her the *real* story. Not the parts I'd conveniently left out while talking to the cops.

And definitely not the ones I couldn't explain myself. There was a good chance she'd think I'd cracked.

Which…fair. I wasn't exactly ruling that out myself. Shaking my head, I typed out a response.

> I'm good. I'm going to bed early. Still on for Sat night?

The plans to hit Crescent Club for dancing and drinks felt like something from another life. The idea of dressing up and pretending I hadn't just been attacked by a death machine felt… surreal. Too *ordinary*.

Then again, maybe that was exactly what I needed. A little slice of normal. One night of pretending things were still okay. That my car accident hadn't caused a paradigm shift I still hadn't recovered from.

The three-dot typing bubble appeared, and I leaned back on the couch just as the TV showed a diagram of the sun. Solar flare coverage again.

I narrowed my eyes. Could that be fake? Just a giant government cover-up to explain away the tech malfunctions?

God, that was a huge conspiracy.

And yet…my phone *had* died. And so had Faith's battery, out of nowhere that night on the country road.

Maybe this wasn't *either-or*. Maybe the flare was real, and the aliens were, too.

I pressed my hot forehead to the bottle's cool glass and sighed. I was going to end up like Kelly. A full-blown conspiracy theory enthusiast, whispering about angry robots from outer space and stockpiling canned goods in my closet.

My phone chimed again, and I nearly fumbled it. The marks on my hand caught the light when I did. I deliberately ignored them and read Amelia's answer instead.

> You know it. Be ready at 8. I'll pick you up and bring you to my place to get ready.

> 😄 Don't want you to get stranded with a dead battery!

She was hilarious.

> 😄 Fine. See you then.

Hopefully. I *hoped* I'd be up for it. For anything. I hoped I could, at some point, move *on*.

I drew my knees to my chest, wine bottle in hand, and stared into the muted flicker of the TV. The glowing lights danced across the grainy screen.

Two days ago, I'd been staring up at one of them.

What if this panicked, jumpy feeling never went away? What if I couldn't bounce back? I had exams to study for, work shifts to show up to. A *life*.

But my brain kept rewinding to the nightmarish scenes in the lab. To those terrible green eyes and the strange, ethereal purple glow of the crystal tablet. My body buzzed like it had been rewired and somebody'd connected things wrong.

"Screw it," I muttered and took another swig of wine.

For now, this would have to do.

LATER, much later, I woke with a start. A gasp lodged in my chest, and I flailed blindly. For a heartbeat, I was somewhere else. Somewhere full of glowing green eyes and hazy, acrid smoke. Luminescent shapes that *meant* something—

Reality slammed back. Home. I was home. Not in the lab.

I scrambled upright, falling back against my wooden headboard. White sheets tangled around my legs, and sweat glued my sleeping shirt to my skin. I clutched at my sternum and forced air into my lungs.

I'd been about to say something. There were words on the tip of my tongue. Gone now. Like the shapes. Those phantom roars. The lab.

God. I drew my knees up and rested my forehead on them.

I was awake. I was safe. In my bed.

Just a little residual panic. A touch of PTSD. That's what this was. Reliving traumatic events was normal. It was just my brain trying to process. I pressed my lids shut, leaning my head back against the wood behind me. Nightmares were a natural response to my shitshow of a day.

But it'd felt way too real.

Hugging myself, I shivered as cold air kissed my damp skin. The bedside lamp glowed softly beneath the scarf-draped shade. I'd slept with all the lights on for the first time in…who even knew how long. Since I was a kid. Since Dad had died.

Too bad it hadn't helped.

The last vestiges of sleep slid away, and I rubbed a shaky hand over my eyes. My marked hand. I glanced at the scars before groping for my phone.

3:08 a.m.

I'd dragged myself to bed after hours of combing alien encounter forums and late-night vlogs. The more I read and watched, the less I jumped each time the pipes creaked or the fridge hummed. The more I came to terms with what I'd seen. What I'd experienced.

Okay, some of that was the wine talking. But still. There was something comforting in the sheer number of normal-seeming folks claiming to have experienced something. And somehow, they kept going. They had jobs. Families. They moved through the world. They functioned.

Sure, a few had bunkers and stockpiles of canned beans, bullets, and vodka. But those were the outliers. Most of them were like me: regular people trying to make sense of it all. Trying to cope.

If there was one thing everyone agreed on—bunker-dwellers included—it was that something big was happening. Sightings had increased. Drastically. Some claimed an alien race had arrived. That they were here. Now. Among us. On this tiny speck of rock we called Earth.

The parts nobody agreed on were the who, what, and why.

I hadn't found any mention of robot aliens, though I'd searched. Plenty of chatter about glowing orbs and saucers. The former struck a particularly nerve-tingling chord.

No mentions of shiny, disintegrating tablets, either.

Could The Willow University, a tiny campus in the middle of nowhere, have held the key to a freaking alien invasion?

No. Not invasion. The last vlog I watched had used a different word: *infiltration*. That sounded less threatening. More like a video game. More like something I could do something about.

At least the bad guys were easy to identify. They were the seven-foot-tall robot jerks with glowing green eyes and grabby six-fingered hands. A little hard to miss.

I snorted and let my arm fall back to the mattress, rubbing at my bruised bicep. Discolorations and scrapes dotted my whole body. I sure looked like I'd survived an explosion.

Biting my lip, I raised my right palm, eyeing it. All the way down to the scars.

The media had already sunk their teeth into the university's explanation. I'd received the official text and email earlier: Finke Hall was closed until further notice due to damage and investigation. Faulty wiring. Solar flare malfunction. Yada yada.

At least they weren't blaming me.

I shook my head and stretched my arms overhead, careful of the deep purple, finger-shaped smudges. My spine popped, one vertebra at a time.

I'd crashed *hard*. The last thing I remembered was inhaling the last pizza slice and face-planting on the pillows.

I pushed the rainbow-colored quilt aside and stood, tugging my baggy sleeping shirt back into place. The room tilted for a second. Maybe finishing off the rest of that wine had been a poor life choice. I waited for the spin to pass, one hand braced against the wall, the other on my roiling stomach.

When the tossing subsided, I padded into the bathroom, used it, then leaned over the sink and stared at my reflection in the mirror.

The bruise on my upper arm looked even worse in this light, a violent bloom of purple and blue. When it threatened to twist up my guts again, I focused on my face instead. My hair was a disaster, but the dark circles under my eyes had faded.

Too bad those marks on my hand hadn't followed suit.

Steeling myself, I raised my palm again. Under the yellow glow of the bathroom's bulbs, the lines were faint. Barely visible, the palest curves and dots. Subtle enough, I wouldn't have seen them at all if I hadn't known where to look.

Filigree. Etched into my skin. Graceful and artistic and…totally not as scar-like as I'd like.

Angling my palm to better see the intricate design, I made my way down the hallway for a drink of water to soothe my dry throat. Those lines flowed in delicate swirls and angles, like decorations seared into my skin. Like something…deliberate.

A lot of the internet accounts I'd read talked about marks left behind from alien encounters. Marks on *victims*. Symbols or implants, unfortunate souvenirs of abductions, some claimed. But I hadn't been abducted.

Had I?

My blood chilled, and I exhaled slowly. Shakily. The white light had knocked me out—and I'd woken up in a different place.

Maybe I had taken a spaceship ride somewhere. If I had, it'd been a short one. Not much time had passed between my descent into the basement and being found by the EMTs and police. I pursed my lips. Strange that they'd taken my book bag for a ride, too.

The thought, while eerie enough to make my belly jump, didn't send me into another tailspin of panic. So that was something. Maybe binging every single alien encounter forum thread I could find had actually worked to desensitize me.

All jokes aside, my head-first dive into conspiracy-land had done something. It'd helped. Just knowing I wasn't alone made a difference, and the curiosity I'd been keeping at bay was slinking back in. I needed to know more.

I wanted answers to the lingering questions: who, what, and why. And, as a bonus, how.

There had to be a logical explanation. Something that made sense. And I was going to find it.

I patted down my frizzing hair. If I wasn't careful, this could easily become an obsession. Both Mom and Amelia said when I got hooked on something, I went all in. I needed to understand and conquer it before I could let it go. That was why anthropology had always made sense. It was, in a way, a career about decoding the biggest questions surrounding human existence.

This was no different. Except this time, I'd be digging for answers about life *beyond* the human existence.

The floor was cool under my bare feet as I crossed into the kitchen. A breeze from the HVAC vent stirred against my nape, and goosebumps swept down my arms. It smelled like night wind.

It reminded me of Sky, strangely enough.

I snorted. At least all this insanity had cut back on my daily quota of bartender daydreams. I curled my fingers over my marked palm and skirted the counter-height bar that passed as a kitchen table, grabbing a water bottle from the fridge. After twisting off the cap, I took a long drink and leaned against the stove.

What would he think about all of this? He'd been tense and oddly curious at the scene of the accident and later at Oasis. Like he'd known I wasn't telling the full story.

Like he hadn't believed I'd seen nothing.

Maybe he'd seen the lights, too. Plenty of people had. Maybe he'd been following one and that was how he'd ended up in the middle of nowhere the night I nearly became his hood ornament.

Maybe, like me, he'd been too afraid I'd think he was crazy.

I breathed a hoarse laugh. That couldn't be it. Sky wouldn't care what I thought. But maybe he didn't want to end up the subject of some Oasis gossip group text.

RE: The Hot Bartender Who Believes in Little Green Men.

My smirk faded as I studied the ugly bruise on my arm. No, not little green men.

Vicious, nightmare-machine aliens.

Still, Sky's opinion didn't matter. I was done spiraling. I'd go out with Amelia. I'd even tackle midterms next week.

But I wasn't done. I was going to get to the bottom of this.

These alien visitors and their *infiltration* had just become my new hobby.

Chapter 15

CONNECTING THE LITERAL DOTS

RAIN PATTERED A STACCATO BEAT AGAINST THE PLATE-GLASS WINDOWS overlooking the lake behind my brother's cute little bungalow.

The storm had rolled in while I was on my way to Maryville, and now I watched lightning lash down over the frothing water past the dock. The battered pontoon boat Dustin had been "fixing up" for ages rocked and rolled on each swell, straining against its ropes like it was trying to escape. The trees, stripped of their brittle, brown leaves by the wind, thrashed like concert ravers jamming out to nature's music.

The next flashing bolt jarred free a memory of blue strands of light crawling over the walls, the ceiling, stinging my flesh—

"You know you're not supposed to stand close to windows during storms, Rae," my mom called from where she was chopping veggies in the cheerful blue-and-yellow kitchen.

I jumped, then blinked, gathering myself enough to shoot her a dry look over my shoulder. "That's mostly a myth, Mom," I said, but it still made me smile.

At barely five feet tall, Mama B, as Amelia called her, was a tiny force of nature wrapped in a riot of color. Her graying hair was long and wild, and today's floor-length dress, red, purple, and pink, should've clashed with the kitchen decor.

It didn't, though. She owned every room she stepped into, a juxtaposition of maternal softness and fierceness I'd found myself striving for the older I got. Still a work in progress. Even now, I tended to fade. Which was fine. Sometimes it was easier to observe things from the background.

And I'd definitely been observing a lot of... *things* lately.

Suppressing a shiver, I turned from the window. Dustin and Lisa's eat-in kitchen opened right into their living room, and with one last glance at the storm, I wandered past the table toward the island where Mom was working.

"It's not that bad out there," I said.

The scent of her cheesy Italian chicken made my stomach growl. I hadn't eaten anything since that pizza binge last night. It was a good sign, I guessed, that my appetite was back.

I leaned my elbows on the counter. "Need a hand?"

"You already made the salad. And that cheesecake you brought." Mom waved her knife like a wand. "Go check on your sister-in-law. Make sure she's not climbing on that stepladder again."

"On it."

I mounted the stairs, rubbing my marked palm with my thumb as I went. No texture. No change, but I knew the markings were there.

Lowering my arms to my sides, I turned the corner, and sure enough—

Lisa froze with one foot on a step stool, both hands full of a stars-and-moon mobile. She winced. "Oh, Rae," she said, easing off the stool. "Hi."

I raised my brow. At nearly nine months pregnant, she was nearly as wide as she was tall, and it was utterly adorable.

"Busted," I said, arms crossed. "I'm under strict orders to keep you off that thing."

She rolled her eyes but conceded, handing me the mobile. "I'm pregnant, not made of glass."

"You're growing my nephew in there. You've earned the right to relax."

I paused to take in the nursery. It had changed a lot since I last visited.

It was oddly fitting, considering current events, that they'd gone with a space theme. The walls faded from light blue to deep cerulean to navy black, like a sky falling into night. Constellations and planets scattered across the ceiling and walls, glowing faintly beneath the soft wash of recessed lighting. Over the crib, the words *I love you more than there are stars in the sky* gleamed in silver script.

Cute. No way in hell Dustin had come up with it.

I saw the changing table and the little gray dresser, both pieces Mom and I had painted together for Lisa's shower, were already in place. It made me smile to see our labors of love on display.

The whole room felt…calm. Soothing. Something I hadn't been feeling much lately. A strange sort of nostalgia settled in, and I turned back to Lisa.

"You guys got a lot done," I said, genuinely impressed.

"Dustin's been nesting harder than I have. He did most of this," Lisa said, flipping a curl over her shoulder. "I had to tell him to take a break."

I smiled. "Sounds familiar." I lifted the mobile. "Where do you want this?"

"Oh, just over the crib. There's a hook already."

I climbed the ladder and stretched up to hang it. The tiny planets and stars tinkled as they swayed. Turning slowly, I took in the rest of the room. A familiar shape on the wall caught my eye: the Big Dipper.

My chest constricted, a soft squeeze. It was like Dad would be here, watching over his grandson.

Then I frowned. Come to think of it, though…all these shapes looked a little familiar.

"Did…" I arched a brow Lisa's way. "Did Dustin actually use real constellations for all of these?"

"Yes." She rolled her eyes, rubbing her belly. "He bought a projector to make sure it was accurate."

"Wow." I climbed down slowly, circling the room. "No wonder it took so long."

"You have no idea. He ordered maps and everything. Remember what I said about obsession? He even…"

I stopped short. Her words faded to a background buzz as my attention snagged on a single star pattern.

It wasn't just familiar. It was *the* pattern. The one I'd woken up with in my head. My stomach dropped.

A rectangle. Off-kilter. Crooked.

My palm tingled.

"Lisa." I turned with a half-formed, apologetic smile. "Sorry to interrupt. But…do you know what constellation that is?"

She followed my gaze, forehead furrowing. "No. I have no idea. That was all your brother."

"Equuleus," said a voice from the doorway.

Dustin. Rain had plastered his hair to his head and soaked through his gray, oil-stained shop coveralls, but that didn't stop him from wrapping Lisa in a soggy bear hug and kissing her shoulder.

"You're soaked!" Lisa squealed. "You're tracking water everywhere!"

"I'm cleaning the carpets tomorrow." He gave her his usual dopey grin, then turned to me. "And yeah, Rae. That one's Equuleus. Why? Want me to come do your room, too?"

"Equuleus," I repeated, the word sticking in my throat. I studied it again.

I'd never heard of it. I'd never even read the word in any textbook. I'd have no clue where to find it in the night sky.

But I'd seen that exact pattern. Burned behind my eyelids. An echo of a dream.

Why was I dreaming about constellations I didn't know?

A nagging voice reminded me I'd been run off the road by a UFO and chased by alien robots in the last week. It didn't take a rocket scientist—or a flying saucer one—to figure out the connection. It had to be related.

Maybe it'd been in my subconscious.

Maybe it hadn't.

I fought the urge to look at my hand.

Oblivious to my existential crisis, Dustin slung an arm around his wife's shoulders. "Yeah, it's a horse's head. You know, like equine."

"Latin for horse," I muttered, still staring at the constellation. I could feel my brother's eyes on me, but I couldn't seem to look away.

"You all right over there?" he asked. "Mom told me you almost got blown up at school yesterday."

"Almost got *what?*" Lisa cried.

I sighed and turned around just in time to see her smack Dustin's arm.

"You didn't tell me that!" she said, spinning toward me with surprising grace for someone that pregnant. Her brows pinched tight over her dark eyes. "What happened? Are you okay?"

An alien infiltration happened.

"I'm fine. Seriously," I said quickly, curling my fingertips to contain the itch in my right hand. "I wasn't hurt at all. Last I heard, the school still isn't sure what caused the explosion. Something about the solar flare." The lie tasted bitter. I shrugged, aiming for nonchalance. "I got knocked out, but the EMT checked me out. I've been fine since."

No need to mention the full-blown meltdown I'd had last night. The wine. The bruises. The dream hallucinations.

I mean, I *was* feeling better. Mostly.

Lisa moved closer and searched my face, still looking unconvinced, so I added, "I even stayed home from work yesterday and took it easy."

She opened her mouth, but my brother cut her off. "Oh, no," he said, circling Lisa to grab my shoulders and peer into my face. His hazel eyes—so much like mine, like Dad's—sparkled with mock concern. "You *called off work?* What is this, *Invasion of the Body Snatchers?* Were you abducted by those aliens everyone says are taking over?"

I almost choked. My eyes bugged, but I caught myself and forced a laugh, shoving him off with more force than necessary.

Because he was my big brother and we used to wrestle daily, he just laughed.

His fingers brushed the bruises on my upper arm, though, as he released me, and I barely checked my flinch. Recovering, I scoffed.

"If I was abducted, they probably would've dropped me back off out of sheer annoyance. Too many questions," I said wryly.

Not a lie at all.

"You've got that right," Dustin said, trying to ruffle my hair. I dodged his hand and sent him a glare. Sometimes I thought he'd missed the part where I was no longer thirteen.

"Did you go to the hospital, at least?" Lisa asked, twisting her hands together.

Sobering, I straightened. "No..."

Dustin and I exchanged a look. I wasn't the only one who'd developed a dislike of all things hospital related. It was a testament of his love for Lisa their birth plan involved Willow Hospital.

"I didn't need to," I said, summoning a smile that felt more than a little stilted. "I really am fine. I promise."

Lisa opened her mouth—but thankfully, Mom's voice rang out, calling us to dinner. With one, final worried look my way, Lisa dropped it and let Dustin guide her from the room. I released a quiet breath, tucking my marked hand into my pocket. My brother chattered about the storm and the lake as I followed them from the nursery.

But not before casting one last glance over my shoulder at the constellation.

Was that actually what I'd seen in my dreams? *Stars?* Or was this some kind of message from them?

Or was I just losing my whole damn mind?

My hand tingled. I'd told Lisa I was fine, but even I was starting to wonder.

There was a chance I was far from fine.

Chapter 16

I CAN'T HEAR YOU OVER THE BASS
AND BETRAYAL

"**You** look *fine*, girl," some stranger yelled in my ear.

My stomach soured as the half-shouted, dubious compliment slashed through my enjoyment like a laser strike. The Crescent Club's bass thumped as I aimed a flat look at the interloper.

Flashing lights revealed attractive-ish features. Surfer-blond, a square jaw, and the kind of smile that probably worked on girls who were into that cocky type.

I wasn't.

In other circumstances, if I hadn't spent my week knee-deep in alien bullshit, maybe I'd have laughed and played it off. Tonight, though, I felt too tense and frayed for this. Setting my teeth, I started to turn back around—not fast enough to miss the guy giving me a blatant once-over.

My annoyance ticked up another notch. I stopped dancing. Somehow, he took that as an invitation.

"So what's your name, babe?" he shouted over the music, leaning in too close. The biting scent of whiskey and too much cologne filled my nostrils.

Babe? Really? I rolled my eyes so hard I almost saw last week. He made a grab for my arm, and I pulled it close to my side, edging away from him. "Sorry. Thanks, but no thanks."

"What?" he yelled, stumbling closer.

Ugh. I knew people came to clubs like Crescent to meet someone. For the night—or hey, maybe even longer. I'd been there.

Tonight, though, I was here to dance. To dance and forget.

Maybe that made me lame. It'd been a while since I'd cuddled with anything that didn't have chapter headings and a title page. But that wasn't what I was looking for.

I just wanted to dance.

Preferably *without* the groping.

But dancing alone apparently broadcasted an invitation. And some guys were pushier than others. As he stepped further into my personal space, I got the distinct feeling this Prince Charming would be one of them.

I searched until I found Amelia. She was leaning against a tall, thin, dark-haired man about our age, her head tilted back at a flirty angle. I vaguely recognized him. Had he happened to be here, or did she invite him?

Guilt prickled. Had she mentioned meeting somebody? I didn't *think* so, but then again, I'd been so distracted lately. Preoccupied. It was taking a toll on my friendships, too.

I swallowed hard and darted a glance at my current problem: the blond-haired man still eyeing me like a carnivore eyes a filet. My lip curled.

Seeing me looking, he opened his mouth, but I gave him my shoulder. I hated to interrupt Amelia, but he wasn't taking no for an answer.

Luckily, she happened to turn her head my way then glanced past me, at the Prince Charming encroaching on my personal space. She gave an exasperated eye roll and nodded, mouthing, *One second.*

My shoulders sagged with relief. Backup was coming.

I waited while she rose to her tiptoes, her leather minidress riding up dangerously high as she whispered something to her dancing partner. He grimaced, his eyes flicking toward me and my admirer, who was currently doing a hip-thrust dance in my direction. *Gag.*

Amelia disengaged and crossed the floor, dodging a group of dancing girls. I let out a relieved whoosh of air when she looped her arm through mine and tugged.

"Sorry," she said to Mr. Pushy, who stopped dancing (if it could be called that) to give Amelia his best slimy grin. Her return look could've frozen lava. "We have to go to the bathroom in pairs."

Before he could respond, she was towing me through the dancers. The DJ booth pulsed in the center like a glowing altar, and the bass vibrated the floor. Around us, lights slashed across bodies, blurring motion and shadowing faces. The effect was eerie enough, I nearly shivered. The thud of music mingled with voices, shrieks, and laughter.

I was getting jumpy again. I fanned myself as we escaped the press of bodies. Amelia steered us toward the hallway leading to the bathrooms.

"Thanks for the rescue," I told her, raising my voice over the bass drop and accompanying cheers.

"No problem." She tossed her dark curls and smirked. "I don't know how he couldn't tell how disgusted you were by the look on your face."

Another reminder of how bad a liar I was. I bit my lip, giving her a sidelong look. "And who's *your* dance partner?"

"Oh." She smile dimmed. "That's Emerick Kensington. His dad works with my dad."

I raised my brows and nearly stopped walking. Somebody from her father's social circle? That wasn't her normal type. She avoided that crowd like the plague.

Interesting.

I studied her as we cut through the line waiting on drinks. Her olive skin was flushed from the dance floor's muggy heat, but somehow her sultry makeup had stayed perfect. She glided in her gold strappy heels like she'd been born in them, while I clomped behind her in my far more sensible boots.

126

We were night and day. Total opposites in a lot of ways. But she grounded me.

I'd needed this night out with her more than I'd realized.

We pushed into the women's bathroom. A few girls mingled at the sinks, checking their lipstick, fixing flyaways, and chatting in too-loud voices. We wove around them, and Amelia stopped at the floor-length mirror.

"Yeah, Emerick's…just fun," she said, her dismissive tone brushing aside any more questions before I could even ask them. She adjusted her skintight tube dress. It did spectacular things for her long legs. Half-turning, she raised an eyebrow at me. "That guy who came up to you wasn't too bad to look at, though. You could've let him buy you a drink, at least. You look like you could use one."

She wasn't wrong. I sighed, turning to my reflection.

I'd been ready to wear jeans, a tank, and a jacket to hide the nasty discoloration on my arm. It'd only gotten worse in the past day. Amelia had taken one look at me and tossed me a slinky silver dress she'd found in her closet. I hadn't put up a fight because… well, it *was* a cute dress, and after spending the last few days pale, bruised, and sweaty, maybe a cute dress was exactly what I needed, too.

Amelia also wasn't stupid. She'd noticed the finger marks while I changed. I didn't think she'd completely bought my claim that they'd come from the explosion at Finke, either. But she hadn't pressed.

It *technically* wasn't a lie. Something had exploded. Just…not what the media was saying.

I'd been stretching the truth an awful lot lately. More so than I ever had with the best friend I thought of as a sister.

My insides twisted. I pushed aside the thought and smoothed the borrowed dress. It clung to my frame in all the right places, and despite how straight-as-a-board I looked next to Amelia's goddess-tier curves, it somehow gave me a hint of cleavage.

Plus, it had pockets. Cleavage and pockets—what more could a girl ask for?

I'd at least won the argument about the shoes. I could walk in my flat black ankle boots. Amelia's deft hand with makeup didn't hurt my look tonight, either. Dramatic smoky eyes, razor-sharp eyeliner, and fire-engine red lipstick. Way more glam than I usually wore. But I hadn't wiped it off.

I contemplated the girl in the mirror. Maybe it wasn't a bad thing to look...different for a night. To *be* someone different. Someone not dealing with all the insanity I had been.

Robots and aliens and whatever the hell was happening with my hand.

I tugged the dress's sleeve down over my arm. With all the marks hidden, I could almost convince myself it hadn't happened. Almost. Not quite. The buzzing panic had dulled with time, but the jitters were still there. So was the compulsion to check over my shoulder.

What *had* happened, though—I'd come to terms with one big truth: there was nothing I could do about *any* of this right now. I couldn't change the mess I'd stumbled into. Nor could I explain it. Not really.

Not *yet*.

I could start looking for the *why*. Solving the mystery.

And tonight, I was safe enough here, in the crowded dance club, wearing this pretty dress and a full face of makeup, dancing with my best friend.

Besides, if aliens were going to stage a full-on invasion, they could've already done it. I'd seen those robots. We wouldn't stand a chance.

They were clearly here for a different reason. And if I was lucky, that reason had broken into a million pieces when that artifact had dissolved.

Really, that'd be the best-case scenario—

"You sure you're okay, Rae?" Amelia's concerned tone cut through my thoughts.

Too late, I realized I'd been staring blankly at myself. I blinked and met her eyes in the mirror instead. Her expression was uncharacteristically serious, her mouth compressed.

She stepped closer, lowering her voice and nudging me with her elbow. "You've been out of it tonight."

When I tried to smile and failed, she turned her attention to her hair, raking her fingers through her curls. Her shoulders drew tight though, before she said, "I know yesterday probably shook you up. You've been under a lot of stress these last few days, with work. Your shitty car. Not to mention midterms. You know if you need to talk or if you need help with...well, anything." She grimaced and dropped her arm, flicking an uncomfortable glance past me. "Even, like, money for Faith or something..."

My jaw dropped open in surprise. "A—"

"I know," she cut in, rolling her eyes. "I'm just letting you know I'm here."

I forced my mouth to close. She'd offered me money. Amelia *never* flaunted her family's wealth. In fact, she hated talking about it. With a passion.

She'd told me before that even acknowledging it felt like bragging. That life, those people, were plastic and fake and far from who she wanted to be. If she could've changed her last name, she would have. In One Willow and Maryville, and in circles where that mattered, *Delarosa* basically translated to dollar signs.

It had been a long time since she'd tried to help me like that. Probably since I'd been applying for scholarships. She'd tried to pay for my schooling from her own trust fund, and she'd been just as awkward about it then. I hadn't let her, of course. I wasn't sure which one of us was more uncomfortable with the entire thing.

But tonight, she'd offered anyway. In case it could help.

My heart gave a thick, hollow thud. She really was the best friend a girl could ask for. And I was hiding *everything* from her.

I fisted my marked hand in my dress and forced my tight throat to work in a swallow. God, for one heart-wrenching second, I wanted to spill it all. The school encounter, the strange tablet, the lights that drove me off the road. The internet rabbit holes. The creeping, exhausting fear.

I *wanted* to.

It all bubbled up, a flood I didn't know I'd been drowning in. My world was fracturing. And with it, I could *feel* the crack forming between Amelia and me, too, this widening chasm in a friendship that had always been bulletproof.

But then I imagined saying it out loud...

Aliens.

It sounded too ridiculous. Too sci-fi. Too *crazy*.

Even Amelia, who knew me better than anyone, would worry I'd lost my mind. And honestly? I wasn't sure I hadn't. Not completely.

I had to wait. I needed proof. Something solid. Maybe even an explanation—or at least a somewhat plausible theory.

Until then, it wouldn't be fair to pull her into this mess. Hell, for all I knew, the robot aliens would be back for me. The last thing I wanted to do was put my best friend in the crosshairs with me.

My chest ached. I made myself release my dress and looked away, forcing a small smile. Unable to look at her, I bent toward the mirror and pretended to fuss with my hair.

"I'm okay." I'd said it so many times lately, I wasn't sure who I was trying to convince anymore. With one more fluff of my fast-deflating curls, I steeled myself and turned around. "Just stressed. I needed a night out. Thanks for doing this."

Amelia narrowed her eyes like she wanted to call bullshit. For a second, I thought she would. If anybody could, it'd be her. She could read me like a book.

But then she simply shrugged. "Of course." She gave her hair a final pat and motioned toward the door. "You ready to go back out there?"

I avoided her eyes. That twisting, empty feeling was back in my stomach.

She knew I was hiding something. I could *feel* it.

But because I was pretending to be normal tonight, I whirled from the mirror and sighed. "Let's go dance. Maybe I can still get a drink out of Prince Charming."

A beat later, her expression cleared, and she grinned, wide and red-lipped. "There you go. That's the spirit."

I followed her out of the bathroom. I didn't resist when she caught my unmarked hand in hers. She cast a coy smile at the group of guys we passed, and their heads turned to follow her.

She seemed fine. The suspicion I thought I'd glimpsed was gone. Maybe it was in my head. There was a chance a lot of things were these days.

But the encounter had killed my buzz. I couldn't shake the heaviness. I trailed Amelia into the press of bodies and pounding music. Like before, in the school parking lot, I had the uncanny sensation the world was crashing around me, and I was an island. Alone with the knowledge—my own personal nightmare.

It was just me, cut off from the rest of the world, surrounded by people who had no idea what was lurking in the shadows. Giant, six-fingered murder machines from the stars. I shivered.

Irritated at the self-pity creeping in, I closed my fingers around the markings on my palm again.

Emerick found us again, and I watched him bend down to speak to Amelia. Her bright laugh was lost to the thud of music as they slipped easily into dancing. I followed suit, but my body felt disjointed. Disconnected.

I tried anyway. Maybe if I pretended things were normal for long enough, I'd start to believe it, too.

MY ADMIRER DIDN'T REAPPEAR, thankfully, and I'd relaxed a little by the time we took a sweaty break to grab drinks. Emerick officially introduced himself, apologizing for not doing so before. He was charming. Nice enough. Not as snobby as some of her other rich friends.

He even whipped out a shiny black credit card to pay for the second round of shots the bartender lined up in front of us. When he turned to take care of the payment, I shot Amelia a raised eyebrow. Leaning back on her elbows against the curving bar, she gave an almost imperceptible shrug, as if to say, *why not?*

"This is a bad idea," I told her, lifting my glass and eyeing the clear liquid. "You know I have work tomorrow—not to mention loads of studying to do."

She snorted and pushed off the counter as Emerick pocketed his card and joined us.

"You need it, Rae," Amelia said, sighing. "You've had a shit week." She raised the tiny glass. When I reluctantly followed suit, she clinked the rims. "Here's to the aliens."

I stiffened, giving her a withering look. Out of *everything* she could've toasted with, she went with that? Her lips curled into a mischievous smile.

Oblivious, Emerick raised his glass, his white designer-label shirt glowing in the black light. "Here's to the aliens."

"Sure," I muttered, saluting them before tipping back the shot.

I shuddered. The minty alcohol burned all the way down. God, I hated shots. I chased it with a gulp of vodka-and-soda to kill the sting. The flavor combination made me wince.

When my vision cleared, I spotted Amelia hanging on Emerick's neck across from me, her face close to his as she murmured something I couldn't hear. His hand was drifting low on her hip. Polite for now, but veering into the flirty lane quickly.

I looked away, turning my empty shot glass over in my hand. The markings on my palm were invisible in the darkness.

We'd toasted to the aliens. The ones who'd almost killed me. Twice now.

The memories stirred a fresh shiver. I forced myself to focus on my surroundings instead. People. Noise. Music. The crowd pulsed with life and movement, a blend of college students and after-work regulars. Laughter and the tinkle of glasses behind the bar melted into the relentless beat vibrating in the air.

It was busier than normal tonight. Good for people-watching, but I couldn't stop scanning the shadows for tall, chrome-plated horrors. Which was ridiculous. There was no way the bouncer would've let a killer alien robot through the front door.

I snorted and drained the rest of my mixed drink.

The song shifted, something dark and pulsing. I was still trying to place the lyrics when Amelia squealed and broke away from Emerick. "We *have* to dance to this one! Come on, Rae!" Her fingers wrapped around my forearm, and she tugged hard.

I barely managed to set down my empty glass before she hauled me from the bar and toward the floor. Emerick strolled after us, sipping from his tumbler. Something expensive and amber-colored —and top-shelf, of course. I lost sight of him a second later when the crowd swallowed us whole.

The alcohol's buzz hit then. Perfect timing. It blurred my thoughts and loosened tight muscles. Laughing, I let Amelia pull me closer. The music slithered through me, an anchor. The song, the club, dancing with my best friend—this was familiar. Loud, chaotic, and safe.

Normal.

No monsters here.

I closed my eyes and dropped my head back, lifting my arms over my head. I let the music take over. Let it scrape away the madness, the lies, the weirdness. For the length of one song, I was just a girl in a pretty silver dress, dancing off a shitty week of midterm and work stress.

The song ended. When I opened my eyes, Amelia and Emerick were twined together, hips moving in perfect sync. I watched them for a beat, more than a little surprised.

Maybe there *was* a spark there. It'd been a while since I'd seen her really into a guy.

For some reason, it made me feel even more alone.

Sighing, I pushed aside the silly self-pity and turned away, giving myself over to the beat again. More of my tension bled away. I relaxed for the first time in *days*. Whether it was the drinks, the dancing, or just pure exhaustion, I didn't care. I was just glad I was finally—

I sensed someone step into my space. I opened my eyes…and nearly groaned out loud.

Prince Charming. Again.

He smiled like we were old friends. I tried to step back—

Except he'd grabbed my wrist.

"Hey, where are you going?" he slurred. Somehow, the alcohol on his breath was even more noxious now. "You're not gonna run away again, are you? Don't be like that."

Irritation flared, dousing whatever contentment was left. "I'm not interested." I tried to pull my arm back. He held on, and I glared at him. "Let. Go."

He did *not* want to mess with me today of all days. The ball of anger in my chest burned brighter than normal.

He must've caught it because his smile slipped and his fingers tightened. "What's your problem?"

"*You,*" I said through gritted teeth.

People were starting to notice now. Heads turned our way. But no one stepped in.

Not that I needed them to. I could handle one jerk with a hearing problem.

I yanked, and this time it worked. I wrenched my arm free, hard enough he stumbled, loose-limbed and clearly drunk. Unfortunately he caught himself before he face-planted on the sticky floor. I took a step back, rotating my sore wrist.

He wasn't done, though. He straightened, and his frown turned dark enough that I stiffened. A flash of blue club lighting flared behind him, shadowing his face as he stepped forward, reaching out like he was going to try again—

A presence warmed my side. A body, moving in close. I jolted when an arm wrapped around my waist. *You have to be kidding me.* I whipped my elbow up, ready to drive it back because what was *wrong* with people in here today—

Then a low, all-too-memorable voice rose over the music. "Hey. I thought I spotted you earlier."

Shock. Pure shock jolted me to the core. I froze with my elbow raised like I was doing half a chicken dance.

I turned my head slowly. My mouth dropped open.

Sky Acosta wasn't looking my way now, though the words were clearly meant for me. His dark eyes were locked on Whiskey Breath.

"Is there a problem here?" he asked in an even tone.

I gawked.

Sky was here. Sky was at Crescent.

I managed to find my voice, though it came out squeaky. "How is it always *you?*"

Chapter 17

WHAT IS THIS, A STALKER ROMANCE?

SKY DIDN'T REACT TO MY WEIRD-AS-HELL QUESTION. He didn't look at me, either.

He did, however, squeeze my side, which obliterated any coherent thoughts like he'd reset my brain. His arm was a warm band—not quite possessive, but definitely a little protective.

I didn't know what was more shocking: his sudden appearance or the hard, unreadable look on his face. His calm, laid-back persona wasn't in the room with us. Instead, something stormy lurked in his eyes as he stared down the smaller man. That looked a lot like temper.

I stood rooted in place like I'd been superglued there.

Meanwhile, the drunk jerk blinked at him, swaying slightly. "Wait, is this your boyfriend? You didn't tell me you had a *boyfriend*."

It was enough to rouse me from my stupor. I turned a glare on him and opened my mouth to deny it, to tell him a girl shouldn't need a boyfriend for him to grasp the word *no*. But Sky beat me to it.

"It doesn't matter who I am." His voice stayed level, but there was steel underneath. "This is your cue to get out of here. The lady isn't interested."

The guy glanced blearily from Sky to me, like he was weighing his odds. Spoiler alert: they weren't good. Sky had a good six inches on him, at least twice the shoulder width, and a sense of equilibrium. Not a fight Whiskey Breath would win.

He was apparently sober enough to realize it, too, because he shrugged, muttering, "Whatever."

And he left.

I watched him stagger away, heart racing. The relief was short-lived, though.

Despite every cell screaming at me to snuggle right in, I stepped out of Sky's embrace and pivoted to face him. The small crowd of onlookers who'd been watching the exchange went right back to dancing. The movement and music swallowed the moment, like it had never happened.

I stared up at my bartender crush. Who was suspiciously good at being in the right place at the right time lately.

Or the wrong one. Depending on how you looked at it.

"What are you doing here?" I asked, raising my voice over the bass-heavy beat.

He tracked the drunk guy's retreat for a second longer before turning back. His ocean eyes moved over me. Flustered, I looked away, massaging the wrist still smarting from that asshole's iron grip.

"Are you okay?" Sky asked tightly.

I raised my gaze back to his. He was watching me rub the tender skin, expression stormy.

Was I *okay*? What a loaded question, considering the state of my life these last few days. I almost laughed but managed to nod instead, letting my hand fall back to my side. Only then did I remember it was the same one with the alien tattoo. I made a loose fist around it. Not that I needed to worry. It was too dark to see anything—

I forgot I even had hands when Sky stepped closer.

The smallest shift, but it was enough.

He was so much taller than me. I was eye level with his chin. His shoulders. His black Henley clung to his tapered chest and outlined all those muscles beneath. How was this man so well-shaped—

His chest shook, and I blinked. It took me a second to register his chuckle. I dragged my attention up in time to see a faint, crooked grin appear.

"We have to stop meeting like this," he said, tucking his hands into his pockets.

"Like what?" I pushed a loose strand behind my ear, then pulled down my dress sleeves before catching myself fidgeting. "When I'm in need of rescuing?"

He lifted a shoulder in a tiny shrug. He could've modeled. There had to be some sexy bartender calendar out there. A shirtless one, hopefully. Because this whole package...

My focus dipped again, trailing down, lower, and—oh no. No, no, no. I did *not* want to be thinking about Sky's...*anything* package.

I snapped my eyes shut.

Oh my God. *What was* wrong *with me?*

"Rae?" he asked, sounding a little bewildered. Most likely because I was standing there with my eyes squeezed shut and hands fisted. "You all right?"

What was it about him that fried my brain cells?

I gathered every ounce of willpower (and maybe a little vodka) and opened my eyes, summoning a small, weak smile. "Yeah. Thanks," I said, swallowing a nervous laugh. "For the save. With that guy."

My throat was so dry, and that was still shock ricocheting through my body. He'd come out of nowhere. Like he could tell I was reeling, his brows tented, humor fading.

I needed another drink. Especially if he was going to keep looking at me like that, with all that intensity.

"Sorry that guy touched you like that," he said quietly, eyes sliding to my wrist once again. Something hard glinted in them for a second. "Some people don't take a hint, and that's not okay."

I smiled up at him less tentatively this time. "I know. I'm fine, though." I paused and glanced around. My rapidly deflating curls brushed my cheeks at the movement, and I pushed them over my shoulder. It'd gotten a lot hotter in here all of a sudden. "So are you here with friends or...?"

Instead of answering, Sky lifted a hand. I froze as he tucked the escaping stray strand of hair back behind my ear again. His finger-tips grazed the sensitive skin at my temple. Fire trailed in their wake.

Breathing became a hell of a lot harder, and my cheeks blazed. Words tumbled out of me.

"What are you doing?"

Like he was wondering the same thing, Sky yanked his arm back and rocked onto his heels, giving me a smile I could only describe as sheepish. Maybe even *shy*. "Sorry. I couldn't help it. I'm not used to seeing it down." He cleared his throat and glanced away.

Down...

Oh. My *hair*.

He was talking about my hair, and he was still standing close. The dance floor's lighting washed him in splashes of neon green, vivid pink, and deep blue. The shifting glow rendered his face in chiseled slopes and planes, shadowing his high cheekbones, straight nose, and strong jawline.

But none of that stopped suspicion from blooming as the shock of his appearance began to fade.

He still hadn't answered me. He still hadn't said why he was here.

Or why, for the second time in as many days, he'd appeared out of nowhere to save the day. First the country road. Now Crescent. Sky Acosta was starting to feel like my own personal knight in shining armor.

The strand of hair he'd tucked behind my ear had escaped, and I pushed it back again, fingers clumsy. Where had that thought come from? I wasn't the damsel type. My thoughts felt like scrambled eggs. Probably from the deadly combo of alcohol and the sheer amount of heat he radiated.

He had to be used to girls melting like this. That thought helped me rally enough brain cells to ask again, "What are you doing here, Sky?" Frowning, I added, "Weren't you working or something tonight?"

I regretted it the second it left my mouth. *Right*, because it's totally normal to assume he lived behind the bar.

He didn't look offended. If anything, he looked amused again, his dimple reappearing. Some of his tension bled away as he raised a brow. "I'm sorry—are you the only one who gets days off?"

"No, of course not. I meant…" I scrubbed my palm against the dress's slinky material and sighed. "What are you doing *here*, here?" I swept out my unmarked hand to encompass the dancers around us, the crowded bar. The DJ bopping away to the heavy beat.

He followed my gesture. "Well, I'm not doing anything right now," he said, raking his bangs back with one hand. He hesitated, then: "So…did you want to dance?"

My mouth dropped open.

"With *you*?" I squeaked. "Right now?"

I had a completely irrational urge to run away. *Sky* wanted to dance with *me*? Here? In front of all these people?

His gaze slid back to mine slowly, and he grinned, a lopsided one with a hint of teasing. "Well, yeah. That's the idea."

He extended his hand. I stared at it, then him.

Dance. *Dance* with Sky? Now, while my life was falling apart?

Maybe I shouldn't question it. Maybe this was the universe's way of balancing things out. After all, these last few days had been less than stellar. I deserved something nice—something *not* extraterrestrial. There was nothing alien about Sky. He was all *human* male.

Ah, what the hell? Why not? I slipped my unmarked palm into his. I was unprepared for the light tug he gave it. A second later, I was in his arms.

And we were dancing…*ish*. At the very least, we were swaying in place.

My hands found his shoulders. His shirt was soft as angel wings. As the fabric of all my hazy daydreams. The contrast with his warm body and sturdy strength beneath nearly made me shiver. So did his featherlight touch at my waist as he nudged me closer. Close enough that the front of our bodies brushed. My heart galloped like it was chasing a world record.

Mouth dry, I raised my eyes to his. I couldn't begin to imagine what he was thinking, but he was focused. On *me*. His thumb brushed my ribcage. His touch felt almost hesitant, like he expected me to pull away.

Which would be insane. This was just as unreal as glowing orbs and robot monsters, as aliens being real and here on our tiny Earth rock.

The thought sobered me enough that I broke eye contact. Club music pulsed and thumped. A group of guys cheered at the bar, clinking bottles together. Spotlights splashed color in flickering patches over the walls, the floor, the dancers moving around us.

Normal. This was normal.

I'd wanted a night of normalcy, hadn't I? Never in a million years would I have thought that included an appearance from Sky, but who was I to question fate? This was nice.

Our movements were tame, a gentle sway compared to Amelia and Emerick nearby. They were wrapped in each other. Enough so that she'd missed everything with drunk Prince Charming. Not to mention Sky's appearance. She'd notice soon, though.

I could only imagine how this was going to go. She knew who he was from visiting me at work, but they'd never *officially* met.

Didn't mean she didn't know *all about him* from me, of course.

I tore my attention from her and found Sky watching me. Studying me. Still moving to the beat with that light hold on my waist.

Another wave of disbelief surged—that he was here, that we were doing this—and suddenly, I couldn't contain words.

"You don't have to do this," I blurted. I knew my face was red. I could feel it throbbing. I was sure I was bordering on a human glow-stick. "He's gone."

"What was that?" Sky tilted an ear toward me.

The song shifted into something darker, blatantly sensual, with breathy, suggestive lyrics. Just the kind of song I'd have pictured Sky while listening to.

That wasn't awkward or anything.

I cleared my throat, rising onto my tiptoes to repeat myself in his ear.

The vodka chose that exact moment to kick in. Off balance, I stumbled forward, erasing all the inches between us—and smacked face-first into the rock-hard wall that was Sky.

Chapter 18

IF YOU'RE TRYING TO GASLIGHT ME,
AT LEAST BUY ME A DRINK FIRST

THE AIR RUSHED FROM HIM IN A SHOCKED HUFF when I crashed nose-first into his front. For one terrified moment, I thought I was going to bowl us both over.

But he moved fast. His arm snaked around me, pressing us together hip to chest. Catching my weight.

I froze.

Sky did, too.

Slowly, like I was surfacing from deep underwater, I lifted my face from his shirt. Whatever apology I might've offered zipped away into the atmosphere, taking my stomach with it.

His lips had parted and his eyes had widened with surprise, but he didn't let go. One hand splayed low across my back, the other tightened on my waist. Mine had flattened against his stomach. Right over a set of hard abs that felt like they'd been designed by some sculptor. They flexed when he sucked in another deep breath.

I'd thought we were close before, but this? This was *kissing*-close. This was I'm-groping-Sky's-abdominals close.

He gave one slow blink, and like he'd just realized the same thing, awareness slid in, darkening his midnight-blue eyes.

But he didn't look away.

Neither did I.

It happened in a single heartbeat and…

We fit.

The thought stamped itself across my brain like a brand.

Which was clearly the vodka talking. The months of infatuation. Maybe stress forming illogical conclusions. It'd also been a while since I'd been this close to someone. And certainly not someone like Sky.

He smelled like mint and *him*, like cool night and sandalwood and spice. I should pull away. Now. Before he pushed me off him. Because surely he would.

Any second now.

…*any* second.

He didn't move.

Neither did I.

Another heartbeat passed before he did, and it wasn't to draw away or put distance between our bodies. Instead, he used the palm on my back to press in, situating me against him.

Not pulling away. Pulling me *closer*.

Laser lights flashed across the floor, slicing beams of rainbow color. His features flickered in and out of focus, but I could see enough. The shock had dissipated from his face, and that calm mask was back in place. His gaze was warm, dark, infinite.

My heart tried to punch its way out through my ribs.

"Okay," he murmured, and it was huskier than he'd sounded a second ago. His mouth curved ever so slightly, crinkling his eyes. "This works, too."

And he started swaying again. Autopilot kicked in. My hips found the beat, syncing with the music's slow, pulsing rhythm.

You know, just…dancing. Casually. With Sky.

I could do this. I just had to keep it together. Act natural.

Natural, as in like it was a totally normal thing to be wrapped around him. Of all people. Of all nights. On this dance floor.

To make it easier on myself, I moved my hands off his abs (*dear God*) and laced them behind his neck instead.

Sky glanced away to scan the crowd and the edges of the

dance floor. Like he was looking for something. I started to follow his gaze, but then his attention drifted back to me. His teasing smile deepened at whatever he saw. Disbelief and awe, most likely.

"You sure this is okay?" he asked, the question rumbling from his chest and into mine. His voice was barely audible over the music.

This was not a fantasy anymore. This was real. Somehow. I'd entered an alternate reality where I'd run into him at the club and now we were plastered together like this.

Our chests brushed. His hips pressed against mine, which threatened to drag my mind in all *kinds* of inappropriate places—

No, I couldn't do that. Not now. Not if I wanted to maintain my composure.

But…kind of impossible not to. After all, this was *Sky*.

How many times had I watched him at the bar? Admired the way his sleeves strained against his arms? Watched that dimple. Melted over that laugh I rarely got to hear. That smile.

There was a chance I hadn't realized how truly far gone I was until now. The world threatened to narrow to only us.

But there was a small, annoying voice at the back of my mind. A nagging reminder that made it impossible to completely surrender to this moment.

"You never did answer my question," I said, way more breathlessly than I'd intended.

Sky tilted his head down, brows slanting in inquiry. "What question?"

He traced his eyes over me—over my *mouth*. Just the briefest glance before he blinked rapidly and looked away. Almost like he hadn't meant to. His teeth sank into his bottom lip, and his fingers tightened a little on my side.

I was suddenly grateful I'd slung my arms around his neck. I wasn't quite sure I could stand on my own.

Focus, Rae. Be logical.

Because if I didn't know better, I'd think he looked flustered, too.

But he was also dodging my question.

Somehow, I made myself form words. "I asked what you were doing here tonight."

"Ah." He dipped his head a little, looking at me through thick lashes. "Dancing with you. Is that okay?"

"Is that—?" My brain stuttered. "But…why?"

"Why are we dancing?" His grin flashed, bright and lethal.

"Yes," I croaked. "No. Uh, kind of?"

He gave a short laugh before sobering. "Honestly?"

"Preferably," I breathed, trying not to notice the brush of his jeans against my lower belly.

My answer drew a faint smile from him, a flicker of one that slipped away just as quickly. "At first, it was because that asshole wouldn't leave you alone and no one else was stepping in." He glanced around us, like he was reassuring himself Whiskey Breath had indeed vanished, and then his attention was on me again. His expression softened a little. "And now we're dancing because…well, I really like your dress. I probably shouldn't say this, but you look really nice, Rae. And I…"

His Adam's apple bobbed with his heavy swallow. Stunned, I could only stare. I desperately needed him to finish that sentence.

He'd just told me he liked my *dress*. That I looked great.

What was *happening* right now?

"What do you mean you probably shouldn't say it?" I asked. A bead of sweat traced down my spine. I couldn't look away from Sky's face.

Because I was watching him, I noticed the way he bit the inside of his cheek and looked everywhere but at me.

Was that redness tinting his high cheekbones or a trick of the light? Holy crap. If I didn't know better, I'd think Sky was blushing.

That couldn't be right. Was he drunk, too? He didn't seem drunk. I didn't smell any alcohol on him, and his gaze wasn't blurry. There had to be an explanation for this.

I was at a loss for one. And words.

After about a million years, he finally looked at me again, running those dark eyes over my face before sighing. "It's complicated. But I also…" He exhaled a soft, self-deprecating laugh and shook his head. "I don't know. I like the way you're looking at me right now. Like you *see* me."

"Like I *see* you?" How the hell could someone miss him?

Also, why did I get the feeling he was holding something back? What was complicated? Dancing? Because he seemed to be doing just fine. I was the one who'd nearly knocked us over. What was I missing?

What was going on?

I stopped moving. It hadn't escaped my notice, either, that he'd said my name for a second time. The *right* name.

This *had* to be a dream. I felt kind of like the clouds had parted and a sunbeam had chosen *me.* Like winning the lottery if the lottery was a long-legged, too-sexy bartender.

I narrowed my eyes. It was my turn to wonder if there was a prank show host lurking in this crowd of sweaty, gyrating dancers. Because that seemed more probable.

I went with honesty. "I, ah, don't know what to say to that."

"Yeah." Sky's mouth twisted ruefully, and he sighed. "I get that."

Since he was still lightly gripping my waist, it took only a nudge of his leg to get me moving again. Because I was a sucker, I let him guide me until we rotated gently in place. My view shifted. Nearby, a pair of girls barely twenty-one shouted the song's lyrics at one another. The lights pulsed in time with the bass's sultry thump.

Another rotation, and his thigh slipped between mine. It was as hard and muscular as the rest of him, which really wasn't helping me find my bearings. I took a deep breath to quell the fire kindling low in my belly and tightened my grip on his shoulders. Also unhelpfully muscular, for the record. I forgot what I was saying.

Sky chose that moment to speak up, his expression torn between curiosity and amusement. "You don't know what to say to which part, though?"

I didn't know what to say to *any* of it. I shook my head. My blood leapt against my skin. The room blurred. I was definitely tipsy. That last shot had tipped me over the edge.

My next exhale was unsteady. Sky must've caught it because his grip loosened instantly, and he bent to get a better look at me. "Do you need some water? Have you had a lot to drink?"

Not nearly enough. My hysterical laugh nearly burst free. I could use some water. Possibly more vodka. Maybe a prescription. I didn't know anymore.

"I'm fine," I said, trying for a smile instead. God, I sounded like a broken record. I disengaged from the object of my fantasies enough to fan myself. It was about a thousand degrees in the center of all these bodies. I made myself keep swaying, if only so I didn't look silly, standing still in the middle of the dance floor. "I've had a couple drinks. It's been a long week," I added, maybe a little more defensively than necessary.

"Sounds like it." He watched me, more serious now. "I heard you called off work because of that explosion at the university."

I stiffened at the reminder. *Explosion.* Right.

"Yeah," I muttered, fanning myself harder. I eyed a girl in a pink sequined dress nearby, the play of lights over all those sparkles. "That didn't help anything."

Sky didn't answer right away. A quick glance up showed his eyes had narrowed a little.

"What happened?" he asked, cocking his head. Green lasers fell in lines across his face. "Were you hurt?"

A thousand bruises, a couple sleepless nights, and a case of terminal paranoia later, and I still wasn't sure how to answer either of those questions. I tried. I opened my mouth, but nothing came out.

Talons. Glowing tablets. Marks etched into my skin.

Somehow, I didn't flinch, but my throat closed. Because Sky was watching me closely again, I dropped my gaze to the partially unbuttoned collar of his shirt. "I wasn't hurt or anything. Thanks for asking."

"Good," he said quietly.

But the conversation had chased away some of my warm, buzzing contentment. I turned my head, searching for Amelia. I hadn't seen her in a while. Or Emerick.

Then Sky asked: "So what *really* happened at the school?"

The words registered and chilled my insides.

Electricity. Smoke. The robot. The light.

This time, I gave up my pathetic attempt at dancing and stopped altogether in the center of the dance floor, not even caring how it looked.

I was too focused on the sick feeling curdling in my gut.

It didn't help that Sky was *pushing* again. Like he had after the accident, and at Oasis. This time I *knew* I hadn't imagined it. He was pushing, and he *still* hadn't freaking told me what he was doing here. Why he'd shown up out of nowhere and why he was looking at me now like I was an equation he needed to solve.

A new, insidious thought slunk in like an oil spill.

Oh my God. None of this was real. He'd turned me into a mushy pile of hormones, and I was dumb enough to fall for it. What if he was just trying to get information out of me?

I was an idiot for believing someone who looked like him would be interested in somebody like me. I'd fallen right for that *you-look-great-in-that-dress* line. Heat rushed into my cheeks—this time fueled by embarrassment.

I stepped back. Cooler air swirled in between us, kissing my scalding face. The vodka sloshed in my stomach.

Sky let his arms fall to his sides, and his brows tented as he watched me put distance between us. If he was acting, he was doing a damn good job. That looked like concern. Real concern. The downward tilt to his mouth, the tightening of his jaw.

I wavered. Maybe he *didn't* have some ulterior motive. Maybe I was just overthinking.

God, this was a roller coaster. I didn't particularly *like* roller coasters. They felt too out of control, which was, oddly enough, a perfect metaphor for my life right now.

I smoothed my dress with twitchy fingers and looked around at the dancing bodies, the swirling lights. It was easier to form coherent sentences when I wasn't peering up at Sky's stupidly perfect face.

"I'm not really sure what happened at the university," I said, stretching my sleeve over my wrist, hiding my marked hand. "I hit my head and...I don't remember anything after that."

The bruises under my dress throbbed, a reminder of how big of a lie that really was.

Sky was quiet for a moment. We were still close enough that I had to crane my neck to meet his eyes when I finally chanced it. He was still watching me. Closely.

"You don't remember what happened at the school?" he asked. "At all?"

I bit the inside of my cheek. There it was again—that tone. I didn't like this. I'd swear it bordered on disbelief.

But what reason would he have to not believe me?

I lifted my chin. "No. I don't remember anything."

"I see." He pursed his lips, gaze sliding to the crowd around us instead of me. But his tone was pointed as he asked, "So…is this kind of like you not knowing what ran you off the road the other day?"

My heart stuttered. The music faded beneath a buzzing in my ears. I gazed up at him, apprehension sloshing over me like a dark tide.

I wasn't imagining shit. That was skepticism.

"I never said something ran me off the road," I replied slowly, shuffling back a step. "I told you I swerved to avoid an animal." I wrapped my arms around myself, pulse hammering at the base of my throat. "Remember?"

He turned his head. His searching stare found mine and didn't waver. "Right. Of course. An animal."

A chill slithered down my spine.

A group of people jostled me on their way by, laughing and yelling. I used the distraction to back up even more. Sky's eyes narrowed, like my retreat bothered him. Or maybe it was my refusal to cave to his interrogation.

Screw it. Gathering my courage, I raised my voice over the music. "I'm just going to come out and ask. Are you accusing me of hiding something? Because I keep getting that feeling. Which is silly. Right?"

Despite the thumping track and loud voices, I knew he'd heard me just fine because the creases in his forehead deepened. I wanted him to agree with me. To laugh it off. He shook his head, opening his mouth, and something in his expression told me he was going to deny it.

Before he could say anything, before I could lose my momentum, more words spilled out of me. "Because it feels like you've been trying to get me to fess up to some secret ever since you gave me that ride home." He closed his mouth. I paused, flushing a little under his scrutiny, and added, "Which I *do* appreciate. It was nice of you to stop and help me." I squared my shoulders. "But what I *don't* appreciate is the insinuation that I'm lying—or that I owe you some kind of explanation."

I ran out of steam and, frankly, balls. I eyed him warily, shoulders heaving. God, where had the air gone in this place?

Sky didn't respond right away. He seemed to be absorbing my rant. Or maybe coming up with an excuse. I didn't know, but he was looking at me, unreadable as ever, bathed in shadow and neon light. The growing gap between us vibrated with tension, bass beats, and unspoken words.

I caught the barest flicker of...*something* crossing his face. Guilt? Frustration? It was too fast to tell. The rapid shift of emotion threw me off.

What would he have to feel guilty about? Accusing me of lying? Well, he *should*.

I mean, I *was*. Lying. But it wasn't like I *owed* him an explanation. It was my business. My life. Even if it was completely off the rails.

I had the overwhelming urge to throw my hands up and scream in frustration. Damn it, I'd just wanted a night of normalcy. Self-pity welled up along with the urge to cry, for some reason. I tightened my arms around my middle, hugging myself.

Like Sky'd glimpsed that surge of vulnerability, he hung his head and balanced his hands on his hips, muttering a curse. It was lost to Crescent's din. When he raised his face, he looked determined, and he shifted his weight. As if he was about to close the space between us.

But I'd put it there for a reason, and that was the last thing I needed to maintain my tenuous grasp on my rationality. When I tensed, ready to back up again, he seemed to think better of it.

Instead, he lifted his hands, palms out. "Raven, I'm not accusing you of anything. This isn't an attack. It's *not*," he insisted more firmly when I took a breath, prepared to argue. His eyes shone with very convincing sincerity. "I'm only saying...if something *did* happen, you could...I don't know. Talk to me about it."

I blinked at him, taken aback by the offer. "If something had happened, *hypothetically*, why would I talk to *you* about it? Of all people."

"Because." He let out a harsh breath, glanced over his shoulder, then leaned in. His dark gaze snared mine. "Because maybe I can help."

I stared at him. *Help?* With what, the evil alien robots? What, was he going to scare them off, too, like he'd scared off that pushy guy? He was intimidating, but he wasn't *that* intimidating. That thing in the lab for *sure* had him on shoulder width. Height, too. Overall scariness.

Certainly on bone-crushing capability.

My disbelieving laugh burst free. "Help how?" I asked, flinging my arms out. "You offering trauma counseling now? I thought you were just a bartender."

His lips formed a tight line. A smidgen of guilt pricked my conscience. *Just a bartender* had sounded way more condescending than I'd meant it to.

I was so focused on this spiraling conversation, I didn't see the couple flailing nearby until one of them collided into me from behind. Hard enough, I stumbled.

Sky reached out to catch me. His fingers landed right on the bruise on my upper arm.

Pain jolted my system. I jerked back, hissing through my teeth. "*Shit!*"

"What?" Sky yanked his hand back. His attention zeroed on the invisible bruise I was rubbing. "What is it? Are you okay?"

"I'm *fine*," I muttered. I wasn't. The entire limb felt like it was going to fall off. "It's just...from what happened at the college."

"I thought you said you weren't hurt." He hadn't looked away from the spot I held. In fact, he was staring at it grimly.

He was right, too. I *had* said that. Minutes ago. He was listening. A little too closely, a little too...*attentively.*

And there was that *tone.*

I hunched my shoulders and slowly released my arm. My heartbeat thudded off-kilter. "It's just a bruise. And it's none of your business."

"Okay," Sky said, tone even. The music's frenzied beat nearly swallowed his words. "That's fine."

It *wasn't* fine. None of this was. Because when his indigo eyes traced their way back to mine, I could clearly see he didn't believe me. A muscle near his temple pulsed.

"You can tell me," he said, confirming it. "I think you'd be surprised at how...open-minded I am, Raven."

Oh, he was good. My actual name, spoken so quietly, in his low, mesmerizing voice...

But the spell was broken, and I was all tangled up now. Confused. More than a little irritated. Had this all been some ploy to get the truth out of me? To get me to admit something?

Why was he so convinced I was lying?

Unless...

Unless he *knew* I was. Because he knew something. Not suspected, but *knew.*

I smashed my lips together, forcing down the sudden lump lodging itself in my dry throat.

Unless *he* was the one hiding something.

Like he felt the weight of my suspicion, Sky's expression closed off, and he eased back a step, giving me space again. Letting that gap between us stretch. He slipped his hands into his pockets, eyes trained on me. He didn't reach for me again. Didn't try to pull me back in. Didn't say a word.

I didn't know whether to be relieved or disappointed. Maybe a little of both. Relieved I could think clearer. That logic was trickling back.

Disappointed that this tiny slice of a dream was over. That cold, harsh reality had come crashing back in. The reality in which I was somehow smack dab in the middle of an alien infiltration.

And meanwhile, Sky…watched. Assessing.

Instincts stirred, prickled. Sunk claws deep.

I backed away from him until I reached the edge of the dance floor.

He didn't chase me. He stood there, still and observant in the blur of moving bodies and strobing light. Only his eyes followed. Sharp enough to pierce right through my pounding chest. Full of awareness of a different kind now.

If I'd suspected it before, if my gut had been hinting at it…now I was certain.

Sky knew something. More than he was letting on. I was sure. He knew more about what happened on the road the other night, the university—*all* of it. *The aliens.*

Me.

And I didn't know what to do with that.

It didn't help that all I could think about was kissing him senseless.

So I spun on my heel and ran.

Chapter 19

DECODING CAGEY BARTENDERS AND OTHER COSMIC MYSTERIES

My RIDESHARE APP SAID TEN MINUTES, but it felt like an hour.

I waited outside Crescent, arms folded tight, glancing over my shoulder every few seconds. I couldn't shake the unsettled feeling.

Amelia hadn't answered my text about leaving. She'd see it eventually, probably once she came up for air from Emerick. Whenever that was.

Sky hadn't come out, either. He hadn't chased after me. I told myself that was a good thing.

My buzz was gone, effectively doused by the reminder of everything wrong with my life right now. All I felt now was tired and cold.

The storm had moved on, but the air was still damp, and the sidewalks slick and gleaming orange beneath the streetlights. Nearby, a knot of clubgoers vaped and chain-smoked, their breath clouds forming a chemical fog.

I shivered harder.

Then, finally…*salvation*. A dark red sedan pulled up, dashboard sign glowing. I half-jogged to the passenger door and climbed in, flashing the driver a muted smile. After confirming my address, he pulled away, and I slumped against the seat, watching One Willow blur past the windows.

The heater hummed, but the chill inside me didn't budge.

Something about Sky Acosta was *not* sitting right.

We'd danced tonight. The object of my fantasies had finally noticed me, flirted with me, touched me, held me. It should've been great. Like, birthday-wish, mall-fountain-coin level great.

So why did I feel so...*gross* about it?

I knew why. It was the timing.

Why now? Why the sudden interest? Why all the questions?

"I think you'd be surprised at how...open-minded I am, Raven."

Right. Not much was going to surprise me after all this. I wouldn't be surprised at all to find my worst fears were true and Sky's entire performance had been strategic.

I *wanted* to believe running into him the night of my car accident had been a coincidence. Technically, it was plausible. One Willow wasn't that big, and there weren't many roads leading out of town. Maybe he hated highways. Maybe long drives on back roads while brooding to weird synth playlists were his thing.

But then there was *everything else.*

The repeated questions about the crash. The pressure. The way he didn't buy my deflections. Tonight, he'd pushed harder about the university, too. He'd said he was just worried, but I'd seen the look in his eyes. He wasn't just concerned.

He was *digging.*

And then there was the fact that he'd shown up at Crescent in the first place. Which, sure, maybe not *completely* weird. It was one of the only decent clubs in town. But I'd never seen him there before. Not once. And Amelia and I had been going there for *years.* If Sky had shown up, I'd have noticed.

My gut sank deeper.

Maybe it wasn't a coincidence.

Maybe...*he'd followed me.*

The thought slid through me like a glacier. I rubbed my arms beneath the thin dress, trying to erase it. It was ridiculous. Sky wasn't a stalker. Right?

...*Right?*

How much did I *actually* know about Sky Acosta? As much as anybody at Oasis. Which wasn't saying much.

One thing was obvious: he was looking for something. Answers.

But what smarted—the worst part of all this by *far*—was the manipulation.

He had to know I had a crush on him. Of *course* he did. I'd been pining after him like a lovesick idiot for six months. Anyone with a pair of eyes and two working brain cells could tell. I turned tomato red every time he said my name. Or, rather, a variation of it. He must've noticed.

Which begged the question: what if he saw an opportunity to use it? Maybe that smile, that damned dimple, the way he moved when he danced...maybe it wasn't about me. It was about *access*. A way to get what he wanted.

The thought made my insides wither with mortification, even as righteous anger flushed my cheeks. God, I was an idiot. I'd really thought I'd caught his attention. I should've known better.

The memory of his thighs against mine, the strength of his arms flickered unwelcome across my mind. I shoved it down. No more. I wasn't wasting another second daydreaming about him.

Resolve stiffened my spine, and I glared out the windshield. He'd picked the wrong girl to manipulate. I might've been infatuated, but I wasn't a fool. And I definitely wasn't a pushover.

Time to get my head on straight about Sky.

The rideshare driver slowed down Cherry Street and rolled to a stop at the intersection. I exhaled, slow and steady. Good riddance. I had more important things to worry about, like finding real answers.

It was time to find out why Sky was so obsessed with my car wreck. With the school. With Kelly's not-so-crazy theories.

With *aliens*.

Was he secretly a blog-lurking ET fanatic? Maybe he ran one of those forums I'd doom-scrolled the other night and was trying to piece things together, same as me.

There'd been something in his eyes tonight, though. Complicated emotion. Almost like he was holding something back.

I imagined confronting him. Telling him everything. The idea made me grimace. Maybe I'd misread the whole thing, but until I knew *his* angle, I wasn't blurting out a damn thing.

He was going to tell *me* what he knew. Not the other way around.

The car pulled up outside Bob's, and I climbed out after a muttered thanks. I paused at the curb, digging in my clutch for my key. My marked palm caught the porch light, the design shimmering faintly.

My stomach flipped. I curled my fingers into a fist. What would Sky say about *that*? Probably launch into twenty more questions.

A cold breeze tickled the back of my neck, and I looked around. My skin prickled. The quiet around me wasn't right. Too heavy. Too still.

I turned in place. The oak tree in Bob's front yard creaked, bare limbs rattling. Across the street, the asphalt gleamed beneath the broken streetlight, the yard beyond shrouded in shadow.

It was late. Most of the windows on the block were dark. Curtains drawn tight. Even the stars were tucked behind a heavy quilt of lingering clouds.

I hesitated. There it was again—that nagging *I'm-missing-something* feeling.

I started for the porch. My boots scuffed across the sidewalk, too loud in the silence. At the door, I paused and looked back, scanning the house across the street.

There.

Something moved. A slinking shape, a *liquid* shadow pulling away from the rest of the dark beneath the trees.

Heart in my throat, I squinted, trying to make sense of what I was seeing.

But nothing else moved. No one stepped out. No robots from outer space. No tall, suspiciously present bartender with too-perfect cheekbones.

Just wind and shadows and silence.

Still, I couldn't shake the feeling of wrongness. I'd seen *something*. Unless I hadn't, and this week had turned me into a full-blown paranoid mess.

Who could blame me? There were aliens, *real aliens*, walking around. Smashing things. Trying to smash people.

Was I ever going to feel normal again?

Probably not. But for now…there was nothing out there but shadows and stars.

I forced a shaky breath and turned back to my apartment entrance, fumbling the key. I shoved it home with more force than necessary. Inside, I slammed the door shut and turned both locks, deadbolt and all.

This wasn't sustainable. I was going to lose my mind if I didn't get control of my nerves soon. The night out with Amelia had been a nice dose of normalcy while it lasted, but it was time to face real life again. The whole, weird mess that it'd become.

I flipped the stairwell switch. Warm light spilled over the small landing, chasing off the shadows. I kicked off my boots and climbed.

And maybe, just maybe…it was time to confront Sky Acosta, too.

Chapter 20

FRIENDS OF THE EXTRATERRESTRIAL RACES

As LUCK WOULD HAVE IT—if you could call it that—I'd get my chance to do both the next day.

A few minutes into my dinner shift, I stood by the employee lockers and listened to the familiar song of Oasis's kitchen. Clanging metal, shouted orders, and the hiss of fryers rebounded around me as I twirled a lock of hair escaping my loose French braid and squinted at the schedule on the wall.

When I found what I was looking for, the ball of nerves in my stomach bounced. I rocked back on my heels, lowering my arm and rubbing my sweaty palm on my apron.

Sky was here somewhere, according to the bartender calendar scrawled in red Sharpie.

I'd decided during the sleepless hours last night that today was the day. If he was working, I'd find a way to corner him. Sky may know how to turn on the charm, but his weird obsession with recent events seemed easier to crack than solving the mystery of an alien infiltration solo.

The thought pulled a dry snort from me. I turned toward the kitchen and nearly plowed into Kelly.

"Whoa—sorry!" she said, stumbling back. When she saw it was

me, she put her hands on her hips and scowled. "I was wondering if you'd be in today. Are you okay?"

"Okay?" I blinked, confused for a second…then I remembered I'd called off because of the university explosion. So much had happened in the last few days, everything was blurring together. "Oh. Yeah. I'm good. Just shaken up."

By alien robots, I didn't add.

She swept her blue eyes over me like she was checking for herself, then rested her pink-manicured hand on her hip. "What's up with you today? You look different."

"Different?" I glanced down at myself. Same hideous neon-green, patterned dress. Slightly dirty white canvas shoes. The mud from the car wreck hadn't come out. Aside from the glowing palm glyph and robot hand-shaped bruise hidden under my sleeve, there was nothing new.

"You're wearing makeup," she said, snapping her fingers. "Eyeshadow."

Oh. That. I flushed. She was right. I was. Just a little. Some smoky shadow and a swipe of lip gloss, but it had made me feel a little more in control before facing a certain bartender.

"It helps you with your tips," I muttered, reaching back to tie my apron.

"Hah. Rae-bae. This—" she swept her hand across her expertly made-up face and body poured into a strategically buttoned dress "—helps with my tips. But hey, I'd give you an A minus for effort."

"Gee, thanks." I rolled my eyes.

Grinning, she fell into step beside me as I walked into the kitchen. Jackie and Tony were already arguing over the finer points of music genres, their voices raised over the screaming hair metal pulsing from the speaker.

Kelly pushed through the swinging doors and held one open with her shoulder. "So, any new stuff on the lights?"

"What lights?" I asked, tongue tucked into my cheek.

She *tsk*ed in annoyance, and I bit back a smirk. It felt good—*normal*—to needle her. Even now, knowing she'd been right about *so much*. Didn't mean I was going to tell her, though.

Not yet. Possibly not ever.

The restaurant was still in its post-lunch lull. Rain streaked the windows, and only a few tables were occupied. Emily was chatting with a booth full of nerdy-looking teen boys, flipping her hair. Across the room, Sara was tending to a pair of women in the corner booth. With her dark complexion, she pulled off the neon dress even better than Kelly. They all pulled it off better than I did.

I didn't look toward the bar while I tapped my fingers on my thigh in time with the steel drum samba thumping from the speakers. The cheerful tune was undercut by a truly unfortunate monkey sound effect. I could *feel* the urge to turn my head like a phantom hand yanking at my chin, but it wasn't time yet. I needed a plan first.

"I don't buy that you're still in denial about the aliens," Kelly said, bringing me back to the conversation. She swatted my hip with her empty tray. "You can't tell me you didn't watch the YouTube videos."

"I saw the videos," I admitted at a grumble.

We reached the server station, and I busied myself with the pre-shift ritual, grabbing straws, checking my order book, counting my coins. Anything to calm the nerves coiling in my chest.

I hated confrontation. But I was determined to talk to Sky tonight.

Kelly leaned a hip against the counter. "*So*," she said, dragging the word out. "You've got to believe me now, right? About the aliens?"

Sighing, I set my molars. "Kelly, I believe something was captured on camera that people are having trouble explaining."

"No. It's easy to explain." She spread her hands. "Aliens."

I looked away, chewing the inside of my cheek. The burning mark on my palm and the bruises on my arm were explanation enough. But I couldn't just...roll over and admit she was right. Since I'd started my own descent into madness, though, I might as well pump her for intel.

"Let's say I believe you," I said, snapping my order book closed and tucking it into my apron. I turned to her and crossed my arms.

"Where'd you get your information? You seem to know a lot about this." Her eyes sparkled with a maniacal gleam of triumph, like me caving was the answer to unholy prayers. I plowed ahead. "So tell me: if there really are aliens, where are they from? What do they want? Why are they here? *Hypothetically*," I added, when her smile spread to Cheshire Cat-width.

It didn't deter her. She rubbed her hands together. "I thought you'd never ask, Rae-bae. Okay. So. I have this…friend, I guess. He's really into this stuff. He—" She broke off, glancing around.

I followed her gaze. Nobody else was nearby, and once she was satisfied, she leaned in. Instinctively, I did the same.

She dropped her voice to a whisper. "My friend is really into this stuff. He belongs to a local branch of FETR." She paused for dramatic effect.

I stared at her blankly. When she didn't elaborate, I raised my brows. "Okay…and what's *fetter*?"

"No, not…ugh, it's F, E, T, R. An acronym for Friends of the Extraterrestrial Races. Pronounced 'Fetter.'"

"Friends of the…" *Friendly* was not the word I'd use to describe the robot that'd chased me through the lab. "What the hell are you talking about?"

She flicked her fingers dismissively, like I was the one being ridiculous. "Just listen. My friend's in FETR. They're this worldwide group of people who research and monitor alien activity."

"Like, what, the Men in Black?" I snorted. *Why* had I thought Kelly might actually be a legitimate source of information?

"No! They're not the government. Come on, Rae. You really think the government would be honest about aliens?"

"They had a whole hearing about it."

She scoffed. "Yeah, and they didn't say *anything*. They didn't confirm *anything*. FETR's made up of regular people, people like you and me, who actually know what's going on. They've got chapters all over the place. And some of their members work at, like, radio telescope arrays. SETI and stuff."

"SETI?" I arched a brow. "Like the Search for Extraterrestrial Intelligence?"

"Oh, so you *do* know about them."

"Yeah, because SETI's a real, science-backed organization." I could see by her imperious look that I was getting nowhere. I sighed. "Never mind. Go on."

"Thank you. So, my friend Cane? He's in FETR. He's an electrical engineer. Graduated from TWU last year. He, like, works for the city now. He's always scanning for electrical or radio-wave anomalies, and this week? He picked up some *weird* readings all over the country. Power surges, random bursts of radio static…"

I slumped a little. "Yeah, Kelly. That was the solar flare—"

"No, Raven." She clamped her hand around my wrist, and I stopped short. She looked… Wow—for once, Kelly looked dead serious. Solemn, even.

"I can show you," she whispered, eyes darting to both sides, like she was ensuring no eavesdroppers closed in. "Come to a meeting. It's not what the news says it is. The signals were *jumping* around, erratic, but not random. FETR cross-referenced it with grid spikes, light sightings, reported anomalies. It followed a pattern. A *path*. Like a…I don't know. One of those scavenger hunts people do on Snapchat."

Like a scavenger hunt…or like a search grid? Ice chilled my veins.

The tablet flashed in my mind, glowing, humming, crumbling in my hand. My palm tingled like it remembered, too. I gently freed myself from Kelly's grip and rubbed my thumb over the nearly invisible marks.

"They're looking for something," Kelly murmured, her blue eyes locked on mine.

I held her stare. She had me now. I was *listening*.

She nodded like she knew it, too. "Cane dug deeper. The anomalies—they led here. To *One Willow*."

My lungs caught on a gasp.

Was *this* the proof? In case I'd had any doubts that the object, that strange tablet someone had stuffed in a Styrofoam cooler, was the actual target. It'd been destroyed, though. I'd watched it disintegrate. Once again, hope rose. Maybe the fact it'd blown up meant this was over. Nobody had spotted any lights last night. No new reels or videos had appeared in my feeds.

But that didn't mean they'd left. There was a chance the robots were hunting down loose ends. Read: me.

Or maybe not. Maybe they'd hightailed it off Earth.

I was going to drive myself crazy worrying without *any* definite information. My arm ached, and my head throbbed. I found myself rubbing the markings on my palm again before catching the motion and forcing my itchy fingers to still.

Instead, I frowned at Kelly. "So what does your friend think this means?"

"Well, it gets better. There's some kind of—"

"Hey!" Sandy's voice cracked through the air like a gunshot. I gasped and looked up. She marched toward us, cutting through empty tables, her frown stormy and her manager's badge glinting under the fluorescents like a sheriff's star. "Is this social hour or a working restaurant?"

Kelly rolled her eyes again, this time with much more dramatic flair. "Well, it's Sunday, so technically both?"

"Cute, Miss Ardmore. Don't you have a section to cover?" Then her gaze landed on me. "And you. You need another day off or something?"

I nearly winced. "No. No, I don't. I'm on it."

I exchanged a glance with Kelly then ducked my head and peeled away from the server station, circling toward the restaurant's main floor. Nobody else had wandered into my section yet.

But my thoughts were spinning.

FETR. Friends of the Extraterrestrial Races. A legit organization, albeit named like it'd been thought up by a late-night Reddit thread. But they were *tracking movements*. Actual patterns. And somehow, Kelly, of all people, had the goods.

How many aliens were hanging around on Earth if they had enough friends to form a damn club?

The idea sent dread slinking through my chest, dousing any remaining urge to laugh.

Maybe it wouldn't hurt to get more information from Kelly after all. Maybe even hear this *Cane* guy's take on it.

I felt a little like Alice—except instead of chasing rabbits, I was chasing flying saucers. Lights in the sky. Possibly even evil robots from outer space. Take your pick.

God. My life was weird right now.

I blew out a breath and smoothed a hand down my braid as I rounded the far corner of the dining area. Half-hidden behind one of our surprisingly realistic palm trees, I had a clear line of sight to the bar. I peered through the silk leaves like a tiger stalking prey.

Only this prey was a cagey bartender.

It was the first glimpse I'd had of him since leaving him on the Crescent dance floor. He leaned across the polished counter, sliding a sunset-colored mixed drink toward a middle-aged woman with too much makeup and a neckline in a fierce rivalry with gravity. She preened, patting her hair and flashing him a coy smile.

He returned it with one of those respectful, guarded grins— reserved, but also smart enough to earn his tips. And that dark curl tumbling over his forehead didn't hurt, either. He casually pushed it back, then strolled to the bar's far end to check on two guys in blue coveralls hunched over beers.

Even that small walk oozed a kind of careless grace. It was a dance I was used to watching him perform. Those worn jeans did *great* things for his ass, too.

Disgusted with myself, I ripped my gaze away and let the branches swish back into place. I wasn't here to ogle. Not anymore. Things had changed. I wanted *answers*.

And this? This was a safe place. Public, familiar. Full of people.

If it went sideways, there'd be witnesses.

Not that it could go sideways, I told myself. This was still Sky. He never raised his voice, let alone his hand. He was always polite. Cordial. A gentleman. The guy had opened my car door for me, for God's sake.

But then I remembered the way he'd stared down Prince Charming at the club. There'd been a flash of something darker.

Colder. Just like there'd been calculation in his voice when he'd asked about the accident.

He was hiding something beneath that polite mask.

Nothing was as it seemed lately. Not my life. Not the truth about aliens. Not even my hot bartender crush.

I squared my shoulders. I was sick of flinching at shadows and overanalyzing every little possibility. This, at least, was something I could control.

I was confronting Sky *tonight.*

I stepped out from behind the palm fronds, lifted my chin, and strode across the restaurant. The squawking calls of jungle birds formed a questionable soundtrack. Nerves leaping, I tugged my uniform dress a little lower on my thighs.

Sky looked up from wiping the counter, and I let go of my hem, inhaling sharply. Our gazes locked, and he paused in mid-swipe, straightening. My steps faltered under the weight of that stare, steady and direct. I wasn't used to this. Eye contact. With him.

He didn't smile. Didn't nod. But something flickered in his expression, quick and unreadable. A flash of tension before that too-neutral veneer slid into place.

He looked away and went back to cleaning, like I was just another customer, though I caught the shift in his posture. His broad shoulders tightened beneath his dark button-up. Like he was bracing himself.

My slow burning irritation flared into something hotter. Recklessness, maybe.

I headed straight for the bar.

Let's do this.

Chapter 21

ALL THAT GLITTERS ISN'T GOLD...OR TERRESTRIAL?

SKY DIDN'T LOOK UP FROM WIPING DOWN THE BAR until I'd nearly reached him. When he did and his dark eyes met mine, I caught a glimpse of wariness before his face shuttered. His movements slowed.

I halted at the drink mat. This was it. My heart rate spiked, and I drew a deep, nerve-steadying breath. I'd *prepared* for this.

But the look he was giving me was penetrating and steady. Too steady. My mind blanked like someone had tugged the power cord, and the words I'd rehearsed all day unraveled into nonsense.

I obviously waited too long to speak because Sky's mouth twitched and he said, "Hi, Raven." Casual as can be. He swiped the rag one final time before leaning on his elbows, brows rising. "What can I help you with? I didn't see any new orders come through."

The false nonchalance zapped my resolve back to life like a defibrillator to the chest.

He was playing it cool, but I'd seen that wariness. If I was right, *none* of this was real. That serene mask—nor the charming smiles. Definitely not that dance at Crescent. A blush threatened to ignite at the memory.

He'd known. He'd used it. He'd weaponized my infatuation with him to get answers.

Talk about a blow to the ego. It cleared the lingering fog from my brain.

"I need to talk to you," I said, proud that my voice came out level.

"Yeah?" His eyes narrowed a fraction. "What about?"

I flicked a glance at the woman at the bar, who was doing a terrible job pretending not to eavesdrop. *"Privately."*

His eyebrows lifted further, and something flashed across his expression. Something that could've been triumph. Maybe even relief.

Like he'd been *waiting* for this.

I faltered, suddenly uncertain, but it was too late to back out now. I'd already lit the fuse.

"Okay. Sure." He searched my face before flipping the cleaning cloth over his shoulder and drawing himself up to his full height.

Feeling at a disadvantage with him towering over me, I rocked onto my heels and shoved my hands into my apron pockets. I couldn't read a damn thing in his expression as he drummed his fingers on the bar and gave me that too-polished bartender's smile. No teeth, all professionalism.

"So, um, where?" I mumbled. When had my throat gotten so dry?

"Give me five minutes," he said, inclining in his head and starting to turn. He spoke over his shoulder. "I'll meet you out back."

Out back meant the employee break area. Picnic table, dumpsters, low visibility.

Great.

The perfect spot to tackle a bartender. Not literally. Well— maybe perfect for that, too. Not that I should be thinking about tackling Sky *at all*, considering—

I shook myself.

I'd tell Sandy I was squeezing in my fifteen-minute break. The dinner rush was late anyway. My insides buzzed with anticipation.

I was doing this. I was about to accuse my crush of manipulating me. Possibly stalking me.

I might even say the word *aliens*.

What if I was wrong?

I swallowed the rising nausea and nodded once. I whirled away —and nearly collided with a pair of customers heading to the bar. The man stumbled back, and the woman clutched her purse.

"Sorry," I muttered, ducking my head and beelining for the back. I *swore* I heard Sky stifle a chuckle, and I ground my teeth.

I wasn't wrong.

Five minutes from now, Sky Acosta wouldn't know what hit him.

Hopefully.

FOUR MINUTES and thirty seconds later, I shoved open the back door. Its hinges shrieked like they were auditioning for a horror film, emitting a screech that bounced off the cinderblock walls and echoed into the parking lot beyond. It did great things for my already shredded nerves.

Huffing, I sidled from the entrance and scanned the area. Empty. The door shut with a thud behind me, sealing off the kitchen's racket. Leaving me alone in the storm.

No one lingered beneath the lean-to. No smokers. No line cooks on their break. Just the rustling hush of the wind and the rain drumming on the shelter's metal roof.

Lightning flickered somewhere out of view, followed by a low rumble of thunder. Wind swirled around the building's side and slapped mist across my face. I wiped it away and moved to the picnic table, checking for wet spots before I perched on the edge and folded my arms.

Another bout of nerves twisted up my belly, and I tapped my toes, pushing the doubt away.

I was right to question him. I *knew* it. My palms were damp and my stomach churned, but I was *done* being jerked around.

A heartbeat later, the door swung open again, and even though I'd expected it, I jolted like I'd been shocked.

Sky stepped out into the wind and rain. He did the same thing I had: scanned the space to confirm we were alone. His shoulders lowered a fraction. Still, tension hardened the lines of his face when he glanced my way.

"Rae," he said in greeting.

I tried to act cool and leaned back against the table again, but my pulse was doing a wild drum solo. I wouldn't be surprised if he could hear it from there, especially when he strolled closer. The door slammed shut once more, and he stopped in front of me, crossing his arms to mirror my pose.

"Did anybody see you come out here?" I asked. Last thing I needed was a rumor about a rendezvous with the bartender.

"I don't think anybody was paying attention. Why?" he asked dryly. "Embarrassed to be caught meeting me by the dumpster?"

I didn't know what to say to that. I pressed my lips into a line. His jaw was tight, like he wasn't looking forward to this, either. Like he wasn't looking forward to talking with me.

Should that feel like a victory? I wasn't sure. It felt kind of like a blow.

I summoned a scowl, despite the blush trying to rise. "Maybe I *am* embarrassed to be caught meeting you behind the dumpster."

"Right." He smiled faintly. When I just stared at him, trying to decide where to start, he tipped his head to the side and arched an eyebrow. "Well, what'd you need to talk about? Need another ride somewhere?"

Was he still toying with me? My anger flared like a struck match.

Maybe he was just ET-obsessed. Maybe he was one of Kelly's FETR weirdos. But whatever the reason, he'd been digging. And I'd been too stupid, too giddy over the attention to realize it.

He'd played me.

That match hit dry tinder, and righteous fury burned bright. I shoved off the picnic table so fast Sky gave a start. I didn't stop. I marched right up to him and thrust out my hand flat between us.

Lightning crackled like a cue. The strange pearlescent glyphs on my palm shone silver in the flash.

"If you want to know my secrets so badly," I said, waggling my fingers, "then here. Why don't you tell *me* what the hell this is?"

His gaze dropped…and widened. He flinched like I'd slapped him.

His wariness vanished, and in its place was pure, unadulterated shock. His lips parted. His face paled. The mask was gone, cracked apart to reveal…

Alarm?

I wasn't sure what I'd expected, but it wasn't *that*. I'd expected denial. Smugness. Not *fear*. God, I wasn't sure if he was even breathing. For a second, the world seemed to hold its breath along with him. I did, too.

Unease shivered through me.

He slowly raised his head, blinking rapidly. Then, as if he couldn't help it, his attention drifted back to my hand.

"How…?" he breathed.

I didn't answer. I couldn't. I was still absorbing his shock.

The rain hammered above us, filling the tight silence. He stepped forward suddenly, hands lifted like he meant to grab my wrist.

The quick movement sent me skittering back a step. Sky checked himself in time and didn't touch me. His fingers hovered, though, close enough I felt their heat.

I whipped my gaze back to his, and I found it dark and searching and full of questions. More questions. His whisper was hoarse. "Where did you get this?"

"Where did I *get* it?" A bubble of incredulous laughter spilled out. My open palm hung awkwardly in the space between us. I curled my fingers. "Oh, you know. Picked it up at Willow Mall. BOGO palm tattoo day."

He didn't smile.

I swallowed hard, deliberately flattening my hand again. "Does this look like something I'd do on purpose, Sky? It's not even…"

Human, I almost said. I couldn't seem to force the word out.

His eyes dropped back to my hand. His chest rose and fell with his uneven breathing.

That was totally fear. Not of me, but maybe *for* me. A chill slithered down my spine.

Maybe I'd miscalculated. Maybe this wasn't the power move I'd thought it'd be. Thunder rolled above us.

I jumped when Sky took a jerky step back, but he only scrubbed his hands down his face, exhaling heavily. I watched wide-eyed as he dropped his arms to his sides and bowed his head. His gaze was trained on nothing, his jaw working.

What the hell was *this?*

I drew my hand back and clasped it in my unmarked one, but it was too late. There was no hiding the marks. Nor this weird reaction he was having to them.

I'd thought he'd deny it, and I'd have to force him to admit he'd manipulated me. Or he'd spout some wacky alien theory, and I could scoff because I knew the *real* truth.

But this...this was something different. He looked like I'd just ripped the rug out from under his feet. Like *his* world had just been rocked, not mine.

When he raised his head again, tossing his bangs from his eyes, his expression had closed. I could read nothing in his stony countenance, but I'd already seen enough.

My pulse stuttered.

Maybe I should've kept pretending. Ignored the artifact, the lights, the weird scars. All of it.

I'd been right, though. He *clearly* knew something. And if *this* was his reaction...what did that mean for me?

We stared at each other. I rubbed my thumb across the markings. It'd become a habit, despite the lack of texture. As if I could rub away this sudden shift in reality.

The skin there felt normal. But it was a lie. *None* of this was normal.

One of us needed to say something, so I licked my dry lips and went for it. "You know something about this, don't you?"

His mouth tightened. "How did you get that mark, Raven?" he countered, tone grave. "I need you to tell me."

I bit the inside of my cheek hard enough to hurt. That question again. He was *still* asking. Still offering nothing in return. And just like that, some of the fear faded, drowned out by smoldering anger.

I had started this conversation. I wasn't going to let him hijack it.

"No. I need *you* to answer the question. What *is* it? And while you're at it, what do you know about..." *Here went nothing.* "What do you know about the aliens?"

A muscle ticked in his cheek, and his nostrils flared, but to his credit, he didn't look away. Instead, he stilled. I saw something spark there, though, a shift in his eyes when I said the word *aliens*.

Confirmation.

Oh my God. I gaped at him.

I'd been right.

He held my gaze. This push and pull, this awareness, sizzled between us like the lightning arcing overhead. The air hummed with tension. It tingled along my skin like static.

"What do you mean?" he asked so softly it was nearly drowned out by the thunder.

I shook my head. "No, don't do that. Don't play dumb now. I *know* you know something." My heart jackhammered in my chest, and I squeezed my marked hand. "The night of the accident, you weren't just out for a country cruise, were you? Were you chasing them down or something?"

His tanned throat worked before he jerked his chin toward my palm. "Tell me about that."

I nearly rolled my eyes. This back-and-forth was getting us nowhere. One of us had to give.

"Fine." I spoke clearly, concisely, showing him my hand once more. "I got these markings when an alien robot at the university tried to kill me. I'm pretty sure it was over a stone artifact that turned into a crystal and then burned the shit out of me—" I broke off, exhaling a humorless laugh. "That's my best guess, anyway." I twisted my wrist and studied the pattern. "I got knocked out or fainted...and somehow woke up in a totally different place. With *these*."

I waved my palm halfheartedly at him before gripping it in front of me again. Silence stretched like thick putty.

Sky didn't answer. He didn't move, either. In fact, he might as well have been carved from stone, too. Only his eyes skimmed between mine like he was searching for something else I hadn't said.

But I'd already laid pretty much everything bare.

Several heartbeats passed, and just when I hit my breaking point, he finally murmured, "And the markings...they showed up that day?"

"Yes. I noticed them an hour or so after coming to in that hallway. But..." I eyed him, my voice trembling. "Sky, why don't you look surprised by any of that...?"

Being right about him wasn't nearly as satisfying as I'd thought it would be. In fact, something icy crawled down the back of my neck, and it wasn't just the rain.

He didn't answer.

"Oh my God," I breathed. "You're *not* surprised, are you? You know about them. The alien robots."

Sky's jaw clenched tighter. He had to be cracking molars. "Rae..." he ground out, the warning unmistakable.

"What do you know about this?" I flattened my hand between us. "Tell me."

The tension between us practically crackled.

I wanted to run back inside. Forget this confrontation. Forget everything. But it was too late for that.

Too late to pretend this wasn't happening. Too late to escape any of this.

I kept falling, diving deeper and deeper into impossible truths. Why couldn't I let it go? Why couldn't I stop pushing?

Sky stared down at me, emotions swimming in his eyes. Another white flash of lightning lit them up, but his face stayed locked in that unbearable tightness. I *felt* it in my own shoulders, a pressure bearing down as I gazed at the man I'd been obsessing over for months.

A stranger.

He wasn't who I'd thought he was. I couldn't summon that righteous anger I'd felt earlier. Not when he was looking at me like that. Like *he* was afraid, too.

I was so wound up I nearly gasped when he asked, "Do you really remember what happened at the university?"

"Do I remember it?" I gawked at him in disbelief. "What kind of question is that? How would I just *forget* an alien robot attack? That's not something that just…" I flung my arms out. "Just *slips your mind!*"

My harsh laugh felt more like a sob. Everything I'd been struggling with for days—it was bubbling up inside me like frothing water. Like trapped steam.

I hugged my middle, but it was a failed attempt at containment. Another bitter scoff scraped out of me. Rainwater slicked stray strands of hair to my cheeks. My skin was buzzing, humming. Too stretched over brittle bones and seething blood.

"I won't ever be able to forget what happened," I rasped, not looking at him. "I've been replaying it over and over. I've had nightmares. I've been alternating between worrying I've gone completely insane and being terrified that some mechanical monster is going to hunt me down and finish the job."

When a phantom stone lodged itself in my throat, I paused, trying to regain the scraps of my composure. My stomach churned.

I risked raising my eyes and found Sky watching me. Assessing. Like I was a bug under a microscope, another sample on the anthro lab table that had changed everything.

The ache in my chest twisted tighter. Became more painful. Like that bubbling, frothing pressure fought to escape.

"Please. Just tell me what you know," I whispered. I'd resorted to borderline begging, and I didn't even care. "*Please.*"

It was enough to crack the mask, apparently, because Sky grimaced, turning his head to give me his profile. The mist had dampened his dark hair, curling it around his forehead and ears in a way that would've been endearing in any other circumstances. If I didn't want to grab him and shake the answers out of his handsomely wrapped skull.

My heart pounded in nauseating thuds. This had gotten all too real, all too quickly. I'd wanted the truth, but this felt dangerous. Like walking the edge of a long drop.

"Sky…" I started, but that was as far as I got before the words dried up.

He squeezed the back of his neck and closed his eyes, breathing deeply through his nose, like he was gathering himself. Then he pinned me with a haunted stare. "Raven, I can't. I can't tell you what you want to know. You don't—" He swore, dropping his head back. "You don't understand."

"*You can't tell me?*" Fury erupted in my belly. I didn't care about the pained look he was giving me. I let him have it. "That's bullshit, Sky. You've spent days chasing me, trying to get information, and now I'm telling you that a…that a fucking UFO drove me off the road, an evil alien robot chased me through the anthro department, and I've got these shapes—" I lurched forward, planting my marked palm on his chest. My fingers slipped between undone buttons, brushing skin hot to the touch.

He flinched, eyes widening at my sudden charge or maybe my chilly hand. But he made no move to push me away.

I wasn't sure what I was doing. Why I was touching him. Maybe I was just trying to form a connection. To ground myself. I was trembling, my vision hazed, the vibration in my blood too much to hold in.

Everything was pouring out, emotions, words. Maybe my insides at this point because I was coming apart at the seams.

"Seriously, Sky. You owe me answers. I know you know more than you're saying, and I want the truth." I glared up at him, gripping his shirt. His chest heaved beneath my fist. "Right now—"

The tension erupted.

Too late, I recognized the charge in the air. The humming in my blood. The static. I'd felt it before, in the lab. Just before the tablet exploded. Familiar and yet not.

Now, it snapped like a rubber band stretched too far.

A white-hot glow erupted from the hand I'd tangled in his shirt.

Heat flared. I cried out, released him, and stumbled back until I hit the picnic table behind me. Swaying, I lifted my palm.

It was glowing.

Light shone through my skin. Bright orange light, pulsing from within. The etched shapes were lined in blinding white. It didn't hurt. Not like before. Only warmth radiated up my arm.

From my *freaking glowing hand.*

I gaped in horror, breath faltering as I wrenched my gaze to Sky. Or what had been Sky.

Air rushed from my lungs.

"What—? Sky...?" His name cracked apart as it tumbled from my lips. A scream clawed its way up instead, but there was no air to back it up. Instead, I wheezed.

My muscles locked. My thoughts screeched to a halt.

Because Sky had changed.

His skin...wasn't skin anymore. Not quite. It shimmered, refracting light like thousands of tiny crystals. Like scattered diamond dust. Glittery and...and *silver.*

I stared, rooted in place by soul-deep shock and a kind of morbid fascination. Lightning glimmered over him in a sheen. His features were sharper, sculpted from moonlight and stone. Not... *human.*

His dark hair was gone, and his scalp shimmered, the same jeweled starlight spiraling with darker patterns, delicate whorls that swept down across his brow.

And yet...

He was still in there.

Paler lips the same shape as his had been a second before. Sweeping ridges traced over his temples, tapering into pointed ears. But that jaw, those cheekbones...

It was Sky, and it *wasn't.* Like I was looking at him through a filter. Like this had been there all along, lurking beneath the surface.

Dizziness swept through me. The world pitched. I was going to be sick.

I could smell the fryer grease still clinging to my clothes. Hear the pattering of the rain. Its cold, clammy kiss misted my slack face. But none of it felt real.

And I wasn't the only one reeling.

The thing that had been Sky gaped down at his shimmer-speckled hands, turning them over slowly. Then he lifted his head, and I saw his eyes.

No whites. Just inky black, swallowing the sclera whole. His pupils glowed, iridescent blue in every shade imaginable. Impossibly bright and jeweled.

And in them, I read panic.

His mouth had fallen open, but he clamped it shut again and staggered back, like he could vanish into the shadowy bushes behind the dumpster. His outline seemed to melt into them, but it was too late.

Far too late. I'd seen him.

We both knew it.

I stood there, gulping air in ragged pants.

Like he knew there was no hiding now, he straightened slowly. His chest rose and fell just as quickly beneath his human clothes. Bartender clothes. A detached part of my brain registered how strange it was, that long, lean body in that fabric with *that* skin...

The glow was fading from my palm, dwindling fast. I couldn't even look at it, though. Rain sliced sideways into the shelter, plastering my hair to my cheeks, but I barely noticed.

It was Sky. And it wasn't.

He was staring back at me. Even in the gloom, his skin glimmered faintly. It was...oddly beautiful. Terrifying.

I couldn't close my mouth.

He shifted his weight, swallowed hard. Cursed under his breath in a voice that sounded strangely resonant. Musical. Human words coming from something that wasn't. The sound struck me to the bone. Jolted free the only thing rebounding in my brain, over and over:

"Holy shit," I whispered hoarsely. "Sky, you're...an *alien*."

Chapter 22

THIS IS FINE. (IT'S SO NOT)

FAITH'S WIPERS SQUEAKED ACROSS THE WINDSHIELD IN A RHYTHMIC SLIDE. They were crooked and missed a spot with every pass. I'd normally be annoyed by that, but right now it was hard to care. Rain slithered down the glass in watery snakes, blurring the lights on the road in front of me, and a clap of thunder drowned out the swish of my tires over the puddle-ridden asphalt.

Holy. Shit.

Sky was an alien.

I readjusted my grip on the steering wheel and forced myself to breathe, despite my panic-cramped chest. I needed to keep breathing. I needed to keep driving. I needed to wake up from this insane dream.

But it wasn't a dream. I was awake. I could tell by the way my head pounded dully.

The urge to smash the gas pedal to the metal and keep going forever was nearly overpowering. Screw it. I could go into hiding. Maybe that whole bunker thing wasn't such a terrible idea after all.

Thank God Sandy had cut someone tonight. The idea of working the rest of the shift like nothing was wrong while Sky—*alien freaking Sky*—slung drinks like everything was fine and dandy made me want to throw up.

I hadn't missed the fact he'd been throwing me quick, cautious looks before I'd taken off. He'd tried talking to me when I was clocking out. I'd practically run away screaming, all the way to my car.

Kelly had said something, too, and I didn't remember if I'd even looked her way. I was too busy chewing over tonight's massive revelation.

The one where Sky was an alien.

Sky was a mother-*freaking* alien.

"Holy shit," I choked out, strangling the wheel with both hands. The stoplight cast red across my rain-slicked window. The engine's rumble and the wipers' squeaks were muffled by the rush of blood in my ears.

A part of me still desperately wanted to believe this was all a dream and I would wake up soon and never eat whatever I'd had for dinner again.

So far, I'd handled all this alien crap with surprising ease. I'd looked at it like a problem. A research project. Something separate from myself I could analyze and investigate and pick apart and, hell, maybe even solve. Like one, big cosmic-sized puzzle.

Even with the burn mark on my hand. I glanced at it, exhaling shakily. At least it was done with its whole glow stick routine. It'd returned to normal.

Sky...his involvement made it somehow even more personal. Made it real.

And you know, maybe it hurt a little.

This was Sky. He'd been a part of my life for months. I'd ridden in his car. I'd salivated over his dimple. I'd fantasized about his biceps.

I'd felt the press of his hard body against mine on the dance floor. I'd wondered what his lips tasted like.

I'd been hurt and pissed when I'd thought he was manipulating me to get answers. But that was before he'd gone all shiny and silver on me. Now I didn't know *what* to feel.

His eyes had looked like they'd won first place in a Hollywood special effects competition. He'd *sparkled*. And not like the vampire guy from that one book. He'd had *silver skin*.

Shit. Did he have a robot form too? Bile rose, and I swallowed hard, forcing it back down. My head spun, and my knuckles whitened around the steering wheel.

I'd known he was hiding something, but...*this*? I'd never seen it coming. I couldn't get the image of his alien form out of my head. One minute, he'd been Sky. The next, he'd been *something else*.

With a jolt, I realized I'd been sitting at a green light. Sucking in a sharp breath, I gunned it. Faith's tires spun out on the wet asphalt before catching, and I sped off toward home. For the hundredth time since I'd peeled out of Oasis's parking lot, I checked the rearview mirror. Headlights beamed at me from a distance. I tensed, panic bubbling up.

What if he'd followed me? What if, now that I'd found out, he was going to come for me and...

Would they kill to protect their secret?

The image of the security guards I'd found swam back. They obviously had no problem hurting and maiming. I had the bruises to prove it, even if those guards supposedly remembered nothing. If the rumors were to be believed, there'd been a flash of light, the explosion, and then they'd woken up in the hallway with no memory of anything else.

Like...maybe like I was supposed to have done.

Only I hadn't.

If Sky's reaction was any indication, he'd expected me to forget. Which was insane. How could I forget anything about any of this?

Wait...*oh shit*. Speaking of forgetting.

Sky already knew where I *lived*.

He'd dropped me off. Oh God. He didn't need to follow me. He could easily find me again. Sweat slicked my palms, and I split my attention between the road and the lights behind me.

Maybe I should skip going home. Maybe I should run. I could just keep driving. Keep going and going...

The headlights in my mirror turned off onto the highway, fading away. I sagged into the seat. False alarm.

Sky wasn't following me.

It's not like he'd tried to stop me at Oasis, either. He'd just stood there by the dumpsters—after his silver skin had rippled and faded back to normal—while I panicked and beat a hasty exit back into the restaurant. I'd caught a glimpse of him right before the back door had shut behind me. I'd seen his eyes, wide and dark, following me, a jumble of emotions playing over his handsome, too-familiar face.

He'd been pale, albeit human-colored, his body rigid.

He hadn't said a word. If anything, he looked more frightened of me than I was of him.

Almost.

I shivered and turned onto Cherry Street. A moment later, I wrenched Faith into park in front of the house and gathered my stuff, shoving open the squeaky driver's door. I splashed through a puddle, soles slapping concrete as I raced over the curb. My fingers shook as I fished out my keys. Nothing moved around me. The heavy rain was a gray, watery curtain, obscuring the world, chilling my already numb face.

I unlocked the door, rushed inside, and slammed it again, turning both the deadbolt and handle lock for good measure. Only then did I pause to breathe, leaning back against the panel, just like I had the night Sky had dropped me off.

Only this time, I wasn't daydreaming about him.

This wasn't a fantasy.

It was a nightmare.

I needed to tell someone. I needed to bring somebody into this with me, or I was going to lose my mind.

Rainwater slid down my nose, and I swiped the back of my hand under it, sniffling. Okay. I could do this. I was home. I was safe.

For now.

I climbed the stairs, fumbling for my phone. It took a few tries to unlock it with my wet thumb, but I pulled up Amelia's number as I reached the top.

I toed off my soaked shoes and shot off a quick message.

> Need to talk. Can you come over?

I hit send.

Only then did I pause and bite my cheek. Maybe that hadn't been the best course of action. Too late now, but still…there were things to consider. As the shock started to ebb, my pragmatic side kicked back in, and I pressed my lips into a line, staring at the screen. I needed to breathe. Just breathe. And think.

Everything was happening so fast.

I squeezed my eyes shut.

It was too late to unsend the text. It was out there. Groaning, I dropped the phone on the kitchen counter and went to my bedroom, where I tugged off my apron and wrestled out of my damp uniform dress. I tossed the wet clothes in a heap on the floor and, not bothering with a clean bra, pulled on a tank top and yoga pants before heading back to the front room.

Shivering from the deadly combo of chilly air and way too much adrenaline with nowhere to go, I snatched up my discarded cardigan from the other day, slinging it on and clutching it close. A quick glance at my phone showed no reply from Amelia. I muttered a curse and rubbed my aching temples. At this point, I was one catastrophe away from never leaving this apartment again.

Maybe it was best she didn't answer. Maybe telling her was a bad idea anyway. It wasn't safe. None of this was. The bruises on my arms and the marks on my palm proved that.

As did, you know, the angry robot I'd tangled with a couple days ago.

No, Amelia needed to stay far, far away from all this. If something happened to her, if someone I loved got hurt because of me… well, I'd never forgive myself.

I stared at the silent phone lying on the counter, catching my bottom lip between my teeth. Maybe it still for the best I keep this to myself. For now.

Just yours truly versus an army of killer robots who could also turn into tall, dark, and handsome liars. Who could also slip into shiny silver skin.

No problem.

"He's an alien" I whispered, lacing my fingers behind my neck and dropping my head back. Saying it aloud didn't help anything. Didn't help it sink in.

I didn't know what to do. Where did I go from here? So far, I'd handled this situation with a certain degree of detachment, but that plan had just exploded.

I'd wanted answers. And I'd gotten them. Sort of. Some, at least. The issue was, these answers raised even more questions.

Like what the actual crap was Sky?

Aliens had been in my life longer than the last week. He'd been hiding in plain sight for months. And now I'd painted a target on myself—

A knock sounded on the door.

The rapping sliced through the quiet and stopped my heart. I gasped, spinning toward the stairwell and nearly tripping over the coffee table in the process. I threw out my arms, barely catching myself before sprawling on the laminate floor.

Somebody was at my door.

Muffled rain hammered the windows. My pulse stuttered, and my strangled breathing seemed extra loud in the sudden, pregnant silence.

Then I remembered the text. Right. I'd texted Amelia.

I blew out a breath, shoulders wilting. Sure, she hadn't responded, but it wouldn't be the first time she'd just shown up. It had to be Amelia. I was just being paranoid.

Still, it didn't hurt to be cautious.

I forced my legs to move. Pulse jumpy, I crossed to the kitchen and yanked open the junk drawer, snatching up the bottle of mace my mom had insisted I take when I moved to the "big city." It had lived there untouched ever since, but, hey, anything was better than nothing. I clamped my trembling fingers around the canister, gripping it tight.

Armed and moderately dangerous, I crept to the stairwell. The steps seemed to stretch forever as I padded down them in my wet socks. The door loomed at the bottom.

Reaching it, I swallowed and squeezed my eyelids shut. "Please be Amelia."

I tightened my grip on the spray, opened my eyes, and reached for the locks before I could talk myself out of it and into hiding in my closet the rest of the night. Muffled thunder rumbled as I twisted the handle tab. Turned the deadbolt.

Bracing myself, I cracked the door open.

And froze. My stomach dropped through the floor. Horror iced my cold feet to the threshold.

It wasn't Amelia.

Sky stood on my stoop.

His head jerked up as soon as I opened the door. Wariness pinched his eyes in the corners as he stared at me, hands in the pockets of his leather jacket, his body hunched against the storm. Rain plastered his dark hair to his head and ran down his tanned face.

His tanned, *human* face.

I bleated like a startled goat, slammed the door shut, and locked it for good measure.

Oh no.

Sky was here. *Alien* Sky.

Was he here to kill me? Or worse, *abduct* me?

I'd left my phone behind, on the counter. I couldn't call the police. If I screamed, no one would hear me. Bob was half deaf and lived across the lawn, a whole house away.

I'd locked the door, sure, but what use was a lock against an alien? He could probably just…beam right in here. Hell, he could probably rip the whole building apart. Blast it with a laser cannon or something.

Maybe he could control alien robots. Maybe he *was* an alien robot.

Oh my God. I was so, *so* screwed—

He knocked again. Gently. Just a soft tap of knuckles.

I screamed anyway.

"No!" I shouted at the door, as if admonishment alone could keep it shut tight. I leapt back and pointed the mace at it like a tiny, spicy bazooka. "Go away!"

Quiet fell. For a wild moment, I thought he'd listened.

But then his voice filtered through, muted but very definitely still there. "Raven, it's okay. I just need to talk to you. Give me a couple minutes, and I promise I'll go."

"It's *not* okay!" I yelled back, the words cracking. "I'm not going to tell anybody. Seriously. You don't have to kill me!"

There was a stunned pause, and then a strangled, "*What? Kill* you? Why...?"

Well, huh. He sounded surprised. As if it were *surprising* I feared my demise at the hands of a freaking *extraterrestrial visitor.* Had he even seen a sci-fi movie? Maybe not. Maybe he found them offensive. I probably would now, too. If I survived long enough to watch any more.

My legs felt strange, weak and trembly, enough so I leaned on the wall, still clutching the spray. Another few seconds passed, during which I eyed the white door panel. The still intact door panel.

For a super advanced robot race, he was being surprisingly cordial about not vaporizing the wall or anything. It almost seemed like...well, like he was actually waiting out there for me to let him in.

I jumped when he knocked again, and I nearly sprayed mace all over the closed door. I checked my trigger finger right in time, swallowing hard despite having no saliva to speak of.

Sky spoke up again, sounding resigned. "Raven, I'm not here to kill you. You know me better than that, right?"

"I don't know you at all!" I breathed a laugh that sounded more like a deflating rubber chicken. "I don't even know what you *are.*"

He was quiet for a second before he said, very matter-of-fact, "I think you do."

Okay, fair. I sucked in a sharp breath, eyes on the door. Silence fell.

He was right, of course. I had a tiny inkling exactly what Sky Acosta was.

A minute crept by.

The door remained whole and door-like between us.

I bit my lip. A tiny niggle of uncertainty began to worm its way through the terror. Maybe he *wasn't* here to hurt me. He honestly sounded…contrite. Maybe a little tired. Certainly not…well, *alien-y*.

Then again, what did aliens sound like?

For a moment, I was in the lab, listening to those terrible mechanical garbled words, and I flinched and gripped the pepper spray harder. But when nothing filtered in through the door but the storm, I leaned forward. Strained to listen.

Sky raised his voice just a little over the hammering rainwater and grumbles of thunder. "I just need to talk to you, Raven. Then I'll go. I swear, I only need a few minutes. I'm not here to…to harm you in any way. I only want to talk." I heard him sigh. "Please let me in."

Ugh. That last part was said so…*persuasively*. That tone, the entreaty in it, combined with the memory of his shocked, frightened face at Oasis had my resolve wavering even further. The blustery storm outside raged convincingly, too, like it was contributing to his cause. He was out there in it, getting pelted by wind and rain.

Could he truly just want to talk?

A sudden, intense sense of surrealism washed over me. This was no dream. I was really standing in my stairwell, and there was an alien on the other side of my door. A being not of this world. An *interplanetary traveler*.

One I'd unwittingly been crushing on for the better part of a year.

There were so many implications that came with that fact…for me, and for the entire freaking human race.

Also regarding my taste in men.

At any rate, if he wanted to hurt me, he would've by now. He'd had opportunities. Before this, even. But there he was, standing out there in the pouring rain and borderline begging for a chance to talk. To me.

I held my breath and eyed the door, gripping the mace hard.

Was I afraid? Hell yes. I was terrified.

But underneath all that, buried beneath the bone-deep fear that came from having my reality shaken to the foundation, there was that latent, burning, *annoying* curiosity. My need to know and under-stand. My gift and my curse.

He wanted to talk, and I...damn it, I had questions. Who was he—who *was* he, really? Or better yet, *what* was he, and why was he here? Was his presence connected to the tablet after all? And what about the robot that'd nearly smashed me to bits?

Had that been *him*?

It was nearly impossible to liken the two, but how was I supposed to know? None of this came with a user guide. Even the Reddit threads hadn't accounted for any of this.

I wouldn't know unless I asked him.

Unless I let him in. Unless I took a risk and let him explain himself and what had happened at Oasis. If I was lucky, he could tell me what this strange design on my hand truly meant. What had happened to me in that gap of time between the lab and waking up in the hallway.

What was happening to me now.

I grimaced at the closed door. This was a bad idea. This was a *bad* idea on so many levels, it was up there with the world's highest sky-rise of bad ideas. This bad idea was about to enter atmosphere on its way right off this planet.

But...screw it.

How many people could say they'd entertained an alien?

My heart in my throat, I reached for the door's knob and eased it open again. The storm hissed and crashed, and when I steeled myself and peered through the crack, Sky ducked his head to meet my eyes. His half-hearted smile came and went.

"It's really raining out here," he said.

Oh, and he really did look pathetic. He didn't look like an alien. Not right now. He looked like...Sky. A soaked-to-the-skin, ashen, worried version of Sky. Rain clung to his long eyelashes and slicked his face, and when he exhaled slowly, it plumed out in a cloud of white mist.

But because I had self-preservation instincts and my common sense was trying desperately to get my attention, I hesitated a moment longer. As if he knew, he squinted against my bright porch light, his brows tented beneath his dripping dark hair.

"Please, Rae. Just give me a minute of your time. That's all I'm asking. I'll be gone as soon as I've said my piece. I'm not going to…" A muscle ticked in his cheek. "I wouldn't hurt you."

He whispered the last part like it pained him to even say it, and maybe it didn't say much about that whole self-preservation thing, but it rang sincere. Something wasn't adding up. I tried again to equate Sky to the violent alien robot I'd encountered at the university and failed.

I had questions. And he wanted to talk. The curiosity thickened and stilled some of the shaky panic, enough so I released my death grip on the door and studied him warily.

He was right. I hadn't known him well, but I'd spent enough time with him…okay, enough time watching him to feel like I had *somewhat* of a grasp on his personality. His habits and mannerisms. Right now, he seemed genuine, his dark gaze steady and possibly even hopeful when I continued to waver in the open doorway. He swiped a hand down his wet face, blinking away droplets.

It was such a…*human* gesture. I sighed.

This was how I ended up getting abducted by aliens. I knew it.

I stepped back and held the door open, gesturing with mace. "Okay. Come in."

Like he hadn't expected me to actually let him in, Sky blinked once before recovering. He eyed the pepper spray but wisely said nothing, pausing only a moment before stepping over the threshold. I peered out into the night behind him. Nothing stirred besides the wind through the leaf-bare trees.

Just me, a tiny canister of pepper spray, and my visitor from outer space.

Here went nothing.

I locked the door and tried not to hyperventilate at Sky existing behind me. When I turned, he stood at the farthest edge of the tiny landing, hands loose at his sides, something like relief softening his features.

This was stupid. On multiple levels. Sky was in my house, and I suddenly remembered I wasn't wearing a bra. A flush crept up my neck, and I turned my shoulder to him, hoping he hadn't noticed the…uh, chilly temperature situation.

"Take your shoes off," I said, for lack of anything more profound, and brushed past him to mount the stairs.

I heard the rustle as he followed my instructions, then his soft steps behind me. Panic licked at me, but I squeezed the mace and made myself keep breathing.

Too late to push the alien back out now. I had no choice but to trust he didn't mean me any harm. At the very least, if he did, I would hope that aliens could also be incapacitated by chemical sprays.

The thought had me practically sprinting the last few stairs, and at the top, I snatched up my phone and whirled. Clutching it to my chest, I backed away and watched Sky follow me into the living space.

He was impossible to read right now. His eyes stayed on mine for a beat before sliding away to scan my apartment. They lingered on the pizza box beside the empty wine bottle on the counter then traveled to the hand-me-down couch, the cluttered coffee table stacked with my laptop, study notes, and too many empty mugs. The janky lamp cast a soft yellow light over everything.

My modest apartment felt much smaller with him in it. Even beyond the whole alien thing, it felt…odd having *Sky* here, in my space. My mess. My chaos.

If I'd known I would be having extraterrestrial guests tonight, maybe I'd have cleaned up. A hysterical snicker threatened to bubble up.

By the time Sky's eyes returned to mine, I had the mace raised. "Okay. You wanted to talk. Here's your chance."

He lifted his hands slightly in an *I'm-a-harmless-alien* gesture. "I meant what I said. I'm not going to hurt you."

"You come in peace?" I snorted. "Original."

He didn't appear to be amused, judging by the compression of his lips. His voice, however, still had that maddening calm note to it. "Raven, I know this is a lot to take in. But this is serious."

"Oh, trust me, I get it." I jerked my chin up, tightening my grip. I lifted my phone with my other hand. "I will call the police if you don't start talking. You've got five seconds to give me a reason I shouldn't spray you and run until someone carts you off to…to wherever the new Area 51 is."

Sky's temple bulged like he was grinding his teeth. Streaks of drying rain glistened on his forehead and cheeks, and he dragged a hand down his face once more, not quite masking his quiet, frustrated grunt. "Okay. Okay, I get it. Just give me a second…"

Once a second passed, I hoisted the phone and mace higher in warning.

"*Okay.*" He raised his palms again, took a slow step sideways, and braced a hip against the kitchen counter. Folding his arms, he stood there, watching me. Drips slid from his clothes and pooled on the laminate flooring in a steady *plop-plop.*

"All right," he said at last, and I snapped my attention up. His brows were drawn, his expression guarded but determined. Like he'd braced himself for something. "I'll tell you everything I can."

This was it. My heart pounded. My insides dipped and climbed like 747-sized butterflies were taking off. Despite the chill in the air, a bead of nervous sweat slid down my spine beneath the tank top and cardigan. I flexed my death grip on the phone.

I wasn't even sure why I was holding it. Would the police even be able to help me if I called them and told them there was an alien in my living room? They'd probably write me off as crazy.

I was close to doing the same.

Meanwhile, Sky's gaze had gone distant, his posture rigid, like he was fighting some internal war. The scent of leather and rain filled the room. Another shiver wracked my limbs, and a clap of thunder shook the walls. In its wake, the silence grew heavier until I couldn't take it anymore, and I opened my mouth—

Sky cut me off. "What I'm about to tell you can't leave this room."

Predictable, but still. I narrowed my eyes. "Can't leave the room? So if I tell someone, what, you're going to abduct me? Kill me? Or like those guards at the university—"

"Will you *stop*?" His voice cracked like a whip, sharper than I'd ever heard him speak. It was so uncharacteristic, I actually jerked and snapped my mouth shut. As if he caught my flinch—and regretted it—he swore softly, looking away and muttering, "Nobody's killing anybody."

Barely daring to breathe, I stared at him. Somebody should've given the murderous robot that memo.

That heavy silence fell again. When he turned his head back toward me, his midnight-blue eyes churned with something that rivaled the storm outside. "I need you to listen to me carefully," he said, a lot more softly this time.

Tilting my head to the side, I contemplated him with my lip between my teeth. This really was a different person, a shift from the laid-back, polite bartender. Voice lodged somewhere in the vicinity of my throat, I bobbed my head again in a nod. I still didn't lower the mace, though.

His attention flicked to it, then back to my face, and he rolled his shoulders like he could shake off his tension. The anticipation was killing me. I tried hard to look like someone who didn't have one foot in a full-blown panic spiral.

"Like I was saying." Sky cleared his throat. "What I'm about to tell you has to stay here. Between us. Not because I'm going to kill you otherwise," he added with faint sarcasm, one brow twitching. "But for your own safety."

My own safety? If not from him, then from whom?

I started to ask just that, only to have him derail my train of thought.

"Raven," he said, his voice low but vibrating with intensity, his dark gaze slicing right through me. "You are in *serious* danger."

Chapter 23

EXPOSITION, BUT MAKE IT EXTRATERRESTRIAL

THE WORDS HUNG BETWEEN US. My heart bucked in my chest like a startled horse.

In danger? Me, specifically? Not the whole human race? Was this because I'd seen him? He'd said he wasn't here to hurt me, but—

"Are you..." My voice cracked. "Are you threatening me?"

"Am I threatening— No!" Sky stared at me like I'd grown a second head, then scowled. Another crackle of thunder rattled the windowpanes.

When I shrank a little against the wall, clutching the mace tighter, Sky blew out a breath and looked at the ceiling like he was summoning divine patience. Like *he* was the one dealing with life-altering reveals tonight.

It was enough to annoy me, and I straightened a little. "Then what did you mean by that? Why am I in danger? Because if it's just because I saw you at Oasis, I promise I won't tell anybody—"

"You know," Sky ran a hand through his soaked hair, mouth twisting, "I rehearsed this conversation in my head. It didn't go anything like this."

The idea of confident, calm Sky rehearsing any conversation

was ridiculous enough, I huffed. "That's kind of how my whole week's been." He sent me a wry look that said, *oh really?* A tremulous smile threatened to curve my mouth. A little of my trepidation faded, and I sighed. "Look, if you're just here to make sure I'm not going to tell anyone, you don't need to threaten me. Your secret's safe. Trust me, I'd rather forget *all* this—"

"I didn't threaten you at all. God, Rae. You jumped to that conclusion. Can you give me a chance to explain things?"

"I *am!*" I protested, throwing out my mace arm. "You're really sucking at the whole explanation thing for someone who just said they were going to tell me everything!"

"I said I'd tell you everything I *could*." He moved toward me, and I immediately took a step back, lifting the canister and phone in warning. He stopped short, a faint scowl tugging his mouth down.

I waved the pepper spray, refusing to apologize. "I let you in, didn't I? You're the one dripping all over my floor instead of *talking*."

As if he'd just realized it was there, he eyed the small puddle beneath him. With a muttered word I didn't catch, he turned away and crossed to the window, flicking apart the blinds and peering out. I breathed in through my nose and out through my mouth, watching his every move.

After a long pause, he said flatly, "A week ago, a scout for an alien race called the Enil landed on Earth."

Despite his oh-so-nonchalant delivery, his words struck like bombs. I'd known it was coming, but it still sucker-punched me.

"A...what's an Enil?" I forced out.

Blank. My mind was blank. It was full of that snowy static, like an old TV. Or Faith's radio if you tried to listen to any station but the local one since the antenna had rusted off.

Sure, I'd wanted answers. I'd *known* they'd be wild. But hearing it *out loud* ripped all the air from my lungs, leaving me light-headed and floaty.

Aliens. Alien *scouts*, no less.

I leaned hard on the wall, keeping Sky in sight. He wasn't looking at me, his attention on the rain-drenched night. He kept talking, though, in that same eerily calm tone. Like dropping life-altering revelations was just another item on his to-do list.

"There are a lot of complicated aspects to all this…too complicated for me to explain, even if I *was* allowed to."

That was enough to snap me from my haze. I clicked my tongue in annoyance. What, had he signed an intergalactic NDA?

"Allowed to? What does that mean?" I asked.

He took me in over his shoulder. "There's only so much I can tell you, Rae."

Definitely an intergalactic NDA.

"You just said…" I tried to steady my breathing, shaking off the dizziness. "Why don't you tell me whatever you're allowed to say?"

"Technically?" He turned away from the blinds, exhaled roughly. "Technically, I'm not allowed to say anything. We have a very strict non-exposure clause. It's part of our Creed. Non-interference."

Oh, great. Now we were getting into sci-fi prime directive territory.

"Okay," I said slowly, dragging out the word. "Then let's try this. Who is…*we?*"

Even as I asked the question, I wasn't sure I wanted the answer. Sky stiffened, and his midnight gaze grew penetrating where he stood in the center of my living room. With his back to the window, he was outlined by my tiny lamp. The glow burnished his dark hair.

He didn't say anything for another moment. I barely dared to breathe. A furrow cut deep between his brows. If I didn't know better, I'd think he was angry.

Like this—this whole conversation—was an inconvenience.

Well, same, buddy. Try this whole *week.*

And yet I couldn't seem to stop staring. For an alien, he certainly had human mannerisms down. He radiated broody, moody man vibes right now.

It was a lie, though. I knew what lay beneath. When I blinked, I could still imagine the silver sheen to his skin, the black-on-blue, inverted eyes. Not a man at all. I shivered.

And yet, *this* version of him looked torn. Frustrated. Almost... pained.

He lowered his gaze to the ground, hiding the emotions flitting over his face too quickly for me to read. The storm's wind battered the side of the garage, rattling windows like a phantom creature was trying to fight its way in.

After an eternity, Sky sighed and braced his hands on his hips. "I don't have a choice," he murmured, shaking his head.

I started to ask what the hell *that* meant, but then he looked up, focusing on me. Despite the several stride-lengths between us, it felt like he'd grabbed me by the collar. My question died on my lips, and I sucked in a breath. Time itself seemed to pause, the entire universe waiting along with me and my ready-to-spray mace.

Sky lifted his chin and let 'er rip.

"My race comes from a planet called Pladia. It's roughly eight lightyears from Earth in a solar system your astronomers haven't located yet. I'm not from there, though. Those of us born during interstellar travel are called the Starborn. I'm one of them. I was born aboard a transport ship in deep space."

My knees decided to melt, and all the blood drained from my head. The room tilted, and I fell against the wall with a strangled wheeze. Fuzzy spots danced in my vision. I blinked hard, willing them away.

I was *not* going to faint. I wasn't a fainter.

Sky didn't know that, though. He jerked forward like he planned to catch me. Pure adrenaline roared through me. I shrank away with a squeak, lifting the pepper spray.

"No," I gasped out. "Stay back."

"Okay." He lifted his hands in surrender and didn't move any closer, simply settled back against the counter again and folded his arms. That broody frown reappeared.

Pladia. Lightyears. Starborn.

My brain stuttered, and I opened my mouth but nothing came out. Giving my head a shake, I tried again. "So you really are..." I licked my dry lips. "You really are an..."

The word got stuck. My knees wobbled. I couldn't say it.

Sky didn't have that problem. He nodded once, slowly. "An alien. Yeah. A Pladian, if we're getting technical."

"An alien. *Pladian*," I whispered. That word *Pladian* seemed to ricochet in my brain, echoing over and over. "How...? How is this real?"

"It's a long story." He rubbed at his temple and sighed, looking, for a moment, exhausted. For some reason, that sliver of emotion grounded me. It was familiar. Human.

It was enough for me to start reasoning out loud. "Okay. Okay, so you're an," *oh God*, "alien. And...what? Is this," I gestured at him with the mace, "like a human suit or something?"

He looked down at himself. A hint of a smirk curled his mouth, breaking through his broodiness like sunbeams through clouds. "Close. My body is bonded with a biological synthesis suit. A synth-skin. So I guess you could say I'm wearing human skin."

"A...what?" My composure abandoned ship. "Wait, *is* that somebody's body? Did you steal someone's skin?"

Was he walking around in some kind of *stolen hot guy body?*

"What? No!" Sky lurched, eyes flaring wide. "Why would you even...? *No*, Rae. It's not like that."

When I continued to stare in horror, he muttered a curse under his breath. "No, it's not somebody's skin. It's a suit. It's tech. The Pladians—my people—we've been explorers for eons. This," he indicated his long, unfairly ripped form, "has been used to blend into local populations so we can observe without disruption. It allows us to explore in a non-invasive way."

Non-invasive. Sure. It was feeling pretty damn invasive right about now.

As if he'd heard the thought—or maybe read it on my face—his mouth pressed into a tight line. To his credit, he kept going. "Before coming to Earth, I went through a merging process. I bonded with the synth-skin and activated its shapeshifting biological interface."

"Uh huh. Shapeshifting," I echoed faintly. "Sure."

His eyes flicked back and forth between mine, as if he tried to gauge my reaction. I was still firmly stuck on *holy freaking crap*.

"Shapeshifting," he said, watching me closely. "But it's more than that. It fuses with its host, all the way down to the DNA. It's my skin now." He presented one arm and pinched the back of his hand. The skin bunched between his fingers, then bounced back when he released it. The white mark faded to red.

I stared at it. It was a hand. With skin. Normal, human skin.

"I can feel that," Sky said quietly, as my panic gave way to cautious curiosity. "I feel temperature, pain. I'm ticklish. The suit restructures my molecules to match your biological signature. Helps that our evolutions took similar paths. That's more common than you'd think."

More *common*? As in, there was an *uncommon* option, too?

Too much. That was too much for the right now. I filed that little tidbit away for later. Focused on the current out-of-this-world exposé.

"Okay." I took a deep breath. "So that's not your real skin...but it is?"

"Exactly. It wasn't always, but it's me *now*."

That ever-present, rational corner of my mind *finally* clicked into gear. Cataloged. Processed.

An alien in a synth-skin suit. And underneath it, he was silver and sparkly.

Got it.

"So I guess to answer your question, Rae," Sky said, tilting his head and relaxing back against the counter again, "I'm as human as you are right now." He held my gaze. "In all the ways that matter."

Something about the way he said that made me blush. I tried to ignore it. "But you're not. You sure as hell weren't earlier at Oasis. What happened there?"

For a second, it drifted back again, the image. That strange glittering of his skin, like he was decorated with tiny crystals. Those depthless black eyes. My stomach swooped.

"No, you're right." Sky pursed his lips. "I don't know exactly what happened back there. The synth-skin malfunctioned. I've never had that happen. Not once in all my years here." He shifted against the counter, and his attention slid to my hand. "I've got some theories, though."

I grimaced and followed his eyes, constricting my fingers around the mace. He didn't know for sure what had caused the glitch, but we both suspected. It had happened after I touched him. With my palm covered with strange markings.

"Okay." One thing at a time. I forced my parched throat to work. "So with this synth-skin thing, could you touch, say…a house cat, and morph into one of those?"

"Uh." He blinked. "What?"

"Animorphs. Old book series," I muttered. "Never mind. Probably before your time…on Earth." Which, while we were on the topic—how long *was* that?

"Ten years," Sky said, like he'd read my mind. Lightning streaked outside the window, illuminating the room in a brief flash of white-blue. "I've been here ten years."

Wow. Ten years. How old *was* he then? I'd have been fourteen when he landed here. I had so many damn questions. They were crowding over themselves, trying to get out.

Focusing on the important ones, I rubbed my forehead with the back of my mace hand. "Okay, back to the human suit. That's it? No other forms…?"

Like, say, a Rock 'Em Sock 'Em from hell? I braced for his answer. If he turned into some kind of killing machine right now, I was toast. Pepper spray wasn't going to cut it.

He was frowning at me now. "I can't shapeshift into other people, if that's what you're asking. Or any other races. That's not how the DNA sequencing works. I'd have to go through the removal of this suit—which is a long, painful process and not always successful—then bond with a new one programmed to the new species. And it only works if they have similar mass. This is my form now."

He looked down at himself then back up at me. "Is that what you mean?"

No. *I was asking if you turn into a murder-y robot.*

I shook my head jerkily.

"Okay." He hesitated, the grooves in his forehead deepening.

"Well, this skin does let me alter my appearance one other way. Only slightly, but... "

He backed into the shadowy corner of my living room. I stiffened, tensing to run. I waited for metal limbs, for claws, for horror.

Instead, his outline shimmered. Darkened. *Blurred.*

His shape smeared, like pencil shading smudged along the edges. My jaw dropped. He was still there, but hard to see, harder to *focus* on. His body bled into the darkness until he became a living, moving shadow.

Essentially, he disappeared.

In a way I'd totally seen before.

I gasped and swayed, colliding with the kitchen counter. Sky snapped back into view, and I lifted the mace in a trembling hand. "*You!*"

Sky halted in place and eyed me warily. "Me...?"

"The lab...and...last night," I rasped, the can wavering. "In the trees across the street. Have you been *following me?*"

He shot a glance at my shaking hand. That muscle in his temple tightened and released. "It's not what it looks like. I just wanted to make sure you got home okay. You seemed upset when you left Crescent."

Upset. That was an understatement. "So what—you *stalked* me like some creepy alien peeping Tom?"

His sigh was barely audible over the storm—and the blood roaring in my ears.

"Just tell me," I ordered, lifting the mace.

"Fine." His stare didn't waver. "Yes. I've been keeping an eye on you, Raven."

"Why? How much of an eye?" I demanded. "You were at the university. Which means you saw that *thing*. And did you *follow* me to Crescent? Is that why you were there?"

He didn't deny it. Instead, his body jerked, and his gaze snapped to mine. "You really do remember what happened at the school."

The way he was looking at me, sharp and assessing, made my pulse jump. I ignored the question, too busy coming to terms with the fact I'd been freaking *right.*

"Oh my God," I breathed. "You *have* been stalking me. Why?"

This was all so overwhelming. Breathing hurt. The question that'd haunted me since he'd gone silver on me at Oasis slipped out. "Do you...have a robot form?"

Sky stilled, then barked a harsh laugh completely devoid of humor. "The Enil," he murmured, raking a hand through his hair, leaving it to fall haphazardly over his ears and forehead. It was starting to curl as it dried. I'd never seen it messy like that. "You do remember the Enil."

I tore my attention from his hair and fixed him with an incredulous look instead. "You keep saying that. Why *wouldn't* I? And you keep saying that word—the Enil. Was that the robot?" I paused for air and flung one arm toward the corner. "And that other person *was* you at TWU, wasn't it? With your...with the skin-suit thing. You yelled my name."

He didn't say anything. He was still studying me. My legs threatened to give out again, and I pressed my lower back into the kitchen counter. My guts were so twisted, there was a distinct chance I was going to throw up. The room needed to stop spinning.

Sky's dark gaze held mine, luminous and so serious. "But the question is, *how* do you remember?" he mused aloud, more to himself than me. Which was fine, since I was having trouble thinking clearly.

He *had* been following me. All my gut instincts about him had been right.

I mean, I hadn't imagined the whole alien-in-a-human-suit part. I'd known *something* was off, but no one could blame me for not considering *that* possibility.

Before I could blink, Sky closed the distance between us. I squeaked, every cell going on Red Alert. But there was nowhere to go. I was wedged between the counter and the looming alien looking at me like *I* was the mystery.

So I stayed in place, breathing hard as he closed the distance between us. I felt too exposed in my tank top and old yoga pants. Like a pinned specimen beneath a microscope. With my phone hand, I yanked my cardigan closed.

Sky didn't stop until he stood right in front of me, and he tipped his chin down, his expression solemn. "You remember everything, don't you?"

"I..." More than I wanted to; that was for sure. I licked my lips, transferring my weight from foot to foot.

Was I supposed to *forget*...? Like those security guards had apparently forgotten everything? Like *everybody else except me* had somehow missed the angry alien robot rampaging through the anthro hall?

I didn't say anything, merely stared up at him. I could feel the heat he radiated. The shirt beneath his coat clung to his torso like a second skin.

Or a third skin, technically.

He was close and he smelled like Sky—rain, leather, that fresh air scent. And that same awareness I'd always felt around him bloomed low in my belly. Made my cheeks heat and my mouth go dry.

Which couldn't be right.

Because that meant despite everything, despite what I'd seen, despite the fact I'd spent the last days narrowly escaping being *killed* by aliens...I was still wildly, stupidly attracted to one.

As if he felt it, too, that pang of *attraction*, Sky's breath hitched— the smallest catch. His eyes swept over my face, pausing on my mouth so briefly I wondered if I'd imagined it. Like it had when we were dancing.

Had that part been real?

I forced myself to focus on the conversation rather than how little space there was between us. "How would I forget something like what happened in the lab?"

Why was it suddenly so hot in here?

Why did I have the inexplicable urge to move toward him?

Instead, I leaned back as far as the counter allowed. Cell phone in one hand, mace in the other. Searching for air that didn't smell like him and failing miserably.

"You shouldn't be able to remember," he said, eyes finding mine again. "When I carried you out to the hallway, I wiped the memory." Now his gaze dropped to my hand. The marked one holding the mace. "Unless…"

"Wait. Back up." I recoiled. "*Wiped my memory?* What are you talking about?"

"It's part of the suit…" He looked away with a resigned sigh. "A neural wipe. The ability to control brain waves via electrical…" He shook his head, sweeping out with a hand like he was brushing that insane sentence away. "It's just a failsafe in case—"

I finally found my voice. "Did you just say *control brain waves?* Are you kidding me right now?"

His eyes slid back to mine, narrowed. "It's harmless—"

"Have you done that to me before?"

"No!" His mouth took on a downward slant, like that question had *offended* him. "No, I haven't. Why would I?"

"I don't know!" I threw my hands up, the movement wild enough that he lurched back to avoid being clipped by the mace. "Maybe I saw your spaceship or something. How am I supposed to know if I don't remember?"

He blinked, then said blandly, "I don't just go around showing people my spaceship, Raven."

No, of course he didn't. My bubble of hysterical laughter burst free, and Sky's frown deepened into something like annoyance. Especially when the giggles kept coming. In fact, I laughed so hard, I had to catch myself on the counter.

"Sorry," I managed, swiping my wrist over my eyes. I flapped the phone at him. "It's just…too much."

He rocked back on his heels and slipped his hands into his pockets. When I could see again, I found his annoyance had dissipated, tucked away beneath the calm mask.

"It's fine," he said, glancing away. His jaw ticked. "This is a lot."

"Yeah. That's an understatement." I snorted. Oddly enough, the laughter had helped, like a pressure valve had released. I took a deep breath, let it out, and went back to it. "Okay. So if you were in the lab, you saw…the robot then."

Looking back at me, he nodded. "That robot—although it isn't technically a robot—was an Enil."

I'd suspected, but putting a name to the thing that'd haunted my nightmares for days felt just as surreal as hosting an extraterrestrial in my apartment. "And what happened to it?"

"I took care of it," Sky said absently. His attention drifted to my marked hand still fisted around the mace.

"Took care of it," I repeated, gawking. "You took care of the seven-foot robot from outer space."

"It's not technically a robot," he said again with a hint of exasperation.

"Not a robot. Sorry." *My bad.* A *robot* from outer space was ridiculous. I leaned against the counter. "And the tablet thing. They were after it?"

"More or less," he said, reaching for me—for my mace, specifically.

I recoiled and clutched it to my chest. "What are you doing?"

"Sorry." He eased back, his voice gentling like I was a skittish animal. "I just want to see the marks on your palm again."

I didn't loosen my death grip. All the shapes and swirls were hidden by the canister. "Why? What are they? I thought it was just scars from a burn or..."

Or at least that's what I'd been trying to tell myself. Before it lit up and effectively ruined that excuse. Now, that theory seemed... highly unlikely.

Sky didn't answer. When I eyed him warily, his expression tightened. Like he was bothered by it.

Yeah, well...so sue me. Frankly, I thought I was doing awesome. I hadn't sprayed a single person—or *Pladian*—with mace, nor had I fainted during this extraterrestrial info dump. I was a champ, thank you very much.

Excuse me for having some reservations about flashing the alien-y looking artwork that'd started this entire thing. I held my ground, knuckles whitening around the pepper spray. My fridge kicked on, humming away in the kitchen. Loud in the silence.

After the standoff stretched another long heartbeat, Sky sighed.

"I'm not going to hurt you," he murmured, his deep voice rasping.

I stared at his shoulder and scraped my teeth over my bottom lip, my heartbeat unsteady. He ducked his head, giving me no choice but to meet his eyes again.

"I promise you're safe with me," he said. The conviction shone in his gaze holding mine. "I'd just like to see the marks again." When I didn't immediately protest, he reached for me, slower this time, watching my face. "If that's okay."

Oh, what the hell. Why not?

This time, I let him. I couldn't quite make myself extend the hand, but I didn't pull away when he touched my wrist.

His fingers were warm. Steady. *Real.* My pulse jumped in the hollow of my throat as I watched them curve around the delicate bones.

They felt…well, like human fingers. Long, graceful, with neat nails and attached to a human-shaped hand. Great hands, really. They made mine look small and pale in comparison.

And because I was a sucker for nice-looking hands attached to nice-looking guys, I let him tug the mace canister free from my loose grip. When I looked up, his frown had faded. He gave me a small, close-lipped smile as he set the bottle on the counter behind me. Like he was quietly celebrating the small victory of not getting doused in the process.

The night was still young.

On instinct, I closed my now-empty hand, hiding the marks, but Sky gently pried my curled-tight fingers open. I didn't stop him from doing that, either.

Once my palm was flat, we both looked down.

The strange symbols shimmered faintly in the light. I held my breath while Sky cradled my hand in his, lifting it slightly, studying the intricate swirls like they held the secrets to the universe.

Which…you know, crazily enough, wasn't outside the realm of possibility.

Speaking of outside the realm of possibility, in case I hadn't mentioned it, Sky was cradling my hand.

Goosebumps prickled across my skin. He'd leaned in enough, his breath ghosted over my forehead. I slowly tipped my face up. His deep blue eyes were intent, his features drawn in concentration. Those cheekbones were ridiculous.

I told myself it was fear. It had to be. That liquid warmth in my gut couldn't be what it felt like. Not now. Not *still*.

But here he was. Sky. My bartender crush. My maybe-alien protector-slash-stalker, and he was holding my hand in his nicely shaped one, and he was looking all broody and thoughtful again—

Holy crap. That feeling. There was something very wrong with me.

He was from another world, and yet I *still* wanted to lick him like a popsicle.

Chapter 24

ANIASI WHATEVER AND OTHER INSANE ALIEN BURDENS

I SHOULD'VE BEEN SCARED. Distracted by the fact he'd just admitted to being from outer space. I should've been...at the very least, too overwhelmed to be thinking with any of my hormones.

But this was *Sky* crowding me against the counter. And because it was Sky and I lost all sense around him, my hormones were still very much involved. They were practically throwing a party.

I'd never been this close to him before. Not really. Crescent had been the exception, and it'd been dark. Here, under the warm lamplight, I could see everything.

Tiny imperfections. A scar near the hinge of his jaw where stubble didn't grow. A cowlick curling at his temple. A faint mole beneath his ear, along the tanned line of his throat.

They were flaws that made my heart stutter.

Human flaws.

Because despite everything I knew...he *looked* human. He felt human. And every cell of my body insisted he was.

But he wasn't.

And for some reason, I didn't care.

Then he brushed his thumb across my palm almost absently, and damn it, it felt way better than it should've. Whether it was some alien reaction or just me being pathetic, I didn't know, but my face heated, and I barely suppressed a shiver.

Amelia was *so* wrong about me not being desperate.

Up close, his indigo irises gleamed with threads of pale blue and silver, the same uncanny colors I'd seen earlier when I'd glimpsed his Pladian form. Otherworldly and breathtaking. They reminded me of trapped starlight. How I'd never noticed before, I didn't know. They weren't quite normal.

"I don't believe it," he murmured, looking up. Those eyes landed on mine, widened a little with shock. Enough so, I stiffened, the dreamy daze fading instantly.

"What? What is it?" I asked, swallowing hard. His hand was warm against mine.

As if he'd suddenly realized how close we stood—or maybe my rising blush had telegraphed my reaction—Sky released me and stepped back. Willing away the redness, I curved my fingers into my palm, clutching my fist in my other hand. My stomach was all sorts of confused about what to feel.

Sky backed up, halting a few feet away. Far enough for me to recall how breathing worked.

"That…tablet, as you called it," he said, grimacing, "was ancient Pladian technology."

My mouth fell open. "What?"

"I know it all happened fast. But did you see the crystal under the stone façade?"

I blinked rapidly, struggling to follow. "Yeah. I did. I touched it. The stone with the writing kind of dissolved and…" I waved the hand still holding my phone. "There was glowing crystal underneath."

"And you touched it?"

"The crystal?" At his nod, I shrugged. "Yeah. I thought it burned me and that's what caused these marks, but…" I uncurled my fingers, looking down at the markings, something cold and hard settling in my stomach. "That's not what these are, is it?"

"No," Sky agreed, something grim in the quiet admission. "I don't think so, Rae."

That ball of dread inside me grew heavier, and I lifted my gaze to his. "What is it?"

He sighed and rubbed the back of his neck. "As far as I can tell, you absorbed the tablet's energy."

"I absorbed..." I stared at him, mouth working. "How the heck would I do that? What *was* that thing?"

He studied my face for a quiet moment, looking torn. The storm battered the windows in the tense silence. A moment passed before he spoke again.

"You have to understand. I'm not supposed to talk about any of this, Raven. The Creed—it's very serious—"

"Sky," I broke in, lifting my palm. "In case it's slipped your mind, I've got alien squiggles on my freaking *hand.*"

"I *know*. Trust me, I know." He pursed his lips, shifting his weight. "That's why I'm here and why I'm telling you any of this."

"Okay." That and the fact that I'd seen his silver sparkly bits. I kept that observation to myself. "So what exactly was that stone tablet?"

I almost didn't expect him to answer, but he did. Albeit with obvious reluctance.

"It was...a greeting, I guess you could call it. An info cache. An organic crystal mainframe designed to impart information using nexus technology and coded molecular..." He trailed off when he caught my blank look. Shaking his head, he braced his hands on his hips. "Basically, it was a calling card the Pladians left here with the hope humans would evolve to access it. Like...like a hard drive."

"Wait—left here? That tablet looked old. Ancient, even."

"Several thousand years old, yes."

"So..." My head spun. "You're telling me your people have already been here. On Earth. Thousands of years ago."

His chest heaved with his heavy exhale. "Yeah. We're...well, we used to be explorers. Scientists. Millennia ago, we surveyed this sector of space and left behind those crystals. On planets we visited."

Earth had alien visitors. *Millennia ago.* Oh my God. The implications of that...for human history, for the *galaxy*...

With effort, I gathered myself. Worrying about the archaeological record having somehow skipped over ancient alien visitors could wait. "So Pladians were here, and they left a...rock with a crystal inside it?"

"One programmed with a message. My ancestors did that when visiting planets with budding civilizations. Think of it like leaving our phone number—except a lot more complicated. Obviously."

"Kind of like leaving your number on the napkin for the waitress."

Sky shrugged. "Sure." His mouth twitched. "That happen to you a lot?"

I sniffed in amusement. "Definitely not to me, but to Kelly, sure." He arched a brow slowly, like he didn't believe me. Blushing, not sure what to do with that, I rotated my palm to study the marks. "So what the hell is this, then?"

"That's the thing," Sky said, growing somber again. "I don't know how it happened, but that's an old Pladian dialect. Like what would be inside the halix."

"Halix?"

"The crystal. The nexus tech," he clarified, crossing his arms over his broad chest, then uncrossing them. Like he couldn't decide what to do with his hands. "That's what it's called."

Sure. Of course. Sounded sufficiently science-fiction-y.

I took a deep breath, and my exhale came out shaky. "I'm not following. So these markings...are, what, burned into me from the crystal going boom while I was touching?"

I didn't miss how Sky's expression closed. The calm mask. That didn't bode well for me.

"Essentially, those markings are the first part of the halix's greeting. In ancient Pladian. It basically says, 'Greetings to those who inhabit this planet.' That'd be a..." He caught my horrified look and grimaced. "That'd be a rough translation."

My ears were ringing. "I've got an alien greeting. On my hand."

"Yeah. Yeah, you do."

"I'm a walking, talking alien greeting card."

Sky watched me carefully. "Basically."

"Basically," I echoed dully. Panic tried to kindle, a tight ball of it cinching in my middle. I pushed it back down. "The stone part of the tablet disintegrated."

"It did. It's gone."

"Why?"

"My guess?"

I gave him an incredulous look. "It'd be better than mine."

"Fair," he said, a faint smile touching his lips. "I think it was triggered by the…other alien tech present. It backfed and shorted."

"Exploded," I corrected, remembering the flash of light and heat and that *pain*, the burn.

Sky bit the inside of his cheek. "Correct. It exploded, and you were touching it. So all that energy…"

He didn't have to finish the sentence. My insides twisted. "You think it went into me."

"It's a hypothesis," he murmured. "One backed up by the fact you emitted energy at Oasis. When you…" He cleared his throat, looking away. "When you touched me."

"When I touched you and you went all silver and shiny."

"Yeah," he muttered, suddenly very interested in my cluttered coffee table.

"And what I saw. That was…you? The real you?" I whispered. I needed to hear him say that, too. To confirm I wasn't losing it and hadn't imagined the whole thing.

His wide shoulders rose and fell beneath his jacket. Slowly, he turned his head. At least an arm span separated us, but I felt the impact of his midnight eyes across the distance. There was a flash of something—vulnerability, maybe—in them and he nodded gravely. "Yes. What you saw…that was my Pladian form."

I mulled that over. His Pladian form had looked shockingly… *homo sapiens*. Well, besides the skin and those eerie eyes. He'd had a nose, a mouth, two eyes. Hands with five fingers. Two legs.

He seemed to have all the parts.

Well, the parts I could see, anyway.

Another flush threatened to crawl its way up my neck. I tried not to think about Sky's parts and battled it back.

At any rate, that had to be what he'd meant by our evolutions taking similar paths. Pladians and humans had a lot in common. At least where physiology was concerned.

Fascinating.

And so *not* what I needed to be concentrating on right now.

"So, if your *hypothesis*," I arched a brow at him, "is correct and I really did absorb some energy from that crystal, what's that mean for me?"

The marks on my palm gleamed faintly under the lamplight. Pladian writing. That's what those little shapes and marks were. A cosmic *howdy*.

When I looked up, I found Sky watching me with a tight expression.

"What?" I asked, tensing.

"It's hard to explain the nexus tech, but the halix was designed to impart information, Rae. So when I say you absorbed the energy, I mean…"

My heart thumped hard, a shocked thud against my breastbone. "You think I absorbed something more than just these marks."

"I think you absorbed the message the halix contained."

He said it gently, but the words rocked me to the core. Rooted me to the floor. I stared at him. He stared back, dead serious.

That couldn't be true. I wasn't some kind of human flash drive. I hadn't downloaded an alien info cache. I'd remember. I'd be…I'd be speaking Pladian and doing advanced physics equations or something, right? There'd be signs.

No, he had to be wrong. I hadn't unlocked any secrets of the universe just because I had some new artwork on my hand.

I scoffed, shaking my head. Everything had been normal. Ish. As normal as my life was right now.

"Sorry," I said, giving him a tight smile, even as my stomach did a little dive roll. "I hate to tell you this, but I think I'd know if I got zapped with alien info."

"You emitted a burst of Pladian energy at Oasis," Sky said flatly.

"What?" I jerked back. "How do you—"

"I ran a scan, and there was a residual signal."

"What kind of scan? How——"

"Not important," he said, slashing a hand through the air. "You'll have to trust me."

"*Trust* you?" I gawked at him. "You tried to wipe my memories and now you're saying I've got some kind of...some kind of other-worldly download in my brain! What message do you think I got zapped with?"

His jaw tightened. "Rae, I can't tell you everything. You'll have to trust me. I'm right about this."

"About my brain being stuffed with new information from an alien crystal info cache that exploded." Words I'd never imagined uttering. "I think I know my own mind."

"Be that as it may," Sky said, still in that calm, sure tone, "that's got to be why you remember what happened at the university and nobody else does. The halix...it changed something in you. Nullified the neural manipulation." I reeled a little at the term *neural manipulation*, but he plowed forward. "Maybe the ancient Pladians messed up and our tech interacts with human brains differently than anticipated. I don't know. There's no way to know without digging into this more——"

"Digging into my *brain?*" I whisper-yelled hoarsely.

"No, I——" Sky broke off on a curse and pinched the bridge of his nose for a second before letting his arm drop and pinning me with an intense look. I'd busted through the calm, it seemed. "Rae, you're in danger. You've got to at least believe me that *something* happened."

"Yeah, I nearly got annihilated by a murder robot!"

He didn't bat an eye. "You haven't had any symptoms at all? Nothing's different?"

I snapped my mouth closed and glared instead. It couldn't be true. I'd *know*, right? I fisted my marked hand tightly. "So is this why I'm in danger, then?"

He didn't answer right away, and when he looked away, I read the conflict in his tense profile. He was struggling again with his damn conscience. That stupid Creed. Annoyance rose beneath the shock and rising fear.

"Come on, Sky." I planted my hands on my hips. "I deserve to know."

He ran his tongue across his teeth and gave in. "Yes, that's the reason you're in danger. The Enil are here for the halix. It's why they're on Earth. They know Pladians left those devices behind when we visited planets, and they've been searching for that one here." His nostrils flared on an exhale. "Since they arrived, they've been scanning for the cache's energy signature. Methodically. And they finally caught up to it here in One Willow."

Chasing it. Tracking it.

Methodically. Like a...like a search grid.

Damn it.

I laughed once. It came out dry and cracked. "You've got to be kidding me. Kelly really was right."

Chapter 25

THE WORST TED TALK EVER

SKY WAS IN FRONT OF ME BEFORE I'D EVEN REGISTERED HE'D MOVED. "Kelly knows about this? Kelly from Oasis?"

I edged sideways just enough to put space between us. He didn't follow, but his eyes stayed glued to my face while I worked through a response.

"Yes. No. Kind of?" I set my phone beside the mace on the counter and scrubbed both palms over my face. That headache had started to throb again. "This group called FETR suspects aliens were looking for something, because of the weird electrical surges and…well, everything else."

When I focused on Sky again, he was watching me intently. He appeared to be processing.

That made two of us. A lot of processing happening tonight.

"So what happens now?" I asked when he still hadn't spoken a moment later.

He sighed. "I wish there was a simple answer to that." I couldn't help but notice he needed a shave. I wished it looked scruffy and gross. Instead, it gave him a rugged, sexier edge. "It depends on whether we can retrieve the information the halix imparted—"

"Oh my God, Sky. How many times do I have to tell you? No

information has been imparted!" I thrust my hand at him. "Just these weird marks!"

He considered them, then my face. "So you haven't been having any unusual dreams? Or any other strange symptoms?"

I stopped breathing.

Last night's dream…

My reaction must've been obvious because his expression darkened with a grim sort of triumph.

"That's what I thought. You don't understand the significance of this, Rae."

"You're right," I snapped, grateful for the anger's burn. It chased away the chills his implication left behind. "I don't understand. So how about you explain it to me? Because your so-called explanation is full of gaping holes."

Black holes, maybe, since I felt like all the gravity in the room was warping. Reality itself.

Sky's mouth compressed again, and I raised my chin. I couldn't help but curl my fingers to tuck the mark out of sight. Then I vented my frustration on my cardigan, yanking it closed and folding my arms over it.

There was no sudden influx of knowledge in my brain. No message. I'd know.

"Speaking of holes." I squinted at him. "You were here looking for this halix tablet thing, and it just *happened* to be at TWU? That's a hell of a coincidence."

His eyes narrowed a little at the subject change, but he only lifted a shoulder. "It would be if I hadn't arranged for the tablet to be brought here. My partner and I have been tracking it for years, chasing down every possible lead. The Enil cracked the code first and found a way to trace the signature much more efficiently than we'd been able to. Like they knew exactly what to…"

He broke off, squeezing his nape. Muscles bunched beneath his shirt. Way more than was fair in this moment, if we're being real.

He let his arm fall to his side and continued. "We'd located it, but it was inside a government research facility. We couldn't figure out how to get in. The only chance we had was to get it moved.

Transferred." He waved a hand in the air, like he was brushing off the work. "So we found a way to connect Professor Stern at TWU with the right people. It took a couple years of planning, but it worked. The military agreed to move the tablet here. To a less secure facility." He looked up, brows lifting in a subtle arch. "So no, not a coincidence. A lot of work and a lot of careful planning."

A couple years' worth, even. Kelly had said Sky had been at Oasis for two. An undercover alien playing bartender while waiting to intercept an ancient alien artifact. That wasn't exactly on my bingo card.

"What happened at the university is my fault," Sky said suddenly—in a rush. As if the words had been pent up too long. I blinked, caught off guard. His jaw tightened. "I underestimated them. I didn't know how many Enil were here—or how close they'd gotten to finding the halix. I sure as hell didn't expect them to get to TWU at the same time I did…" He huffed a bitter laugh. "I suppose it getting destroyed is better than the Enil getting their hands on it, though."

I frowned at that. I was missing an important part of this puzzle. "You said it was just a greeting. Why is that so important?"

His eyes flicked to mine, then away. "I can't tell you that, Rae."

"Part of it is literally tattooed on my hand. I think that earns me the inside scoop."

"Maybe we can find a way to remove it," he said, dodging the question. He turned on his heel and began to pace. "Maybe we can extract the information. Bast would know. He's better with tech than I am."

"And who is Bast?"

"My partner," he said over his shoulder.

"Exactly how many Pladians are roaming around Earth?"

He sent me a sidelong look. "Just us. Bast and me. We're a Pair."

Two more than I'd anticipated before this afternoon. Well, that was fine and dandy. It didn't matter. I didn't want Sky, this Bast, or any other potential alien visitors extracting *anything* from me.

So I tried again, this time more gently. "There's no information, Sky. I'm telling you. I don't feel any different. Weird dreams are totally normal considering how weird *everything* is right now. In case you haven't noticed, my life's become pretty insane."

"I know. For what it's worth, I'm sorry." He paused in his pacing to peek out the blinds again. "But even if you don't recall anything now, there's a chance you will with time."

"Recall *what*? I wouldn't even know what I'm looking for!" Irritated, I tugged on my frizzy braid, tossing it behind me. "Was I supposed to start speaking Pladian or something? I told you, everything's been normal since the lab. The UFO on the road, the lab—"

"You *did* see the Enil scout probe on the road," Sky cut in, spinning around to face me. "I *knew* it wasn't an animal. You're a terrible liar, you know."

So everyone kept telling me. I rolled my eyes.

"Yeah, well, we all can't be a locked vault of alien secrets." At my pointed scowl, he merely raised an eyebrow, and I shook my head. "That doesn't change the fact that besides the shiny version of you showing up today, things have been relatively normal the last few days. I haven't shown any signs of anything else. Just these marks."

Dragging in a steadying breath, I lifted my hand. The pearlescent etchings gleamed faintly in the dimness. Alien symbols. I felt the weight of Sky's gaze, but I couldn't look up.

Alien markings. Alien visitors. Alien *robots*.

To think two weeks ago, my biggest stressors were exams, Faith, and fifty-cent wing night.

When I raised my head, Sky was still watching me, his expression unreadable. Lightning blazed through the slats, bathing him in blue light, hollowing out his handsome features into something starker and striking.

He was a Pladian.

And yet his face was so familiar.

"You killed the Enil in the lab," I said, battling a shiver at the thought. "Didn't you?"

That familiar face shuttered completely. "I took care of it."

"By...killing it?"

At the question, his eyes darted to mine, then slid past. He shoved his hands into his pockets, shifting his stance like he was uncomfortable. He didn't answer, but…

"So that's a yes," I whispered. The realization settled with a metallic clang in my gut, as if a giant robotic dinosaur foot had planted its weight on my middle.

Just what exactly was he capable of if he'd taken out that Enil?

Apparently a lot more than slinging whiskey sours and pouring local drafts.

As if picking up my sudden apprehension, Sky exhaled through his nose, closing his eyes. "I've never told anyone any of this, Rae. If it wasn't so important that you understand the danger you're in—if I didn't fully believe you'd absorbed the halix—I wouldn't be here."

I believed him about that, at least. He looked borderline distraught. Breaking that Creed of his really *was* bothering him. I wouldn't have pegged Sky for such a rules stickler. It'd be cute if my life didn't hinge on whatever part of this he was keeping to himself.

With that same, defeated expression, he elaborated, "Technically, no, I didn't kill the Enil. But I neutralized the one you saw at the lab. And I haven't picked up any more activity in the area since. For now, at least."

Well. That was good to know. On one hand, glad they weren't lurking around every corner.

On the other, *he'd taken out a killer robot.*

So Sky wasn't just an alien. He was an alien badass.

He chose that moment to step closer, and I stiffened before I could stop it. He halted a few feet from me, face tightening. Tension arced between us, thick with words—spoken and otherwise—the revelations of the night. All he'd dumped on me.

Everything had changed, including how I saw Sky. That'd never go back to normal. The version of the man I'd pined over for the better part of a year was gone. Maybe I'd mourn it if I wasn't so overwhelmed.

And yet when he took another step, I froze, stuck somewhere between backing away and staying right there, waiting for him. The simultaneous urges tangled up my insides. Just like my thoughts, I couldn't begin to pick apart the mess of confusing feelings when it came to *this* Sky.

He seemed to know, too. Or maybe he was feeling just as tangled. Hard to tell. His hands twitched at his sides like he wanted to reach for me, but I was glad he didn't. My nerves were strung tighter than harp wire. I couldn't guarantee I wouldn't snatch up the pepper spray and blast him in the face. I was holding on by a thread.

It was either that or kiss him. Maybe vent all this wound-up tension into *that* instead. At the thought, my stomach flipped.

...alien, Rae. He's an alien.

"This is a long, convoluted explanation for what happened today," he murmured. That fatigue was back, tugging at the skin around his eyes. "It's complicated, and I'm sorry I can't tell you more. I would if I could. Believe me. But I'm telling you the truth when it comes to those marks."

He tipped his chin toward my palm. I tugged my cardigan sleeve down over it, self-conscious for some reason.

His dark eyes found mine again. "You need to lie low until I figure out what's going on here. With the markings. With the Enil. Most importantly, how to fix the signal you're emitting and whatever else the halix's done."

Another denial tried to surface, and I clicked my tongue in protest, but he didn't let me get a word in.

"I know it's a lot to ask, but I need you to stay out of sight. Stay here, if that's what you'd prefer. Where I can keep you safe."

Even though I felt a floaty little flutter at the protectiveness, I shook my head. "Out of sight isn't possible. I have work. School. A *life*. I've got midterms this week. I can't just skip those."

"Tell them you're sick. Figure something out. I told you, the Enil are tracking the halix," he said, his pointed gaze dropping to my palm before rising slowly to mine. "Its *energy*, Rae."

Oh. *Oh.*

Oh no.

I took a step back, like I could outrun what he was suggesting. I was almost embarrassed it'd taken so long to catch on. "You think the Enil can track *me* now."

"Yes." Sky's throat worked in a heavy swallow. The blood drained out of my head so fast, I swayed. He caught it, judging by the apologetic tilt of his full mouth. "I'm sorry, Rae. But yes, that's exactly what I think. And I know you don't want to hear this, but that energy pulse at Oasis was strong enough to scramble my synth-skin. Something I didn't even know was possible. I have no idea what the range is on the Enil scanners, but…"

I'd seen my own hand *glow*. I'd seen his alien form. I couldn't deny something had happened, and it'd happened the moment I touched him with my marked palm. Too much of a coincidence to argue against the correlation.

Which meant, as much as I hated it, I couldn't refute his asser-tion that something had changed. That didn't mean I was ready to agree I was a Google Drive for an alien info cache. But my hand *had* shone like a star. Something was up.

As if reading my grudging acceptance, Sky nodded slowly. "I know this is your life we're talking about. I know you're over-whelmed, and I'm asking a lot. And I really am sorry this happened. I never wanted you of all people to get dragged into this."

I wanted to ask what exactly he meant by that, but he wasn't done. His voice hardened.

"But you don't know the Enil. You don't know what they're capable of." He stepped even closer until I had to tilt my head back to meet his intense gaze. "They won't hesitate to kill you to get what they want. They'll tear you apart to extract whatever has changed inside you. Even if it breaks you. Even if it *kills* you. They won't care."

I shuddered. Sky stared down at me, a muscle tightening in his cheek God, he painted a vivid, horrifying picture. Vivid enough, my insides pitched and rolled. If he was hoping to scare me, he was doing a great job.

Not that it took much. I could imagine all too well what the Enil could do. Those clawed hands. That iron grip. The visceral fear while being hunted by a mechanical monster—it all slammed back.

The bruises on my arm were nothing compared to what it could've done. This part, at least, I had no trouble believing. I could believe they weren't burdened by pesky things like a conscience.

A darker thought crept in. *Sky* was an alien, too. How was I to know *he* felt things like I did? Mouth dry, I took him in with newfound trepidation.

But as the doubts rose, I remembered the distress he'd shown at Oasis when I'd seen his real form. That had looked real enough. And so did the regret in his eyes now, as he watched my emotions play out on my face.

Like before, I tried to compare this version of him—the true version—with the one I knew. His calm, steady presence behind the bar. That polite, dimpled smile. He charmed old ladies as easily as he breathed. Then there was the way he'd helped me that night he'd found me run off the road. His quiet concern and his competence. Hell, he'd even opened my car door for me and waited to make sure I got inside my apartment.

Like a good guy. A good alien. A good, alien guy.

I knew he'd hidden his true self, but if that'd *all* been acting, he deserved an intergalactic Oscar. Beyond the whole shiny-skin-and-murderybot-killer thing, he'd really passed as just another nice Midwestern guy. He served drinks. Drove an SUV. Had a butt that looked like it'd been engineered for denim.

So then…what *was* real?

It had to be somewhere in the middle.

Was I looking at the real Sky? This tense, stressed-out version with a day-old beard and worry shining in his too-blue eyes? The mysterious alien visitor with the weight of the world on his shoulders who was pacing my living room and pleading with me to let him protect me?

That fluttery feeling was back, coupled with curiosity that itched like a rash I shouldn't scratch. I shook both off. I couldn't afford to wonder about him. About his past. About his species. About any parts of his…*anatomy*. Butt or otherwise.

This was my life. Not his mission.

"No," I said, tightening my arms across my chest. "I'm not skipping midterms. There must be another option that doesn't involve messing up my future."

"Hard to have a future if you're dead," he muttered, clenching his teeth.

The retort hit home hard enough I flinched. When I gaped at him in dismay, he winced and hung his head.

"Sorry. That was uncalled for." He inhaled deeply and seemed to gather himself before raising his face and trying again. This time with less vehemence. "But even if I'm wrong and the Enil *can't* track you directly, the last place the halix was seen was the university. You can bet they'll be watching. There are probably more Enil on their way here already. That one in the lab was just…one. Of many." He scrubbed a hand over his mouth before fixing me with a resigned look. "I'm telling you the truth. It isn't *safe*."

I tried not to focus on the idea of an army of angry mechanical creatures from outer space and instead on the fact *this* particular alien was arguing against my autonomy. I wasn't stupid. I understood the stakes. But surely…surely there was a compromise here. If he could track the Enil, he could keep an eye out. That meant I shouldn't have to become a paranoid shut-in like those people I'd read about on the internet.

I squared my shoulders. "I appreciate that you're trying to keep my brain matter intact, but Sky, I can't just hole up in my apartment indefinitely or until this invasion is done or whatever."

"It's not indefinite." He swiped a hand through his hair, gritting out, "And it's not an invasion."

"Potatoes, pot*ah*toes," I muttered, brushing off the flat stare he angled my way.

I still had a thousand unanswered questions, but my mind felt foggy. Probably because of all the new info I'd been cramming into it. The truth was so much more complicated than I could've anticipated.

But that didn't mean I was about to blindly follow orders from some overprotective alien with a savior complex. I shook my head again. "No, Sky. I can't."

Challenge glinted in his eyes, a flash of stubbornness that sent equal parts apprehension and exhilaration zipping up my spine. I held his gaze, though. I was proud of the fact I didn't waver.

An impasse. A good, old-fashioned standoff—except instead of the Wild West, we were in a sci-fi thriller.

A chill ghosted down the back of my neck. What happened if we couldn't come to an agreement? Would he stop me? Would he *make* me stay? Would he steal me away inside his flying saucer?

A lump lodged itself in my throat, but something, my trusty gut instincts maybe, told me...no. He wouldn't. After all, why bother trying to reason with me or explain any of this? If he was going to abduct me, that spaceship would've already sailed.

Maybe that was against his Creed, too, abducting humans.

Sniffing, I looked away. Another bright flash of blue lightning snuck through my blinds, evidence the fall storm was still going strong. Crazy weather for a crazy night.

And it *was* crazy. Insane. This whole thing.

This was what I got for not letting it go. For going after Professor Stern. For poking the UFO-shaped bear. Now I had a cryptic alien burn mark, an agitated extraterrestrial in my living room, and killer robot stalkers.

God, what a week.

When I turned back to Sky again, something in him had shifted. That tense frustration had drained from his expression. He gave a long-suffering sigh and squinted at me. "Okay. Fine. If you're insisting on still going to class, then I'm going with you."

"You're...what?" I blinked at him. "You can't just *go* with me to class. That's not how college works. There's no *Take Your Alien to School Day!*"

He leveled me a cutting stare, obviously not a fan of my hilarious sarcasm. "If you're set on going, I'm coming with you. That's the compromise, Raven."

The way he growled my name in that low, irritated voice wasn't helping me stay impartial. With effort, I persevered. "So now you're just my alien bodyguard? We've graduated from lurking to full-blown shadow status?" When he simply folded his arms, jaw jutting obstinately, I pushed away from the counter, scooping up my phone and narrowing my eyes at him. "All because I've got some fancy alien tattoo I can't even read, and you refuse to tell me why it matters? You realize this is completely insane, right?"

"Is it?" He squared up to me, eyes sharp. "Which part is insane, exactly? You *know* I'm right. Something happened to you. You saw your hand glow."

He had me there. The hand in question tingled.

"Then there's the fact you withstood a memory wipe," he continued tightly. "And there's the signal you emitted. I saw the residual readings with my own eyes. Is that enough for you?"

My pulse quickened, and I ground my molars. He was being infuriatingly rational. I, on the other hand, wasn't entirely sure why I was pushing back this hard.

Maybe it was because everything felt like it was spiraling so out of control, and this was just *one more thing*.

Sky's eyes slid back and forth between mine, too astute. Too perceptive. "You might not remember anything yet, but something's in there, Rae. And until we figure out what, or at least until we figure out how to block the signal from the Enil, you're in danger and I'm sticking close."

We were back to staring at each other again, back to that stand-off. He had me. A phantom fist wrapped my heart, squeezing tight enough to make breathing tough. It was the uncanny sensation of being trapped.

Sky searched my eyes, and like he saw the hopelessness threatening to swell up, his expression softened. "Come on, Rae. You're smart. One of the smartest people I know. You know I'm right."

I bit my cheek. Well, wasn't that just sweet? If I wasn't damn near miserable at being told my life wasn't going back to normal anytime soon, I might have basked in the genuine compliment coming from Sky Acosta. Nothing was better than a guy admiring your brain.

Unless he was admiring it because it held alien secrets, that is.

I buried my face in my palms, shoulders slumping, suppressing the urge to yell in frustration. Dropping my arms, I sighed. "Fine. I won't go waving my hand at any Enil." He started to relax, but I pinned him with a tight stare. "But if this is all so dangerous, why won't you tell me what they want with this tablet? Or what *you* want with it, while we're at it."

He turned his face away. "I just can't. It's better if you don't know."

This time I did move closer, shifting to the side until he was forced to look at me. "When is ignorance ever the better option?"

"I *can't*, Rae." White lines formed around his mouth before he bit out, "I told you. It's complicated. *Please* don't push."

He looked miserable enough, I relented. If only because he'd obviously smashed his rules to bits tonight giving me this much.

I filed it away, though. Bet your ass I'd be trying again later.

"Fine," I whispered, and his eyes sprang open, lips parting in surprise.

"Fine?"

I spread my free hand in a shrug. "I'd rather not end up as robot bait, so…whatever you need to do to prevent that from happening."

"Great." His smile was quick and bright—and damn that stupid dimple. I was still recovering from it when he twisted and gave the living room an assessing glance. "I'll take the couch."

Whoa, *whoa.*

Everything went quiet. My brain. The storm. Possibly my heartbeat, because I was pretty sure I'd just keeled over and died.

Did he mean what I thought he meant?

"The couch?" I repeated, breathing faster. "Are you saying you're staying *here? Now?*"

He turned back around and frowned at me. "Well, yeah. That's the easiest way to make sure you're safe. Right?"

Seeming not to notice me staring in mute horror, he peeled off his jacket. A bolt of heat flashed through me. His shirt beneath was still damp and stretched tight across his shoulders as he walked away from me, carrying the wet leather into the kitchen.

I turned my attention to the blank wall.

If his synth-skin really mimicked human biology, did it also go out of its way to include *underwear model* upgrades?

But when he returned from draping his damp coat over the

counter, I risked another glance. He appeared annoyingly relaxed now, like he'd decided and that was that. Like he'd already claimed squatters' rights to my throw pillows.

A flare of panic launched in my belly. Sky couldn't stay here. I needed to be alone. To think. To think *alone.*

I couldn't do that with Sky being here, all confusing and mysterious and—what was wrong with me—*still so hot...*

"No," I said firmly. "You don't have to...stay here. I appreciate the offer and all, but that's not necessary."

He ignored me. When he didn't even turn from adjusting my couch cushions, I marched over to him.

"Did you not hear me? You're not *sleeping with me.*"

My mouth formed an O of horror. Lightning flashed. Thunder boomed.

That—that wasn't what I'd meant to say. A faux pas. A Freudian slip of the highest order.

And now...silence. Sky, too, stilled mid-pillow fluff, his back to me. Any hope he'd missed it vanished. He'd heard what I'd said.

Every one of my cells screamed in silent, abject misery. Why was I forever making an idiot out of myself around this man?

Around this alien. Alien man. Whatever.

"That's not what I meant," I whispered, face flaming. "You're not sleeping *here*. In this apartment. Like, with me here, too. That's what I meant."

Too late. It was far too late.

He set down the throw pillow and turned to face me, brows raised. "Well, yeah. I didn't think you were offering to share your bed. I just admitted I was from another planet." He waited a beat, then cocked his head, a small smile toying with the edges of his mouth. "But you know, if that's your idea of staying safe, I'm open to negotiations."

That smirk deepened. I gazed up at him. "Negotiations..."

I was sure he was good at negotiating. I'd bet he was outstanding at *negotiations* of all kinds.

When I continued to gaze stupidly up at him, having turned into a stone, his grin faded. "I'm kidding, Rae. It's just the couch."

I jerked, coming back to life. "Right. Of course."

Of course he was kidding.

I shouldn't be thinking that way, either. I shouldn't be imagining doing any…negotiating with him.

This was Sky. Alien Sky. From the stars. The sparkly-skin, Enil-fighting, mind-wiping bartender.

Who was now in my living room. Still kind of wet. Being hot. Being…*flirty?*

Oh my God. He'd been flirting with me. And now he was staring at *me*, eyes slightly narrowed, like he wasn't sure what I was thinking.

Bad thoughts.

I pressed my lips together and went into defense mode because it was a much better choice than abandoning all my standards and wrestling him onto my couch.

"Good. I'm glad you're kidding. Because not in a million years, Starboy," I said, backing away. I fixed a sneer on my burning face for good measure. "My life is complicated enough. I don't need alien STDs, too."

His eyes widened, like I'd stunned him. Then he let out a rich, genuine laugh that did funny things to my insides. I'd only heard that laugh a handful of times in the six months I'd known him. It transformed his face, flashing white teeth and crinkling the skin around his eyes.

Broody Sky was attractive. Happy Sky was gorgeous.

I wondered briefly what it'd take for happy Sky to make more appearances, then pushed aside the thought. That wasn't something I needed to be worried about right now.

I needed to be concerned with the Sky currently trying to camp out on my couch.

"For the record, I can't carry anything, remember?" he said, his grin lopsided and maybe a little chagrined. "The suit?"

My face was on fire and having absolutely nothing to say in response to that tidbit of knowledge I could've done with never being privy to, I could only stare.

His smile fading, Sky angled his chin to assess his rumpled shirt and reached for its buttons. "But you're right. Any of...*that* would complicate things." His fingers stilled and he huffed a weak laugh. "Well, complicate things more. It's best we keep our distance if we're going to work together to fix this."

He darted a glance at me, then back down. I opened my mouth to respond, came up blank, and shut it again. Well, at least we agreed on no sexy time. Because that would be, like, the *worst* idea.

...right?

I didn't have a chance to analyze what my urge to argue said about me before he began working his way down his shirt. Only then did I realize he was unfastening buttons. It fell open and suddenly I was faced with a chiseled chest and a flat, tanned stomach rippling with eight whole abs.

I swallowed a squeak and spun around. Partially to give him privacy and partially to give myself a breather.

Because damn.

Sky was telling me to keep my distance while stripping in my living room. That seemed counterintuitive. It was also suddenly very hot in here again, too. I gulped air and stopped just short of fanning myself.

"Seriously, Sky. I don't know if it's the best idea for you to stay here," I said, glad my tone came out cool despite my racing heart and very *not* cool face. "I...I think I need to be alone."

After that display, possibly with BOB, the battery-operated boyfriend.

ALIEN, Rae. He's an alien.

Over the blood rushing in my ears, I heard Sky's frustrated exhale.

"I'm not going to force it, obviously. This is your choice." It came from much closer than he'd been a second ago, meaning he'd brought his chest and abs with him.

Steeling myself, I turned around. He had closed the distance between us, and all humor had vanished from his expression. I didn't miss the flash of disappointment. "But at least consider it, okay? For your own safety."

I kept my eyes firmly fastened on his face despite the fact there was an awful lot of very human-looking skin on display in my periphery.

But he radiated heat. And he smelled good.

"My safety. I like safety," I whispered weakly. So much skin.

He was looking at me now, too, his arms at his sides. There was caution and something else lurking behind his mask, something that looked like it could be curiosity—

But then a pounding sounded at my door.

Chapter 26

UNINHIBITED FLIRTING OBJECTIVES

I SPUN TOWARD SKY. Forgetting, for a second, his mostly naked state in lieu of panic.

The knock faded into silence. Sudden, waiting silence filled only by the hissing rain and my own unsteady breathing. Neither of us moved for a full ten seconds.

Then I broke free of the shock and whirled to face the stairwell instead. My pulse stuttered. The microwave clock read eight-thirty at night. Who would be stopping by now?

Amelia hadn't answered my text, had she? A glance at my phone told me no.

"Are you expecting anyone?" Sky asked, eyeing my phone grimly when I set it back down. His shoulders had bunched. The vivid ice-blue chips in his eyes looked brighter than normal.

"No," I whispered, like my words could carry down the stairs and through the door. "I texted Amelia a while ago, but she never answered."

"Okay. Get behind me." Without waiting for an answer, he strode around me and headed toward the stairs.

It took me a heartbeat to catch up. "Wait—hang on!"

He didn't, so I surged forward and grabbed his arm, pulling. He paused at the top of the stairs and, at my tug, turned. I tightened my grip on his forearm. The tense muscles felt like iron.

I took a deep breath. "If it's Bob or Amelia..." I didn't know how to put my reluctance into words, but I wasn't ready to explain this to anyone. Explain *him*. Being here. Not yet, anyway. I licked my lips. "Just let me check first, okay? I don't want you answering my door. Especially with you...well, this." I gestured vaguely at his half-open shirt and all that other...stuff.

He looked down, then back up. A flicker of complete confusion crinkled his forehead, like I'd just handed him a math problem in Sanskrit. Except he could've probably figured that one out.

He eventually figured this out, too.

"You're...embarrassed to have me here?" He said it slowly, like the concept was foreign. He blinked at me once, twice. "Why? Nobody knows what I am. Except you."

I flushed. Especially because his reaction brought back, *in vivid HD*, that one time I'd told him I didn't want his number.

"Do you not usually bring people here...?" Sky stilled suddenly, like something had occurred to him. His gaze darted to mine. "Do you have a boyfriend or—"

"*No!*" I blurted, a strangled laugh escaping me. I realized I was still holding his forearm and released it hastily. "No, I bring...well, I *have* brought...sometimes..."

I trailed off. Sky was studying me intently, and I couldn't for the life of me determine what he was thinking. Not that it mattered. I was *not* talking to him about my love life. Or lack thereof.

Especially not when there was a potential threat at my door.

Flustered, I pulled my cardigan closed and set my phone back on the counter. We were up here having a discussion, and the FBI could be at my door.

"I just want to answer my own door, okay?" I told him. "I shouldn't have to explain myself." I wasn't sure I could. "You can come down with me, but *I'm* answering it. So stay back."

He held up his hands as I brushed past. His footsteps were quiet as he followed me into the stairwell.

We'd made it halfway before another knock sounded, sharper

this time. Impatient and loud enough, I jolted and snatched the banister, narrowly avoiding tumbling down the rest of the way.

"Careful," Sky murmured.

Yeah, no kidding. Licking my lips, I called out, "Just a second!"

No one answered. I sensed Sky sticking close as I made short work of the rest of the stairs. My heart thudded against my ribs by the time I reached the bottom.

My hand hovered over the deadbolt. *Note to self: install a damn peephole.* I hesitated and glanced back. Sky had joined me in the narrow entry, standing off to the side and out of sight, ready and waiting. He gave a single nod.

Here went nothing. At least killer robots probably didn't bother knocking.

I unlocked the door and eased it open. Relief hissed out of me like a popped tire. Amelia stood there, scowling.

"What the hell, Rae?" She adjusted her sleek black umbrella, her cheery yellow raincoat gleaming under the porch light. "Took you long enough. It's pouring. What were you doing in there?"

Arguing with a shirtless alien. A slightly deranged laugh got stuck in my throat, but just then, Amelia moved to step forward. I leaned out to block her.

She stopped. Her eyes narrowed. "What's going on?"

So much. I couldn't think of a single lie. I tried to smile. "Sorry. I was, uh…in the shower."

"Ri-ght." She snapped her gum, very obviously taking in my dry hair and loungewear. "I was around the corner studying at Joanie's when I got your text. I thought you were working tonight. So can I come in or what?"

"Now's not…a great time." I could *feel* Sky behind me. He was quiet but impossible to ignore. Just like our unfinished conversation.

"You texted *me* to come over like an hour ago— Wait." Amelia's amber eyes narrowed further into slits, then flew wide. Her lips curled into a slow, delighted grin. "Is somebody in there with you?"

Damn it. She knew me *way* too well.

I tried to summon a denial, but she tipped closer and dropped her voice to a stage-whisper. "You have a guy over or something?"

I recoiled. "What? *No.*" Not technically a lie. Pladians didn't count as guys, did they? I laughed, and this time it sounded genuine. Mostly. "Nobody's here."

She rocked onto the heels of her rainboots with a dramatic sigh. "Damn. I was really hoping you were finally taking a shot at that sexy bartender you work with."

Lightning flashed across the sky like a bony hand ready to slap me into the next dimension. Which could be exactly what I needed. I gawked at her, horrified.

Oh…oh no.

A soft thud sounded behind me, like Sky had bumped against the wall. My pride shriveled up and died. I shook my head frantically, mouth working, but words wouldn't come.

Luckily for me, Amelia didn't have that problem.

"I haven't gotten a chance to talk to you about this! I saw you guys dancing before you ghosted me at Crescent. I get it now. You weren't kidding when you described his ass." I lifted a hand like I could physically shove this conversation away, but Amelia only tilted her head, peering at me from beneath her dripping umbrella. "You should do it. Go after him. You've spent the last year panting for him, and I bet he's a good time. They say if a guy can dance…" She grinned like the devil herself.

Which made sense because this was hell. I was in it. I gazed at her, arm falling limply to my side. My throat had closed. Helpless, I tried to will her into silence with my eyes, but it didn't work.

She plowed on like a charging bull dressed in couture. "That's what you need, you know. You've been super stressed. And it's been, like, ten months since you've gotten laid."

What? *Ten* months?

That was enough. I tried to scoff, but it got stuck, and instead I choked out a garbled correction. "No, it hasn't. It's been four!"

Okay, six. *Fine,* seven.

Purely a coincidence that'd been when my last relationship had ended and…when I'd started at Oasis.

Fine. I'd been too stuck on Sky since then to entertain the idea of anyone else. I wasn't admitting that right now, though.

With him. Hearing *all* this. I wondered if it was too late to call the Enil to come crush me.

Desperate to derail this descent into my own personal nightmare, I spewed words. "I'm not— I mean, I'm over him. I definitely have *not* been lusting after him."

"What are you talking about?" Amelia snorted in disbelief. "Uh, yeah, you have. Last time you got drunk, you spent half the night having ChatAI name your future children."

Well, I was going to die now. Killed not by alien murder robot, but by humiliation. I closed my eyes. Any minute now, my ghost would leave my body. Death was imminent. I welcomed it.

"That...I never did that," I whispered. Cold sweat beaded on my forehead.

When I opened my eyes, I saw she'd raised a brow. "You did."

"Right, but that was before." I tried for a scoff. "Really, A, I'm over it. He's got some real, um, issues. The kind that make him very, very...*not* someone I'd want to do...that... with."

"Yeah, well," *snap* went her gum, "as long as his issues aren't bad dick—"

"Okay!" I said loudly, cutting her off as Sky let out a shocked laugh behind me. Hopefully the storm drowned him out. "*Well.* I'll keep that in mind! Thanks for stopping by. I'm fine. Great. Everything's fine."

Amelia angled her head to the side. "You're acting weird."

"Yes!" I smiled. It felt like baring my teeth. "You know me. Just weird. Going to take a bath. Early night. Alone. Very alone."

"I thought you just took a shower." I stared at her with wide eyes, and she took a step back, pursing her lips. "O-okay. Whatever. Well, text me if you need me."

"Will do. Bye!" I slammed the door shut and slumped against it, forehead to wood. I could feel Sky's eyes burning into my back. My face was on fire again. My neck, too, this time. Everything. My whole life. One big dumpster fire.

"I've changed my mind," I muttered. "You can go ahead and kill me now."

Sky chuckled softly. The sound was unfairly sexy. Talk about kicking me while I was down.

"Oh, come on. It wasn't that bad," he said, but I could hear the smile in his voice. Maybe even a little smugness. Like that'd been good for his alien ego.

That was great for him. It also happened to be the single most humiliating experience of my life.

Did she have to mention the ChatAI night? I'd completely forgotten about my hypothetical children, Hamilton and Stella Acosta.

I groaned, burying my face in my hands. "That wasn't...what she said wasn't what it sounded like." I winced into my palms. "Would you believe me if I said she was talking about a *different* bartender I work with who I *also* happened to dance with at Crescent last weekend?"

He hummed as if giving it actual thought. "Well, considering Derek and his husband are on a beach somewhere this week, Ashley was working, and I happened to be off—and at Crescent—you're kind of out of options."

Right. He'd been there because he'd been following me. Dropping my hands, I closed my eyes. Maybe if I didn't move, he'd disappear.

But when I opened them, he was still very much there, leaning against the stairwell wall. His jeans sat dangerously low, framing his tapered hips and the hard cut of his abs disappearing beneath the waistband. I hadn't thought that V-shaped hipbone thing was *real.* I'd been sure it only existed on romance book covers.

But there it was.

Then I realized I was staring at his hipbones and hastily dragged my gaze to his face. Unfortunately, his raised brow and faint smile told me he knew exactly where I'd been looking. Great.

He pushed off the wall, moving toward me until he was close enough to touch.

I didn't. Touch him, that is. But I wanted to. The way he looked at me, eyes glinting with laughter and...something like *interest,* my belly flipped.

Alien. Sky was an alien. I shouldn't still want to—

"Things probably don't even work the same, right?" I blurted before I could consider the words. The second they slipped out, I stiffened.

What the actual hell was wrong with me?

"Uh." Sky drew back. "What do you mean?"

I stared at the wall over his shoulder. "N-never mind."

I could see him studying me from the corner of my eye, though. Intently. Like he, too, was wondering what my problem was.

Then he leaned in—so suddenly, I gasped. He kept leaning until he braced one hand on the door above me, crowding me back a step.

My heart skidded to a stop. He still smelled like rain. Like Sky. Like a mistake I very much wanted to make.

A heated thrill settled low. I dragged my gaze up past his perfectly sculpted pectorals to his face, only to find the humor had drained from his features, replaced with seriousness.

He wasn't gazing passionately at me. My cardigan had slipped down, and he was staring hard at my upper arm. At the marks left by the Enil.

I balked when he reached out, but he stopped just shy of touching me, fingers hovering above my skin. His frown deepened as he took in the bruising wrapped around my bicep. The six, individual fingers drawn in blotchy purple and blue. The clearly defined handprint stood out, thanks to my skimpy tank top.

Along with my very obvious, very chilly nipples, which was just great.

"Is this from the Enil?" he asked quietly.

I assumed he wasn't talking about the nipples. The mention of the killer robots chased away the awareness, replacing it with coldness. I bit the inside of my cheek. "Yeah. From when it grabbed me. Right after I pulled the tablet—the halix, I mean, out of the box."

I was lucky it hadn't snapped my arm in two. I shuddered at the memory of shrieking metal, the storm of electricity, and the sheer terror. That painful grip.

But it all faded when Sky's gaze lifted back to mine. Warmth prickled up my neck. He was near enough, his chest nearly brushed mine when I sucked in a deep breath. And he was—*lord*—so stupidly attractive. The awareness was back, and the liquid ache in my belly made it excruciatingly clear I was still affected by it. By him.

Despite everything I knew, despite everything he'd said, I still wanted him.

Alien, alien, alien, I chanted silently. It didn't help.

I shouldn't still want to kiss him. I didn't even know what parts of him were…well, *human*.

But I sure wanted to find out.

I was willing to explore the possibilities on behalf of the entire human race.

My mouth went dry.

Clueless to how deeply I was spiraling into inappropriate interest in his physiology, Sky sighed. "I know I've apologized a million times, but I never meant for you to get caught up in this mess. The lab…everything just happened so fast." That was regret shining in his eyes now, when they slid from the bruising and found mine. "But I should've done better. They never should've touched you."

There was that protectiveness again. It made me all soft and gooey inside. It didn't help that his gaze sparkled with that alien light, like it held swirls of nebulae.

"It's okay," I managed to whisper.

"It's not." His murmur came out hoarse. "I hate that they hurt you."

I blinked, caught off guard by his vehemence. "It's just a bruise." One that still throbbed if I laid on it wrong, but still. "And it's not your fault. You couldn't have known I'd be there."

He gave his head a little shake. My attention slipped down and caught on his lips. They were awfully close. Mere inches from mine.

And they looked human enough.

There were a thousand reasons why thinking that, standing this close, and noticing how easy it'd be to smash my mouth against his were all terrible, *terrible* ideas. But I couldn't recall a single one. Common sense had fled the scene.

I only realized I'd been staring when his mouth curved into a crooked, knowing smile.

"Rae…" he said softly, a tinge of that regret coloring his tone. His voice had deepened, though. Enough a shiver passed through me.

"Yes?" I yanked my eyes upward to meet his again, cheeks scorching.

Something had changed. Beneath that ghost of a grin, I read a struggle in his tightening jaw, the sudden tension in his shoulders. I had the reckless urge to raise up on my toes just enough to wipe it away with—

I should be running far away. Calling the FBI. Hiding. Not leaning in.

But I didn't want to do any of that. I wanted to press my lips to Sky's.

He broke eye contact and looked down at the bruise again. This time when he reached for me, he didn't stop. His knuckles grazed the discolored skin, light as butterfly wings and reverent. I bit back a gasp.

My belly tightened. It was my arm, for God's sake. Not exactly an erogenous zone. But my mouth was a desert anyway as I asked, "What are you doing?"

He didn't look up. "Not sure. Not keeping my distance like I'd said we should, though."

Sky raised his head. His expression was impossible to decipher.

The stairwell seemed to melt away, like we were floating in soft shadow. The sound of the storm outside was muffled beneath my shaky breathing, my racing pulse.

He didn't move. Neither did I. His heat made me want to lean in, but because he wore a faint frown, I didn't. I'd give anything to know what he was thinking right then. Because it *seemed* like he was feeling this, too, this electricity. But that was clearly conflict—

I nearly gasped when he cupped the side of my face. My heart stopped beating as he bit his lip and gave his head the tiniest shake, eyes darkening.

"Just this once," he murmured, gaze lowering to my mouth. "You make it really hard to follow my rules, Raven."

Before I could even grasp what he'd said, what he was saying, he kissed me.

Sky Acosta was kissing me.

Time slowed. My soul left my body.

I decided I also hated rules because I never wanted this to end.

His mouth brushed mine in a gentle, teasing slide, and I gripped his shoulders for balance. To catch myself because my legs went weak and my head was a spinny, dizzy ball of fluff. No thoughts. Only feelings.

He captured my lower lip between his, giving it a slow and deliberate tug, and I stopped breathing.

How many times had I dreamed of this moment? Too many. More than I'd ever admit. The reality was better than I'd ever imagined. *So* much better.

Like he'd registered my blazing green light, Sky tilted his head, deepening the kiss. I met him in it. Sparks spread and heated my blood.

I *knew* there was a reason not to do this. An extraterrestrial reason.

But right now, it couldn't hurt to just...try it out.

You know, for science.

Tentatively, I brushed my tongue against his.

With a muffled curse, he pulled back. An invisible bucket of ice water dumped over my head, and I collapsed against the wall, breathless, gaping.

Holy crap. He'd just *kissed* me.

Like he, too, was shocked by it, Sky backed up a step. Mouth slack, eyes wide. I flattened my marked hand over my pounding heart, as if that'd stop it from leaping out and chasing after him. My lips tingled.

"I'm sorry," Sky muttered huskily, dragging his fingers through his hair until it stuck up in wild tufts. He sank his teeth into his bottom lip again and turned his head, closing his eyes. "I shouldn't have done that. I...I crossed the line."

I was struggling to form coherent thoughts. My attention kept wandering back to his mouth, captivated by the way it moved. It'd been so soft. "Line? What line?"

"What line?" he echoed, breathing a laugh that sounded a little pained. That mouth twisted as he turned an incredulous stare on me. "Rae, I just told you I'm an *alien*. That I'm the reason you're being hunted by the Enil."

Oh. Right. That. If only that did anything to silence the Marvin Gaye chorus coming from my nether regions.

When I didn't reply, only gazed up at him, he frowned. Nobody should make confusion look that good. But with that flush riding his cheekbones and his kiss-swollen mouth, here we were.

I could still taste him. I was having trouble thinking around it.

And I wasn't the only one affected. His breathing was a little ragged. His pupils were blown. The stairwell's shadows played over the dips and swells of his lean upper body and his taut face as he studied me almost warily. Like he didn't trust me—or maybe himself.

God, I hoped it was the latter.

Screw it. I pushed off the wall, and he stiffened.

I had Sky Acosta half-naked in my stairwell, thick hair mussed, eyes glassy with what I was praying was lust, and this would probably never happen again. After this, I'd go back to being sane, careful Raven. The logical one. I'd remember that he was an alien and I was possibly radioactive just from touching him.

But *right now*? Holding back felt like a waste of a once-in-a-lifetime opportunity.

His eyes widened as I threw my arms around his neck and yanked him toward me. He stumbled, caught himself with a hand on the wall, and started to speak, but I didn't let him. I lifted onto my toes and pressed my mouth against his.

This time, there was nothing tentative about it.

No slow burn. No teasing.

Just a woman who'd been crushing on the hot bartender for a year and now had him up against her in a stairwell.

I thought he'd resist, but he didn't. He responded immediately, his fingers tangling in my braid, a raw groan catching in his throat and tumbling past my lips.

That sound lit me up like a supernova.

I touched his jaw, fingertips scraping over stubble then gliding lower, down his chest. Beneath his open shirt, he was all warm skin and hard, twitching muscle. Synth-skin or not, he *felt* real.

His soft exhale wasn't quite steady as his hand slid deeper into my hair, tipping my head back. My belly flipped as his tongue tangled with mine. His heart pounded against my palm, matching the frenzied cadence of mine.

In a night that'd been filled with impossibilities and nothing short of the unbelievable, *he* felt real.

And I very much needed something real.

Like he agreed, he sank deeper, kissed me harder. An embarrassingly needy whimper slipped out of me, one I hoped he translated correctly as: *yes, more of that.*

He appeared to be fluent in horny Raven because, with a muffled curse, he dropped the arm braced above my head and bent, gripping beneath my thigh. The world lurched as he lifted me, and my back hit the wall with a soft thump.

It shocked me enough, I gasped into his mouth.

He'd just...hoisted me like I weighed nothing. All without breaking the kiss. Somehow, I didn't combust, but I did moan, because he settled my legs around him...and he'd just answered a few very *pressing* questions.

It sure felt like his physiology was compatible. *Very* compatible, if that friction told me anything. And it was telling me all sorts of things. Mainly that we were wearing way too much clothing.

I clamped my knees tighter around him. Combustion was now a very real possibility.

Sky's hand flexed on my thigh, and he broke the kiss, just long enough I caught the faint gleam of his heavy-lidded eyes, felt the rush of his breath on my cheek, and then he claimed my mouth again. His hips gave the tiniest roll, pressing me harder into the wall, and my thighs trembled around him at the answering burst of sensation.

Perfect. He felt perfect, tasted perfect, and this was so incredibly reckless. Such a terrible idea. Such a wonderful, terrible idea.

I didn't want it to end.

My fingers found his hair—just as silky as I'd thought it'd be—and my marked palm skated across his bare torso. His skin pebbled beneath my hand.

Speaking of hands, his were wandering. The one on my thigh had found my hip, and the other drifted down my side, toying with my shirt's hem. I gave him an enthusiastic wiggle, rubbing against the hardness trapped between us.

"*Raven*," he choked out against my lips. That sent a pulse straight through me, and it settled between my legs.

I knew then I wasn't going to stop this. I couldn't. I was all in. Alien or not, I didn't care. It was still Sky.

And I was on fire. He was on fire, too. *We* were burning.

I could feel it in my blood.

I could feel it buzzing—

Wait, *buzzing*—?

My breath hitched, and I jerked back. My hand rested on his stomach, and my palm…

Holy shit—my hand was glowing *again*. White light, brilliant and unmistakable, spilled from me and shimmered across his skin.

His silver, *alien* skin.

My lips parted in shock. Under my fingertips, the disguise had slipped. Vanished. His abs glittered like diamond-studded metal.

It'd happened *again*.

Sky inhaled sharply, breathing it out as an oath that sounded just as stunned as I felt. But I couldn't look up yet to see his expression. I could only gape at the sight in front of me.

His stomach was as warm and hard as ever beneath my hand—but it felt different now, subtly textured. Up close, his Pladian skin was even more intricately detailed, beautiful in a frightening, impossible way. Like layers of stardust painted over all that muscle.

I was touching alien skin.

Like I was in a dream, I finally lifted my spinning head.

Most of him still looked like human Sky…except for his eyes.

The whites had darkened to black, just like they had behind Oasis. Incandescent cerulean swirled in place of his irises, and his lips— still kiss-swollen—parted in what looked like wonder.

That was enough to snap me out of it.

Realizing he still had me pinned, I squirmed. He got the message and let go. I slid back down to my feet and collapsed against the wall behind me, gawking between my still-glowing hand and Sky's alien parts.

"What...?" I whispered, throat drying out. I fisted my hand around the fierce glow.

Sky lurched back a step, widening the gap between us. "I don't understand." He looked at me, then down at himself. "How does this keep happening?"

I assumed it was rhetorical because hell if I knew. We both stared as the silver dissolved, his skin becoming tan and whole and...human once more. His abs flexed when he craned his neck to watch his own stomach smooth back out.

It was like it hadn't happened. Well, almost.

Orange light leaked from the cracks between my fingers. The light flickered rapidly, though, dimming like a dying flashlight. Within the span of one heartbeat and another, gloomy shadows swallowed the stairwell again. And us.

The reality of the entire situation crashed back. I slapped my unmarked hand over my mouth.

Holy shit. I'd been dry-humping an alien in my stairwell.

Somehow, that seemed like the least of my worries. Flattening myself against the wall, I tried to process the glowing hand, the silver skin. But that kiss...

Could it be physical contact that caused the marks to glow? My own raging hormones? Because they were raging, all right. Still. Despite the fact he'd gone partial Pladian on me.

Or maybe it was *his* hormones?

He'd kissed me. I'd kissed him. *We'd kissed.*

Sky spoke then, and I jerked, wrenching my gaze up from the hand I'd just had pressed to his silver abdominals.

I'd just touched alien skin. After kissing an alien.

"It has to be the halix's latent energy somehow affecting the synth-skin," Sky muttered, running a hand down his torso, as if checking to make sure everything was back to normal. In a daze, I followed the movement a little too closely. "It only happens when you touch me."

That brought my eyes back to his, and I nearly let out an incredulous laugh. Oh, I'd been doing a lot more than just *touching* him.

I'd wanted to keep going, too.

I crushed the back of my hand to my mouth, the other pulling my sweater back into place and tugging it closed. My lips still tingled. His taste lingered on my tongue.

A clearly confused, traitorous bolt of need shot through me again.

He was an alien. And yet...

When I didn't say anything, he looked up. His strange eyes hadn't returned to normal. They glittered in the dim light, eerie and jeweled.

"Are you all right?" he asked softly.

I lowered my hand. I couldn't look away from that mesmerizing blue. "Yeah. Yeah, I'm fine. Has this," I motioned to his exposed torso, "happened before?"

"Just at Oasis, but——"

"No," I cut in, a blush crawling its way up my neck. "I mean, like before, when you were—*if* you...I mean..." I licked my lips and tried for a casual shrug. "I mean...have you...with humans?"

Sky blinked once, mouth parted. My blush reached thermonuclear levels, and I quickly held up a hand, wincing. "Sorry. I'm sorry. Don't answer that. It's none of my business."

What kind of a question was that? I studied my stocking feet and the tile floor beneath them. I blamed the exhaustion. Words just kept *falling* out.

Silence stretched. Long enough, I reluctantly raised my head. The blackness had bled from Sky's eyes. His star-flecked indigo gaze was trained on me, his face unreadable.

"I've been on this planet for over a decade," he said quietly. "I've spent that time learning what it means to be human and..." He paused, glancing up at the stairs. Looking away, like I wasn't the only one uncomfortable. "I've, uh, had the full experience. I've…" He exhaled, rubbing the back of his neck. "I've slept with humans in this form. And no," he indicated his abdomen, "that's never happened before." His eyes pinged to mine, then away again. "I think it's safe to say it's related to the markings, Rae. The halix's energy."

Safe to say. Yeah. I pursed my lips and eyed the shapes on my palm to distract myself from my raging blush.

Well, that answered *another* question, too. That hadn't been wishful thinking before. *Things worked the same.* With this version of him, anyway.

Which I'd assumed because I'd felt his hard—

I squeezed my eyes shut. I did not need to be thinking about hard anythings right now. That was decidedly not appropriate with, you know, a glowing crisis on our hands.

The strange, sinking jealousy wasn't either. I'd had sex before, too. Also with humans.

He was an alien, sure, but it made sense they had…needs. It was a biological imperative in most species to procreate. Sky having mating urges checked out.

Unfortunately, the thought of Sky doing any mating threatened to make my insides liquify again. Especially because, for an alien, he sure had kissing down. Was that how Pladians did it, too? Or had he just adapted to life on Earth *that* well—

My pent-up breath spilled out in a rush, and I made myself focus on Sky's voice instead.

"I'm willing to bet you just emitted a signal again, and I don't know why this keeps happening," he was saying when I tuned back in. It took me a second to realize he wasn't talking about the kissing. He burrowed both hands through his messy hair and frowned at me, oblivious to my private analysis of his race's mating habits. "I don't know what's triggering this." He jerked his chin at my hand before meeting my eyes again, expression grave. "But I think we need to find out, because whatever the reason, it puts you in danger."

Oh, I was in danger, all right.

For more reasons than I could count.

There were alien robots chasing me. My hand was doing a very weird glowy thing.

And there was a very confusing, half-naked alien in my stairwell.

Who, for some insane reason, I still very much wanted to kiss some more.

I was in serious danger, but especially when it came to the latter.

Chapter 27

ATTACK OF THE KILLER SWEATPANTS

I SHIFTED FROM BUTT CHEEK TO BUTT CHEEK on my worn couch. Despite the half hour that'd passed, the awareness hadn't gone anywhere. It had only gotten worse. Like not acknowledging it had made the awkwardness grow exponentially.

Not even my panic-order of Chinese comfort food had helped.

It'd arrived right after my very cold shower. Now I surveyed it from my spot beside Sky, resisting the urge to look at him. Mostly because every time I did, I remembered the soft, tortured sound he'd made when I'd kissed him and how those long, graceful fingers he kept running through his hair had gripped my thigh—

Clearing my throat, I twisted the hem of the baggy concert tee, curling further into the couch's arm. My damp braid soaked into the shirt's back, and I tugged it over my shoulder, toying with the end.

Sky was spread out on the couch's opposite end, one arm slung over the back, his long legs crossed at the ankles. Because I was a masochist, I gave in and risked glancing his way.

Which was a mistake.

Not because he was frowning in confusion at the excessive spread of takeout littering my coffee table...but because while I'd taken the chilliest shower known to man, Sky had changed into a white T-shirt and gray sweatpants.

Gray. Sweatpants.

He'd had them in his SUV, he claimed. Why he was carrying around thirst-trap clothing, I couldn't begin to guess. The threadbare shirt clung to his torso, and the sweatpants...well, they weren't doing *me* any favors.

Clearly, the universe hated me.

I jerked my attention away from the fabric molded to his muscular thighs and focused instead on his hair. It'd dried the rest of the way into soft curls and messy tufts. He usually wore it so neatly. This tousled version made him seem...younger. Approachable.

Too approachable. Especially now that I knew how silky it was—

Sky moved then but only to look between me and the dozen takeout boxes. He appeared concerned. Understandably. I'd ordered enough for four starving people. And I wasn't even hungry.

I couldn't take this tense silence anymore.

"So—" I began.

At the same time, he said, "What—"

We both stopped. I sniffed a laugh. My nerves were tripping over themselves. I drew up my legs and adjusted my position until I faced him. He watched me with a slight, guarded smile.

"Go ahead," I offered.

"Well," he said, exhaling. He sat forward, and one of those endearing curls fell over his forehead as he steepled his hands. "I think we should talk about what happened."

I had a feeling I knew what he was talking about: that kiss. And this wasn't awkward at all. Telltale heat stung my cheeks.

"Which part?" I asked anyway, resisting the urge to fiddle with my braid. I had no idea what to do with my hands.

He contemplated me for a second, as if picking up my anxiety. It was probably written all over my face. Sitting back, he transferred his attention to the entirety of the Chinese restaurant menu spread out before us. "First things first. Which one do you want?"

I shrugged because I wasn't sure I could eat at all. Not with my insides twisting and turning like they were. He began popping lids anyway.

"Orange chicken. Chow mein. Beef and broccoli. Shrimp fried rice." He frowned at another container, lifted it, and sniffed its contents. "No idea what this one is."

"Egg foo yung," I whispered, tucking a frizzed strand behind my ear. I made a valiant effort to avoid noticing every casual twitch of his body. And failed. "I'll take the fried rice. I don't like noodles...so, you can have those. If you like noodles."

"You don't like noodles," he echoed, as if making a note, passing me the rice box. "I like them just fine."

Casual food talk. I could do this. That is, until our fingers brushed, and the blush roared back. Full steam ahead.

Kissing him had not helped this ever-present awareness. Not even a little. It'd made everything *much* worse.

I threw myself into opening my chopsticks, and when I took a breath, I caught a whiff of the rice. Maybe I *was* hungry. Despite the absolute insanity of my day, my stomach grumbled. I didn't remember the last time I'd consumed anything that wasn't caffeine-based.

Even with the gnawing in my midsection, though, I couldn't bring myself to take a bite. I stared at the food in my lap while silence closed in again.

Until Sky broke it. "Rae."

That was a serious tone. Heart skipping, I looked up. His expression matched. Here it came.

"I'm sorry," he said, holding my gaze. "I shouldn't have kissed you."

My stomach dropped with the weight of those words—and the humiliation that rose with them. Of course he regretted it.

Clinging to my pride, I forced myself to keep looking at him and willed those emotions to stay tucked inside. "It was just a kiss, Sky. It's...it's okay."

He shook his head, mouth downturned. The dark curl flopped over his brow. "No, it's not."

"It's not," I repeated, voice thin. My throat was tight, and I didn't know what stung worse: the rejection or the regret in his eyes.

He raked the curl back. "I...I can't."

Wait. I blinked, stunned. *He couldn't?* Oh. *Oh.*

I'd just assumed—especially after what he'd said earlier, about being with humans. Had I gotten it wrong? Had I totally misread the situation? I'd practically launched myself at him in the stairwell.

I was an idiot.

"I'm-I'm so sorry," I stammered. I couldn't even look at him. This made things ten times more awkward. "I thought things worked the same. Well, you'd said you'd...you know...with humans—"

"No, that's—" He loosed a sharp breath and transferred the container he held to one hand so he could pinch the bridge of his nose. A strangled huff that might have been a laugh escaped him. "No, Raven." He lowered his arm. His mouth twitched like he was fighting for composure. "Things definitely work the same. Almost exactly the same for Pladians and humans. And even if they didn't..." He gestured at himself. "Like I told you, the synth-skin makes me human. In *every* way." He bit his lip and glanced up at me. "In case you didn't notice."

Oh, I'd noticed. A whimper tried to escape, and I swallowed it down, tearing my attention from him before I succumbed to the pull of the Gray Sweatpants.

I'd noticed *all* of it seemed human enough to work just fine.

Then the rest of what he'd said sank in. Had he just said *things worked the same way for humans and Pladians?*

Oh my God. My pulse lurched. I suddenly needed to know more. That shouldn't turn me on, but it kind of did. It had to just be the thrill of the unknown.

I didn't want to prod too much at what that—the fact I was sitting here, contemplating what it'd be like to do the horizontal tango with an actual alien in alien form—said about me.

"...ah," I said, eloquently. My brain had abandoned me. That old, familiar flustered feeling I'd always gotten around Sky was still going strong and now was *also* accompanied by the fact that I knew he was a fantastic kisser. "Sure. Okay."

"Sure?" Sky watched me cautiously. There was a hesitant note in his voice, too, when he asked, "That doesn't...bother you?"

"That it...that it works the same?" More redness crept up my neck.

No, it didn't bother me. No, I was *very* interested in exploring that little detail. Thoroughly.

He stared at me for a second before a crooked smile tugged up the side of his mouth. I frowned in confusion.

"No, Rae," he said, grazing a hand over his face like he was erasing the amusement. Lowering it, he fixed me with a narrow-eyed look. "What I meant was, doesn't it bother you that I'm an alien? That you kissed *an alien?*"

Oh. That. Funny, I'd been asking myself that question since it'd happened. Possibly before.

And I'd come to some conclusions. If he meant, did it change the fact that I still wanted to see him naked, the answer was no. Firmly. Still fully on board for naked Sky. For some messed up reason, that hadn't changed at all. But I certainly wasn't going to tell *him* that.

So I chewed the inside of my lip and settled on, "Define bother."

He leaned back, lips parting, like I'd stunned him. When I gathered my courage and met his eyes, a flash of *something*—interest or heat or maybe just shock—flickered across his face before he lowered his gaze.

I twisted my braid around my finger and looked everywhere but at him. The Chinese takeout waited, but neither of us touched it. The clock on the microwave said we were well past my study time already.

"Sorry," Sky said, after a moment of strained silence. "That, ah...wasn't the response I'd expected."

He was staring at the floor. What had he expected me to say? It wasn't like I hadn't known what he was when I kissed him.

"Anyway." He breathed a faint laugh and finally lifted his head again, though he didn't quite meet my eyes. "That doesn't change the fact that we can't cross that line. I shouldn't have kissed you. I meant what I said about keeping our distance. We need to work together to fix it, and we—*I*—can't afford distractions."

He said all of it in such a reasonable, composed way. Like it was logical and obvious, and it probably was. It still wasn't fun hearing it.

"Then why..." Unable to keep looking at him, I took in the sad shrimp count in my rice box. There were never enough in there. "Why did you? Kiss me, I mean."

Because he *had* kissed me first. I'd definitely initiated that second one, but the first time? Sky had kissed *me*.

When the silence went on a heartbeat too long, I looked up.

He gave a helpless, full-body shrug. There was something in his eyes when they finally slid my way. Something a little...bashful? That couldn't be.

"Because I've been thinking about it for a long time," he said so quietly, I leaned forward, sure I'd misheard. "And I wanted...well, I guess I wanted to know what it was like."

It was my turn to be shocked. My mouth dropped open. I had to have misunderstood what he was saying.

He took in my flabbergasted expression, and his small smile flashed dimple. The rain pounding on the roof was louder than ever.

"Are you telling me...?" I started, but that's as far as I got. He didn't say anything, and I shook my head slowly. "No. That doesn't make sense. You called me *Rachel*. Like a week ago."

He sniffed, running his fingers along his jawline. "I know. It's dumb. I've always called you silly names that start with R. Lame way to flirt, but..." This time, his grin was definitely a little shy. "It got your attention, and you usually ignored me."

Ignored him? *Ignored him?* Is that what he'd thought I was doing when I was *short-circuiting in his presence*?

"So you're trying to say you called me the wrong names on purpose?" I managed an incredulous huff. "You're joking."

He wasn't laughing.

My eyes bulged. "You're serious."

"Well." He averted his gaze, cheeks coloring. "I'm trained for infiltration, not flirtation."

That surprised a laugh out of me, a real one—but I wasn't so sure I believed him. He seemed to have zero issues in the flirtation department.

He gave me a quick, answering smile then grew serious, adjusting his grip on his takeout box. "I don't know. I guess I wanted you to correct me. Tease back. You were always so guarded around me."

I scoffed. *Guarded?* I turned into a complete *moron* around him! He'd clearly misread everything. How was that possible?

His long sigh drew my attention back to him.

"But…" He set his chow mein on the coffee table and eased into the couch, twisting toward me. "My life is complicated. Very complicated. As you are now aware." He scrubbed his palms over his thighs. I tried not to look. Gray sweatpants were a menace to society. "Somebody like me, with the mission and the secrets, not to mention the dangers…well, I can't afford attachments. Especially considering how dangerous this could be if I'm right about the halix."

I swallowed hard. There was that note again in his voice, the same thing I'd just glimpsed in his eyes. Maybe loneliness.

I understood more than I wanted to. Right now, despite the fact that only a foot or two separated us on my dingy couch, the distance felt vast. Like I was floating alone in a void. In fact, I'd felt that same isolation this past week since I'd stumbled into this extraterrestrial mess.

And I wasn't from a different planet. I could only imagine how he felt.

Even so, that shared emotion also felt too intimate. Almost more so than the kiss in the stairwell. I didn't know what to do with it or the soft way he was gazing at me. Like he was full of regret for something that hadn't even happened.

"Right," I murmured, wrapping my braid around my finger again. "Of course."

"I noticed you the very first day you came into Oasis, you know."

His words took a second to register, but when they did, I snapped my attention to his face. He was lying. Surely.

"You don't believe me." He read my skepticism, and his grin was slow. Leisurely. "Is that so hard to believe?"

"Kinda, yeah. That was months ago." *And you're you.*

"Six months ago. Almost seven."

"Seven," I corrected, eyes wide. Holy crap. He was throwing me for another loop, here. How had he remembered that?

He lifted a brow in challenge. "You were waiting at the bar with your bag, a bio-anthropology book sticking out of it. Your hair was in that braid you do…" He indicated my drying French braid, and I smoothed a hand over it self-consciously. "You were dressed up. White button-up. Very professional, especially for Oasis." Still smirking slightly, he leaned his head back, resting it on the couch cushion, his gaze settling on the ceiling. "You smiled at me, but I could tell you were nervous. I've gotten pretty good at reading people, and you were doing that thing where you chew your lip." He sent me a sidelong glance. "Like you are now."

Caught, I pried my lip from between my teeth and pressed my mouth into a line. Despite my better judgment, I found myself wavering.

Because out of a day full of crazy reveals, this one—if he was telling the truth—might've topped them all.

Chapter 28

STAR-CROSSED ROMANCE FOR
DUMMIES

No WAY HAD HOT BARTENDER SKY—*alien* Sky—noticed me all this time.

I gaped at him, shrimp fried rice forgotten. If he was lying, he was doing a damn good job. Because I remembered that day clearly, too. Remembered seeing *him*.

"How do you…?" I started to bite my lip again, then caught myself. "You're right. I had to bring my school bag because I ordered a ride from class. Faith broke down that day."

Sky had been impossible to miss. Even with the impending interview weighing on me. I'd been nervous, not *dead*.

Now, his attention was back on the ceiling. "You got hired on the spot. Started the next week." He lifted one broad shoulder, letting out a long sigh. "I don't know. You were just…different, Rae. The way you move through the world is different."

Different. Yeah, that was one way to put it. I always went with weird.

I puffed out a laugh. What was he *saying*? That this whole time I'd been sneaking looks at the out-of-my-league bartender coworker, he'd been doing the same thing? It wasn't possible.

He angled his face my way, eyes sweeping over me, narrowed

slightly in contemplation. "There's something about how...*aware* you are. You study things. You watch. Like you're absorbing and experiencing. You're present in a way...well, in a way most people on Earth don't seem to be."

People on Earth.

There was that little jolt, that little reminder of who he really was. I used it to close my mouth.

"I noticed," he said simply, temple resting on the back of my couch, "because it's how I feel living here. Watching it all. Experiencing it."

Something cracked a little behind my breastbone. I answered him honestly, because I was too shocked to do anything else. "I... have no idea what to say to that."

He *had* to know I'd been obsessing over him. If not before tonight, he did now. Amelia had cleared up any confusion when she'd stopped by earlier and oh-so-helpfully spewed my deepest, darkest secrets. If he'd had any doubts, me attacking him in the stairwell should've driven the point home.

Even though this was the answer to every one of my daydreams, I knew it came with a giant, looming *But*. And he was about to give it to me.

"It's okay," Sky said, giving me a slight, close-lipped smile that faded quickly. "You asked why I kissed you—and that's it. That's why." He sat up with a sigh and squinted down at his hands. "And why I shouldn't have, too. Because despite any...well, feelings, I have a mission. It's got to come first. Once that's done, I..."

He formed loose fists. Head still bowed, he didn't finish, but he didn't have to. Right. He was an *alien*. He had a home planet out there called Pladia.

He didn't have time to flirt with a waitress from his undercover job, even one who happened to get herself wrapped up in a giant, interstellar mess.

Once his task—whatever that turned out to be—was complete, he'd be leaving, wouldn't he? That made sense.

It didn't change that I was feeling *all the things*.

Or the fact I had *so* many questions about him. For him. They crowded in, clamoring for release. There were so many more things I needed to know before that time came. Before he was *gone*.

I'd only *just* begun to see the real him. The real Sky, who was born on a ship in deep space. Whose world was eight lightyears from Earth.

I tilted my head, looking at him. Really looking at him.

For example, why *him?* What was he doing here, and why had he chosen to take on this task? Or had it been chosen for him? And when he'd come to Earth, had he left people behind? Family? Friends?

A…a lover?

I tried to imagine leaving everyone I knew—Dustin, my family, Amelia, even the Oasis crew—and a pang of sympathy wedged beneath my ribs. God, no wonder he was lonely. He'd said before that he'd never told anyone the truth he'd spilled here tonight.

What would it *feel* like to live on a completely foreign planet where no one knew the authentic version of you?

Granted, he'd mentioned a partner. Bast. But that was one person. In a sea of strangers. A sea of stars.

It was overwhelming. Crushingly lonely.

But none of that changed what he was gently telling me right now, that whatever was between us couldn't happen.

I'd deal with the little ball of hurt ricocheting around my chest later. *Later.* I'd stuff it down with all the other things I'd be screaming into a pillow about once I got the chance.

For now, I had the opportunity to ask some of the million questions spiraling through my brain.

I just had to keep cool. To let this gentle rejection roll off me. And I could do that. I was a big girl.

It wasn't like I didn't have *tons* of practice pretending to be unaffected by Sky Acosta.

I turned back to my shrimp fried rice and grabbed a pair of chopsticks, pitching my tone light. "Well, if we're not going to pass the time making out, I have questions."

Out of the corner of my eye, I saw him staring, as if my sudden acquiescence had surprised him. Then his light chuckle broke the tension, and he shook his head, reaching for the chow mein again. "I know you hate hearing this, but I can't tell you much. The Creed we follow is very specific. I've already broken so many rules telling you what I have." He winced, like the reminder was too much. "So many."

I cocked a brow as I hefted my utensils. "You don't think they'd make an exception for extenuating circumstances?"

"You don't know Pladians," he muttered, and I couldn't argue with that. I knew exactly one, and he did indeed appear to be really into rules.

"Okay then." I paused, pinching a piece of shrimp and looking over at him. "Was it really a solar flare, or is that all a big lie?"

He ran his tongue over his bottom lip, hesitating.

When he stayed quiet too long, I rolled my eyes and gave an exasperated growl. "Come on, Sky. You can't drop bombshells like *'you're not alone in the universe'* and then give me nothing—"

"The Enil use the sun's energy," he interrupted, exhaling through his nose. He grabbed one of the soft drinks and slurped it loudly enough to make me blink. Swallowing, he studied the Styrofoam cup. "They use solar energy to recharge their engine power cells. So yes, your sun's energy is fluctuating because of their interference, but that's not the whole truth."

I waited, brows high.

He rattled the ice in his drink. A silent battle of wills commenced until he relented with his own eye roll. "Fine. Yes. As you've probably guessed, most of the unexplained things happening lately are connected to the Enil. They use a world's existing resources—technology, in Earth's case—to create their suits. The robot, as you called it." He leaned forward to set the cup down. "Their ships also absorb ambient electricity. That's what's been disrupting your power grids."

Power grids. Phone batteries. *Car* batteries.

It'd been aliens. This whole time. I swallowed hard. "So it *was* one big conspiracy."

Sky pursed his lips but didn't say anything further as he reached for an egg roll and crunched into it. It took me a few heartbeats to organize my thoughts.

An actual conspiracy. An alien invasion—*infiltration*—had been happening this whole time.

The vlogs were right. Kelly's stupid reels, too.

When Sky swallowed his bite, I decided to push my luck. "If the Enil use a planet's resources to create those suits, they'd look... different on different planets?"

That one, he didn't seem against answering. Expression clouding, he nodded. "Which is why no two look the same here, either."

I'd only had the pleasure of seeing one so far. Hopefully my luck held. "If the robot body is just a suit, what do the Enil actually look like?"

Sky paused mid-chew, eyes darting my way. When his jaw began to work again, it was more slowly. I waited. He took his time, like he was putting together his answer.

"Even the Pladians...don't really know," he said haltingly, after a moment. "Sending biological forms into deep space at the speeds necessary to travel those kinds of distances...well, it's difficult." He hefted the rest of his egg roll, examining it. "The Enil found a workaround. They don't send bodies. Just minds. Programmed consciousnesses, transferred from their scout ships into the mechanical suits they create after landing." He lifted his eyes to mine.

I gawked at him. "So then that means..."

He nodded once, slowly. "Yeah. The suit doesn't have a body in it. Just a mind. That's what I meant by I hadn't technically killed that Enil in the lab." He polished off the rest of the appetizer and brushed crumbs from his fingertips, speaking around the mouthful. "There's only a programmed consciousness inside."

"If that's not how the Pladians do it, how—"

"I'm really not supposed to tell you any of that, Rae," Sky interrupted, mouth twisting. Something like a plea softened his voice. "I've taken an oath."

"Who am I going to tell? The government?" I waved my marked palm. "They'd probably lock me up too, considering this."

"That's not the point…" He looked away. His posture had stiffened, shoulders tightening.

I'd reached his limit, it seemed. Okay, so no discussing his people. Got it.

"Fine. Something safe then." When he didn't protest, just eyed me sidelong—warily—I leaned in, unable to stop my eager tone. "What's space like? You said you were born there, right?"

"I was." He eased back into the couch, seeming to mull it over.

Probably deciding if telling me broke any of his rules. I held my breath.

Sighing, he turned his head. He wore a faint smirk. "I should've known you'd have a million questions."

I pursed my lips, adjusting my grip on the chopsticks. "Sky, you're an alien. *Anybody* would have a million questions."

"Not everyone would handle it this well, though," he murmured, canting his head and examining me. "Why haven't you freaked out?"

"Oh, trust me." I scoffed. "Been there. Done that." I sent a pointed look at the very large, very empty bottle of wine. "At least you didn't have a robot form. That was a concern."

"Wait." He raised his eyebrows. "A robot form? You thought *I* was an Enil? That's what you meant earlier?"

I flushed a little, then made a face. "I wasn't expecting Earth to be teeming with alien life. UFOs, robots—then my bartender cr— um, coworker turns out to be an alien?" I picked at my rice and willed my blush to die down. "Can you blame me for jumping to conclusions?"

I could see him studying me, still wearing a tiny smile. "No, I guess I can't. No robot form, for the record."

"I know that *now*." I ate a piece of shrimp, sliding him an expectant look. "You were telling me about space."

"I was. You're right." His eyes went hazy. Faraway. "I don't know how to describe it, really. When you're born there, it's just a… fact of life. Like dry land is for you." He swirled a finger, encompassing the room, then leaned forward and grabbed one of the white takeout boxes. "But sometimes, when you *do* remember or think about it too deeply..." He looked down at the food he held, brow furrowing. "It makes you feel small. Like you're a single grain in something vast and unknowable."

He blinked slowly and raised his head, gaze finding mine.

"It's the same feeling I imagine you get when you look up at the stars. Just *magnified*. There's something about being among them, standing at the edge of that kind of vastness, that changes you. It reminds you that you're part of something much bigger." He set the box down again without opening it and folded his hands loosely in his lap. "Which I am. This whole mission...it's part of something greater, Rae."

I stared at him. That was more profound than I'd expected. Much deeper.

A reminder, too.

About who and *what* was sitting here beside me, sharing greasy takeout food and slurping drinks like he didn't understand straws. It was hard to ignore when he spoke like *that*.

Feeling suddenly vulnerable and more than a little overwhelmed, I looked away.

He *was* part of something greater. Now so was I. And in a way that wasn't exactly safe.

Suddenly not hungry, I jabbed my chopsticks into my rice. "You really can't tell me what your mission is, can you?"

A beat passed. I set the box back on the table. In the silence, a gust of wind rattled the side of the garage, splattering raindrops against the windowpanes.

When Sky answered, it was with a quiet sort of finality. "No. I would tell you if I could. It'd help you understand."

"But you can't. Because of your Creed."

"Right."

I frowned and bit the inside of my lip. "What *is* it? The Creed, I mean. Some kind of blood oath or...?"

He laughed. "No, nothing quite so barbaric." His appetite didn't appear to be affected. He gave his attention to his food, digging in with his chopsticks. He was shockingly efficient with them. "It is one of our ultimate laws, though. Think of it as a collection of the standards Pladians hold themselves to. My race is very…" He brandished the chopsticks, searching for the word. "I guess you'd say straitlaced."

Straitlaced. Well, that certainly explained a lot.

Although he hadn't exactly seemed straitlaced when he'd had his tongue in my mouth earlier.

I shifted uncomfortably, watching as he wrangled a single noodle with his utensils. "You're good with those."

He glanced up, following my gaze. "Oh. Yeah. I spent a couple years in Asia."

I sat up straighter, nearly dropping my shrimp fried rice. Duh. I hadn't even *considered* that—all the things he'd seen, the places he'd been. He'd only been in this city for two years. He'd been on this *planet* for a decade, searching for his tablet.

It still blew my mind it'd ended up in *One Willow*, of all places.

"Searching for the halix?" I asked, examining him closer. "Where did your ancestors originally leave it?"

He halted in his chewing and slid a glance my way, hesitating. Like he was trying to decide if answering violated anything. Apparently not because he went back to eating. "The Middle East."

That made sense. The cradle of civilization. Those markings had looked close to Sumerian cuneiform, one of the earliest forms of writing.

The implications of Pladian presence at the dawn of humanity were still…staggering.

Hell, *Sky's* presence was.

Despite my roiling stomach, I picked up my food and forced down another bite without tasting it. My emotions were a mess tonight. I was full to the brim, and they'd begun to spill out in ways I didn't intend.

"That brings us full circle," Sky said, lowering whatever he'd dug into after polishing off the chow mein. "Until we know what the halix did to you, I'd like to stay close. If you'll let me."

He didn't say it, but I knew what he was asking. Again. The rice turned to dust in my mouth. Giving up, I put it on the table and focused instead on the alien.

He'd turned to face me, and he pointed behind him, at the stair-well. "The Enil won't be stopped by door locks, and they're not going to wait for an invitation. They'll tear down any obstacles—or people—to get to what the halix contained."

To get what he believed my brain contained.

Great.

My stomach heaved, and I hugged myself. Suddenly cold, I wished I'd put the cardigan back on after my shower.

"Don't sugarcoat it for my sake," I muttered, tightening my arms against a shiver.

"I want you to understand the risk. Which is why…" Sky paused and waited until I'd looked at him again. "Which is why I really wish you'd agree to let me stay close. I wish you'd listen to me about lying low, too." He searched my face, eyes soft but filled with convic-tion. "If there was another way, one that didn't upend your life like this, I'd take it, Rae. But too much is at stake. More than you know. More than I can tell you."

I worried the inside of my cheek, unable to look away. Beneath the worn tee, his shoulders were tight again. He looked…so very grave. Like life-or-death, world-on-the-brink grave. *Worlds*, maybe.

"I need you to let me keep you safe." He leaned in. "If you don't trust anything else, at least trust me with that."

And there it was. The problem. Because I wasn't sure I trusted him. Or myself. Or anything, really.

Because aliens weren't just real. They'd been here. For *years*. They were in my life.

And now they were after me.

Exhaustion rolled over me like a wave, threatening to pull me into the undertow. This had all happened so fast. The UFO encounter. The lab explosion. Sky's big alien reveal. My life had detonated in real time over the past week.

I drew in a deep breath and dragged my hands down my cheeks.

"I need to study," I said, letting my arms fall back to my lap. "And then I need sleep. It's been a long day."

It wasn't an answer to his unspoken question, his gentle prod about staying. But Sky surprised me by not pushing. He only nodded and set his empty takeout container down. I stared at him while he finished off his soda. Loudly.

Did he not know how to avoid *slurping* like that?

When he set the cup down by his empty box, I gaped in shock. Wait. He'd left behind multiple empty boxes. Somehow, he'd polished off three of them and just as many egg rolls. While I'd barely managed one bite. Did his alien super-suit come with a built-in metabolism boost? Because if so, that was a load of crap.

Sky stood, and I forgot about the food as he rose to his full height. He brushed his hands off, and I tipped my head back to meet his gaze, trying to ignore the gray sweatpants front and center. Was he doing this on purpose?

He didn't appear to be. His midnight eyes were serious as they swept over my face. "Are you sure?"

"Sure of what?" I asked. Because the answer was probably no. I wasn't sure about anything at the moment. Except the fact he shouldn't look that good in rumpled, comfortable clothing.

"Are you sure you don't want me to stay?"

I puffed out my cheeks, turning my head toward the blinds. It was dark out there. The storm had quieted finally. Now, only gentle rain pattered against the roof. The kind that'd be great to fall asleep to...if I didn't have hours of studying to do.

Sky wanted to stay to make sure I was safe. I forced myself to consider it objectively. *Logically.*

I wanted space. I needed time to scream into that pillow, cram for my test, and possibly spend two full days in a Tylenol PM-induced coma. I'd always needed alone time to process, and that would be impossible with a Pladian attached to my hip. A Pladian whose hips I wouldn't mind being attached to...

I tucked my tongue into my cheek. See? Already the thought of having him around was making it difficult to concentrate.

But then I remembered that creature in the lab, and the thought of being alone—*truly* alone and exposed—made my skin crawl. The Enil had been frightening before I knew what to call them. But after talking with Sky, after all he'd had to say, it was infinitely worse. Now I knew what the monsters were and what they could do...

If he'd wanted me to be afraid, he'd succeeded. If he was right and I was putting off some kind of signal they happened to trace, I had no doubt the Enil would tear this garage apart like tissue paper. And then they'd tear *me* apart.

Sickness climbed its way up my throat, and I shivered.

Maybe it was that fear. Or maybe it was the fact that I craved *something* familiar. Or better yet, maybe it was the fact that this entire night felt like a strange, murky dream that, for some reason, I didn't want to end.

Whatever the why was, I'd come to a decision.

I swallowed and looked up, meeting Sky's patient gaze. "Okay."

"Okay?" He blinked a couple times, like he hadn't expected that. He wasn't the only one. "You want me to stay?"

"Yeah." I twisted the hem of my shirt. "Yeah, if that's okay. Just in case…well, just in case."

"Sure." His grin slid into place slowly, devastatingly—one of those real ones that were *way* too appealing—and my belly fluttered in response. I couldn't help but smile back, though I turned my head and tucked it into my shoulder, shy suddenly.

Because he was staying here. In my space. My home.

He was the last person I'd ever expect to have a slumber party with. Talk about a descent into the unbelievable.

"Well," I said, standing and tugging down the baggy shirt. "So do you…" I faltered, flustered.

Oh my God. Sky Acosta was sleeping over my apartment. I was playing Airbnb host to an extraterrestrial.

I nearly giggled, a terrible sign I was getting slap-happy. I stifled the completely inappropriate urge and instead faced him. "Do you need anything? A toothbrush? I've got an extra from my last dentist visit, I think. Never opened."

"Oh." His smile slid crooked, and he surveyed the coffee table between us. "No—thanks, though. I've got my bag. It has everything I need."

First clothing, now a toothbrush? I narrowed my eyes as he began to gather the empty takeout boxes. "You just happened to bring stuff? What would you have done if I'd said no?"

He paused in stuffing the trash into the to-go bag and gave me a rueful grin. "Slept in my car outside your apartment."

"What?" I stopped short, staring at him. "Seriously?"

He shrugged and finished cleaning up our dinner, setting the crammed-full bag back on the coffee table. "I wasn't lying about the danger," he said as he straightened and slid his hands into his sweatpants pockets. "About how important this is. To the mission, I mean."

Right. The mysterious mission. Which I was somehow now a part of.

"Okay. Well, thank you?" That sounded lame, but I had no idea what else to say. I pressed my fingers to my forehead. "I've got to study for my test tomorrow. Make yourself…comfortable, I guess."

I turned to leave. Paused.

Then spun back around and spoke in a rush. "I work the lunch shift, too, before the afternoon class. That's…my schedule. Since you…I mean, if you're going to be coming along for it. I know I said I didn't want you to, but…"

Some emotion flashed before he bobbed his head in a single nod. "I would like to, yes." It was said so politely. Calmly. His bartender voice. That stray curl slid into his eyes, and he pushed it back. I couldn't read him.

It bothered me now for some reason. Like I could see it for the mask it was.

Sleep deprivation. That had to be it. I needed sleep. So much sleep. My bones were *aching* for it.

I must've said it out loud because Sky made a shooing motion toward the hallway. "I'm fine. Go ahead. You won't even know I'm here."

This time, I barely swallowed my snort. Right. Like I could forget there was an alien sleeping twelve feet from my bed.

An alien I'd made out with a mere hour ago.

I flushed and gave him my back. "Night."

I'd taken one step before he stopped me with a single word. "Rae?"

Pausing with my hand on the wall, I glanced over my shoulder.

"Thank you."

A blush rose at the way he was looking at me, his small smile. I found my voice. "For what?"

Letting him stay? Not pepper-spraying him? Not calling the FBI on the actual extraterrestrial who'd dropped a cosmic info dump on me over takeout?

He balanced his hands on his hips. "You handled this a lot better than most people would have. Thanks for giving me a chance. Thanks for listening. Telling someone who I am…" He looked away and scratched his nose. "Well, I'm just glad you listened. So thanks."

Feathery wings fluttered in my midsection. Was I imagining the redness staining his cheekbones? It had to be a trick of the light.

Flustered all over again, I turned and spoke over my shoulder. "Don't thank me yet. That couch sucks."

His quiet laugh followed me out of the room. In my bedroom, I fell into the loving arms of my textbooks, hoping that maybe, just maybe, academics could help me forget he was just outside. Maybe also just how much of a tangled mess I was.

And if I was lucky, what an alien's kiss felt like.

Chapter 29

HOUSE GUESTS OF THE FOURTH KIND

MY ALARM'S CHEERFUL RINGING yanked me out of an exhausted, nightmare-riddled sleep. That couldn't be real. I'd only just closed my eyes. I groaned in protest, swatting at my phone until the sound died, then slumped back into the pillow.

The sun was up, though. I could see it through my eyelids. The alarm had been right, after all.

I'd had another nightmare. This one with glowing eyes and echoes of something I couldn't hold on to. Strange shapes and fragments of words that dissolved like mist the further I strayed into wakefulness. Vanishing like sunspots.

Still gritty-eyed and half-conscious, I shoved back my quilt—which sent pencils and flashcards skittering across the floor. Perfect. With a mumbled curse, I staggered upright and stepped over them, tugging down the hem of my sleeping shirt.

My jaw cracked with a huge yawn as I opened the bedroom door—

And nearly ran straight into Sky emerging from my bathroom.

I froze mid-yawn.

Oh. Right.

Sky was here.

In my apartment.

Because he'd spent the night.

And there he was. Still here. Tall and broad, he took up most of the bathroom doorway. His dark hair was tousled like he'd spent hours tossing and turning, which he probably had because I hadn't been lying about the couch.

Stubble shadowed his strong jaw, but his sapphire eyes were somehow clear and bright.

When I just stared, he rocked back on his heels, a smile tugging at the corner of his full lips.

Lips I'd attacked last night.

That memory alone was enough for me to snap my mouth shut with an audible click.

"Good morning," he said.

Oh God. His morning voice was rough and low. All gravelly and husky. Sexy enough to jolt every hormone in my body awake.

"I made coffee," he added.

"Coffee," I repeated faintly. My alien houseguest had made coffee. Somehow I managed not to swoon.

His attention slid over my blushing face then down, lingering, unmistakably, on my bare thighs beneath the hem of the Metallica shirt I'd crashed in last night after ditching my leggings.

Too late, it occurred to me what that meant. I wasn't wearing pants.

A confusing mess of embarrassment and awareness churned in my belly. Way too much churning for this early in the morning. I tugged the shirt's bottom down as far as it would go.

Not that Sky was paying attention now. He shifted from foot to foot, rubbing the back of his neck and looking everywhere but at me.

"You have a...uh..." He pointed in the general vicinity of my stomach while squinting at the hallway ceiling. "You're wearing a note. About agenda-setting theory."

"What?" I looked down. Sure enough, a sticky note from last

night's study session clung to my shirt. A yellow one scrawled with half-legible media theory ramblings.

Okay, maybe he was paying a little bit of attention, after all.

Blushing even deeper, I peeled it off and managed a weak laugh. "Thanks. Study note." I shook it in the air for some reason then gestured vaguely at the bathroom. "I'm just gonna…"

"Oh. Sure. Sorry." He moved aside quickly.

I did a little awkward shuffle-step past him, sliding toward the bathroom door without looking directly at his face. My hallway felt so much smaller with him in it.

"I'll be out here," he said behind me.

I muttered something I hoped passed for human language and shut the door, leaning back against it with a dejected sigh.

It was *way* too early for this.

And I hadn't slept nearly enough. Those dreams…

I dragged a hand over my face, trying to chase the fragments. They felt heavy. Important. Familiar in a way that made my chest tighten. But I couldn't for the life of me recall a thing.

Were they what Sky had implied yesterday? Were these glimpses of something I hadn't quite remembered yet? Something I couldn't quite summon back to my conscious mind but had been planted there…?

A creeping unease coiled beneath my ribs. Whatever they were, they were gone now, scattered like leaves in the wind by the shock of finding Sky in my hallway.

That, too, felt dreamlike. Too strange to be real.

Maybe the dreams were just stress from…*that*. Maybe the power of suggestion had made my subconscious stage some kind of cosmic theater production. I had enough material for it. Midterms and a possible apocalypse. Oh, and the fact that I'd kissed a literal alien yesterday.

My stomach swooped, and I bit my lip.

It had been a hell of a kiss, too. And now I was supposed to just…act like it hadn't happened.

I stared into the mirror, unwinding my sleep-rumpled braid while studying my reflection. My shadowed eyes and still-reddened cheeks. My face trying very hard to pretend everything was normal. I braced both hands on the counter and drew in a long breath, holding it. Closing my eyes, I exhaled slowly.

I could do this. I could find my equilibrium.

My worldview had completely shifted yesterday. Which meant I had to define my new normal.

It was fine. Everything was fine. I could survive midterms. Face Sky. Untangle alien weirdness, decode impossible dreams, and *still* show up to work on time. All that. I could handle it.

No pressure.

None at all.

I buried my face in my hands and wheezed a laugh.

So much pressure.

I FELT MODERATELY BETTER after a pep talk beneath scalding-hot water. It was my second shower in twenty-four hours, but hey, I was now extra clean. I did my best thinking under the spray.

By the time I'd dried off, I'd moved through panic, disbelief, and some more panic, and I'd mostly arrived at anxiety-laced acceptance. Not that I had much of a choice. I had alien scribbles on my palm and an intimate understanding of just how not alone we were in the universe.

First things first. Sky was here. And together, we needed to come up with some semblance of a plan. I'd feel much better with a plan.

Acutely aware of his presence in my front room, I tamed my hair and got dressed in actual clothes—*with* pants this time—before going in search of coffee.

I rounded the corner into my living room, anticipation simmering at the prospect of caffeine and the reality of facing my houseguest. When I saw him, though, I nearly turned back around to go hide in my room.

I'd somehow missed it in my sleepy haze, but Sky still wore The Sweatpants. The white T-shirt, too. He was sprawled on my couch, one leg bent, the other stretched out. He frowned faintly at his phone and chewed his lip as his thumbs moved over the screen. Looking comfortable and…yeah. Still lickable.

Somehow, I kept moving, and when I emerged from the hallway, he lifted his head.

"Hey," he said. He sat up in an easy movement, swinging his legs around the couch's edge and putting the phone on the coffee table.

The *clean* coffee table. I stopped short. The takeout bag from last night was gone, and there was no longer any junk on its surface. Or on my kitchen counter.

Had Sky taken out my *trash?*

I transferred my stare to him. He smoothed his palm over his messy hair, and his brows tented. "Everything okay?"

"What? Yeah! Of course." I made a beeline for the coffee pot. I injected as much cheerfulness into my voice as I could manage. Like it was totally normal to find Sky cleaning my apartment and lounging on my couch. "Did you take out the trash?"

"I did," he said, tone light. Easy. Like it was totally normal to clean my apartment and lounge on my couch. "I picked up a little. Hope that's okay. I was up early."

"Oh, that's fine. So fine. Thank you. That was…" Why was my heart beating so fast? It was *nice.* He'd made coffee and picked up and, damn it, that really wasn't helping me *not* want to do any sort of licking—

I rummaged for a mug, bypassing the one that said, *I like my coffee like I like my men: sweet and hot*, because that seemed *way* too on the nose. I pulled down a chipped blue one instead. "Thanks for making coffee, too."

Sky's phone buzzed, and I glanced over as he picked it up.

Who was he texting? His partner? Did he have other friends? After last night, it sounded like he kept everybody at arm's length. Like he'd been completely focused on his mysterious mission here. But he'd *also* said he'd…*experienced* being human, so—

None of my business. I focused on pouring coffee. Not on analyzing Sky's social life.

"No problem," Sky said, sparing his phone screen a quick look before offering me a distracted smile. "Coffee is one of Earth's best inventions, in case you were wondering."

I hadn't been, but that was good to know.

Feigning a scoff, I dumped an indecent amount of creamer into my cup, just the way I liked it, before carrying the steaming mug into the living room. "I'm not sure I believe you. Have you had a pizza roll?"

He laughed at that. He was still grinning a little when I crossed to the couch, and he scooted over to make room for me. I tried not to remember how he'd looked stretched out as I perched near the edge, like a nervous intern waiting for feedback. Meanwhile, he reclined in the far corner, crossing his ankles and sliding his phone into his pocket.

I cupped my coffee. Blew on it. Tried not to gawk at Sky's stocking feet near mine. A slightly stilted silence settled between us.

Why did this feel like the awkward morning-after dance, minus the fun hook-up part?

I quickly derailed that train of thought. Murky light filtered through the blinds and slanted in soft stripes across the laminate flooring. The sun tried its best to burn through the overcast sky, but it wouldn't last. Storms were due again today, more moody fall weather. Very on-brand for my life lately.

"So," I said finally, unable to stand the quiet. I adjusted my cupped hands around my chipped mug when the ceramic got too hot and chanced a glance at Sky. "What now?"

He tipped his coffee back, watching me over the rim. He drank it black. Another sign he wasn't from Earth.

I tested a sip of my own.

"Well," he said, "I'd like to try some experiments."

I choked, sputtering. The coffee burned its way down the wrong pipe, and I wheezed, barely avoiding a full spray all over Sky.

He jerked upright, nearly spilling his coffee in his lap. "Whoa—"

"*Experiments?*" I croaked, pounding my fist against my chest. I glowered. "Really, Sky? You can't just casually suggest *alien experimenting* on someone!"

He stared at me for a second before chuckling. I wasn't entirely joking, but he didn't seem to pick up on it. He set his cup down on the clean table, slanting me a dry look. "Funny. Not like *that*. I meant I'd like to see if we can help you remember anything the halix may have conveyed. Since we have some time this morning. I've been brainstorming ways I can jog your memory."

I forced another cough to expel the remnants of coffee from my lungs. Breathing much easier, I shook my head. "Sorry, but I told you, I can't remember anything…"

But that wasn't entirely true, was it?

Shapes. Lights. The echo of something behind my eyelids when I woke up. Distant and half-formed. I'd had dreams last night.

None of them had made sense. None of the images were coherent or resembled organized information that would, say, be stored in an alien info cache, waiting for humanity to access it.

They were just stress dreams, I told myself again. Stress did weird things to the brain. Science backed that up. Studies. Peer-reviewed journals. Real, *reasonable* things.

And currently my life was sorely lacking anything resembling reasonable.

I believed Sky that something was happening. After all, the glowy hand kind of made that difficult to argue. Still, it didn't make it easier to accept I'd been blasted with an alien encyclopedia or whatever he thought.

I took another long sip of coffee to buy time and soothe my scratchy throat.

Elbow resting on the couch's arm, Sky watched me. Waiting, I realized, for an answer.

It seemed a bit early for alien experiments, but I supposed now was as good a time as any. At least I'd had caffeine first.

"Okay," I said, swirling my mug to mix in the egregious amount of creamer. "I'm not agreeing, but for hypothetical purposes…how would you do that? Help me remember things, I mean."

Sky made a thoughtful noise then stretched his arms overhead. His chest muscles and shoulders bunched in the process. The shirt was thin enough to leave nothing to the imagination. Not that I needed to imagine after last night. I'd seen it in all its eight-pack, gym-bod glory.

Did he even need a gym? Or did the synth-skin just ensure he was always ripped like that?

I wrenched my eyes away when he rubbed a hand over his sternum and leaned forward, picking up his mug. "I have a few ideas."

I was tense, wound up, and suddenly nervous, so I tried for humor. "For the record," I attempted a sneer, "I'm not on board for probes of any kind."

"I see." He tucked his tongue into his cheek and considered his coffee cup. Then he tipped his head my way, and his lips curled up in the corner. "Of *any* kind?"

If I'd been drinking, I'd have choked again. That smile was just shy of criminal. I opened my mouth then closed it. On second thought, exceptions could be made.

But as if he'd just realized what he was doing, Sky's flirtatious grin vanished as quickly as it'd appeared. A beat of eye contact passed, during which we both silently acknowledged the boundary-setting conversation we'd had last night, before he looked away.

"Sorry," he muttered, attention dropping to his mug again. "No. No, ah, instruments involved besides your mind. Minimal touching. If you don't mind me using…well, the synth-skin's abilities."

I froze with my coffee halfway to my mouth. "Like…the memory wiping?"

I lowered the mug slowly, and Sky shifted, glancing away like the reminder of what he was capable of somehow made *him* uncomfortable. "

"Not like that," he said, rubbing his neck. "Just…just a little bit of a neural interface. Nothing too invasive."

Oh, just a little *neural interface.* "How is interfacing with any of my neural-*anything* not invasive? How exactly does this work?"

"It's hard to explain…" At my disbelieving huff, he swiped his hand across his mouth and peeked at me from beneath his lashes. "Low-grade electrical interference? Directed through your nervous system to your hippocampal cortex. It'll stimulate memory pathways and hopefully promote recall."

My *hippo* what? He'd just dumped a whole lot of big words on me, and I'd gotten a little stuck on the mention of low-grade electrical interference being aimed anywhere near my brain.

I took a massive gulp of coffee, not even caring when it burned all the way down. My heart pattered against my breastbone. Swallowing, I lowered the mug and took a deep breath. "Okay. So basically, *probing* my memory banks." I raised a brow.

"Basically." Sky seemed to be fighting a smile again, though there was something cautious in his expression. Like he was waiting for me to laugh and say *hell no*.

Figures. All this stimulating and probing, and none of it sounded like the fun kind. "Will it hurt?"

"No!" He leaned in, serious again when he caught my eyes. "No, Rae. You probably won't even feel it."

"Probably," I repeated, gnawing the inside of my cheek. "You're really selling this."

"I know. But I've..." He pursed his lips. "Well, I've never tried this with someone who actually knew what I was doing."

Right. Because he'd never told anybody what he was. Belly twisting, I set my empty cup aside again, the thunk of ceramic against cheap faux-wood loud.

I felt Sky studying me. I didn't look at him. Sitting back, I dropped my chin and twined my fingers in my lap.

He wanted to zap my brain with Pladian skin-suit tech. I should be running in the opposite direction.

But if it helped solve this mystery—if it proved one way or another whether this halix of his had actually stored something—it had to be worth it.

Besides, I was a *little* curious. And he said it wasn't going to hurt...

Curiosity was really going to be the death of me. Steeling myself, I raised my head. "Fine. I'm not saying I think this will work, but I'm willing to try."

"Okay." Sky's eyes roved my face, as if trying to glean my thoughts. Maybe he'd be reading those soon, too. God, I hoped not.

"Okay," he said again, adjusting to face me. He tucked one leg beneath him, the other balanced on the floor. "I'm going to try some light hypnosis. More of a…suggestion for your mind to open itself. Hopefully let things come forward naturally."

"Light *hypnosis?*" I snorted. "You're going to Jedi-mind-trick me? Really?"

"I think I'm flattered you've put me in the Jedi category," he said, smirking again, though this time with much less wickedness.

I didn't know if I was more surprised that Sky had seen *Star Wars* or how relaxed he seemed. He was in a good mood. It was a stark change from the tortured, broody Sky who'd shown up at my door last night.

Maybe he was a morning person. I could see it. I normally was, too, when my night hadn't been filled with late studying and finding out I was at the center of an intergalactic womanhunt.

Or maybe he was just relieved. Maybe, under that tough, alien-on-a-mission exterior, he'd needed to talk to somebody. Maybe, like humans, Pladians sometimes had to get things off their chests. Their wide, muscular chests.

I forced my attention away from the chest in question and back to Sky's now-focused expression. I needed to know before we did this: "You're not going to be able to…like, read my mind or anything, right?"

Because the last thing I needed was him finding out just how deep this fascination with his shoulders went.

"No," Sky said, with a breathy chuckle. I exhaled in relief, and he shook his head, dark tufts of hair shifting with the movement. "Not at all. Like I said, it's neural manipulation via electrical stimulation. I can't actually *see* the memories or anything. I'm just sending electrical impulses."

I fought the urge to shudder at the wording. "And you know what you're doing."

"Trained for years." He held my eyes. "I've never used it quite like this, but we'll start slow." Queasy, I stared when he held out a

278

hand. "I want you to close your eyes. I'm going to touch your wrist. Your pulse point. Think of that as grounding. You might feel a little tingle."

Little tingles were pretty normal when it came to Sky touching me. Big ones, too. I didn't tell him that.

"We're going to try to relax your mind and step back into your memory," he said, when I continued to hesitate. "To the moment you touched the halix. And go from there."

I gave a sniff at that, settling further into the couch. "Do I want to know how you learned to hypnotize humans?"

He shrugged a little. I took that as a no. Dragging in a deep breath, I tried to tamp down another swell of nerves. I'd never been hypnotized before.

Then again, I'd never been zapped by an alien before, either.

My insides twisted into a knot, and I swallowed hard. I still wasn't convinced there *was* anything for us to dig up, but I'd agreed to try. So try I would.

I braced myself and extended my arm. The couch groaned when Sky shifted to face me more fully. The light brush of his fingertips on my wrist sent a frisson of electricity up my arm, and my gaze snapped to his. Was that it?

His eyes were closer to cerulean in the dim morning light. That messy curl slid over his temple when he nodded gently. Encouragingly. The pads of his long fingers pressed against the thin skin over my pulse point.

"Go ahead and close your eyes," he murmured. I silenced the cynical, anxious clamor in my brain and obeyed. "Good. Now, take a deep breath."

I nearly smiled, biting it back just in time. His voice was oddly soothing—and he almost sounded like he knew what he was doing. Maybe Sky dabbled in psychotherapy between bartending, battling evil robots, chasing down artifacts, and being forced to rescue me.

I did as he instructed, drawing in a lung-stretching breath, holding it, then letting it out, slow and steady.

"Again," Sky said, barely above a whisper.

His light touch *was* grounding. That low, rumbling voice was also nice. He could've read me a terms-and-conditions page, and I'd have enjoyed it.

Focus, Rae.

I pulled in another breath, even deeper this time. Slower. To my surprise, the tension in my back started to ease. I slumped a little, collapsing into the couch.

"You're doing great. Just like that," Sky said, and in *that* deep timbre, the slight rasp…

I gasped when a faint buzzing vibrated up my arm, and I rolled my lips into my suddenly dry mouth.

"Doing okay?" Sky asked, fingers flexing on my wrist. The tingling stopped.

"Sorry," I whispered, cracking an eyelid. He was studying my face closely. "That just felt weird."

"We can stop," he said, brows pinching. His grip loosened. "We don't have to try this."

"No." I straightened my shoulders and squeezed my eyelids shut again to block out that concerned stare. "No, let's keep going."

"Okay. If you're sure. If it gets to be too much, tell me. Try to relax." His fingers slid over the soft skin inside my arm, and I fought a shiver.

Right. Relax. Sure.

Amelia had dragged me to enough yoga classes that I fell into diaphragm-focused inhalations easily enough. Now, if only I could stop focusing on the fact that Sky Acosta was holding my wrist and whispering like a sexy audiobook narrator.

"Keep breathing," he said, and I resisted the urge to huff.

That faint buzz started up again, and when I forgot that it was being generated by the guy I'd been crushing on for seven months, it was actually kind of…soothing. Relaxing warmth. It didn't hurt at all.

I lost track of the number of deep breaths I took. Gradually, I sagged into a hazy, tranquil slouch. This wasn't so bad.

It wasn't bad at *all*.

I'd almost forgotten Sky's fingertips resting on my wrist. There was just pleasant heat. For the first time in…God knew how long, I felt peaceful. Like maybe the midterms bearing down wouldn't be so bad and aliens weren't *that* big a deal. Like maybe I could just take a quick nap.

I had no idea how much time passed. Maybe minutes. Maybe hours.

"Now," Sky said eventually, from far away, "go back with me to the lab. The anthropology lab. Recall what you were feeling and seeing, and focus on the moment you touched the halix."

The lab. The tablet. The white-hot fire. Electricity everywhere, and the mechanical groans of a robotic monster.

A thin thread of that relaxation unraveled. Frowning slightly, I summoned the memory. The rough, stone outer layer had sloughed away under my palm like sand sliding off that pulsing, amethyst-like core.

"It's glowing," I whispered. My voice sounded strange and slurred. Muffled. Detached, just like my mind.

"Yes. It is. You touched it."

I bobbed my head in a jerky nod. "I touched it. It felt hot. And…my skin is tingly."

"Yes," Sky said, a note of anticipation bleeding into his voice. "Your hand was on it when it exploded."

I stiffened.

That moment rushed back with jarring clarity. Like I was there again, living it. The blinding flash, the molten surge that melted into my hand and burned through me.

That light flooded in. Blinding white fire. Shapes. Glyphs?

Symbols I didn't know. Somehow also familiar.

Planets? No, a planet. Blue, green, glimmering like a jewel in an ocean of glittering, unfamiliar stars.

A flash of silver.

Words. *We're here. Come find us.*

Pain split my skull like an axe blow, severing the connection to the light, slicing through the haze. Full consciousness roared back, and with it, a red-hot poker jammed itself behind my eyes.

"*Shit!*" I cried out hoarsely, hands flying to either side of my head. It felt like my poor brain was fracturing into a billion pieces. I tasted iron.

"Raven!"

For a second, I didn't know where I was or who was shouting my name. Only pain.

And then—Sky. That was Sky's voice. Sky gripping my wrists in a near-bruising hold.

"Rae, you're okay," he bit out. "You're here. You're safe."

I realized I'd been flailing and pushing at him, and I pulled back. When I peeled my eyelids open, I could make out his blurry outline over me.

"Sky? What..." I gasped. My face felt wet with perspiration. Or maybe those were tears. Hard to tell. I was trembling uncontrollably. "Was that supposed to happen?"

"*No.*" He was holding my shoulders now, fingers tight. "Absolutely not."

That coppery tang. Oh. Oh, *shit*. That tasted like *blood*.

I touched my tongue to my lips. Sure enough, it was running from my nose and into my mouth. Possibly past my chin. A whole gushing mess of it.

Blurry Sky swore, releasing me and shooting to his feet. "Hold on. Stay here."

"Not going anywhere," I said through my chattering teeth. I caught the gushing flow in my cupped hand and curled forward, breath ragged. My vision cleared enough for me to make out Sky rummaging frantically through my kitchen drawers.

A second later, he was back, pressing something against my face. I reached for it instinctively. My dish towel. Soft. Plain gray. I'd gotten a whole pack on sale for three ninety-nine.

"Here," Sky said, guiding my hand to the towel. Gently, he helped me press it against my geysering nose. "Tilt your head forward."

"I thought it was back," I muttered into the fabric.

"That's a myth." He planted his palm between my shoulder blades and guided me forward. "Like that."

I doubled over and squeezed my eyes shut. "Was that…was that because of whatever you were doing?"

"I wasn't doing *anything* at the end," he muttered. "Once you were under and in the memory, I cut the current."

He was rubbing small, soothing, and very distracting circles on my upper back, but I frowned anyway, adjusting my grip on the towel. So if all this wasn't because of his brain ray, what the hell had just happened? I tried to think back, but my head rang like a giant warning bell. Shapes, color, light…

I'd seen something. Felt something. But it was gone now, buried in a haze of pain and buzzing dissonance. Like static.

"Are you okay?" Sky asked, an edge to his voice. The hand on my back stopped moving.

I opened one eye a sliver, breathing through my mouth. The morning light outlined him. His shoulders were tense beneath his thin white tee, and his big hand still rested over mine, keeping the wadded towel against my nose. His face was tight.

A flare of embarrassment crept in.

"I think so," I mumbled, muffled. "I'm sorry."

"For what? Bleeding?"

"It didn't work," I told the towel.

At least, if it had, I didn't remember it. The eerie sensation of forgetting something scratched at the back of my skull, annoying and chilling all at once.

Sky's incredulous huff was accompanied by a quick headshake. "Don't worry about that, Rae. *I'm* sorry." I slid my eyes his way again. He looked annoyed, but I didn't think it was at me. His jaw flexed, and his lips pressed into a white line. "I shouldn't have pushed that hard. Are you okay?"

Good question.

I assessed. The pain in my temples had started to recede. My nose didn't feel as gross and gushy, either.

I gently disentangled my hand from Sky's and drew the towel away from my face, grimacing at the deep crimson stain. That wasn't coming out. So much for the three ninety-nine special. I'd liked that towel, too.

But when my nose didn't spurt out any blood, I cautiously sat up. Sky's hands hovered. A groove pinched between his dark brows, and he was a little pale. Maybe he wasn't great with blood.

Human blood, anyway. Was Pladian blood red, too?

"Are you okay?" he asked, cutting into my disjointed thoughts. "Do you need something to drink?"

Yeah, maybe a shot of whiskey to chase some Excedrin.

"I'm okay," I said instead, managing a wobbly smile. The headache had subsided to a dull, pulsing throb. Better than it had been, but pain medicine was definitely on the agenda. I should have some in the medicine cabinet. I'd been going through it quickly lately between stress headaches and going toe-to-toe with our Enil friends.

I sat up the rest of the way, and this time, Sky touched my arm to steady me, careful to avoid the bruises visible just beneath my sleeve. He released me as soon as I made it into an upright position, settling back on the couch beside me.

The room spun once, twice. The muted morning light felt too bright.

"You sure your neural whatever didn't cause that?" I asked, tossing the towel onto the table and swiping my other hand through my hair. I probably looked like a not-so-hot mess.

"I've never had anything like that happen." Sky's scowl was etched so deeply into the lines of his face, it looked permanent. "But it doesn't matter. We won't be trying it again."

For once, we were in complete agreement. I preferred my brain *not* leaking out my nostrils. I let out a noisy sigh. "Sky, I know you'd hoped I could…"

Recall something. Anything. And I thought I had—if I wasn't imagining things—though, it hadn't lasted.

I shook my head, rubbing my temple. "I thought it'd worked, but it's gone. Whatever happened, it was like…" Like my mind was an Etch-a-Sketch and somebody'd just given it a shake.

"Like it's too much for your brain to recall," Sky supplied much more eloquently, his expression grim. "I think that's exactly what just happened. The neural interface worked, but the memory was too much."

My heart stumbled. That sounded...a lot more ominous than a shaken children's toy. Did that mean I had some kind of ticking time bomb in my skull I needed to never, ever think about?

He held my wide stare, that calm, unreadable mask sliding into place. "This may not have solved the issue, but I'm not giving up hope. You probably don't want to hear this, but I think this is just more proof the halix did what it was meant to do. Something's in there. We just have to find a way—a *safe* way—to extract the information."

I made a face. "*Extract* doesn't have the best connotation, Sky. Especially after all...that." I gestured vaguely at the bloodied dish towel.

He followed the motion, jaw ticking. "I said a *safe* way. We'll find a safe way."

I bit back another protest. After what I'd just experienced, I wasn't convinced there *was* a safe way. But one look at Sky's determined expression, and I knew he wouldn't be hearing that.

Whatever had been inside that halix thing, he was determined to access it.

Which meant accessing my brain.

Restless, suddenly uncomfortable, and all too aware of how close we were sitting, I took a breath and pushed to my feet with the couch's help. I needed some headache meds pronto—

As soon as I straightened, the world tilted. The floor gave a slow, undulating roll beneath me, taking my stomach and equilibrium with it. My knees melted.

But Sky was there, moving with that uncanny speed. Before I could draw a breath, he'd snatched me around the waist. Strong arms caught me against him.

"Hey," he murmured. "Careful. Not so fast."

I braced my hands on his chest. Whether it was the residual effects of what'd just happened or his closeness, I didn't know, but breathing was suddenly difficult.

He searched my face, mouth drawn in concern. "You okay?"

The dizziness faded, but my pulse didn't slow. I could feel the steady thud of his beneath my palm, too, and the warmth of his body against mine. He was so tall, my nose barely reached his chin.

His mouth was *right there.*

"I'm fine," I whispered, dragging my eyes up to his. "Just a little dizzy."

He watched me like he didn't quite believe me. "You sure?"

I nodded. His grip didn't loosen. He studied me long enough— intensely enough—that my cheeks heated.

"You can let me go," I said, turning my face away. "I can stand."

He didn't, though. "I'm sorry. I didn't mean for you to get hurt." He paused, and then muttered darkly, "Feels like I'm saying that an awful lot lately."

It was enough to make me turn my head back toward him. Lines bracketed his lips beneath the shadow of stubble. That muscle fluttered in his temple. He looked genuinely upset. Stressed, even.

That was kind of sweet. I mean, considering it was the alien mess that'd caused all that in the first place.

"I'm *okay*, Sky. No long-term damage." I tried to smile, but it didn't quite form.

Because neither of us knew that for sure, did we?

The way he was looking at me told me he'd thought the same thing. His obvious worry sank claws deep enough I nearly shivered.

"You really can let me go," I said again, emphasizing it this time with a light push against his chest. "I'm going to go wash up." I dropped my gaze, unable to hold his searching look anymore. And stiffened. "Shit—Sky, I…"

I'd left a bloody handprint on the front of his shirt.

He followed my gaze. The dark smear seeped into the white cotton, a stark, spreading stain.

He loosened his grip enough for me to slip out of his hold, and he plucked at the fabric. "Least of my worries. I'll change back into my shirt from yesterday. It's fine."

"Okay. Sorry." He gave me a dry look—most likely because I'd apologized for bleeding again. I let out a breath, jerking a thumb toward the hallway. "Right. I'm gonna go…take care of this."

This time, he let me go without comment.

A moment later, I was bent over the bathroom sink, scrubbing my face with hot water. Steam curled up around me, fogging the mirror. I stared at my blurred reflection, at my matted hair, pale skin, and the blood still clinging to the edge of one nostril.

I was fine. Of course I was fine. Bleeding and confused and brain-scrambled, but *fine*.

…right?

I swallowed hard and, for a moment, all I could see was the handprint. Crimson against white. Pressed to his chest.

It felt like a warning. A symbol of something dark and ominous.

A sign of what was coming.

And it didn't bode well for either of us.

Chapter 30

FIRST ANNUAL TAKE YOUR ALIEN TO WORK DAY

"**So**...NO TO TELEPATHY, RIGHT?" I asked.

The SUV's wipers scraped away another sheet of rain, revealing the storm-darkened street. Red lights gleamed dully on the wet road ahead, casting a soft glow over Sky's profile as he sent me a sidelong look. One that made it clear what he thought of my question.

He'd changed back into jeans and yesterday's button-up, the one he'd discarded during the alien-exposition-followed-by-striptease routine last night.

I'd done my best to forget the bloodstained handprint on his white shirt, as well as this morning's brain-melting nosebleed. So far, I was doing a decent enough job. Judging by Sky's annoyed expression, though, my coping mechanism—nonstop inquiries—wasn't winning me any points.

I couldn't help it. The emotional whiplash of waking up to an alien in my hallway, nearly breaking my brain, and then *not* immediately dying had left me craving something solid. Something grounding and logical. Like figuring out the puzzle that was Sky Acosta.

"No," he said, lips flattening. "I already told you I can't read minds. And I'm not sure how many times I need to say it, but I'm really not supposed to talk about the details—"

"Okay, fine," I cut in. "Can you at least tell me what your spaceship looks like?" *Or even better...* I sucked in a breath, twisting toward him. "Can I *see* it?"

"Raven."

It was said quietly, but his grip flexed on the steering wheel. So that was a firm no. Of course it was.

I sat back on a sigh, sipping my third cup of coffee. Because if I was going to die of a psychic nosebleed, I might as well be fully alert and caffeinated.

The memory made my stomach lurch, and I gripped my thermos tighter. The normalcy of packing my books, changing into my uniform, and dodging Bob, who'd peeked out at the unfamiliar SUV in my driveway, had helped me feel better.

I'd told Sky I wanted to maintain my routine, and I meant it. I was taking one thing at a time: lunch shift at Oasis then midterms.

Totally normal day. Just with an alien chauffeur. And alien stalkers.

No big deal.

I glanced across the center console. Sky was the picture of focus, one hand on the wheel, the other resting along the window. His mouth was tight, eyebrows slightly drawn, probably from resisting the urge to shove me out of the moving vehicle.

This Creed of his must be ironclad. Pladians took their secrecy *very* seriously. It seemed silly they couldn't make an exception, considering how deeply I was involved. I mean, I'd seen Sky's real form. Couldn't get much more...*involved* than that.

I was even sporting a Pladian tattoo. I fisted my marked hand. Surely being up to my eyeballs in this mess meant I'd earned the full picture.

At least Sky didn't seem quite so inflexible. He'd bent enough to fill me in.

To kiss me in the stairwell like his life depended on it.

A blush tried to crawl up my neck, and I quickly looked away. I really needed to stop thinking about that.

Maybe I could get him to answer just a few more questions instead. We'd reached downtown One Willow and would be at Oasis soon.

I cleared my throat, sliding my eyes his way again. "You said your biology was a lot like mine. Exactly how similar? Do you need, say…sleep?"

Sky didn't look at me, but his mouth compressed further. Enough to form white lines. "Do I need *sleep*?" His turn signal clicked as he veered onto Second Street. "What kind of question is that? Of course I need sleep."

"I meant, like, the same amount of sleep." My flush was back. I tucked my lip between my teeth. "I know your suit makes you mostly human, but…"

There were definite differences, considering he'd just used it to do a little early-morning brain stimulating.

My attention flicked to his forearm, the tanned skin exposed beneath a rolled-up sleeve. That was a synthetic skin. I should've been grossed out by the idea. Instead, I found myself fascinated by the subtle shift of muscle and veins as he tightened his grip on the wheel.

"Synth-skin," he corrected sharply. I snapped my gaze up and met his narrow-eyed glance. In the gloom, his eyes were the color of ink. "It's called a synth-skin. A synthetic dermal implant. And yes, I need sleep. I also require sustenance. Specifically, dihydrogen monoxide and nourishment in the form of proteins, carbohydrates, and fats. Just like you." In the pause, his cheek bunched like he was grinding his molars. He returned his attention to the road. "And in case you're wondering, yes, I produce waste. I don't like pickles, green beans, or tuna fish. I eat normal human food. No Soylent Green. I breathe fine in your nitrogen-oxygen atmosphere. I drink Earth water without dying. *You're* the one with the glowing fingers. I don't lay eggs. I don't reproduce by face-hugging. Does that cover the bases?"

He'd taken me by surprise. I bit the inside of my cheek against a shocked laugh. *Green beans?*

I fought it down, though, when guilt surged immediately after.

Especially because his nostrils flared with his forced breath. He didn't look happy. Apparently, I'd struck a nerve.

I turned my head toward the window and sipped my coffee. I wasn't being fair, pushing him. He was doing *me* a favor by sticking close like this. Driving me. Staying over. The least I could do was respect his boundaries.

All of them. Even if I couldn't stop thinking about that damn kiss.

The SUV sloshed through a deep puddle when Sky slowed at a red light and came to a stop. He balanced an elbow on the steering wheel and twisted toward me, and I lowered my cup, glancing over.

With the full force of his gaze trained on me instead of the road, I could see the dangerous gleam in it. He wasn't just unhappy. He was borderline pissed. My throat tightened.

"Since you're so interested in my physiology," he murmured, running his eyes over me, "you may have also noticed I can experience sexual arousal."

I choked on my own saliva. "I…"

Any response melted when Sky leaned a little closer, into the space between us. His voice dropped an octave. "I can even orgasm," he said, holding my gaze. "In case you were wondering about that, too."

Was that a challenge? A promise? I didn't know anything for certain other than the fact I'd forgotten how to breathe.

Fantastic. Now I was thinking about Sky and orgasms and orgasms *with Sky*, and all the ways I was totally on board with all those things. My coffee nearly slipped from my numb fingers, and I caught it just in time, tightening my grip to avoid dumping it in my lap, unable to tear my wide eyes from his face.

He watched me fumble with a faintly arched brow, like he'd done it on purpose. Maybe he had. Maybe this was a defensive reaction to my prodding.

I recovered enough to sit back and managed to close my mouth, though I didn't look away. Neither did he. A charge vibrated between us. His lips parted like he was about to say something else—but then he scraped his teeth over his bottom one, muttered something under his breath, and turned back around.

Hands on the wheel, he went back to staring out the windshield.

The silence stretched.

I eyed his profile, a little shocked, a smidge turned on, and more than a tiny bit confused.

But then he exhaled again, quieter this time, and ran a hand through his hair. I'd never seen Sky actually angry. It didn't exactly feel great, being responsible for almost getting him there.

"Sky," I started, intending to apologize, but he cut me off.

"I've got the same basic needs as you," he said without looking away from the red light. He sounded resigned, like he'd accepted answering *some* of my questions—if only to shut me up. Or maybe this was an apology for dangling the word orgasm in my vicinity. "The only real difference is the suit's ability to manipulate and generate electricity, the cloaking mechanics—which include the interference with recording technology. And my enhanced immune system." His gaze darted my way then back to the road. "My body runs at…peak performance, I guess you could say. I heal a little faster. Can't get infections or viruses. Metabolize quickly…" He turned his head. That calm, reserved expression was back, but his firm tone held finality. "But I'm really not supposed to talk about it."

"Yeah, I know. I'm sorry." I slid deeper into my seat. My face still burned. Had he just told me his body runs at *peak performance?* "I get the picture. I'll stop pushing."

"Thank you," he said, subdued.

My pulse hadn't settled quite yet, mostly because the tension lingered. Sky was quiet as the light turned green, and we took off again.

He couldn't entirely blame me, though. Anybody would have questions. How many people could say they'd interviewed an actual alien over a to-go coffee cup?

Well…considering how many aliens I'd discovered were hanging out on Earth, maybe more than I thought. Maybe FETR had the market cornered on alien dialogues. I wouldn't be shocked if they had a podcast or something.

Regardless of who was doing any interviewing, I couldn't be the only one who knew about this. Somebody high up had enough information to come up with a cover story, after all. But even that lie would only last until the Enil decided to make a more public appearance. Hard to cover up a seven-foot-tall angry robot busting through walls and shooting pink lasers.

Then I remembered Sky was worried they were after *me,* and the two and a half cups of coffee churned in my stomach. I tightened my hold on my thermos.

But that was why Sky was here. In case he was right, and the Enil were still a threat. I risked glancing at him. He didn't look irritated anymore, just pensive. Brooding, even. That was better than mad.

The silence felt a little awkward, though, filled only with the thump of his dark industrial music and swish of tires. I had a whole day of this, being in his presence. Being around him.

And I couldn't decide if that fluttering feeling was anxiety or… anticipation. Maybe a little bit of both.

I went back to chugging my coffee.

THE RAIN HAD SUBSIDED to a misty drizzle by the time Sky pulled into the pothole-ridden employee lot behind Oasis. A few cars were scattered across the spaces marked with fading white paint, including Tony's souped-up street racer and Kelly's pink two-door coupe.

I nearly sighed. I wasn't sure I had the energy for her this morning, but it didn't look like I had a choice.

The clouds hovered, heavy and gray, promising more storms. I dodged one of the parking lot's many puddles as I climbed out of Sky's SUV and smoothed down my work dress, rubbing my arms against the chill. I really should've grabbed a coat.

I heaved my bag's strap higher as Sky shut the driver's side door. He looked my way, pocketing his keys. The wind tugged on his dark hair, and while he said nothing, his questioning look was enough— as if he was asking if I'd be okay.

I shifted from foot to foot, gripping my shoulder strap. I *was* okay, but...I felt strangely uncomfortable at the thought of being apart from him.

Which was ridiculous. He'd be right upstairs. An Enil wasn't going to crash-land on top of Oasis.

Maybe I'd gotten kind of *used* to him being around. It didn't help that it felt like there were still unspoken words hanging between us. Lingering tension. As if everything that'd happened had created this tether pulling me to him. Like I *saw* him—

I didn't get to analyze that any further because my gaze slid past him and locked on Kelly behind her windshield.

She was staring at us staring at each other, her eyes wide.

Oh no. We'd just shown up together, first thing in the morning. I knew what it looked like. Or at least what she'd assume.

Which...was exactly what we'd done. Technically. He'd slept on the couch, but still. Close enough.

But how did I explain that?

I nearly groaned. So much for a calm, easy shift.

Maybe I could dodge her. I turned and power-walked toward the restaurant. I'd only made it a few steps before Kelly's car door slammed. Her footsteps sped up.

She was coming.

I cast a desperate look Sky's way as he rounded the SUV. He flicked his brows in a *you're-on-your-own* slant before heading in the other direction. I watched him stride for his apartment stairs. He didn't look back, the alien traitor.

I turned around just as Kelly descended on me with bouncing curls and the widest of smiles.

"Good morning, Rae-bae," she said, tone positively chipper. Her eyes sparkled with razor-sharp curiosity. "Details. *Now.*"

Resigned, I sighed, adjusting my bag's strap again and falling into step beside her. "Morning, Kelly."

The gravel crunched under our shoes as a gust of wind blew in the scent of petrichor and frying bacon from the kitchen vents.

"So," she said casually, "are you, like, banging the hottie bartender or what?"

Heat flooded my face. "Seriously? You couldn't even wait until we're inside?"

I glanced over my shoulder, but thankfully, Sky had already disappeared up the back steps leading to his door. He was nowhere to be seen. For now. I exhaled, relieved.

"No, I'm not sleeping with Sky," I said, turning a glare on her.

"Why not?"

Yeah, why not?

I cleared my throat, shoving back my hair. "Because. We're just...friends."

Friends. If that was what you wanted to call two people—a human and an alien—stuck together thanks to a mysterious mission from the stars and my inability to keep my hands off extraterrestrial things.

...all extraterrestrial things.

"Friends," Kelly repeated, the word dripping so much skepticism I was surprised we weren't leaving a trail.

"Yeah, friends." I shot her a look. "Two people of the opposite sex can be friends, Kel."

"Okay. And why were you riding to work with your friend today?"

We neared the break area, which smelled faintly of stale cigarette smoke. Tony must've had a pre-lunch-shift puff. Kelly stepped through the cloud and pulled open the employee entrance door, raising a brow when I didn't answer right away.

"I've been having car issues," I said, shrugging and nearly dislodging my bag in the process. I hitched it back up. "Remember the other day?"

She nodded, eyes narrowed, and I forged ahead, the lie gaining steam. "He, uh, gave me a ride home after my accident and offered to pick me up today."

Kelly snorted, flipping her hair over her shoulder as we stepped inside. "Well, if I'd known that's all it took to get his attention, I'd have slashed my own tires months ago."

A snicker escaped me before I could stop it, and I elbowed her. "Stop. You would not have. You wouldn't stoop that low."

"Okay, fine. You're right. I don't usually need to." She stopped at the back server station's touchscreen and eyed me speculatively. "But some guys are worth a little desperation."

Desperation. Gnawing on my lip, I watched her punch in her code and wondered, not for the first time, if *I* was the desperate one. After all, I couldn't seem to shake my fascination with Sky—nor my attraction. *Despite* everything I knew.

Kelly moved aside, giving me access to the screen for my own clock-in. I typed in my numbers.

"What's he think about the aliens?" Kelly asked, and I missed a digit. The screen flashed red, and I couldn't suppress my snicker.

"Oh, he's got *very* strong opinions," I said, biting my cheek hard as I started over.

This time, the numbers took, and when I turned back to Kelly, she was watching me with barely disguised glee. "Really?"

"Yeah." Before she could dig deeper, I leaned in. "Speaking of. This friend of yours…the FETR guy?"

"Cane," she supplied, the gleam in her eyes becoming nearly maniacal.

"Yeah, him. Does he know…well, have you guys actually *made contact* with any extraterrestrials? Hypothetically, I mean. I still don't know if I believe in any of that stuff," I added for good measure.

Which was clearly a lie. I didn't have a choice now, did I?

"Well, look at you." Kelly leaned back against the server station, bracing her elbows on its edge. Her smirk was sharp, knowing. Triumphant. "You're, like, hooked, aren't you? Did Mr. Sexy Bartender finally convince you?"

If she only knew.

"No, Sky didn't have anything to do with it." *Sky had everything to do with it.* "I'm just curious."

"Uh-huh." Kelly gave me a look but let it slide. "Cane said FETR has contacts inside the License 16 branch of the government."

"License what?"

"License 16," she repeated, slower. Like that was the issue.

When I just stared blankly, she rolled her eyes and lowered her voice. "They're the real-life Men in Black. Duh."

Okay, now we were drifting back into far-fetched territory.

I arched a brow, pressing my lips together. "Is Will Smith a member?"

"It's serious, Rae."

I schooled my expression. "Okay. And what's MIB think about our alien invasion?"

Kelly grew somber. Which was a strange look on her. It brought me up straighter.

"Actually, Rae…they're supposedly worked up about it, okay?" She glanced around before crowding closer, and her mood shift was sudden enough that I followed suit without really thinking about it. Satisfied no one was close, she continued. "I just know something has the powers-that-be worried. The FETR network's on high alert. Cane said something big is going on, and he and the other Skywatch Spotters in the area were all activated. Apparently, there was some kind of alert message last week…"

Skywatch Spotters? It sounded so ridiculous, I wanted to laugh. I *wanted* to roll my eyes and crack a joke about paranoid YouTubers and tinfoil hats. To make fun of it.

Maybe I would have a week ago. But that was before I'd seen what I'd seen.

Before weird alien glyphs had been burned into my hand.

Before a Pladian had told me I might be carrying alien information in the inner recesses of my mind. Before I'd touched said Pladian and watched him transform.

I curled my fingers, hiding the nearly invisible marks. It was hard to keep up the act when I *knew* these FETR people were at least partially right. About some of it, anyway.

As much as I hated to admit it…the Friends of the Extraterrestrial Races had guessed correctly. Something was happening.

And I'd somehow crash-landed right smack in the middle of it.

Chapter 31

FIRST ANNUAL TAKE YOUR ALIEN TO SCHOOL DAY

LUCKILY, WORK WAS HECTIC ENOUGH THAT, for a few short hours, I was able to forget it all.

Sky had yet to return from his apartment, but I knew he would. He'd made it clear he didn't want me out of his sight. We were stuck together. At least until we could come up with a better plan.

I found myself glancing at the door, searching for him, more times than I wanted to admit. I told myself it was out of self-preservation. *Not* anticipation.

The brunch rush hit the fast-forward button on the morning, and by the time I checked my phone during a lull, I was nearly through my shift. Which meant it was nearly time for my communications midterm.

I grimaced. I'd managed to cram last night, but I didn't feel remotely ready. I'd been slacking this past week. Schoolwork had taken a serious backseat to all the *running for my life* I'd been doing lately.

I swiped a tip off my empty table and grabbed the dishes to help the busboy, Adam. When I turned, I caught sight of the tall figure perched at the bar. I stopped short. My insides fluttered.

I would've recognized those shoulders anywhere. Sky was finally back. Absorbed in his phone at the moment, but there he was, leaning on one of the high-top stools, hip braced on the bar counter.

His hair was still damp and curling from beneath a black ball cap, and he wore a matching long-sleeved shirt and dark jeans. The combination wasn't helping the sudden heat flooding my face. He looked long and lean, and the pang of attraction hit me square in the middle.

I tightened my grip on the dishes.

Ashley, the afternoon's bartender, approached him, and he looked up and pocketed his phone. My mouth went dry as he leaned over the bar, pointing at something behind the counter, one boot propped on the footrail, those jeans pulling tight over the world's best ass. Or maybe it was the galaxy's, considering.

I tore my attention from his backside when Ashley nodded. He offered her that polite, professional smile before tapping the counter and straightening, turning—

His eyes snagged mine. Where I stood in the middle of the dining room, practically gaping at him. I was so busted.

His faint smile faded to something more intent as he pushed off the stool and moved toward me in easy, long-legged strides.

Realizing I was still gazing stupidly at him, I bobbled my load of plates and hurried toward the kitchen. He veered into an intercept course and cut me off halfway there.

"Almost done?" he asked, already pushing up his sleeves. He reached over and relieved me of most of the plates before we made it to the swinging door.

"You don't have to..." I trailed off when he gave me a look and fell into step beside me. "Thank you," I mumbled instead, clutching the trio of glasses and lone chip basket he'd left me with.

Well, this was it. If Kelly hadn't already spread it everywhere, people were going to notice that he wasn't on shift and clearly here with me. Helping me carry dishes. We'd shown up together and were getting ready to leave that way, too.

If I wasn't careful, people were going to get the idea we were more than friends.

We passed Emily at the server station. She'd frozen halfway through tying her apron and watched us pass, clearly stunned. Her wide eyes shone with disbelief behind her glasses.

I flushed. Okay, *that* was a bit much. Wasn't it truly so far-fetched that Sky might actually be interested in me?

I wasn't sure whether to feel validated, considering that'd also been *my* reaction...or insulted.

Maybe both.

Oblivious to the looks we were getting, Sky pushed open the kitchen door and held it for me with his shoulder. "You ready to go?"

Once I'd slipped through, we deposited the various dishes where they went.

"Almost," I told him, wiping my sweaty hands on my apron. "Give me a couple minutes."

"Okay. I'll be at the bar," he said, glancing around us at the suspiciously quiet kitchen. Tony was staring at us, but when Sky noticed him, he quickly looked away. Sky frowned a little and turned back to me. "Come find me when you're done, and we'll head out."

"Sure." I went to work stacking my chip basket while he left through the swinging doors.

After grabbing my bag from the employee lockers and finishing my close out, I made my way back through the kitchen. Tony and Jackie were waiting. Tony didn't waste any time, either.

"*Oooh*," he said and, at my eye roll, began making kissing noises.

"Real mature," I muttered, making a face at him. But when I turned, I found Jackie eyeing me sidelong, too. "What?" I snapped, hefting my bag. "Why's everybody *doing* that?"

Jackie held up their hands, feigning interest in the menu board. I huffed and gave them both my back, marching toward the exit. Ridiculous.

These people seemed more surprised to find Sky willingly interacting with me than the prospect of aliens being among us.

This was doing real stellar things for my ego.

. . .

I WAS STILL MULLING that over as I finished getting ready in the bathroom.

There hadn't been a Kelly in sight—thank God. She'd vanished somewhere once her last table had left. I'd changed into the same jeans and long-sleeved blouse from earlier, and now I stood at the bathroom sink, palms gripping the counter's edge.

Now that the shift was done and I'd had a moment to breathe, that surreal feeling returned. The full weight of what I was dealing with. The reason the hot bartender-slash-undercover alien was waiting for me in the dining room.

I took a long breath and stared at myself in the mirror, patting down the damp weather-induced frizz.

I had to push it aside. As wild as exploding tablets and alien mech-suits were, I still had a *very real* midterm to take. One that had *very real* consequences for my *very real* degree.

Exhaling slowly, I straightened my shirt.

I still had a future. I still had a life to live. That was what grounded me now. I might've *wanted* to run home and hole up there until this threat was gone…but I wasn't doing that. I wouldn't run. That wasn't what Raven Barrister did. I'd never shied away from a challenge.

Which meant I had to stop hiding in the bathroom.

So I left it, and I took a deep breath before rounding the corner. Sky was at the bar like he'd said he would be, peering at his phone again. Texting, it looked like. Again, curiosity rose, but I tucked it away when he looked up.

"Hey," he said in greeting when I reached him. "Ready?"

Suddenly nervous—everything outside this tiny bubble of normalcy felt unsafe—I swallowed hard and nodded.

"All right." He glanced back down, thumbs tapping a few more words before he slipped the phone into his pocket and straightened.

Maybe that was Bast he was texting. His partner. What exactly did "partner" mean? Because if they were bonded, or mated, or whatever the space equivalent was, then…he was right about kissing me being a mistake.

Hadn't he just given me a lecture, though, on why he couldn't afford attachments? It hadn't seemed like a lie, either. He'd seemed genuine.

God, we were getting ready to brave evil alien robots. Why was I fixating on Sky's love life, of all things?

"What's wrong?" Sky asked, and I jumped, realizing I'd been staring at him.

"Oh. Nothing. Sorry." I tightened my grip on my bag. "Just lost in thought."

He paused to scan my face, lingering. Concern formed a line between his brows. "Are you sure you want to do this?"

This was certainly a broad enough generalization for…well, *everything*. Starting with spending the rest of my immediate future with Sky.

But I forced a smile. "That midterm isn't going to take itself."

He waited another second, as if giving me a chance to change my mind. When I didn't, he nodded and jerked his head at me to follow. "All right. Let's go then."

I kept to his heels as we made our way to the side door, studiously ignoring Emily and Kelly, who'd appeared from the kitchen and were now gaping with the rest of them. God, even Ashley was watching with raised brows.

I held my chin high.

Outside, the rain had lessened to a soft mist, but the sky was still gray and swollen with the promise of storms. We crunched across the damp gravel toward Sky's SUV. I glanced once over my shoulder at the building. As we passed into the shadow of the structure, something cold crawled over my skin. Something a lot like foreboding.

Imagination, I told myself. *Stress.*

The product of too much caffeine, too little sleep, and far too many glowing alien objects. I hunched my shoulders against the chill and picked up my pace.

First, I needed to survive this midterm.

Then I'd take on the Enil.

One thing at a time.

I climbed into the SUV and buckled in. Sky's music spilled from the speakers and wrapped around me, a slow, glitchy melody that sounded like outer space dreaming. That tugging feeling of danger settled deeper in my chest.

Maybe it wasn't foreboding. Maybe it was inevitability.

Or maybe it was the understanding of how much everything had changed.

The memory of that bloody handprint drifted back. I focused instead on Oasis disappearing out the window before turning my attention to the road ahead.

Chapter 32

BEAM ME UP, ANXIETY

MURMURING VOICES AND BURSTS OF LAUGHTER ECHOED through Kepler Hall. I wove through the commotion, bag secured to my shoulders. The afternoon classes were always more crowded, which made the common area busier. So many people.

I felt twitchy. So twitchy, my skin itched.

I resisted the urge to glance back at Sky. I knew he was there, following me past the hallway openings, scattered tables, and cushioned benches. Somehow, his quiet presence made it a little better. He was quickly becoming my personal alien safety blanket.

I needed to get it together. This anxiety wasn't going to help me pass this test. And I'd need all the help I could get.

I paused at the corner by the elevator and took a deep, steadying breath. The scent of baked pretzels wafted from the tiny snack shop, reminding me I'd only consumed a handful of Hula fries and too many cups of coffee today.

I didn't trust my stomach, though. It hadn't been quite right since this morning.

I lifted my phone and checked the time. I still had fifteen minutes until my midterm. Fifteen minutes to calm down. Swallowing hard, I tightened my grip and glanced around.

Everything was too bright and loud. Movement and echoing voices. A man walked past, earbuds leaking tinny music. A janitor pushed a mop bucket through swinging doors across the way. A group of people at the next table dissolved into cackles so suddenly I jumped. My heart gave an extra thump, and I shoved my phone back into my pocket with more force than necessary.

It was all so...*normal*. Gripping my bag's straps, I dug my nails into the fabric. How could they all act so normal?

I supposed it wasn't hard without garbled voices, strange lights, or creaking, chrome-plated death robots lurking in the shadows.

This was a *me* problem. *I* felt out of place inside this normalcy. I'd felt that way all day. At work, in traffic. Now here.

It felt like...like I didn't belong. Like the world was suddenly too big and ominous, and danger—

"Are you all right?" Sky asked—and I jolted, barely biting back a gasp.

Definitely a me problem.

Willing myself to calm down, I looked up to find him peering at me from beneath his ball cap. It was the first thing he'd said in a while. He'd seemed lost in his own head on the drive here, and he'd been just as quiet since we'd made it inside.

Now, though, he was watching me like he could see I was barely holding it together. His brow furrowed in concern. Like he saw it and *understood*.

He was also waiting for an answer, so I made myself nod. It must've looked as unconvincing as it felt. He narrowed his eyes, shifting his body to block out some of the people, the lights.

"What's wrong?" he asked, more quietly.

Normally, I would've laughed, because where did I even begin? Did he want a list?

To start with, I had no idea where to go from here.

Once I knocked out this midterm...then what? Did I just...hide out in my apartment? Twiddle my thumbs until Sky figured out how to prove, one way or another, if I'd absorbed something from the halix? Hoping, while I was at it, that there was a way to fix it that didn't involve severely damaging me in the process?

The crimson-stained T-shirt reminded me it might be too late for that.

I closed my eyes briefly. God, *could* we fix this? Was there a way to escape any of this unscathed? Or was that nosebleed just the start of something much worse?

This pent-up, strung-tight, ready-to-explode feeling was *not* sustainable. My life was spinning off its axis. Out of control.

Maybe coming here had been a bad idea, after all. What was the point? Some half-cocked bid to hold onto my pre-alien life goals? Maybe I should've listened to Sky, who was now looking at me with his eyes crinkled in worry beneath the shadow of his hat—

"Rae!"

I yelped, spinning so fast, I nearly toppled into Sky. He steadied me with a hand on my waist and released me as soon as I'd regained my footing.

Amelia stood there, eyeing me like I'd lost my mind. Which wasn't necessarily far off.

"Hi!" I rested a hand over my thundering heart. Sky stepped a little farther to the side, putting some space between us. I pretended not to notice. "Sorry, A. You scared me."

"*Hi?* Just hi?" she repeated incredulously, scanning me from head to toe. "Are you okay? You didn't answer *any* of my texts today, not to mention you were weird last night when I stopped by. And today you look like you did after we watched *Paranormal Activity* and you were so convinced you were going to sleepwalk, you refused to sleep for…" She trailed off as her gaze drifted past me, and she blinked. "You're Sky."

"Yeah," he said, transferring his weight. *I* flushed at the charming half-smile he aimed my best friend's way. His arm brushed mine when he offered her his hand. "I didn't get to introduce myself at Crescent. Nice to meet you. Amelia, right? I'm Sky Acosta. I think I've seen you before, when you stopped in to see Rae at work."

"Uh huh. I know who you…" She caught herself and pursed her lips. "Nice to meet you."

She shook his proffered hand, but her attention slid to me and she slowly raised her eyebrows. Her *tell-me-now* look.

Oh boy. I nearly winced. If Sky thought my questions were a lot, an Amelia tirade would be a real shocker.

"Sorry," I told her again, biting my lip. "Didn't mean to ignore your texts. It's been kind of a crazy few days." *Hah.* Understatement. "And last night was…" *Easily one of the weirdest nights of my existence.* I coughed. "Busy. Then I worked today and…I had stuff."

I gestured vaguely at the university around us, like school was the *stuff* keeping me from texting. *Not* a galactic crisis.

"Sure." Amelia eyed Sky with obvious doubt.

He wore a tight-lipped smile.

Oh, God. My brain chose that moment to recall all those humiliating things she'd said through the door. Was he remembering them right now too?

It was too late to do anything about it. He knew my feelings. The cat was out of the bag.

But still. I'd never meant for Sky to find out about Hamilton and Stella Acosta. Not by any stretch of the imagination.

I'd never imagined Amelia and Sky meeting like this, either.

Or, you know, that he was secretly an alien.

I gripped the straps of my book bag like I was holding onto a ledge. It sure felt like I was.

Amelia tilted her head to the side, and I knew that look, too. It was her digging look. "I didn't know you went to TWU, Sky. Rae never mentioned that."

"Oh, no," he said, tucking one hand into the front pocket of his dark jeans. "I don't. I'm just here to hang out with Raven."

"Oh, *really?*" Amelia rocked back on her heels. Her brows climbed even higher beneath her curtain bangs.

My face grew warm. The pressure of his shoulder against mine was doing weird things to my belly.

When I said nothing—*words? What are those?*—Amelia tucked her lips and flipped her phone face-up, like she was checking the time. "You've got a midterm now, don't you?"

I nodded, pouncing on the subject change. "My communications one, yeah."

"Great," she said, tucking the phone into her Louis Vuitton purse. She glanced Sky's way before turning back to me. "Meet me for coffee after?"

I knew what she was really asking. She wanted to get me alone so I could spill everything about this admittedly wild situation she'd just found me in.

A sinking feeling settled in my gut. I couldn't tell her. I didn't even need to ask Sky. It'd been like pulling teeth for him to tell *me*, and I was carrying an alien tattoo around on my palm. There was no way he'd be okay with telling Amelia.

Not to mention there was a risk. To her.

I couldn't tell her.

I had to keep lying to my best friend.

The handful of fries I'd eaten pitched in my stomach. I cast around for something—anything—to say.

And then Sky cut in. "We've got a date."

My mouth dropped open, and I pivoted to him slowly. "We... do?"

Despite everything, the robots, the scrambled brain, the impending doom, and all that...my insides fluttered at the thought. A date. With Sky.

He looked sincere. His lips were still curved into that small, pleasant enough smile, his posture relaxed, but the quick look he shot me spoke volumes.

Because of course it was an act. And he wanted me to play along.

And I got it. I did. Fake dating the undercover extraterrestrial. This was about safety. Staying close. Finding a solution for my shiny squiggles.

But this was also Amelia standing in front of me, and I suddenly badly wanted to get that coffee. Couldn't I just spend time with her without spilling his secrets? Without spilling mine? Because if I could, I'd cling to her like a life raft before I *drowned in this mess—*

"I should still have time," I blurted, looking at him. I didn't miss his barely perceptible headshake.

When I didn't take it back, his brows gathered. "I thought we agreed."

"We didn't agree to...that." I frowned back. "It's just coffee."

"We agreed to this."

"But not that."

"Rae, we agreed—"

"Sounds like a lot of disagreeing for all this agreeing," Amelia interrupted, eyes swerving between us. There was confusion written all over her face. "Is everything okay?"

Only then did I realize I'd swung around toward him, and he'd done the same. We were scowling at each other. Like the unresolved tension from earlier had come bubbling back up.

Catching myself, I shuffled back a step, turning to my best friend. "Sorry. Yeah, we've, uh..." I felt Sky looking at me. "We sort of have something to do after this."

"It's really not a big deal," Amelia said slowly, squinting at me like she was trying to decipher a code. "I've got a tech lab at the array tonight. How about I call you and we meet up later? After that something you agreed on." She sent Sky a suspicious look.

"Sure." An ache lodged in my throat. Even as I said it, I knew it probably wasn't going to happen. "That sounds...good, yeah. I'll catch up with you later."

"Sorry," Sky interjected, though whether that was directed at me or her, I didn't know. I only knew that sinking feeling was growing heavier, tugging my heart down with it.

Amelia backed away. I wanted to reach for her. Wanted to grab her arm and whisper: *This isn't what it looks like.*

But it was even weirder than she could imagine.

"Nice to meet you...I think?" she told Sky.

He murmured something back.

She cast one last, loaded glance my way before stepping into the elevator. I stood frozen as she turned. Her eyes held mine until the doors shut.

She left a vacuum in her wake. Lonely and empty. I took a deep breath and held it, throat aching.

More lies. More of a chasm.

More distance forming between me and everything I knew.

Because it was easier, I turned a glower on Sky, gripping my bag's strap. Frustration heated my chest. "So I can't see Amelia now?"

The elevator dinged and opened again, spilling out a group of students. They parted around us. I moved closer to Sky, my shoulder brushing his sternum, and his hand hovered at my waist again, stopping just shy of touching me.

When they'd passed, I stepped out of the half-embrace and looked up at him expectantly.

This time when he reached for me, he grasped my wrist, tugging me into the corner, away from the flow of foot traffic. Only a trash can and recycling receptacle could overhear us here.

"I'm sorry," he said, and this time there was no doubt it was directed at me. He still held my wrist lightly, fingers on my pulse. It reminded me of this morning, and for some reason, I didn't pull away. "It's not that I don't want you to see your friends. I'm not trying to come between you. Trust me. I know how isolating this all is."

I swallowed, a twinge of empathy rising. I'd wondered about that more than once, how he must feel. I saw the understanding in his dark eyes, too, as they searched mine.

"But you *can't* tell her," he said, with a hard note that stung.

My shoulders sagged. I knew that. I did. But it still felt like a punch to the gut.

I turned my head and pressed my cheek into my shoulder, unable to look at the quiet regret softening his expression. A couple ambled past holding hands. To them, Sky and I probably looked like that, too. A couple huddled in the corner, whispering.

If only this were a conversation about something as mundane as romantic feelings.

I realized he was still touching me, and I tugged my arm free.

Sighing, he pulled off his hat, pushing his hand through his wavy dark hair, leaving it sticking out in tufts before planting the ball cap back in place. Focusing on the common area instead of me, he leaned against the wall and crossed his arms.

He didn't say anything. Like he was giving me a moment to process. When my traitorous eyes flitted his way again, I found him contemplating me with a faint frown, his mouth pulling in at the corners. There were bruises under his dark eyes, too. He must've shaved earlier at his apartment because there was nothing to obscure the tightness of his jaw. He looked tired. Tired and on edge.

Which checked out. That couch he'd slept on *was* pretty shitty.

Not only that, but he had protecting me *and* the burden of his mission weighing on him. The stakes of which I probably couldn't fathom. Not knowing the rest of this story frustrated me, but maybe I had enough on my plate, worrying about my own skin. I probably didn't need to be worrying about his, too. Silver or otherwise.

Which led me full circle. I hated it, but Sky was right. Even if I didn't take his Creed into account, I couldn't bring Amelia into this. I couldn't risk it. *Her.*

That didn't make this any easier.

Another round of elevator riders boarded, and I watched the door slide shut, bitterness coating my tongue. God, why was I even here in the first place? What was I trying to prove by playing at normalcy? Nothing was going to be normal until we could figure this out.

I licked my lips and turned back to Sky. "Maybe I should just skip this midterm—"

"No," he said. Firmly enough, I peeked up at him. He shook his head slowly. "No, Raven. We're already here, and it's important to you. I know I seem overprotective—and I wish I could tell you why this matters so much. Why *you* matter so much. But I can't. I can only say...if the Enil get to you, Rae, it's not just your life at risk. It's bigger than you can imagine."

"So you've said." It came out snappier than I intended. I fisted my marked palm instinctively and tried to lessen the bite. "And I get it. You can't tell me everything."

Sky dipped his head in confirmation. "No. But I know it makes it more difficult for you to trust me. I want you to. Trust me." He hesitated, and when I tried to look away, flushing at the direct, intent stare he was giving me, he bent until I met his eyes again. "I *want* you to trust me."

Something about the way he was looking at me, like I mattered —and not just because I was possibly carrying a Pladian info cache, for once—threatened to make that lump in my throat rise again. It had to be because I was so overwhelmed.

A large group of girls rushed by, talking loudly, their words a jumble. When they passed, I glanced up at the clock on the wall. Five minutes left before my test began.

I did trust Sky. Enough. I mean, I didn't have many options, but there was something about him. Something easy about his presence, even knowing all I knew. Something dangerously comfortable, too. If I wasn't careful, it was liable to get me hurt in a way that didn't involve mech-suit attacks and glowing tablet burns.

Unable to help myself, I slid my attention back to him. We stood close enough now, tucked in the corner, I could see flecks of other-worldly glitter in his dark blue irises. Even worn-out and frowning like he was, he was still beautiful.

See? Dangerous.

I lifted a shoulder, not sure what to say. I didn't really have a choice but to trust him, did I?

Once he saw he had my attention again, he sighed. "I've got a mission, and you're a part of that now. An important part."

A mission. I tucked my tongue into my cheek. How romantic. Just what a girl wanted to hear from the guy she'd been pining after forever.

But Sky was my best bet for staying safe. For getting answers and solutions. After all, he was the only one I happened to know who could take on an evil space robot.

"Okay," I said, managing a small smile. "I'll do my best. And I *do* trust you. For the record."

Mostly, anyway.

He searched my face for another breath before pushing off the wall. "Good." He cast a quick look around us before his gaze came to rest on me again. "I'm sorry about Amelia. Maybe we can figure something out once we get a handle on things. I'm still waiting to hear back from Bast on some options."

"Yeah. Maybe." I didn't have much confidence in that.

From now on, I was committed to getting this alien mess figured out. The faster we did that, the faster I could go back to normal life and coffee dates with Amelia and maybe even sleeping through a whole night again.

And then Sky could do what he'd come here to do…and go. Back to the stars.

Speaking of confusing feelings.

He moved then, angling closer and lifting his hand. His fingertips were warm as they skimmed my cheek, and I froze in place. He brushed a strand of hair behind my ear. Barely a graze, but it was the first contact we'd had since the ill-fated hypnosis attempt this morning.

I stopped breathing, wide eyes tracing up his tanned throat to find his. He stiffened a little, like he hadn't meant to touch me. For a heartbeat, we stared at each other, the sounds of the university hallway fading.

Sky looked away first, lowering his eyes and stepping back. My skin tingled where he'd brushed it.

He may not have meant it as one, but that tiny touch was a reminder. Everything around me was a spinning, churning mess, but…I wasn't alone. Not completely.

Not entirely.

He was here, too. For now.

Which was a whole other complication in itself.

When I tipped my head back, I caught the barest flicker of emotion crossing his face before he turned away. "Come on. We're already here, so let's ace this test."

I came back to myself, drawing back too. Before I did something I'd regret. Like lean on him.

Because we might've been in this together, but there were boundaries. Boundaries that were somehow just as confusing as everything else.

God, I was a mess.

It was test day, and none of this had been on the syllabus.

Chapter 33

WHAT HAPPENS IF HE'S RIGHT AND OTHER IMPOSSIBLE TEST QUESTIONS

Yeah, this was going just as swimmingly as I'd thought it might.

I hadn't even made it a quarter of the way into the exam, and the questions were already blurring together. I rubbed my eyes with one hand and tapped my pencil with the other before staring blankly at the paper test this old-school professor insisted on using.

I didn't remember half of this from the study guide.

One glance at the clock made me squirm in my chair. Time was draining away.

It was like my brain had dumped all the media communications information to make room for words like *Pladia* and *halix* and angry Enil set on performing lobotomies. I shuddered.

"Focus," I whispered under my breath, hoping it might help. It didn't.

It did annoy my neighbor, a bushy-haired girl who shot me a glare. I mouthed an apology and trained my eyes downward.

Why do we need market research...

Why do we...

Blank. Buzzing blankness filled my head. I tightened my grip on my pencil, lead hovering over the question bubbles. My palm was just visible, the shapes etched into my skin glimmering.

Alien writing.

With an effort, I turned my attention back to the test. Market research helped…it helped with…

Rushing erupted from the vent nearby, and I jumped, biting back a gasp. Air stirred the fine hairs escaping my braid. It was just the HVAC. A bead of sweat trickled down my spine, and I tucked the swaying strand behind my ear.

Just like Sky had done before I'd come in for this test.

That whole interaction hadn't helped my ability to concentrate.

I turned to look at the closed door. I couldn't see him through the tiny window, but I knew he was out there. Standing guard. He'd been leaning with one boot braced against the wall, hands in his pockets, his ball cap pulled low over his eyes when I'd rushed into the classroom with thirty seconds to spare.

Oddly enough, he'd looked completely at home in a college hallway. He wasn't kidding about his ability to blend in. At least, until you noticed how alert he was. How closely he watched everything. Like he was searching for a threat.

Which, to be fair, was exactly what he was doing.

A very real threat.

The longer the test dragged on, the more jittery I felt. Like the passing of each second wound the coiled dread in my chest a little tighter.

Tearing my gaze from the door, I looked around the classroom instead.

Were any of these students *involved* in this alien madness? Were there FETR members among us? Did anyone else know the threats hidden in the sky above?

At least…I assumed they were up there. Where were the Enil when they weren't in their robot mech suits? In those balls of light like the one that'd run me off the road? I hadn't gotten around to asking Sky. There wasn't a guarantee he'd tell me, of course, but…

God. I wasn't paying *any* attention to this stupid test. It was dumb to even be here. What was one midterm in the middle of all this—

Suddenly, I realized my hand was moving.

I inhaled sharply and yanked the pencil away from the paper. But it was too late. The damage was done.

The writing utensil slipped from my numb fingers and clattered onto the floor. Heads turned my way, but I didn't care.

Because I'd scrawled alien scribbles all over my paper's margin.

My heart skidded to a stop before pounding double-time.

I had *no memory* of writing any of it.

"No way," I whispered, picking up the paper. I brought it close enough that it brushed the tip of my nose. My hand shook.

"*Shhh!*" Bushy Hair hissed at me.

I ignored her.

The lines weren't random. Not a doodle. They were…strangely familiar.

Maybe because I was wearing them. They were the same kinds of shapes on my hand. Pladian writing.

I'd just written *Pladian* on my comm test.

"Holy shit," I whispered, clutching the paper tightly enough that it wrinkled.

My neighbor's glare drilled into the side of my face. "*SHH!*"

And then—

Pop.

The lights went out.

My fingers spasmed on the test, and I stiffened. Gasps and titters rose around me. The blinds had been pulled shut on the three rectangular windows, and the murky beams of sunlight sliced through the cracks.

"Relax," the bored professor said from where he'd been surfing the internet on his work computer. His screen was dark now, too. "It's just a power surge."

That didn't make me feel better. Mainly because I knew those power surges were just a flimsily constructed excuse.

A cover-up for something much worse.

Seconds later, the emergency lights flared on, casting everything in an eerie, pale glow. Washing out faces into skeletal visages. Like something from a haunted house.

Also not exactly reassuring.

I gripped the edge of the desk with my free hand, breaths shallow, and looked toward the door. My fingers trembled, and I accidentally wrinkled the test even more. I still couldn't see Sky through the narrow window. The hall was dark, too.

"Everyone, stay calm, please," the professor called over the murmurs increasing in volume. "We should be used to this by now. This is likely residual from the solar flares. Let's give it a minute…"

I stopped listening. Because a prickling, tingling feeling was gathering beneath my skin. The hair on my arms and the back of my neck stood on end. The air was coming alive.

I knew that feeling.

It was unmistakable. I'd felt it before, once in the road, when I'd seen a UFO. Then again, in the lab.

Which meant—

I bolted to my feet, slinging my bag over my shoulder. A tremor shook the floor, a subtle, nearly imperceptible vibration. But I registered it. It settled hard in my gut, hollowing it out.

We were *so* screwed.

"Raven? What are you doing?" my professor asked, clearly startled when I whirled and began to move quickly.

I didn't spare him a glance, weaving through the rows of desks. I nearly kicked over a woman's purse in my haste. People were staring.

The wall-mounted TV burst to life in a fizzing blaze of static. Sparks spat from the connection in the wall. Someone screamed.

Screw this.

I broke into a run, shoving the crumpled test deep into my pocket. Later. I could worry about that later. I almost crashed into a student by the door, but I shoved past him and reached for the handle—only to stop short, gasping.

Not *again*.

My palm was glowing.

The brilliant white glow seeped from beneath my skin, illuminating the bone, sinew, and blood vessels beneath. It turned my flesh translucent and cast an ethereal halo of light around me, a veritable beacon.

318

The guy I'd nearly run into stumbled back, eyes wide. "What the hell—"

"*Shit*," I agreed.

I made a fist. It did a total of nothing since the light streamed out between my fingers. Giving up, I reached for the door with my other hand, ripped it open, and stumbled through.

"Sky!" I yelled before I'd even made it two steps.

The hallway shuddered.

My startled yelp snagged in my throat as I spun in a circle. The walls shook, raining down dust. Terrified shouts and cries rose through the din. The fire alarm activated, its shrieking horns joining the chorus of screams and pounding feet rounding the corner.

The fear that surged through me was slick and cold, forming a ball in my chest and stealing my breath.

I heard them before I saw them—pounding feet, panicked shouting. Coming from around the far corner. Before I could move, running, frightened people flooded the hallway. Someone clipped my shoulder, pushing me off to the side. I flattened myself against the wall and frantically searched the faces streaking past.

"*Sky!*"

A wide-eyed man grabbed me. "There's a— I don't even know, but you've got to run!"

Run. Running sounded great. But Sky was here somewhere.

Pushing free, I yelled his name again and gave the stranger a light shove back into the fray. He didn't wait around, and I didn't blame him. Especially as another ominous rumble shook the building.

I hesitated, every cell urging me to follow the crowd. But I was safer with Sky. And he *had* to be here somewhere. He wouldn't have left me.

…right?

Movement in my periphery stole my breath—

And there he was.

Sky melted from the shadows, his outline solidifying between one blink and the next.

"Holy *crap*," I whispered, staring. Forgetting, for a moment, the imminent doom bearing down on us.

That invisibility was a handy trick. He'd demonstrated it in my apartment, but it was wholly different now, with the adrenaline riding high in my veins and that battle-ready tension he radiated.

His chest heaved like he'd been running, and his eyes glinted every shade of blue in the white light pouring from my palm. His attention dropped to it before lurching back to my face.

"Did it light up before the power went out?"

"No," I said, fisting my blazing hand. "Or wait—maybe around the same time."

His hat was gone, and nothing hid his grim expression. He looked deadly serious, focused, and *intense*.

I'd never seen him like this. Even when he'd found me on the side of the road. Even when he'd shown up at my apartment. Gone was any of the softness leftover from when he'd asked me to trust him and tucked my hair behind my ear with gentle fingers.

Which was probably for the best because a second later he bit out, "The Enil are here. One of their mech-suits just assembled in the boiler room."

Oh my God.

Terror rooted me in place until Sky grasped my shoulder, pulling me out from the path of more fleeing students. It was enough to jolt me from my shock. I abandoned my pride and threw my arms around his waist, clinging to him in a way I'd undoubtedly be embarrassed about later.

Had these people seen it? Was that why everyone was running and screaming? Evil, murderous robots would do that. Maybe this was finally the incident that couldn't be explained away and lied about.

There was no way all these people would forget seeing a rampaging Enil in the halls. Especially without Sky to do his brain-zapping thing.

Which he wouldn't be here to do because surely we were *also* about to get the hell out of here.

But when Sky didn't move, I eased my grip and leaned back,

peering up at him. "Why aren't we running, too?" I shouted over the screams and blaring alarm.

He opened his mouth, but a distant *boom* answered before he could. He swore instead, tensing against me as the building rocked. I buried my face in his shoulder. Emergency lights blinked, and dust fluttered like snow from the vents.

And then I heard it.

A roar. Far away and muffled under all the other noise. But unmistakable.

That same mechanical, garbled sound that haunted my nightmares.

My insides tightened, panic clamping my throat shut. I squeezed Sky's waist harder, slowly raising my head again.

"It's too late," Sky answered finally, when the shaking had subsided. There was resignation gleaming in his eyes, in the thin line his lips formed. "Stay close to me, okay?"

Stay *close*? I couldn't get any closer, unless I crawled inside his skin. Which, admittedly, might be safer.

I flinched when the building gave another almighty shudder. With a crackle, the nearest emergency light exploded, plunging us into dusty darkness. Distant sunlight filtered in beams from the hall's mouth and open doors. It did nothing to dim the glow my palm gave off. It shone even brighter in the gloom.

"Are they here for me?" I asked Sky, gripping his shirt with my non-flashlight hand.

He wasn't looking at me, and he didn't respond. He didn't need to. I wasn't stupid. I knew the answer.

I'd come to the school despite his warnings. Naively thinking I could pretend, even for one afternoon, that this nightmare wasn't real. I'd been trying to cling to routine, and look where that'd gotten me.

"We need to go," I said again, pulling away. Running had to be better than just *standing* here.

"There's no use," Sky said, his face hardening. His eyes were on the distant hallway opening. The one all the scared people had come from. "They tracked you. If we run, they'll just follow."

Oh God. *Tracked* me. I uncurled my fingers. He'd been right. We were trapped, and they'd come for *me*.

My hand radiated light like a signal flare. Like a lighthouse. Except instead of guiding ships to me, it was summoning alien robots. Sickness roiled in my gut. "So what do we do?"

"You stay here," Sky said, turning away. He paused long enough to look over his shoulder at me. "And I eliminate the threat."

"Eliminate the…" I sagged against the wall, staring at him. He was going to *fight* them? *Here*? "Wait, Sky—"

"Stay behind me, okay?" With that, he swiveled to face the hallway, settling into a waiting stillness.

I gaped at him, clutching my shining hand to my chest. He seemed oddly calm for someone about to take on a giant Megatron. Like he did this every day.

Did he do this every day, in between mixing martinis?

It suddenly occurred to me that I had no idea.

Tearing my attention from him, I cast a frantic look around for something, *anything*, to help. It was useless. Nothing would help against the thing I'd encountered in the lab days ago. I was a liability.

Maybe *I* should run, and he could stay here and do whatever it was he—

All thought drained away when the air vibrated. Every hair on my body lifted. Pulse pounding, I sent one more longing look toward the hallway's end, where everyone had disappeared.

A metallic groan echoed beneath the droning alarm. Close. Closer than it'd been a second ago.

My chest caved beneath crushing fear. In slow motion, I turned. The lights strobed, but the disorienting flickers did nothing to mask what waited.

An Enil had shown up in Kepler Hall, and it wasn't here to take a midterm.

Chapter 34

EVEN MORE RUNNING AND SCREAMING

My imagination hadn't exaggerated what I'd seen in the anthropology lab. Time hadn't warped the memory of how horrifying it'd been. Not even a little. I'd seen a monster then, and I saw one now.

But Sky had been right; this one looked different from the Enil I'd seen before.

The first creature I'd encountered had looked like a praying mantis made of junkyard scraps. This one wasn't the same shape. Not even the same size.

Still a disturbing twist on the familiar, though.

It moved with loping, fluid menace on four sleek legs built from piping. It'd come from the boiler room, Sky had said, and sure enough, there were gauges and valves melted and melded together, like some kind of Salvador Dalí painting.

But that wasn't the horrific part. Its elongated head—like a wolf's skull rendered in polished steel—swung side-to-side as it stalked forward with predatory grace—despite being forged of clunky metal parts. Tiny grotesque limbs jutted from its chest, tipped in needle-sharp appendages. *Fingers.*

It had gnarled little arms. Like someone had combined a Mecha

T-Rex with the Big Bad Wolf. Surreal and ridiculous and it might have been comical if those arms hadn't ended in scalpel-like claws designed to tear into flesh. Probably brain matter, too.

I tucked my brightly shining hand behind my back.

The strobe lights bounced off its mishmash of alloys and scrap, casting it in staccato bursts of white and shadow as it prowled from the hallway entrance. There were recognizable shapes embedded in there. An air filter frame, a microscope, a cracked, warped flatscreen. So strange.

The word robot didn't quite fit. Sky was right. It moved like no collection of random parts should. Like it was part animal, part machine. All really bad news.

The Enil had found me. *They were here.* And this time, they weren't sneaking in shadows.

They were coming right for us.

The awful groaning, clanking noise grew clearer the closer it came. A pair of green, pulsing orbs locked on where I stood behind Sky, my palm still burning bright and steady. I tucked my hand behind my back, but it was useless. It gave off enough light to cast our shadows on the tiled floor.

The Enil emitted a sound, all grinding metal and warped modulations. It took me a second to recognize: *speech.* It was talking to us. Or maybe it was chatting to the other Enil via some alien walkie-talkie tech. Maybe it was cursing in Enilese.

Whatever it was saying, the sound of its language was as terrifying this time as it'd been before. Almost more so now that I knew what this thing was. What it was capable of.

Lungs heaving, I glanced at Sky. If he understood anything the Mech T-Rex Wolf had said, he didn't respond. He simply adjusted his stance, coming forward onto the balls of his feet and rolling his shoulders back.

Like he was preparing.

Apparently, the Enil took that as an answer.

It angled its massive body. Blade-like protrusions glinted along its limbs. Its serrated jaws opened, and it loosed a digitized roar loud enough to drown out the fire alarm. Loud enough to rattle my teeth and make me slap my hands over my ears. I would've staggered back if I hadn't already pressed myself into the wall.

Before I could recover, it charged.

I screamed as tile cracked under its claws. It moved so fast, it was a blur of metal and death. The crunch of its footfalls mingled with the clanking, groaning squeal of impossibly bending joints.

It was coming right for *me.*

"Rae, go!" Sky tore his eyes from the charging alien long enough to give me a push.

I wasn't ready for it.

My ankles tangled, and I hit the floor hard, my backpack taking the brunt of the impact. Air whooshed from my lungs, and stars burst behind my eyes. Dazed, I rolled to my side and looked up.

Sky had planted himself between me and the threat.

But that wasn't the craziest part.

The craziest part was that he was *covered* in electricity.

Before, when he'd said he could manipulate it, I hadn't quite grasped his meaning. Now I did. Strands of energy crackled over his hands, crawling up his arms, wrapping him in snaking tendrils. They shone neon against the darkness. The scent of ozone filled the hallway, the burnt, biting scent of a gathering storm.

Except it wasn't a storm. It was a Pladian in a skin suit.

He'd caused all that electricity that day in the lab. Not a severed wire. *Sky.*

Unfortunately, now wasn't the time to marvel over finding out just how much of an alien superhero my bartender coworker had turned out to be. The Enil was almost on him. On *us.* Heels scrabbling for purchase, I scrambled backward, but Sky didn't flinch. He didn't back away.

Instead, he dropped into a ready stance, arms at his sides, knees bent, like a sprinter before the starting gun.

The Enil took one step. Another.

Then Sky *moved.*

He was a blur of bright blue and dark clothing. A streak moving to meet the creature head on. Another cry caught in my throat, this time a wordless warning. Alarm. Because that was a

325

vicious killer robot and this was Sky, and those claws were *so sharp*—

In between one strobe flash and the next, he disappeared.

He'd vanished.

"What the…" Still wheezing, I shoved myself up to my hands and crab-walked backward, my panic-slicked palms sliding on dust and pieces of ceiling. One hand slipped. I fell onto my elbow, grunting at the stab of pain, unable to look away.

His suit. He'd used his suit's cloaking ability again.

The Enil seemed just as shocked. It reared back, skidding, joints and gears flexing and whirring. Debris flew as it dug in its metal paws and ground to a halt, chunks of tile rippling out like a wave, its tiny, stupid hands clutching the air. Levers clanked inside its frame when it rotated in place. Its green gaze roved the empty space Sky had occupied a second before.

Sooner or later, it was going to spot me instead. Lying there with my beacon-hand shining away. I needed to get up—

A blazing, violently churning orb of blue exploded from the darkness, crashing into the Enil's side. So bright, I threw up a hand to shield my eyes.

Sky.

The blow hurled the roaring creature sideways into the cinderblock. The wall fractured, cracks spreading as the Enil collapsed into a heap of metal limbs. I covered my head as chunks of tile rained down, dust coating my tongue, blinding me.

When the rocking faded, I risked raising my head, peering through the murk with watering eyes. I couldn't see anything. Nothing but flashing lights and vague shadows. I rolled onto my hands and knees with my heart hammering against my ribs and hacked up a lungful of dust into my elbow, searching the gloom.

Where was Sky?

A moment passed. Panic began to settle in, and then…There. The world settled enough for me to make out his silhouette in the center of the blown-out hallway, rubble scattered around him like tombstones. His back was to me, and flickering blue and crackling sparks rimmed his outline, clashing with the disorienting strobing. He was a lean silhouette in the middle of it all.

But past him, the Enil dragged itself upright. Still going. Bits of cinderblock slid off its back. One of its tiny chest-limbs hung limp. Sparks burst from its front leg, sizzling like a frayed wire.

But it bared its jagged teeth anyway. As if to say, *Nice try, buddy*.

Sky raised his hands. A hot current stirred my hair, lifting a wave of goosebumps. A second ball of energy swirled to life between his palms, hovering there.

Hunkered in the hallway, I forgot, for a heartbeat, to be terrified. He was actually wielding lightning. Like freaking *Thor*, no hammer necessary.

The Enil also seemed impressed. It hesitated, those green, alien eyes trained on the roiling sphere. I couldn't see Sky's face, but his back was tense, his body coiled. That ball between his hands pulsed and snapped.

The Enil sank low, and Sky eased to the side, keeping it in his sight. Meanwhile, I knelt on the cracked linoleum, afraid to move. Barely daring to breathe.

Then, without warning, Sky flung the fiery orb straight at the Enil, and it detonated like a bomb.

White-blue fire engulfed the world.

I hunched over and shielded my face, choking on a scream as the gust of heated air and grit engulfed me. Through it all, I caught a glimpse of the Enil's form convulsing, seizing in midair before it crashed in a sparking, smoking heap.

Sky stayed where he was, arms half-raised. Still ready. Static curled off his body like steam.

A second passed. I waited another before I straightened and lowered my arms. My throat was paper-dry.

"Is it dead?" I called over the alarm's drone, voice hoarse. I'd breathed so much dust.

Sky didn't say anything. He didn't even look back, but he did motion to me with one hand, a quick, *stay-back* gesture.

He didn't need to tell me twice. I backed up a step on shaking legs. The alarm strobed in slow, rhythmic bursts, illuminating the piles of debris, the massive fissures in the walls, and the gaping ceiling. The corridor had become a barely recognizable battleground.

And the Enil still hadn't moved. Maybe it was done. I started to relax, relief unfurling. That hadn't been *so* bad—

With a shriek of grinding metal, it sprang back to life.

"Look out!" I yelled, but Sky was on it.

He ducked a swipe from its massive claws and sidestepped with flowing grace to avoid a snap of those vicious, sharp-toothed jaws. Spinning, the Enil gathered itself and leapt straight for him. Sharp talons spread.

Sky's body rippled and disappeared.

The Enil's claws met air, and it landed with a thunderous, floor-shaking *crack*. I staggered back as a low, warped growl rolled from it. If I hadn't known better, I would've thought it was confused. Its limbs creaked and groaned as it whirled, searching.

Now was my chance. It was distracted. I could run. Was I supposed to wait for Sky? Or was it every woman and alien for themselves?

I took too long to decide.

The Enil's sickly green gaze landed on me.

To be fair, I was hard to miss. Even with the flashing and smoke, the pure white light radiating from my palm was pretty damn obvious.

Slowly, the thing turned to face me, the single, working set of its sharp, grabby chest-fingers opening and closing. Its step in my direction crushed a fluorescent bulb that'd fallen from the ceiling beneath one gleaming, knife-blade talon.

My knees locked up. The empty hallway seemed to contract between us. My stomach dropped out.

It was coming for me.

I stumbled backward, toward the hall's exit, too afraid to tear my gaze away, like if I took my eyes off it, the Enil would pounce. My soles slid on the dust-coated floor. Sweat rolled down my temples.

Sky hadn't reappeared.

The creature moved slowly at first, careful, stalking steps. Then faster. And *faster*. Until it was loping like a cheetah—straight for me. That *crunch-creak-whir* of shifting gears rent the air.

Nope.

"*Shiiiiit!*" I turned and took off. I didn't stand a chance, not with this stupid mark glowing and the alien mech-wolf thing at my back. It was *so much faster*—

Sky materialized beside me and lunged past, intercepting the robot monster on my heels. By the time I'd reeled around, he'd fired a thick bolt of blue straight into the Enil's chest. Crackling light streamed between his hands and the creature's scrap-heap body.

The Enil's distorted roar sounded desperate. Furious. Its foreleg collapsed, but it snapped vicious jaws Sky's way, trying to fight through it.

He didn't let up. He poured a steady stream of light into the creature's shuddering body. I gasped as he bore down, straining, like he pushed everything he had into that power.

The air was on fire. Electricity arced *everywhere*, stinging and hot, and my teeth chattered. I stumbled, nearly tripping as pins and needles swept down my legs. But it was *working*.

The Enil's spine arched, limbs juddering. It opened its mouth, and another garbled whine poured out along with billowing smoke. The energy Sky forced into it shone through cracks in its body, lighting it up. Frying it from the inside out. The bitter smoke stung my nose, my lungs, bringing tears to my eyes.

And still Sky advanced, the stream of electricity pouring from him undulating and bleeding sparks.

My lungs ached. It was too bright—much too bright to look at. Turning my head, one hand raised to block the glare, I shuffled back another handful of steps as the storm went on and on—

The Enil loosed a keening, garbled cry, one that sounded like a death shriek, just before the blue glow winked out, throwing the hallway into sudden murky dark lit only by gloomy sunlight and my hand.

My chest heaved as I came to a wary stop. The alarm still shrieked, strobes pulsing like a heartbeat. Blinking through the black spots crowding my vision, I looked up just in time to see Sky sag. He caught himself on the wall and hung his head, breathing hard.

But it wasn't done. Movement stirred in the dark.

Somehow, impossibly, the Enil was *still* going. Scorch marks covered its metal parts, but its internal mechanisms whirred back to life. It lurched upright, mismatched limbs bending and wobbling before it gained its footing. It faced us once more.

"You've got to be kidding me," I muttered, inching back. Why wouldn't this thing just *die* already? It was worse than a cockroach.

I risked a glance over my shoulder. I'd almost made it out of the hallway. The common area was *right* there. We were so close.

But Sky wasn't running.

No, he pushed off the wall, and electricity ignited and slithered along his arms again, those blue sparks rippling out until he was encased in it. Stray bolts lashed out, striking the walls. The remaining strobe lights and alarms in the hallway erupted with tiny pops, dying in a shower of fading sparks.

Then, before I could blink, he'd leapt straight for the Enil.

Metal shrieked as the creature spun, jaw opening, those teeth and claws gleaming. Sky flung his arm out, and I was deaf to everything but the screech of gears and claws on linoleum and my own strangled scream—

His blast of electricity went right down the Enil's mechanical throat. Ropes of energy snaked across the floor, crawling along the walls and ceiling. A strand arced down and struck the ground next to me, scorching tile. Narrowly missing my toes.

I backpedaled, but my eyes were locked on Sky, on the glow swelling around him. *From him.* Terrifying and awe-inspiring, all at once. I needed to run, but I couldn't seem to make myself turn—

The light burst, flaring white. Heat slammed into me like a truck, lifting my feet from the tile. Limbs flailing, I hit the ground hard enough that I nearly bit my tongue off. My tailbone took the brunt of the impact, and the jolt reverberated in every vertebra.

Swearing, I rolled once and came to a stop on my side. The books in my bag jammed into my ribs and spine. I lay there, too stunned to move, facing the hallway.

The air tasted thick and gritty. I couldn't see a damn thing. A chunk of ceiling crashed down as the structure shuddered ominously. Like it was going to cave any second.

Silence fell, though, filled only by my panting, the distant, still-blaring alarm somewhere in the building's recesses, and the high-pitched ringing in my ears. In the murky dark, everything was painted in chalky gray, cluttered with drywall pieces and debris.

Nothing moved. No mechanical wolf thing. No Pladian. Nothing.

"Sky?" I called, pushing up onto my elbow.

Smoke shifted, and then...I saw him.

He looked like some kind of avenging angel. Like something otherworldly and dangerous and powerful—which was fitting. It's exactly what he was. Goosebumps broke out as I slowly sat up, unable to stop from gaping.

He stood over the fallen Enil, breathing hard, his hands at his sides. His shirt was torn across his broad chest, revealing a thin gash beneath, and a fine layer of dust coated his shoulders and tousled hair. But he was standing. Somehow he was still standing.

He swiped the back of his hand over his forehead, shook off dust, and then looked up.

Our eyes met.

Only then did I notice he held something small and metal in his other hand. Orange sparks dripped from it like blood. A piece of the Enil. He'd ripped something out of it. The creature lay in a heap, dark and motionless. The green glow had vanished from its eyes.

He'd done it.

I couldn't seem to look away. Sky had just taken down an entire alien robot *by himself*. And he barely seemed ruffled.

I, however, shook like a leaf in a tornado as I pushed to my feet. My knees somehow held. Sky tossed aside the part he held and began to make his way toward me. As he got closer, I realized he *was* moving slower than normal. Like he was running on empty.

Understandably. It was still impressive that he was still standing—

Another mechanical roar echoed in the distance.

Sky froze. I stiffened, clutching at my middle. Dread iced my veins.

No. No way. There was *another one?*

Then a second sound, another garbled howl. Distorted and unmistakable.

Oh God—*two.* Those were two distinct noises. Two *Enil.*

The cracked floor vibrated beneath my shoes. The air began to hum again, that same, telltale charge skittering over my skin. My hand's glow intensified.

I felt them before I saw them, but I turned anyway, shuddering.

Past Sky, two sets of green orbs appeared at the far end of the hallway.

"Go!" he yelled, breaking into a sprint.

I was already whirling, darting for the exit into the common area. Hauling ass as fast as possible because there was no freaking way I was sticking around for another round of *that*—

I'd only made it two steps before something warm and hard slammed into me. I shrieked as strong arms clamped around my waist and yanked me tight against a solid chest. Sky snatched me to him, and we hit the wall.

Just in time.

A searing pink beam sliced through the space where I'd been a second before.

I knew that light. That was the same weapon from the lab. The Enil had just shot at me with that laser beam.

As if robot claws and teeth weren't enough.

"Run!" Sky shouted, bodily spinning me and giving me a solid push toward the hall. "Go, Raven! I'm right behind you!"

And so I ran.

My shoes slapped tile, but it felt like wading through molasses, like one of those dreams where you couldn't move fast enough to escape.

The floor lurched, and the ceiling groaned above me. The creak and squeal of mechanical joints cut through my gasping and the distant alarm. The Enil were giving chase.

Meanwhile, my palm glowed like a miniature sun.

I didn't look back.

The common area loomed ahead. Almost there.

Faster.

I rounded the corner and hurtled into the open space. As soon as I did, I risked it, throwing a glance over my shoulder, checking to make sure Sky was there—

Bad move. My foot caught the leg of a fallen chair. With a cry, I pitched forward and slammed into a table. Pain lanced through my thighs as I hit the edge, and I barely caught myself on my palms.

I cursed, shoved free, and struggled through a tangle of fallen chairs. *Too slow.* I was moving too slowly.

But I was almost there. The exit was ahead. Sunlight shone through the wall of windows. I was so close, I could make out the trees, buildings, and concrete sidewalk beyond. People. There were people out there, though I could see them scattering as the building gave another mighty quake.

The Enil—this fight—was going to bring the whole thing down. We had to get out of here.

"Rae!"

My name. Sky was shouting it, just like he had that day in the lab. Heart stopping, I stumbled and twisted in time to see it.

His body tumbling from the hall.

A metal arm had flung him off his feet, launching him halfway across the room. He flew through the air. His limbs were limp. His spine bent in a way that *couldn't* be right—

He crashed through a table. The surface split apart beneath him, cracking in half. Wood splintered and metal twisted, and he disappeared beneath the broken pieces.

He didn't reappear.

"Sky!" The scream tore out of me, raw and jagged. *Get up.* He had to get up. We had to go. We were so close to being out of this, to escaping.

Any minute now…

On autopilot, I started forward.

Just as another of those deadly pink beams exploded from the hallway.

Driving straight through the wreckage where Sky had landed.

The blast rippled out. I staggered back, pain slicing deep, as if that beam had driven into me, too. I couldn't breathe. A delayed wave of blistering heat rolled over me, followed by slinking cold. Numbness.

The broken table ignited instantly. Red-hot flames burst to life and licked greedily at the wall, climbing up plaster and wood. Metal warped, and plastic melted and dripped. Steam and boiling chemicals hissed like some great beast.

Smoke and fire enveloped everything.

No. No way. I'd just watched him wield *lightning*. I'd watched him take on an Enil and survive. He'd been a steady, immovable force through all this. He couldn't be…

He couldn't be…dead.

But if he'd survived the impact, there was no way he'd survived that.

Hungry flames climbed toward the ceiling. The table was nothing more than a lump of charred, blazing wreckage.

My pulse thudded. I needed to move. I knew that.

But I couldn't. All I could do was stare at the blackening metal, the rapidly expanding fire. Precious seconds ticked past. Sky didn't emerge from the destruction.

They'd killed him. Sky was dead.

An Enil lumbered from the sagging hallway's mouth—no, two. Tall and spindly, they looked eerily similar except for the slight reddish sheen to one. Like villainous robot twins on stilts, made of multi-jointed, too-long limbs. Even their faces were elongated, blank metal plates set with unfeeling green eyes. I could make out their distorted speech over the roar of flames.

They split up, one going for the melted debris where Sky had landed. The other came for me.

God, was it even worth trying to run?

Flames rippled along the ceiling like orange waves, a tide

sweeping closer. Alarms shrieked. Something popped, and water began to fall. Sprinklers, but too late to do much good.

The red-tinted Enil bore down on me. Its steps shook the floor. Water flowed into my eyes, running into my mouth and plastering my hair to my head. I watched it come. My hand's glow was muted in the fiery light, but it was still there. Still a signal drawing them to me.

Sky had been right. I hadn't listened. The midterm—it hadn't been that important. Not worth dying over. Not worth losing *him.*

Green eyes found mine through the haze. The advancing Enil threw aside a table like it was made of cardboard. The pressure in my chest caved my lungs.

Sky had told me to run. He'd bought me that chance with his life. If I stayed here, if I forfeited now…

Well, then he'd died for nothing.

Even if I didn't stand a chance, the least I could do was make them work for it.

I turned and ran for the doors, feet sliding. The floor was a mess of waterlogged ash and chunks of plaster. I leapt over a chair, pumping my arms.

The air stirred—the only warning I had.

I threw myself to the side. Claws sliced through the place I'd just been and gouged deep into the floor instead, furrowing tile. Close. *Too close.*

The Enil were too fast. Too big. I didn't stand a chance against two. I couldn't make a dent in that metal armor. My flesh stood no chance against those talon-tipped fingers.

A reddish gleam flashed in my periphery, and I ducked instinctively, staggering sideways. My spine lit up as my backpack slammed into the wall, bouncing me into a vending machine forehead first. Hard enough that the whole thing swayed, and energy drinks, candy bars, and packs of gum rained down. Sucking in air through my teeth, I spun around, flattening against the machine's front.

The Enil towered over me. Joints and gears spun and ground together as it leaned down, like it was getting a closer look at the specimen of helpless humanity. The green glow of its eyes filled my vision, and twisted, garbled speech spilled out of it. I was pretty sure I didn't want to know what it was saying. I shrank as far back as I could, but it was no use. There was nowhere to go.

Sleek swaths of welded metal and stitched-together parts shifted as it stepped closer. Close enough for me to smell the engine-grease, fried-electrical scent it gave off. Alien and somehow also familiar. A flattened, blue Ford logo bent across its chest. Bizarre, seeing something so recognizable forged to the front of this extraterrestrial robotic being.

I braced my palms against the vending machine's cracked side and slowly tipped my head back. Water stung my eyes, blurring everything. I could see enough, though. Its neon gaze was trained on my hand. My shining, blazing hand. The reason for all this destruction.

For all this death.

My throat closed, and I looked past the bulky creature, to where the molten pile of metal and burning things lay. I could barely make it out from here, through the water and smoke and my streaming eyes. I couldn't even see Sky's body.

Hopelessness welled up. There was nowhere to run. Nowhere to go. They'd trapped me. Those multi-jointed arms were too long, those claws too sharp. I could try for the door, but I wouldn't make it.

Breathing hard, I curled my fingers around the markings, but it was no use. The glow seeped through, anyway, like I'd stolen a star. My throbbing head spun.

I should've listened to him. Should've stayed away. Stayed safe.

But a small voice said at least *this* way, it'd be over. I'd be done looking over my shoulder. The Enil would have what they wanted. Maybe they'd even leave Earth. My family, friends—humans in general—would be safe.

It helped a little to know that. Maybe it'd make what would inevitably be a slow, painful death worth it. Make Sky's death worth it.

My chest squeezed.

I turned my head, a gasped sob escaping. The water was cold, icy, pouring in sheets off the Enil, pinging on metal that reflected the fire in an orange sheen. Long talons flexed, twitching, as if the creature couldn't wait to dig them into me. As if it was ready to root around in my brain for the information everyone seemed to think was there.

I, for one, hoped it was sorely disappointed.

Squeezing my eyes shut, I cringed against the rattling vending machine and readied myself for the crushing metal grip, the slicing of those scalpel-tipped fingers.

Instead, a warm, hard body flattened to the front of mine, pressing me back.

My eyes sprang open at the same instant a dark form materialized.

A tall, lean form. One I *knew*—

Sky.

I may have shouted his name, or maybe I only whispered it because I couldn't breathe, couldn't think, because how the *hell was he alive?*

He slammed both glowing palms into the Enil's chest plate. The metal dented beneath the blow, and the force of it drew a grunt out of him and shoved his body into mine, squishing me between his back and the vending machine.

But it worked. The robot's furious roar drowned everything else as it launched away from us, colliding with the wall of windows.

Glass exploded in a shower of crystalline fragments. The metal frame buckled, and the ceiling sagged. I screamed and covered my face as shards and rubble rained down in a glittering storm. My legs felt strange, wobbly.

Light and heat and water. Everything seemed muffled. Maybe I'd hit my head harder than I thought, because when I lifted my face, a hazy grayness gathered at the edges of my vision.

Or maybe it was just that Sky was here, and he was somehow *alive*.

I stared up at him as he spun and reached for me, pulling me against him. Shielding me. The building, the air—everything—

shook and fractured, but somehow, I managed to lift my head from his chest.

He looked down, and his midnight-blue eyes met mine. Blood streaked the side of his face, vivid red against his golden skin. A thin trickle of it ran from the corner of his mouth. He was covered in soot and dust and scrapes.

But he was alive.

Too many emotions clawed their way to the surface, but I couldn't get out a single word. I clutched handfuls of his shredded shirt, going limp in his grip. My legs were completely numb.

"We have to go," he said, gripping my waist and tugging, urging me to move. It sounded like he was far away. Fading.

He was so pretty with sparks falling and water slicking his hair. Even frowning. His mouth moved, forming words I didn't catch. Somewhere, an Enil roared, and Sky looked over his shoulder, tensing against me. Water and smoke swirled and blurred everything.

I'd hit my head, and…

"I think I'm going to faint," I tried to say.

I didn't get it out before everything went black.

Chapter 35

CAN YOU CALL IT AN ALIEN
ABDUCTION IF I'M ON BOARD?

SOMEBODY WAS POUNDING A SNARE DRUM. Loud, hammering thuds in rapid succession. I groaned, then grimaced at the grit coating my tongue. My aching head felt like it had been stuffed with cotton. My mouth, too.

Then memory slammed back: the midterm, the Enil, *Sky*.

I gasped and bolted upright.

Only to be yanked back by a strap across my chest. Exhaling shakily, I reached for it as my vision cleared. Seatbelt. One of these days, I'd unbuckle before trying—

Wait. What was that?

I held up my arm. A thick, purplish-blue band of metal wrapped the wrist below my marked palm, gleaming dully in the dim light. It looked like it had fused right there, molded close but loose enough to slide up and down a few inches. No clasp, no buckle. Just smooth, seamless, *otherworldly* metal.

I curled my fingers around the edge and tugged. It didn't budge.

"What the hell?" I whispered.

"Easy," said a rough but familiar voice.

Slowly, I looked up...and locked eyes with Sky.

My heart gave a hard thump against my ribs.

I was in the passenger seat of his SUV. That drumming was rain beating on the windshield. Night had fallen, and taillights blurred past in streaks of red, flying along a highway I didn't recognize.

Which meant we'd been driving for a while.

He was dead.

I nearly died.

"Sky?" I rasped. "What is this thing? Where are we? How…?"

He tore his eyes from the road long enough to glance my way again. "The cuff is an inhibitor. A signal blocker. And we're safe for now. Are you okay? You fainted."

Fainted. Or knocked myself out on the snack machine. One or the other. Either way, my head hurt like a bitch. I touched it gingerly. No blood, but even the barest pressure hurt.

Was I *okay*, though?

Yeah…

Well, no. I didn't know. Something was building in my chest, growing too fast. Squeezing like an iron vise.

He'd died. The Enil had come for me. They were *after* me.

Panic. That was what this was. It was a volcano of…of *feeling*—

"*No*," I wheezed, scrabbling for the seatbelt. Nope, I was *so* not okay.

I was going to be sick. Right here. I needed air. There wasn't enough air.

"Shit—hang on." Sky let go of the wheel and reached for me, but I cringed away.

I didn't want him to touch me. I might shatter if he did. I was too brittle, too wound up, too stretched out and thin.

My stomach heaved. I slapped a hand over my mouth, breathing in stilted gasps through my nose.

Sky drew back, wrenching the wheel. "Hang on, I'll—"

We swerved. That panic clawed its way up, scraping my throat.

"Air. I need air." I fumbled blindly for the window control, then the door handle. I needed to feel the wind and rain. My body tingled, and a creeping numbness was spreading.

I'd nearly died. The Enil really were after me, and I'd thought Sky was *dead*.

I was a walking, talking *alien beacon*. Sky was right. Nowhere was safe. There was nowhere I could go. I'd tried to fight it, and I'd nearly gotten killed. Nearly gotten *him* killed. Had anyone else been hurt at the university?

Because that was my fault. My fault for not listening.

My vision began to tunnel. I finally got my fingers curled around the handle, and I yanked. The car's alarm dinged, but I barely heard it. I was going to throw up if I didn't get out of this damn seat *right now*. Wind blasted in through the cracked door, bringing with it icy droplets.

"Hang on, Rae," Sky bit out. The SUV lurched as he slammed on the brakes, and I was only vaguely aware of shapes and lights flying by as he cut across lanes of traffic, jolting onto the shoulder.

The moment the car came to a stop, I shoved the door open the rest of the way and half-fell out, ignoring his shout.

Wind and water slammed into me. I gulped air, clinging to the chill, the stinging on my bare skin. Doubling over, I braced my hands on my jelly knees. I couldn't seem to *breathe*. Rain soaked through my shirt, my jeans.

The storm raged, so cold and so alive.

I was alive.

Somehow, I was alive.

My heart beat like it was trying to punch its way out of my ribs. Straightening, I managed two staggering steps away from the SUV, puddles splashing my ankles, before Sky rounded the hood.

"Rae!"

I looked up, weaving a little. Bright headlights tore by on the highway beyond. Two of them. Like green eyes bearing down. Sharp claws—

I clutched my chest.

And then Sky was there, tall and broad, blocking some of the fierce wind as he pushed close.

"You're having a panic attack," he said, tone pitched low and calming.

I shivered as he reached for me slowly, but this time I didn't shrink away, and his warm hands closed on my upper arms, dodging the lurid bruise on my bicep.

His fingers tightened, and he bent to meet my eyes. "It's okay. You're safe now. I've got you. Try to breathe."

Safe. That word—and his touch—jolted me from the shocked haze. Just enough. Some of the blind fear faded, and without it, I was left with a tangle of feelings far too complicated to begin to sort out.

He was still holding me. I grasped his wrists in shaking hands, searching for an anchor. The rain swirled over us, driven to needle-sharp pinpricks by the cold wind. I trembled so hard my teeth clicked, but I forced words out. "They came for me. You were right."

Thunder grumbled like a distant warning. Sky's breathing was shallower than normal, like me nearly leaping from a moving vehicle had shaken him up.

"I know." He gave me a light squeeze. His face was tight, eyes shadowed by the SUV's headlights. The downpour had washed the blood away, but the scrapes and bruises remained along his temple and cheekbone, the left side of his forehead. With the injuries and his ripped, charred clothes, he looked like he'd survived a war.

Which was close to the truth. The memory of him crashing through that table, of flames leaping high above where he'd fallen…

"God, Sky." I tilted my head back, chest constricting. "I thought they'd *killed* you. I thought you were *dead*."

His throat worked, and he looked away, at the cars rushing past, the raging gale. Beads of water gathered on his lashes. He blinked them away before refocusing on me.

"They didn't." His lips twisted into something between a grimace and a dry smile. "It was close, but…they didn't." The trace of humor vanished. "Which is why we need to keep moving."

"Toward what?" I pried my stiff grip from his forearms and hugged myself instead. The cold was sinking into my bones. "Where are we going? Where are you taking me?"

"I'll explain everything." He swiped a hand over his hair, slicking it back. His heavy exhalation came out as a white puff, and he reached for me, my shoulder this time, stopping short of actually touching me. "Let's get out of this."

"You mean you'll explain everything you *can*," I muttered. I hadn't meant for it to come out bitter, but there was *so* much, and this was *so overwhelming*. Waking up alive and all-too-aware of how much *my entire life* had changed—

"No," Sky said quietly. He dropped his arms. Somber. "I mean everything."

That stopped me dead in my tracks. Squinting up at him, I licked my lips, tasting rain. Was he saying what I thought he was saying? The lightning washed his slick face in white, revealing his expression. Resignation. That was resignation.

"I'll tell you everything," he said again, this time a bit more forcefully. "If we're going to do this—*survive* this—you need to know what we're up against. I'll deal with the Creed's consequences. We need to stay alive first."

It shocked me enough that the rest of the panic faded. He was going to break his rules. I stared up at him, that confusing knot of feelings tangling up even *more*.

Wind buffeted us, slashing my hair across my face. Another bolt of lightning speared through the sky, and we both flinched at the accompanying ear-splitting thunderclap. That one was a little too close for comfort.

"Ah, maybe we could do it in the car, though...?" Sky turned to look at the SUV. "If you're ready to get back in."

He didn't push. Didn't force anything. Just faced me again and waited, despite the fact he looked like he'd taken a quick dip in a pool with his clothing on. Now that the anxiety had lessened and I could feel my body again, I was freezing.

But I still hesitated.

Something about getting back in that car felt like acceptance. I wrapped my arms tighter around my middle, huddling against the cold and...well, inevitability.

"Come on," Sky said when another moment had passed. He motioned me toward the vehicle. "You're soaked."

"So are you," I pointed out, but I fell into step with him, picking my way through mud and puddles until we reached the SUV. He opened the door for me and waited until I'd poured myself into the passenger seat before closing it.

The thud when it shut felt like the period at the end of a sentence. Maybe one that said, *Here we go.*

After the howling storm, it felt oppressively quiet inside the car. My clothes and shoes were soaked—ugh, *soggy socks*—and I swiped my wet sleeve across my eyes, clearing water from them before I tilted the car's vent my way. The warm air trickling out wasn't nearly enough, but it was better than nothing.

When I drew my arm back, the shiny metal bracelet I wore slid down. Mouth dry, I eased back in my seat, spinning it on my wrist. It was kind of pretty in the dim light, shifting shades of iridescent purple and pink. Not bad for alien bling.

Everything.

Sky was really going to tell me everything. I was finally going to find out why these marks were so damn important, why Sky was actually here, and what the hell the Enil wanted badly enough to crash my midterm and destroy the university.

Because I'd been stupid enough to be there in the first place.

Wind and rain tunneled in as soon as Sky wrenched open the driver's side, jerking me from my spiral. I looked up as he leapt inside, and he muttered a curse, slamming the door. Shaking some of the water off, he blew into his cupped hands.

"Sorry," I mumbled, looking away. My chilled cheeks heated. "I don't know what happened back there." The panic attack—if that was what it was—had hit hard. I'd never had one before.

"Don't be." Sky glanced my way before adjusting the thermostat. More blissful warmth poured out. "I think you've earned a few freak-outs."

I exhaled a wobbly laugh at his wry tone, tucking my stringy hair behind my ears. He wasn't wrong. Honestly, I was surprised I'd lasted this long without a full-on meltdown.

Sky lapsed into silence, like he was gathering himself. I let him, wiping condensation from my window and taking in the view. My earlier assessment was right. I didn't recognize this part of the highway at all. How long had I been out? Long enough, apparently, for Sky to get us out of TWU, slap this fashion accessory on me, and cart us both out of One Willow.

Had he carried me? Something about that thought made me squirm. I did my best to ignore it.

It helped that the heat had finally begun to thaw me out. When I turned back, I found Sky watching me. He'd reclined against the window, one knee bent, forearm resting on it.

"Do you feel better?" he asked.

I nearly snorted. If he meant had I mostly come to terms with him being right, me being in danger, and almost *dying*—absolutely freaking not.

But instead of saying any of that, I focused on the shiny cuff. "You said this is...an inhibitor?" At my quizzical look, he nodded, and I twisted my wrist to look at it from all sides. So strange that it had no seams. How the heck had he gotten it on me? "If it's hiding a...*my* signal from the Enil, why didn't you give it to me sooner?"

That would've saved us a lot of headaches. Literally. My forehead still smarted from where I'd smashed it on the vending machine.

Sky studied the cuff then me. The dashboard's display washed everything in an ethereal blue-green glow. His torn, drenched shirt clung to the lines and swells of him as he took a deep breath. For once, I was almost too cold to notice.

Almost.

"Bast *just* ironed out the design details," he said, shoving a hand through his dripping hair. I tore my gaze from his upper body. "We're not even sure how long it'll hold. Which is why I'm in a hurry. I had to throw it together with what I had on hand, and he's much better with this type of thing."

"With what you had on hand," I repeated, raising a brow. "Which happened to be...what, alien metal?"

A short laugh escaped him, almost reluctantly. "Yeah. It's Pladian alloy. The last of what I had to work with."

Pladian alloy. I was wearing *Pladian jewelry*. I held it away from me, eyeing it. I didn't exactly have a great track record when it came to touching strange alien artifacts.

But…I blinked, forgetting my worries about radiation and brain melting for a second as I turned slowly to Sky. He'd volunteered that information without a fight.

Maybe he *was* serious about explaining everything.

Another bubble of anxiety rose, this one laced with anticipation. This, too, felt like a turning point.

Sky held out his hand, and, confused, I glanced from it to him.

"Can I see it?" he asked, nodding toward the cuff.

I shrugged and extended it between us. He wrapped his palms around it, rotating it from side to side, like he was checking for something. He bent close enough that his wet hair dripped onto the center console. A few drops slid over the back of my hand, too.

When his fingertips brushed the inside of my forearm, I nearly shivered.

A semi-truck raced by, and its tailwind rocked the SUV. In the silence that followed, Sky spoke without looking up. "It's a map."

He trailed one finger along the curved metal. I could've sworn colors shifted beneath the surface, and the band warmed slightly. A subtle pulse of heat. I tilted closer and…nope. Not my imagination. Something was *moving* in there, and it almost looked like symbols or writing—

Then his words registered, and I straightened, frowning. "Wait, what's a map?"

With his head tipped toward the cuff, I couldn't see his expression, only his forehead furrowed beneath that floppy curl. He gently turned my hand over, exposing my marked palm. Goosebumps rose as his fingertips traced the shapes and swirls, a featherlight caress. My pulse skipped, and I bit my inner lip. This time the shiver escaped.

He must've felt it because he stilled. When he spoke again, his voice was rough, like the words were being dragged from deep in his chest. "The halix contained a map."

I waited a beat, mulling it over. A map? He'd said it was an informational cache…

"I thought you said it was a greeting," I said, my frown deepening.

"This is." He tapped my palm before easing back. His fingers slipped from my wrist.

I clasped my marked hand in the unmarked one, unable to look away from him. My skin tingled where he'd been touching me. Like the phantom pressure lingered.

When he finally looked up, there was something achingly raw about his expression, the emotion in his dark eyes. "The halix contained a greeting and sort of a… You could call it a roadmap to Pladia. We wanted humans—or any species we'd left the messages for—to find us. Pladians have always been obsessed with gaining knowledge, and the chance to learn from another civilization…"

He leaned back against the door again, gaze skipping toward the watery windshield, where the wipers squeaked over the glass. "I guess the *why* isn't important. Just that the halix contained a map. And that map is the reason Pairs like Bast and me were sent to all these worlds to find any caches left behind. It's why the Enil are hunting the halix, too."

"But *why*?" I swallowed, my stomach twisting. Unfortunately, I had an inkling what he was getting at. Thanks to my handy new palm tattoo, he thought I had this map now. He didn't need to spell it out. "Why would they need a map to Pladia? Why do *you*? Isn't that where you're from?"

"No." He turned his head, and his attention slid to my marked hand again. I balled it up into a fist in my lap. "I'm not from Pladia. I was born in the stars, remember? Bast and I both are Starborn. Part of the generations born in space."

"Yeah, you did tell me that," I said slowly. Something about the way he was looking at me, somber and weary, made it hard to breathe. "But then why…"

"This is going to be a lot, so…" He sat up and rubbed his hands on the thighs of his soot-stained jeans, flicking a glance at the highway. "Just…bear with me. I've never—well, I've never done this."

Told anyone. Trusted anybody enough—or maybe needed *their* trust enough—to break his code.

I nodded and tried for levity, spreading my hands to encompass the car. "You've got a captive audience since I've been, you know, abducted by aliens." His serious expression wavered, and he shot me a dry look. I managed a weak laugh and wrapped my arms around my middle. "Take your time."

"Thanks." He squeezed the back of his neck with one hand and sighed.

The car's interior seemed to shrink. The seat had begun to warm beneath me, but I couldn't relax into it. It took all I had not to lean toward him.

"The ship I was born on is trapped here in this sector," he said, lowering his arm. "It's a very long story, and I'm going to try to keep it short." A pause, during which he pursed his lips. The rain's song was nearly as hypnotizing as his gaze. Dark and unreadable, it searched mine, and then he said, "The Pladians and the Enil have been at war for almost a century."

I jerked back. "At *war?*"

"Yeah, at war. The Enil..." He rubbed his knuckles beneath his chin, scrubbing the stubble there. "The Enil are what you'd call a culling race."

"What's a culling race?" I was turning into a parrot in my shock, repeating everything he said. At least it wasn't a chicken this time.

Sky shifted, rolling his shoulders as if he could shake off whatever unpleasant thing he was about to say. "Basically, their goal is to find planets like their own and evaluate any life found there. If they believe it doesn't measure up in some way, they wipe it clean and plant something else. Something in *their* image."

A block of ice settled in my stomach. "So—wait. You're saying they'll *wipe out* existing species and..."

I couldn't finish. That made it sound like the Enil had some sort of...some sort of twisted god complex. It was horrifying enough that it didn't even sound *real.*

But it was, if the darkness in Sky's eyes was any indication.

"Yes. That's what I'm saying." He settled back in his seat again, balancing his wrist on his bent knee. "They've ended entire thriving civilizations because they didn't fit their mold. Because the Enil believe they're the highest form of life."

"Oh my God," I whispered, clutching at my burning throat. "Is that what they're trying to do with *Earth?*" Fear licked down my spine, colder than the rain had been outside, but Sky shook his head.

"No. No, they're not here for humanity. They're here for the halix, too."

That didn't exactly make me feel better. My palm gave a phantom prickle. "But why?"

He opened his mouth then closed it. Instead of speaking, he blew out a slow breath and tipped his head back until it bumped the window, studying the SUV's gray fabric ceiling. "This is even harder than I thought it'd be," he said, after a long moment.

Breaking his oath or telling his story? Either way, I felt for him. I did. But I also wanted these answers. Needed them to help make sense of this new reality.

I edged closer in wordless encouragement.

Sky tilted his chin down to meet my eyes in the muted dark. "I told you before that Pladians were—are—explorers, right?" At my slow nod, he turned his attention to the storm-wrapped_highway. "The ship I was born on was once part of those science fleets. The ones that discovered and documented other worlds."

He plucked at his wet shirt, shifting in his seat. He radiated restless energy. So unlike him. He always seemed so damn *calm*, it was disconcerting to see him twitchy.

But he kept going. "The Pladians were in a sector of space not far from here when we encountered the Enil for the first time." Outside the window at his back, lightning cracked apart the clouds, a jagged slash of cold light through the rain. "They'd found a race they'd decided wasn't worthy and were already reshaping the planet, the first step to seeding it. Which also meant they were killing... everything."

My mouth went dry. "They were reshaping an entire *planet?*"

They could *do* that?

"Yeah." Sky's expression hardened. "We tried reasoning with them. It didn't go well. Can't exactly reason with mindless purpose."

I tightened my fists on my thighs. Listening to this felt a little like falling into deep, dark water. Scary, monster-infested water. The Enil were even worse than I'd imagined. And that was saying a lot.

Sky ran a hand over his drying curls. "But Pladians being Pladians, we couldn't sit by and watch an entire world get wiped out of existence like that. So the science fleet intervened. Or tried to." He let his arm fall back into his lap. "The Enil are more advanced than us, and their technology outmatched ours. They didn't appreciate our interference. And—well," he spread his hands, "it started the war."

I was barely breathing, too busy absorbing all of it. Pieces began to fall together.

Sky watched a set of headlights streak past, voice going husky. "The conflict went on for a while. Our fleet got torn apart. We lost..." His voice hitched. He swiped his palm over his mouth like he could erase the emotion. "We lost a lot of people. And so many ships, too. Close to the entire science fleet that'd been out here."

I knew that emotion. Grief. I saw it when his eyes flitted to mine, then away, full of stars and galaxies and an old ache I knew all too well.

He'd lost people close to him. I wondered who but couldn't bring myself to interrupt.

"It became pretty obvious we weren't going to win," he said, finally lifting his face again. His gaze grew distant. As lost in his story as I was. "We were down to one ship, and it was falling apart. So..." He blinked once, like he was resurfacing, and he fiddled with his wiper setting, kicking it up a notch to battle the downpour. "So our leaders came up with a last-ditch plan. An attack meant to fry the Enil mothership's onboard computers—and hopefully disable their drones long enough for us to get away. And it worked. Kind of."

His Adam's apple bobbed with a thick swallow, and he dropped his chin, staring out at the storm. For some reason, I braced myself, some instinct telling me we were coming to the story's culmination.

I wasn't wrong.

He spoke quietly but clearly. "But the attack also fried *our* onboard computer and almost destroyed our ship. We were able to salvage basic systems, but we lost all the long-distance comms and nav data. Everything. All the logs. All our past jump points and everything we'd used to map routes through the stars…"

A stone landed in my stomach. I dug my fingers into my thighs as he slowly turned back to me.

"Including," he said, his eyes boring into mine, voice steady, "the location of Pladia."

Holy. Crap.

There was no saliva left in my mouth. Or air in my lungs. "So you're saying…you don't know how to get home. You don't know where Pladia is. And the map in the halix is— And *you* think…"

Sky nodded gravely. He'd stopped fidgeting. Like now that he'd gotten the words out and it was done—his oath broken—he'd receded into that calm again.

That made one of us. I felt anything but calm.

Because what he was saying…what he was *implying*…

"Space is huge," he said, in that same soft, even tone. "It's not as easy as just pointing your ship in the right direction and hitting the gas. And the mothership—the last Pladian ship, the one I'm from— wasn't built for long-term deep-space travel. Let alone decades of war. It's barely holding together."

"So…" I flattened my marked hand to my sternum. Underneath it, my insides were writhing. "That's why you're looking for these halix things."

"Yes. Because the info caches hold the coordinates to Pladia. Coordinates we need."

Which meant—*oh God*—he thought *I* was the key.

The key to getting home. And not just for him, but for *all* of them. Every single Pladian stranded on that ship.

No wonder he didn't want to let me out of his sight.

And just like that, I was back to wanting to throw up again.

Chapter 36

TO FLORIDA AND BEYOND

I GULPED A DEEP BREATH and leaned forward to flatten my hands on the dashboard. Mainly to stop myself from sliding limply right down onto Sky's floorboards.

"Holy *shit*," I managed to force out.

Sky thought I was the key to saving his people.

Lightning flickered blue through the watery sheen and condensation gathering inside the windows. We'd been sitting here long enough for the car to grow stuffy. Hot.

Or maybe that was the gravitas of his confession.

Suddenly, that icy cold rain beating down outside was looking real good again.

"You think I can get you home," I whispered, staring at the smeared, fogged-up glass.

"I'm sorry." I could feel Sky looking at me, and his quiet tone was just as apologetic. Like he knew what he'd just thrown my way. "That's why I didn't want to tell you. I know it's a lot."

A lot. *So* much. Swallowing hard, I twisted my head to look at him, wide-eyed. "And the Enil? Why are they chasing the halix?"

"That one is a little more complicated," Sky said, leaning back against the door. He was still watching me closely, like he, too, was wondering if I was going to throw myself out of the car and run screaming into the night. A distinct possibility. "We aren't entirely sure why they're chasing it. We think they've figured out we're after it—clearly, since they're scanning for its signal—but we're not sure if they know *why*. The Enil aren't stupid machines. There's a chance they've put it together, and they're hoping to get their hands on the info cache first." He gripped the steering wheel with one hand, biting the inside of his cheek. "Which would be very, very bad. Right now, they don't know where our home world is. And if they did, if they found Pladia first, after how brutal this war has been and how *we* technically started it…"

A new kind of dread crept in, and I sat up. He was worried they'd wipe out his whole world. It wasn't only about getting back to his planet. It was about potentially *saving* it.

This kept getting better and better.

He tracked my movement—and the understanding that I knew had dawned on my face—adding grimly, "We don't even know if Pladia knows what happened out here, since we have no way to communicate. They'd have no warning."

Blood roared in my ears, and I pressed my fingers into my temples. My head ached, and I didn't think it was only from head-butting the vending machine.

He wasn't kidding when he'd told me this was bigger than I could imagine. Talk about out-of-this-world stakes. He'd basically just plopped a whole planet on my shoulders.

This was it. His mission. He was here to save his people—possibly his whole damn *world*. No wonder he was stressed out. And so desperate to protect the map to his world that he thought was inside my *brain*.

A map. I rolled the idea around in my head. The shapes I'd been seeing. That constellation I'd recognized at Dustin's. The things I'd doodled on the test.

The test! I'd completely forgotten about it.

"Sky!" I bucked my hips up and tried to jam my hand into the pocket of my wet pants. Waterlogged jeans were the worst.

Groaning in frustration, I wiggled my fingers, forcing them deeper. "Damn it."

Sky's grip slid from the wheel as he reared back, frowning in confusion. It only deepened when I produced a sodden, crumpled piece of paper and shoved it across the center console at him.

"Look at this." I shook it.

When he only stared at it, I clicked my tongue and tried to peel it open, ripping part of it in the process. Sensation hadn't completely returned to my cold fingers—especially after all he'd just revealed.

"I wrote it during the test. I didn't even realize I was doing it. Like I was in a trance. But…"

I unfolded it enough that a few of the smudged symbols became visible. Sky's eyes flared wide, and he snatched the paper from me, tilting it so the dash's light washed the waterlogged page. He muttered a word that didn't sound like English.

"What's it say?" I asked, leaning closer. Close enough that our shoulders touched.

"It's hard to tell." His brows pinched. "What I can read looks like ancient Pladian. Like the symbols on your palm. Another part of the greeting."

He looked up. Our noses nearly brushed, and I started to pull back, cheeks heating.

He stopped me by tucking his knuckles below my chin, tilting my face up. I let him because his fingers were warm, and his touch felt more real than really *anything* right now.

"This means I was right." His words whispered over my lips. He lowered the paper to his lap without looking away. "You've got to believe me now. After what happened at TWU. And this." His eyes skimmed between mine. We were sharing air. "The halix did some-thing to you, Rae. The map is in there."

In my *brain.*

God, this was overwhelming. The pressure, what it meant. Being so near him. That earlier panic threatened to creep back, tightening my chest.

But he was right; I *couldn't* deny it. I couldn't keep lying to myself.

Something had happened to me when I'd decided to manhandle that stone tablet. When I'd touched the crystal slab beneath. The white-hot light that'd followed. I could dismiss each individual symptom—the dreams, the weird reaction to his hypnosis, my mindless doodles—but together? Together, they were too much of a coincidence.

And whatever it'd done put me in danger. Me—and anyone around me. It'd nearly gotten Sky killed today. I could be responsible for other people getting hurt.

What would I have done if it'd been Amelia? Or Dustin or Lisa? I'd never forgive myself.

My stomach plunged off the edge of an invisible cliff. The growing lump in my throat ached.

There was no going back. Not yet. Not now.

I couldn't even say goodbye, because how was I supposed to explain any of this?

As if Sky had seen that acceptance, and the cold, harsh slap of reality that came with it, his expression softened. "I'm sorry. But we can fix it." He let go of me. He didn't pull away, though.

I didn't move either—or bother to hide my shaky laugh. "How the hell do we fix this? We tried your suit powers, and it nearly melted my brain."

He winced a little at the reminder but shook it off, fixing me with an imploring look. "Come with me. Let me take you to Bast. He's a god with technology, and we'll figure out a way to extract the halix's data from you. *Safely,*" he added when I flinched.

"Stop saying extract," I muttered, pulling back. I raked my fingers through my hair, getting tangled in the remnants of my braid. It was drying in a frizzy mess.

"Fine," Sky said, breathing a chuckle. "Remove, then. We'll find a way to safely *remove* the signal—the map. The information the halix gave you. And then you can go back to…to a normal life."

Right. Because normal was possible after finding out he was an alien in a human skinsuit and there was a whole galactic war happening somewhere overhead.

I couldn't help my snort. "Normal," I whispered, glancing outside. "Sure."

"Something like it, yeah."

Even if we managed to do what he was proposing, things would never return to normal. I would never be the same. Not knowing all I knew.

I turned back to him and raised my brows. "Nothing says normal like defeating alien robots from outer space, right?"

Sky's mouth curved upward, flashing that damn dimple. His hair was beginning to dry, too, but in tousled waves and curls. Even drained, dripping, and looking like he'd been through a tornado, he was still unfairly attractive.

Flushing, I dropped my eyes, but then my heart stopped when he leaned forward. I sucked in a sharp breath and tipped my face up. Our faces were kiss-close.

Intensity had replaced his smile, and for a wild moment, I thought he'd do it. That he'd kiss me again. I *wanted* him to. Badly. If only to make me feel something besides the sensation of falling.

But he didn't. He fixed me with an entreating look instead. "I asked you before, Raven. I'm going to ask you again: do you trust me?"

It was barely louder than the rain. A soft question.

One that felt rhetorical at this point, because somehow, despite the hidden truths, the revelations, despite the fact he wasn't even *human*...I *did* trust him.

After today, after seeing him nearly die defending me—even if it was just because I might be carrying the salvation of his race—how could I not? He'd still risked his life. He'd risked everything.

Hell, I trusted him more than I trusted *myself* lately, when it came to life-and-death decisions. I felt safest when he was there.

But because I couldn't—*wouldn't*—tell him any of that, I cleared my throat and asked, "Exactly where is Bast?"

"Florida." Sky shifted back a little. I had the overwhelming urge to chase his heat. Hope lightened his expression, like he knew I'd already made up my mind. "Is that a yes?"

"Your super-secret alien base is in *Florida?*" I deadpanned.

Sky's grin bloomed, a little lopsided. "I wouldn't call it a super-secret alien base, but yeah, I guess so. For now, anyway."

Florida, of all places. I would've loved to say it was surprising. But it kind of made tons of sense.

"*Is* that a yes?" he asked, serious again. "Will you go with me? We'll have to move fast and keep our heads down. That means going dark for a few days. I don't know how long that cuff is going to work, and I have a feeling what happened at the university is going to attract more than the Enil."

I didn't doubt it. I'd already seen those people in suits once, after the lab incident. Kelly's FETR friends thought the government was involved, too. I absently twirled the metal encircling my wrist.

This rabbit hole was getting deeper. A hell of a lot more crowded, too. It wasn't going to be easy, making it all the way to Florida with both Enil and—if Kelly's information was right— *License 16* after us.

Us.

God, I was doing this. I was throwing in with an alien, going on the run. Nerves twisted tight in my belly. Nerves and something else, something fizzy and light that felt a lot like excitement.

Because I was going on the run with *Sky*.

"No more secrets," I said, turning to him. I waited until his eyes met mine again. "I get your whole Creed thing, and I know you broke rules to tell me all this. But I want to be partners, Sky. It's my life on the line here, too. I want to know exactly what we're up against and why. I *need* to if I'm going to stay sane."

"I can understand that." He didn't look away. "And I agree. It's not safe for you—or for me. From now on, we're partners. Okay?"

I swallowed hard. "Partners."

That smile began to creep back. Unfair. How were his eyes so many shades of blue? "Maybe even friends?" He tilted his head. "Can't say I have a lot of those. Not who know the real me."

My cheeks heated. The real him, like the silvery-sparkly version?

The one on a life-or-death mission? The self-sacrificing, capable, broody alien super soldier?

The one who kissed like a dream in a way that was not at all *friend*-like?

"Kelly would disagree," I muttered, biting back my answering smirk. "You have a whole club, you know. The Friends of the Extraterrestrial Races."

"The what?" Sky frowned, looking bewildered. "Work Kelly?"

A laugh burst from me. That was a story for another day. "Never mind."

Friends with Sky. Sure. What else would I call the visitor from outer space I was embarking on a road trip with?

He had my life in his hands, after all. And I apparently had his entire race's well-being in mine.

"Okay." I drew in a deep breath through my nose, held it, then exhaled in a rush, squaring my shoulders. "Okay. I guess let's go save a couple worlds." I glanced his way. "Friend."

I didn't usually lust after my friends—but whatever. Something to work on. Maybe a couple of days trapped in a car with him would lessen the appeal.

His smile faded a little, and he was looking at me in a way that made me wonder if he was also thinking about the stairwell and maybe some lust. Which wasn't going to help matters. I lost the fight against my flush.

Friends, I reminded myself.

But then he seemed to catch himself, and he leaned both elbows on the console and shot me a crooked smirk. "All right then, Rachel. Let's go save some worlds."

"*Not* funny," I said, narrowing my eyes. I had to bite my cheek, though, because it was a little.

"Thank you," Sky said suddenly, and I blinked and slid my gaze back to his.

That was a *real* smile, not the polished, bartender one. A real, grateful smile he'd trained on me. It melted me a little.

"For what?" I asked, clearing my throat. I dialed my googly eyes down a notch.

"For trusting me. And for agreeing to come."

I let out a puff of air. "Yeah, well." I settled back into my seat and reached for my belt. "I didn't want you to abduct me in your spaceship or something instead."

That killed the pretty smile. He heaved a sigh instead. "I don't abduct people in my spaceship, Raven."

"Just your SUV," I said, with a pointed look.

"Uh huh. Just my SUV." He turned on the defrost setting and gripped the steering wheel. "Ready?"

Was I *ready*?

Ready to run from space robots and the real-world version of the MIB? Ready to see if I could dig an intergalactic info cache out of my skull, one that might save a whole species from annihilation? Ready to go meet a mysterious Pladian named Bast, who lived in the Sunshine State?

All while trapped in a car with the guy I'd been secretly fantasizing about for the better part of a year who—oh yeah—was also an alien and had just put us *firmly* in the friend zone?

Sure. I was born ready.

I buckled my seatbelt and said cheerfully, "Let's go."

After one final, searching glance my way, as if giving me one last chance to change my mind, Sky put the SUV in drive. We pulled off the shoulder and merged with late-night traffic. Just another car in a stream of headlights cutting through the storm.

If this experience had taught me anything, though, it was that appearances could be deceiving.

I had no idea what would come next. Amelia would notice I'd vanished. She probably already had. Eventually so would my mom. Dustin. Lisa. The Oasis crew. Even Bob.

I'd need to let them know I was safe. At some point. A look at my phone showed it was dead. Drained, most likely, from being in the Enil's vicinity.

For now, it was just me and Sky.

I stole a glance at him, at the soft curls forming, the tiny cowlick at his temple. The firm line of his strong jaw and the pensive set of his mouth. He looked tired but also determined and lost in thoughts a million miles away. Maybe even lightyears.

As if he felt my stare, he turned his head.

I looked away, back out the window. But I couldn't stifle the quiet thrill that zipped through me. We were in this together. Whatever *this* was.

And for now...I was safe. As safe as anyone with a glowing alien tattoo and a cosmic map embedded in her brain could be. Hopefully, anyway. It was hard to be sure of anything right now.

Well. That wasn't *entirely* true. I bit back a smirk.

There was one thing I was sure of.

I'd been wrong all those days ago in the diner. Kelly had been on to something.

Because it was *definitely* aliens.

And somehow, I was weirdly okay with it.

Acknowledgments

WRITING IS THE WEIRDEST, MOST PAINFUL, most rewarding thing ever. I've had this idea for the IDNA universe for…over a decade, really. In various shapes and forms.

During 2020, when the entire world was going crazy and me extra so since I was trapped in the house, I needed an outlet. I channeled all that weirdness into Sky and Raven's story. It's been through several (*several*) drafts and changes since, but it was during that time, when everything felt like the beginning of a sci-fi movie anyway, that this story truly came to be.

However, it wouldn't have become an actual book people could read without my husband's (and family's) support. I could wax poetic about all he's done for me—but suffice to say, you're the very best, babe. I am forever grateful for your existence.

To my friends and my family, *thank you* for all the gentle encouragement and excitement and cheerleading. Especially when imposter syndrome hit me with the one-two punch. We're only in round one, guys, so I'm going to still need you for that one.

A particularly giant thanks to my mom, who's been my biggest fan since I wrote that lost kitten story. I'm sorry about the spicy scenes that are coming, but I'm going to get you a redacted copy.

Diane, too—thanks for lending your critical eye. This whole series exists, in part, because of our countless hours spent watching *Roswell* and obsessing over science fiction worlds. Love you.

To my dad, for instilling the love of written word in all forms. If it weren't for you, I never would've fallen in love with storytelling.

Also big thanks to Danielle for her editing magic. Somehow, she always hurts so good. I don't know what I'd do without you and all the work Design by Definition does for my weirdo book babies. You truly are a saint.

I also need to thank all the people in the FaRo Discord. None of you know I'm there because I don't ever talk, but I'm lurking and learning.

And to my "Sci-fi Romance Chat" girlies! I know we only recently found each other, but you guys have kept me sane in these last few months. So glad we found each other in the promotion void.

Lastly but biggest of all... thanks to you, dear reader! Thank you for taking the time to enjoy my strange little sci-fi romcom. Sky and Rae's story isn't done, and book two will be here faster than you can say *Starborn*. It only gets better, too.

(OMG. *Wait until you meet Bast!!*)

I'd love to stay in touch. Connect with me on Instagram, TikTok, Facebook—or via email on my website. If you'd like updates on the rest of this series (and it's about to get crazy!), including sneak peeks, giveaways, and other top-secret transmissions, you can join my Facebook group or subscribe to my newsletter at https://elledeyesso.com/!

If you liked Stardusted, please consider leaving a review! Indie authors like me rely heavily on word of mouth to promote their books, and I could use all the help I can get.

In the meantime, find your local FETR group and keep your eyes on the stars.

Until next time,
    Elle

Want more aliens, angst, and adventure?

Sky and Rae will be back in the next installment of the *It's Definitely Not Aliens* universe, set to release Valentine's Day 2026! Preorders are live! Hope you're ready for more spice…and more hot aliens, too.

For more info (or to snag your copy now), make sure to visit www.elledeyesso.com. Join the newsletter mailing list and then head over to Facebook to become a member of *DeYesso's Reader Den,* the spot to hang out and chat all things IDNA universe, sci-fi romance, and get sneak peeks of all the top-secret gossip.

If you liked this book, please consider leaving a review! It would mean the world.

Thanks so much for reading, Earthlings! See you soon. 🛸

About the Author

ELLE DEYESSO writes sci-fi and fantasy romance and has a soft spot for sarcasm, found families, and complicated characters who banter their way through problems.

Her stories blend romance, action, and out-of-this-world adventure.

An avid lover of all things sci-fi and fantasy, Elle lives in the Midwest with her family and is powered by iced coffee and binge-reading every genre imaginable. When her nose isn't buried in a book, she enjoys video games, cooking, hiking, and convincing herself she can keep a houseplant alive.

Stardusted is her debut novel and the first in the *It's Definitely Not Aliens* series, a love story full of spacey swoon, slow burn to spice, and aliens totally worth phoning home about. 👽

You can find her on Instagram, TikTok, and Facebook, and she absolutely wants to hear from readers.

For more sneak peeks and to chat with other IDNA universe fans, join the **DeYesso's Reader Den** *Facebook group linked on her page!*

www.ingramcontent.com/pod-product-compliance
Lightning Source LLC
Chambersburg PA
CBHW071246250626
47163CB00002B/351